MATTEO

THE CASTILLO FAMILY
BOOK THREE

FIONA MURPHY

Matteo

By Fiona Murphy

Copyright © 2023 by Fiona Murphy

Cover design by Cheeky Covers

✽ Created with Vellum

Matteo

Within weeks of my thirty-ninth birthday, I lost my thirty-ninth patient and all feeling. I was certain it would pass, only it continued into the next day and the weeks after.

In order to treat my patients, I needed to feel *something*. Without feeling, I couldn't stay. Not in oncology and not in Baltimore.

So, I'm back in Dallas after more than twenty years gone. Home, my mother keeps saying with happiness.

Happiness I still can't feel more than four months after that day. I'm beginning to accept feeling isn't coming back.

Until the moment I walk into an exam room and look into her eyes. All at once, feeling comes rushing back as suddenly as it disappeared.

She's my patient. It's all kinds of wrong to want her, no matter what television portrays. Add in the fact she's running from an abusive husband. I should be staying far away from her, not taking her and her daughter home with me.

But I can't walk away from her. They're living in a crappy motel, barely surviving. I have a room, a safe place for her to recover and heal. She needs time and patience before she's strong enough for me to tell her the way I feel.

I'll give it to her. And hopefully, she'll grow strong enough to trust in me and fall in love with me the same way I've fallen for her and her baby daughter.

***Trigger warning for domestic violence on page. I apologize in advance to all those who've gone through abuse (I have as well, and it hurt like heck to write.). This will break your heart. But I promise it will be put back together by the end.

Another warning for my long-time readers. I'm sorry to say this is a slow burn. Nothing else made sense after all she's been through. But I promise, it's still a me story, and once we get there...it's all there. All the yummy bad/goodness you expect to find in every story I write.

CHAPTER 1

*M*atteo

I sigh with relief as my mother and grandfather leave. Rafe chuckles as the door closes behind them. Damn, he looks different. He's no longer wound so tight I worry he'll have a heart attack before he hits fifty.

Javi laughs. "Why the hell did you do that without warning us?"

"What, I wasn't supposed to ask if Mom was finally going to divorce Dad now that she and Abuelo are getting biblical? It's a valid question, considering they're now three years in. Especially since she and Dad are more than twenty years legally separated." I shrug.

"Yes, it's a valid question. However, you only asked so they'd leave. That's what makes you an ass." Rafe sends a dark eyebrow up. "You want us to leave too? It was a long flight from Baltimore to home."

Typical Rafe, calling me on being an ass while giving me an out for my behavior. I always knew he was going to be a great father.

Since he was one to us growing up, even though he was only two years older than me. He was a better father than our actual father.

I shake my head. I'm not ready for them to leave—to be left alone with the emptiness.

Am I home? My mother kept going on and on about me being home. It's why I said what I did, aware it would send her running. I wasn't sure how I felt yet about being in Dallas after more than twenty years gone.

Over the years, there were times I thought of Dallas as home. Only because my family is here. After almost fifteen years in Baltimore, it's hard to think of anywhere else as home.

"You sure?" Javi asks as he eyes me.

Running a hand over my face, I nod. I'm up at the window that looks out over an enormous pool and a large green grass area residents were assigned and could use for a garden, but no one uses for much of anything.

I shake my head again. "I should be asking you for the number of a therapist, not…"

"Talk to me." It's an invitation spoken softly yet also a demand. The iron hand in the silk glove Rafe has down to an art. "You left Johns Hopkins weeks before you called me to tell me you were coming back to Dallas."

I shouldn't be surprised he knew. The last thing I want to do is talk about it. And maybe that's why I should. "I lost another one. Nine years old, the sweetest thing you've ever had the misfortune to encounter as a doctor treating her for leukemia. As cancers went, her case should have been a walk in the park—a gloomy as fuck park, but nothing I couldn't handle. I did everything right. And she

2

still died. I'm standing over her calling time of death, and I didn't feel a thing."

Even now, the memory of that day is fucking with my head. "Almost fourteen years I've been doing this. My thirty-ninth birthday was two days before she died. She was the thirty-ninth patient I lost. I couldn't feel a thing. No sadness, no anger at myself for losing her. Not a damn thing... I was positive it would come back. It had to. I needed it to do what I do."

Rafe and Javier share concerned looks I pretend I don't see.

"Except it didn't come back." Unease is still in me at the lack of feeling, even now. "After a week, I gave in to what I had known in the back of my mind as I walked away from the hospital—I was done. I sent an email with my notes on my cases and told them I wasn't coming back. Then I laid in bed for a week while I tried to figure out what to do next."

"Just a week?" Javi's eyebrows are up. "It's okay if it was longer than a week."

"It might have been a little longer than a week," I admit.

It was more like a day in bed and two weeks on the couch trying to figure shit out. "I was lost on what is there for me if I'm not doing oncology. Since the only reason for me to be in Baltimore was Johns Hopkins, it didn't feel like there was anything left for me there. I'm hoping a new environment will jumpstart the desire for me to do something."

"You don't have to do anything. Not a fucking thing." Rafe is firm. "What you did day in and out is going to leave cuts no one can see. If you never want to set foot in a hospital again, there's no shame in that. If you want to come by the office and see if you're interested in having one of your own in the building, we'll welcome you with open arms. And I have the number of a great therapist."

The idea appeals as much as running a cheese grater over my face.

Rafe doesn't miss a thing and chuckles. "I get it. I'm sure Abuelo would love it if you took over the running of the charity he started. I don't know if you were aware it went from focusing on breast cancer to a broader stance on women's general health. The women's center here in Dallas is also an option. I've heard rumblings about the current administrator. I know they would welcome you immediately. It's a warning, so you can brace yourself for him to ask. His focus has moved to mom, so they've contacted me for direction and attention."

I consider it. "Are you sure you aren't soft asking me to ensure they no longer contact you?"

He chuckles. "Maybe."

"I'll take those calls. It might help fill the days."

"Come on, let's cut into the enchiladas my wife had me bring you. I had to beg her to make more so we could have some for the house. She's an awesome cook." Javi licks his lips as he opens the refrigerator.

I sit down at the table, separating the living area from the kitchen. Javi waxes lyrical about his wife and two kids. Although I came back to Dallas for Rafe's wedding a few years ago, I couldn't get time off for Javi's wedding last year since there was so little warning—only a week before the day.

Rafe gets in on showing me pictures. I've yet to meet their daughter, Elena, or their newest daughter, Stella. Carrie has sent me pictures of them over the years. I have better text conversations running with her than I did with Rafe. She kept me updated on what was happening in our family, like my mom and Abuelo, Rafe taking the weekends off, and when Ava appeared in Javi's life.

Guilt hits me. How had it been so long since I was with my family to see what it became? It's been years since I came home for Christmas or any holiday. Since my patients were so young, I hated leaving them alone on holidays—some of them didn't have parents who could spend time in the hospital with them.

About eight years ago, I got caught with a patient who wasn't stable enough for me to leave for longer than a day, let alone the week off I planned. Once I went into the hospital that Christmas Eve and saw the listless, sad faces of my patients and others in the pediatric oncology ward, my conscience wouldn't let me leave them at Christmas. At the time, I didn't regret missing out on time with family to be with my patients. Now I wonder what it cost me in my relationships with my brothers.

Rafe's glance at his watch is only the flick of his eyes. "Go on. Carrie is probably wondering where you are." I order Rafe. "You too. Leaving your wife alone with a new baby." I mockingly shake my head at Javi. "You'll be lucky if she lets you back in."

"Whatever, she's going to yank me through the door so fast my head will spin." Javi is glowing.

After they're gone, I go onto the massive rooftop deck to look over downtown Dallas. I'm grateful Javi is letting me stay here until I figure out where I want to live. My mother made it clear she wished I was staying with her, not in Javier's place. I love my mother, but the idea of living with her, even briefly, is not something I could bring myself to do.

Do I want a condo or a house? If I had a house, do I want to fill it with anything? A wife, maybe a couple of kids.

Over the years, my relationships were mainly with nurses and other doctors. They understood I didn't have regular hours, and making plans often ended with me getting called away. The women were selected because of convenience. We both knew it was nothing more than the need to scratch an itch.

I wasn't willing to give up time for anything besides my work. A wife meant getting home at a decent hour. A baby meant midnight feedings. A child meant parent-teacher conferences and dance classes or soccer games. If I gave time to them, there wasn't enough to give to my patients.

Do I want what my brothers have? I don't know. It doesn't feel like I know anything right now. Rafe said I didn't have to know. Except the lack of a plan—a purpose—is fucking with my head. I'm hoping like hell once I create a new purpose, the feeling will come back.

* * *

MATTEO

Scanning the restaurant, I find Rafe and Javi in the corner of the elegant dining room. The hostess guides me toward them. Javi's eyes are hopeful. Rafe's are concerned.

"What do you think?" Javi prompts me the second my ass hits the seat. "You want to take over running the center?"

I shake my head, and his eyes dim. Rafe doesn't look surprised. "I'm not ready to sit behind a desk. And that's what running the center would require."

"But it helped you recognize what you want." Typical Rafe, it's not a question.

6

"Yes. I want to open a clinic like the women's health center—for everyone. We can do X-rays and fill some prescriptions at no cost. I also want to include mental health so it's more like a community health center."

Javi loses his smile. "You're going into a shitty area, aren't you?"

"Where else do they need regular health care more? Ninety-five percent of low-income clinics are a revolving door of doctors going in to get their internship out of the way before moving into a practice. Patients do better with regular doctors who give a shit about them, not someone coming in to get their time and get out."

Rafe sighs. "You're going to fund it completely and work fourteen hours a day, seven days a week, as penance for leaving oncology."

His words hit hard because they were exactly what I admitted to myself it would become. The hours were going to be eight to eight, and, of course, we would be open on the weekend for greater availability. It would be my duty.

I must make up for not doing the work of the life I left behind. I'm a billionaire because of my family's wealth. I didn't earn that money on my own. Therefore, I needed to pay for it by giving back in other ways. It wasn't enough to give away what I could—my grandfather restricted what I could donate to charity. He knew I would give it all away if I could. Besides, giving it away was too easy.

"It doesn't have to become that." I force the words out.

"No, it doesn't. You paid every due there could be. It's okay for you to stop and enjoy life." Rafe almost sighs the words.

"If I stop, I don't know if I can get myself to begin again," I admit.

AMY

The blow sends me off my feet. Pain radiates through my whole body, and I fight not to vomit. I'm not sure if the urge to be sick is because of him hitting me in my stomach or if the pain is that bad. I can't breathe through the pain, and I'm grateful because if I do, I'm positive I'll be sick.

"What have I told you? You stupid, fat bitch. Keep the brat quiet. Fucking waking me up and shit."

Layla screeches in fear. An unintelligible pleading for comfort I can't give her.

I watch helplessly as he turns on her. *No. No.* He can hit me all he wants, but not her. She's only six months old—a baby. Fear sends a shot of adrenaline through me to get to her first. I cover her with my body. "I'm sorry. Please. I'm sorry. I'll keep her quiet."

I feel him looming over us.

Please. Just this once, answer a prayer. I'm begging a god I lost belief in decades ago as I clutch Layla to me.

With a final curse, he swipes a rough hand at my head without any of the power of his previous blows. He learned not to hit me in the face, not because he cared if anyone saw my bruises—the bone hurt his hand with how hard he hit me.

"Stupid bitch." He mutters. "I'm going to Jack's to get some sleep. His woman knows how to keep her kids under control. Clean this place up before I get back."

Squeezing my eyes shut, I don't move until he slams the door behind him. He was going to do it. Danny was going to hit Layla. If he had, he would have broken something in her small body. At almost six feet and a former construction worker—only not working because he hurt himself at work—he's strong with thick meaty hands.

It's almost every day now. He used to only hit me once or twice a week. But over the last few months, Layla couldn't breathe without him losing his temper and hitting me. I tried so hard to keep her quiet, to please him. I've gotten so stressed out I've dried up, unable to breastfeed Layla the way I wanted to. The way I needed to because formula is insanely expensive.

Layla pats my face with tears in her own eyes. How could I have been so stupid? This is what I grew up with—a father who yelled and screamed and hit my mother. Then he moved on to me and my two older brothers. I promised myself I would do things differently. That I would never end up with a man like my father.

For the first two years, there was the typical male lack of empathy, like forgetting birthdays, not getting me anything for Christmas, and never cooking or cleaning, but he always half-heartedly apologized and promised to do better. The way he would tease me about going to school and how hard it was for me to read and study with dyslexia. He would 'joke' about what I ate and my weight.

The abuse started slowly, only after we moved in together. I didn't see it as abuse. After all, it was minor things like the joking and teasing that became meaner—mocking and belittling my weight and dyslexia, throwing a dish when he hated what I made for dinner. Gradually, there were fewer apologies and more accusations I was too sensitive.

But I was never afraid of him.

We were both shocked when he slapped me for the first time. I wanted to leave then. Except I was seven months pregnant, and he was on his knees begging for forgiveness.

9

I also had nowhere to go or money to do it with. I hadn't found a job after our move to Waco. He told me that I didn't need a job and didn't want me working when the baby we planned for came anyway. The reason we moved to Waco was so he could earn more money for me to be a stay-at-home mom, he reminded me.

There was no family for me to run to. My older brothers fled our home and didn't look back after my mother died from an overdose when I was fourteen. I had few friends in the small town we left. We weren't close enough I felt comfortable asking them for help. I had no friends at all in Waco.

Stupid. I shouldn't have stayed after the first time he hit me. I should have paid attention to how quickly he stopped caring about me or the baby after he found out it was a girl.

At the time, I was so excited. All I was focused on was my pregnancy and preparing for the little girl I always wanted. I'd heard about dads not being excited over having a girl and then falling in love with them when they were born. Of course, he would love her when she got here.

Then Danny got hurt at work when I was six months pregnant. There was no money coming in, so I had to go back to waitressing.

I worked up until the day before I went into labor. He drove me to the hospital, dropping me off at the ER entrance. His promise of going in after he parked the truck was a lie. He never came.

Even when the nursing staff called him to tell him that I needed an emergency cesarian and wanted him there with me because I was terrified. My calls and texts were ignored for the almost three weeks that I was in the hospital with an infection. Layla should have gone home after only a few days. But since he wouldn't come get her, she stayed with me in my room.

Danny wouldn't even pick us up to bring us home. One of the nurses took pity on me. She gave me a ride home and the car seat and baby carrier she no longer needed.

I was terrified he wouldn't even let me into the apartment. Thankfully, my key still worked.

When he walked in, he was surprised to see me but acted like it was any day. He shrugged off my questions and ignored Layla.

From the day I got home, the verbal abuse was constant. He didn't want me breastfeeding because it was gross. But we couldn't afford formula, so I hid with her in the bedroom—keeping her out of sight. He treated Layla as though her presence offended him.

The first time he hit me with intent was two weeks after I was home from the hospital. He ordered me back to work because there was no food in the house. I was astonished he thought I could work. There was no way. I was recovering from a cesarian and in pain. He'd taken my pain pills and threw a bottle of Tylenol at me when I begged him for them. How could he tell me to go to work?

The words were barely out of my mouth when he backhanded me. I was stunned, unable to speak or even move. Then he did it again and again until I was on the floor. None of it made sense. It wasn't happening, it was a bad dream.

Except it wasn't. He was standing over me, threatening me with a worse beating if I didn't go to work the next day and bring home money and something to eat. Or I could leave, pack up my shit and the brat and get the fuck out.

All I wanted to do was do exactly what he said: pack up our things and leave. But I had nothing and nowhere to go. As I lay there, I promised myself it was the last time he would hit me.

It was a promise I couldn't keep, but I made another promise to myself: I would go back to work and, with the money I earned, leave him. Except he took all my money. The minute I walked out of the restaurant, he demanded my apron.

I've managed to squirrel away nine hundred dollars, hiding tips in my bra—I didn't need to worry about him seeing me taking my bra off. Ever since I was six months pregnant with Layla, he thought I was too fat for him to touch.

I've taken it all these months and would have continued to endure it until I had enough money to leave. What I have saved is almost laughable. I have no idea how far I can go on it. I wanted more money to escape with. The plan was for two thousand.

Except I don't have time. He would have hit Layla. Deep down, I know next time he *will* hit her.

Danny didn't care about her. Sometimes, I think he hates her. He's never held her once. I don't understand it. She's a good baby, calm and smiling, only crying when she was hungry or needed her diaper changed. I had to pay a girl next door to watch her when I was waitressing because I was too scared to leave her alone with him.

Rocking Layla, all I can think is that I'm failing her. I'm failing at everything. In a week, I'll be twenty-seven. The only good thing I have to show for my life is Layla.

I spot the keys to his truck on the table. It's more than ten years old, with almost a hundred thousand miles on it. The truck is in my name because when he wrecked his after a night of drinking, I was the only one who could be financed for it. When my car died, there was no money for me to finance another. Yet I was never allowed to drive it—not even for a late-night run to get formula or diapers. Despite the age and miles, I know it could get me out of here, away from Danny.

Layla cries in fear when I put her down on the couch. For the first time, I ignore her cries and run to the bedroom. Packing up her stuff takes less than ten minutes. My things take about the same time as I jam everything into two suitcases. I grab the miserable nine hundred dollars. It's not enough, only there's no more time left to get more.

Putting the truck in gear, I squeal out of the apartment complex and head for I-35. I don't know where to go. Right takes me south to Austin, left takes me north to Dallas. Indecision has me slowing down. Fate decides for me. There's a wreck on I-35 South, so I turn left, north to Dallas, and pray it isn't worse than what I've left behind.

CHAPTER 2

*a*my

Almost three months later, I'm not sure if this is better than what I left behind.

When I drove into Dallas, I didn't know where to go. I chose the exit for downtown. My first stop was at a convenience store to get gas and ask the cashier if they could tell me somewhere I could rent that wasn't too expensive.

She looked me up and down with dull brown eyes and shrugged. I tried again at a small grocery store down the road and had better luck.

Looking around the tiny motel room, I'm not sure the word I should be using is luck. I'd managed to get a job as a housekeeper at the place in exchange for a tiny salary and a place to sleep. The only good thing about it is I can bring Layla with me while I clean.

Whatever luck I had, I'm now out of it. I'm sick. I've tried telling myself over the last week that I was wrong. It's allergies. Except

14

my sore throat has gotten worse every day, and the fever that started four days ago tells me I'm wrong. Since I didn't need to clean yesterday, I spent all day in bed—hoping it would help me get better. It didn't.

The owner of the place eyes me as I go in to collect the cart and towels. "You sick."

He's not exactly a warm guy. Somewhere between fifty and eighty, his eyes don't miss much. I shrug. "I think so."

He sighs heavily. "There's a new medical clinic opened up a few weeks ago down the street. A walk-in place. They don't charge nothing. Hours are eight to eight. When you get done, head on over there. I don't need you getting me or anyone else sick."

I nod as I try to focus on staying on my feet. Putting Layla on the cart, I keep my eyes on her and remember she needs me. This should only take five or six hours. As soon as I'm done, I'll go. I don't want to get Layla sick, too.

Three hours later, the room swims around me as I try to straighten from bending over to make the bed. Layla claps and speaks gibberish to me. I work to focus on her. *I'm almost done.* I repeat over and over to try to keep going. It doesn't help.

The owner is in the open doorway of the room shaking his head. I'm not sure how I came to be on the floor. "Go on, get to the doctor. I'm docking this from your pay. The place is two blocks up and to the right."

Closing my eyes, I repeat the instructions until they're in a loop, even if I don't understand them. Two blocks? Two blocks from where?

Layla squeals. The sound pulls me from the dark. I just want to sleep. I'm so tired. Everything hurts, especially my throat. Two blocks up and to the right. Once I go two blocks and turn right, I'll feel better.

Oh god, I almost drop Layla in her car seat carrier. She laughs, thinking it's a game as she plays with my purse. Two blocks up and to the right. I make it to the truck and strap Layla in. She pats my cheek. I grasp her hand and hold it against my cheek, grateful for the cool touch.

Two blocks and to the right. I find it. It's busy. In the time it's taken to get here, Layla's car seat has somehow become ten pounds heavier—I almost drop her again. All I can do is drag her seat. It's too heavy to carry.

The receptionist's eyes go wide when she sees me. "Are you okay?"

I shake my head and run my hand over my throat. "Hurts." I croak out at her.

"Do you have a fever?"

I nod. Talking hurts too much.

"Let me get you into a room. We don't want you out here getting others sick." She's around the desk, taking the car seat from me. "Got you, sweetie. Let's get you and Mommy to a room."

Everything happens from far away. She helps me onto an exam table, readjusting the pillow beneath my head and pushing the table a few inches so it's pressed against the wall. "We don't want you falling off. I'll tell the doctor you're in here."

I made it. It's safe here. I could hear it in the woman's voice. Everything will be okay. It's my last thought as I let the darkness overtake me.

* * *

16

MATTEO

"Doctor, I put a patient in room five. She's probably got strep. The poor thing is out of it. She has a baby, too. Might want to check her and make sure she's not sick also." Willow informs me as I pass her in the hall.

"What?" I'm trying hard to keep my temper. "Why didn't you let Camilla triage?"

The procedure is supposed to be that a patient gets checked in and tells Willow or Amara why they came in and if they have an appointment. Then Camilla or Lupe triages. If symptoms indicate it could be a case of strep, they get a culture for a rapid strep test. It's worked for the last three weeks.

I have one other doctor, Diane, who is off today. I also have two nurse practitioners, Tomas and Imani. Imani is also off today. Camilla is an RN who can handle a patient as well as me or Diane. Lupe is an LPN working toward her RN and has already left for the day.

Two of our lab techs are also out sick today. There are four techs total to handle laboratory testing. I was able to get the X-ray machine I wanted, and there are three techs for it. With one of them out sick today, I'm realizing I need to hire another.

Since I have to hire techs and a radiologist for the CT machine, I was able to purchase and will be delivered by the end of next month. It's going to be easier if I can find a tech who also has X-ray certification since it's a common step up to earn more than an X-ray tech salary.

The last few weeks, everything ran smoothly, but today it feels like the whole neighborhood is sick with either strep throat or the flu.

There's also the fact Christmas was two days ago, and people were still getting together even when they were sick and spreading it.

She shrugs. "The lady was about to keel over. The baby is a sweetie. She was asleep almost as soon as her momma."

Shit. If nothing else, it's good they're both asleep.

Two hours later, it's time to close the doors. Even though there's another half hour before the clinic closes, we're not going to be able to see anyone else for the day. As it is, we're going to be here late, clearing people out.

Cleo stops me on my way to a patient waiting. "Doctor, I had a pharmacy tech come over to let me know we're running lower on amoxicillin than they thought. I'm not sure we'll have enough if even six more patients need it. We're getting a delivery first thing Monday, but it's good we're closed tomorrow."

I sigh and nod. To get Rafe off my back, the clinic isn't open seven days a week. We're closed on Sundays, and we're only open today on Saturday from ten to seven instead of the eight to eight we are during the week. "Let Tomas and Camilla know to give penicillin shots to those who are willing to take one. Remind them to tell the patient it hurts like hell, but it will resolve the illness sooner."

While there's also a pharmacy within the building, I don't usually need to interact with the three pharmacists and their techs. We talked earlier today, and they let me know they placed another order for antibiotics.

I'm just grateful my pharmacists are on top of things. The pharmacy is always as busy as we are—sometimes more. We contacted local hospitals and clinics to let them know they could send their patients to us. The medications we offer for free are basic and high-cost treatments: antibiotics, steroids, inhalers, insulin, immunosuppressives, and HIV and AIDS treatments.

It's almost eight o'clock, and everyone else is already gone. As I walk the last patient out, Cleo stops me. "We have a problem."

"What?" I run a hand through my hair as I fight not to yawn.

"There's a patient in room five. She's asleep and there's a baby in there with her, also sleeping." She hands me a file.

"Are you fucking serious?" How the hell could a patient be forgotten?

Cleo gives me the stink eye I deserve. "If you're done. Tomas got a throat culture from her. It came back as strep, but the woman was dead to the world when he tried to find out if she was allergic to penicillin. He told Camilla to see her. However, Camilla didn't."

Sighing. "I apologize. I'll see to her now. Go home. I'll close up."

I'm also going to talk with Camilla later. I can't believe she didn't complete patient care. I will note that.

"All right. Have a good night, and take the day off tomorrow. Don't be coming in here to work." It's an order.

I'm grateful as hell that Cleo is my manager. The woman's hard work kept me from living here the way I thought I would. Because of her, I didn't need to. However, there were things, such as charts and some paperwork, that only I could do. I often came in on Sundays to finish everything I hadn't completed for the week to start Monday off right.

Reviewing the file, I see she also has an ear infection. Tomas noted the fever had lasted four days, and she was in so much pain from her throat she wasn't even aware of her ear infection. This is exactly the kind of patient I opened the clinic for—people who needed to be seen and were afraid of going to the emergency room because they couldn't afford it.

I open the door to room five and find a woman curled onto her side.

"Ma'am?" I say loudly as I close the door behind me. Damn, she is dead to the world.

The woman's olive skin is flushed from fever. Her features are delicate. A heart-shaped face with a small chin is tucked into her chest. Her mouth is full and wide beneath a cute, upturned nose. Long, pitch-black hair is in a frayed braid.

I study her. Her black leggings, which cling to her short legs, are worn. The plain black shirt she's wearing swamps her. Small holes are scattered throughout the shirt, and the hem is worn. Her small hands are rough from work, and her inexpensive shoes are more worn than both her shirt and leggings.

A little sigh pulls my attention to the baby in the carrier at my feet. On my haunches, I study the baby. She's adorable, her mother in miniature down to the thick black hair. I run a hand over her forehead, checking for a temperature. There isn't one. I'm glad she's not sick too.

The baby is wearing a faded yellow sleeper, slightly stained. A large black purse is gaping open in the baby's lap. There's a lone diaper, a baggie of wipes, a tired wallet, a bottle, and another baggie, this one half-full of formula. A thick bundle of yellow folded paper catches my eye, I take it out. They are receipts for a room at the weekly motel a few blocks away.

The place is a shithole. Only people who were desperate lived there. She's definitely living there because there are multiple receipts dating back ten weeks.

What's worse, and tells me she'll be trapped there, are the receipts showing as housekeeping. She's trading housekeeping for a place to live. The pay would be so little that she would barely exist on it. It wouldn't be enough for her to save to leave.

There's a burner cell phone. I turn it on. Thankfully, it isn't locked. Not everyone remembered to add in the ICE—in case of emergency. I'm not too surprised to find hers empty. Only there's no one in her contact list to call in an emergency at all. There are no entries for mom, dad, or even the name of a friend—someone who cared she was here and needed help. All the contacts are for staffing agencies.

Is she really all alone? Where is the father of the baby? The only way to find out is to wake her up and ask her.

Louder, directly above her. I try again. "Ma'am. Hello. Ma'am."

I'm relieved when she blinks blearily up at me. She pushes up from the bed. It takes a few attempts for her to sit up completely. If the wall weren't behind her, I have no doubt she wouldn't be able to stay up in the position.

"Who are you? Oh." The words are barely a whisper.

Her eyes are dark chocolate. I feel them as heavy as a touch as they run over me. They widen at the sight of my white coat and the stethoscope around my neck.

I've never been able to leave the lesson of dressing professionally from my grandfather behind. I wear a suit every day and leave the jacket off once I begin seeing patients. Today, I'm wearing a dark blue button-down shirt, a light blue tie to go with my navy wool suit, and a blue and silver checked vest where my tie is tucked to stay out of my way.

Meeting those dark eyes head-on sends a frisson of electricity down my spine. For the first time since my patient died more than four months ago, I'm feeling something. Something I don't understand.

The electricity has shocked every cell in my body to life from a long-dormant sleep that I had no idea they were in—or maybe it's they are alive for the first time. Whatever it is, those cells need to be fed. A fierce hunger claws at me from deep inside, desperate to get out. They recognize she is the reason they're awake. Every-thing in me longs to touch her, to taste her, to *consume* her.

This is nothing I've felt before. My libido—even before the loss of feeling—would embarrass most men. Sex was like my other appetite, it didn't happen often. Once it was satisfied by a woman or my hand, I rarely thought of it again for another few weeks or even months.

She runs a hand over her face, breaking the connection. The loss of it is abrupt, and I immediately want it back. When her mouth opens only to close again, it's clear her attempt to speak causes her pain. The thought of her in pain yanks me out of the chaos rioting within me and causes a tug to my chest. What the hell is that—any of what's happening to me?

A hand goes to her throat. Pain, she's in pain. I need to fix it. Forcing it all down, I go into doctor mode of professional and polite. "Hi, I'm Matteo Castillo. I'm a doctor here at the clinic you came to. Your culture came back, and you have strep throat. I'd like to give you a penicillin shot. Are you allergic to penicillin?"

Shaking her head. "No." Is croaked out.

Relieved, I nod. "Good. Is it okay if I give you a shot? I need to make sure you know it's going to hurt. However, even if we weren't running low on pills, I would want to administer a shot. It will help you feel better in only a day or so. The best place would be your hip, which should help with the pain—for some patients. If you don't feel comfortable with that, I can write a prescription for an oral antibiotic."

Some patients were afraid of needles, and when it came to the penicillin shot, it was understandable. The solution is thick, so a bigger gauge needle is necessary. I've found the pain was less if given on the hip—not the buttock the way some still gave it.

She considers the question.

"I'm sorry there's no one else to administer the shot. Everyone has left for the day."

Her eyes widen. "It's not. Pain." She shakes her head. Pointing to her throat, "I want a shot. No pills."

"Ah, you were more worried about the pain of the shot than me being the one to give it to you."

She's nodding before I finish.

I make the decision—it's not something I usually offer, but I hate the idea of the shot hurting her. "Are you allergic to lidocaine?"

Another shake of her head.

"Good. I'm going to add a little lidocaine to help with the pain then. I'll be right back with the shot."

Her eyes are on her daughter. "Is she okay?"

I nod. "She's good, no fever. I'll be right back."

Closing her eyes, she lets her head fall back against the wall. "Okay." Is nothing more than her lips forming the word.

23

Her eyes slide closed, and I hate it. I want to see her beautiful eyes again, to feel them on me. *What the hell is the matter with me?*

Prepping the shot takes a few minutes. I should be ecstatic I'm feeling something. Except it's wrong. Because a patient made me feel it, patients are off limits. Whether I'm treating her once or on a regular basis. As in, I could be facing sanctions if I do anything my body is begging me to do.

Back in the room she's managed to fall asleep again. Unable to take my eyes off her if I wanted to, I spot the thin line of sweat along her hairline from her fever. While the shot can work as quickly as eight to ten hours, she let it go too long. It's unlikely she will recover soon enough to be up to take care of herself—let alone her daughter as soon as the baby needs her to.

The plan solidifies. It's *not* because of the weird feelings thrumming through me. I've taken patients and their families home with me when they had nowhere else to go. She's no different from any of the others. I can give her a safe place.

My home as a safe place has to come without strings. And it will. All I want is to give her a place to recover. I'll take care of the baby while she does. She doesn't need to worry about anything but herself, which will make it easier for her to get better. At least Javier left all the furniture in the place. There's even a crib for the baby. It's just until she's strong enough to find something else.

"Ma'am, it's best if you lay back down so I can give you the shot."

Her eyes pop open, meeting mine without searching. Chocolate disappears as her pupils dilate. I read it as clearly as I feel it in my bones—she felt the crazy feeling, too. She blinks, and it's gone.

Nodding, she lays back down and pulls down her leggings and plain white cotton underwear several inches past mid-hip.

I focus on finding the perfect spot, not on the skin on show. Rubbing the site with the alcohol swab to clean it, I remind myself that she's off-limits.

"Sorry," I mutter, hating the idea of hurting her as I depress the plunger. I'm ready to hold her down if I need to.

All she does is moan and whimper.

When I remove the needle, she goes to touch it.

"Hold on. Let me get a band-aid on it." I show her the little round band-aid I stuck to my thumb. Placing the band-aid in place, I rub gently, and she sighs. Trying to ignore the way the sigh slides down my spine, I cover her again.

"Being a baby, sorry." The words clearly cause pain as she swipes at her throat.

"Don't apologize. It's a painful shot. I'm going to get the car seat out of your car and put it into mine. Give me a few minutes."

Her eyes pop open wide. "What? Why?"

"Because you don't have anyone to take care of you and watch your daughter while you're sick."

Double blinks and her mouth opens wide, then slams shut, confirming it. "What makes you so sure?" The words are nothing more than a croak.

I send an eyebrow up. Daring her to lie to me. "I checked your phone to get the number of an emergency contact I could call to come get you and your daughter. There are no contacts besides staffing companies. Which tells me there's no one to call. I found the receipts for the motel you're living in. It's not a good place for you or your daughter, even if you were healthy."

She pushes off the exam bed. Once her feet hit the floor, she sways. It takes everything in me not to grab her. Her hand is already on the bed to keep her standing before I can get to her. "I can take care of myself and Layla."

I'll give her points for trying. Both eyebrows up, I run my eyes over her. She's not quite as small as I thought, five foot three, maybe five-four. Still almost a foot smaller than my own six foot two.

"I'll tell you what. I won't argue with you. I'll even drive you back to the motel myself if you are able to stand on your own for longer than sixty seconds." I bring up my watch to time her. "Push away now."

Sweat collects along her brow. She tries. More points for trying. She falls back. Her hand goes down to catch herself. "I can take care of myself."

I shrug. "Maybe yourself, but not your daughter too. This isn't charity. It's also nothing I haven't done for other patients before. My first time since I've been back in Dallas. However, it's far from the first time. You will each have your own room, and they come with locks on them."

Tension eases in her ever so slightly when she hears the lock thing.

"Don't cut off your nose to spite your face. That's only allowed when it comes to you. Right now, this is about your daughter and what she needs."

My words hit home. Her eyes fall to her sleeping daughter.

"Or I can take you to a shelter." I offer. Despite the fact that I don't want to. Shelters are no place to recover, and sure as shit, no one will take care of her there.

She flinches and shakes her head. "Okay, your house."

"Good. Can I get your name now?"

She blushes and nods. "Amy."

"Hi, Amy. I'm going to grab some diapers and other things for her. What size is she, and which formula does she prefer?"

It's hard for her to speak as she gives me the information. The baby is nine months old? She seems too small for her age.

I grasp her arm to guide her to the chair beside the bed, worried she'll keel over without support. Holy fucking shit. This is worse than I thought. The hunger is back—I'm desperate for more of the feel of her skin beneath my fingertips.

She jumps at my touch. Fucking hell. This is not good. Not good at all. I don't dare let her see it, keeping my face as bland as I can.

"I'll be right back. Let me get your keys to grab the base of the car seat."

"Wait."

CHAPTER 3

*M*atteo

I sigh. "I thought we covered this."

"We did but... I don't have the base. My ex—he broke it to keep me from leaving." Her eyes are down, ashamed.

It's bullshit she's ashamed when he's the one who should be. An ex who wasn't a contact in her phone. A man who tried to trap her with him. Everything in me clenches tight at what she had to have gone through for her to flee him with a small baby. That it was so bad a place like the motel she's at was better than staying with him.

"We have car seats. I'll grab one. Have a rest. It will be a minute." I assure her.

She nods and lays her head on the exam bed next to her.

I go into the freebie room. Everything was donated. There are cans of formula, baby food, diapers in every size, bottles, pacifiers, a few sleepers, white shirt onesies, and a few plain white shirts. Snagging a large pack of diapers, I fill a diaper bag with five sleepers and as many onesies, along with odds and ends for the baby.

After studying the car seats, I grab one and took it along with the bag to my car. All my vehicles are purchased with safety as the most important thing in mind. After several months of working a rotation in the ER, I saw more deaths from car accidents than anything else.

I'm now regretting my decision not to go with the safest vehicle, which was a luxury vehicle. Because of my height and the need for comfort, I stayed with an SUV. However, I was concerned about how it would appear to the patients coming to the clinic to see me arriving in a vehicle that was more expensive than what most of them would make in a year.

After today, I'm going to use the luxury SUV my mother purchased for me—she was aware of the only criteria I previously used. I don't give a shit what anyone thought if it meant Amy and Layla would be as safe as they could be.

I find Amy asleep again in the room. The baby is awake, though. She studies me with dark brown eyes like her mother. "Hi, sweetheart. Have a good nap?"

She chuckles as her hands go up to her mouth, and she begins sucking on them. "Hungry? I'll get you home and a bottle real soon. I promise."

Her chubby baby hands clap at the news. I unfasten her from the car seat. Damn, she needs to be changed. Snagging the lone diaper and the wipes, I set the baby girl on the exam bed. Layla—she said the baby's name was Layla.

"Hi, Layla. I love your name." She chuckles around the fingers in her mouth.

I unbutton the sleeper from the bottom up and scoot it out from under her, only to find her diaper leaked onto the sleeper. It's a good thing I grabbed some sleepers for her, too bad they're now in the car. She's got a little white shirt on.

I find the wipes are actually damp paper towels. Layla doesn't seem to mind, as I clean her with them. I put on the new diaper and pick her up to take the sleeper off.

Carrying her with me, I go back down the hall to the freebie room. She's so light. The first thing for her will be a complete workup to confirm she's healthy. It's to the point I'm studying sleepers for six months. There are dozens of sleepers. She reaches for them.

"What do you think? How about this one with ladybugs on it? Do you like ladybugs?" It's brightly colored, and her little hand opens and closes for it.

Lady bugs it is. I grab it and take her back into the exam room. "Mommy is sleeping. You're going to be a good girl for me, aren't you?"

When I lay her down, she shows me a gummy smile. "Yeah, you're a good baby. Sleeping away so Mommy doesn't have to take care of you."

"Mama," she chuckles.

"I'm so proud of you, talking at only nine months. You're so smart." I talk to her as I get her dressed in the sleeper. I decide to take her outside first in case I need to help Amy out of the clinic.

Settling her into the car seat, I'm relieved when she only gives me a wave when I tell her I'll be right back with her mommy. What a good baby, I marvel as I go back into the clinic.

Back in the room I find Amy is still asleep. I hate waking her. Except the sooner I can get her home, the sooner I can get her into a comfortable bed where she will sleep better. "Amy, I've got Layla settled into the car now."

She stirs, then blinks a few times. "Layla?"

"She's in the car. Can you make it to the car by yourself?" I ask as she attempts to stand.

Nodding, she straightens and takes a step away from the chair. She would have gone down in a heap if I weren't as close as I am. I don't let it happen.

Catching her to me, I lift her in my arms. And my world comes crashing down around me. It's a thousand plates, a million glasses, all shattering around me at once. The sound is so loud and real to me that I run my eyes over the ground, wondering if I'll step on something.

I blink again to confirm there's nothing broken around me. My heart is pounding too fast, heat rushes over me, and my palms feel sweaty. I don't understand. What the hell was that?

"Doctor?" Is a croak from Amy.

Words are too hard to string together. My chest is heaving as it works to get air into my tight lungs.

Her eyes are wide in surprise. Blinking a few times, she sighs. I see her hand moving, yet the touch of her small hand to my cheek shocks me. She runs her hand down my cheek. Closing her eyes, she sighs. Then snuggles into me and promptly goes back to sleep.

I'm not a man who cuddles—ever. Yet the way she snuggles into me has that damn tug thing happening in my chest again. It isn't only the weird sensation in my chest. My skin is hot and tight. I

31

want to hold her closer until there is nothing separating us—until I can inhale her into not only my lungs but beneath my skin. Nothing in this world has ever felt more right than holding her.

I shake my head as I try desperately to understand what is happening. Closing my eyes, I take a deep breath and exhale slowly as it all becomes clear. This woman is mine. It doesn't matter that it makes no fucking sense.

I'm a doctor. A man of logic. Twelve years of education at the best universities in the country combined with another fourteen years of continued education and reading research. I don't have faith in...anything.

I don't believe in what I can't see and touch. While there have been things that I wouldn't believe were possible. I believed in them because they happened. The why doesn't always have to be explained.

Looking into Amy's eyes, I was lost in her. In touching her, holding her in my arms, every cell in my body recognizes her as mine. The woman who I will care for until I take my last breath.

It didn't matter that I don't believe in destiny or fate. Those things didn't need me to believe in them to exist. The date on the first receipt for her checking into the motel was the day I purchased this building—when I finally felt like I was where I should be.

I was meant to be here when she needed me. For the first time since my patient died, I feel again—for Amy. The how or why of us coming together doesn't matter. It simply is.

A little sigh comes out of her that reminds me so much of Layla —shit.

Once I have Amy in the car, an odd relief comes over me hearing her soft snoring and Layla babbling behind me. It feels like it could be any day driving my family home.

Family? Home...the word feels different from when my mother declared me home—from even an hour ago. Now home means Amy and Layla.

My head is spinning on the fifteen-minute drive. The building is in Deep Ellum, an area of downtown Dallas known for its hip, almost bohemian vibe—a vibe completely at odds with the slick, monied veneer most of Dallas wore.

Javier's condo, where I'm still living, takes up the whole top floor. I appreciate the quiet of the place. There are only three other floors of condos and only two per floor. It's peaceful for a place in the middle of the city.

Pulling into the garage I park as close to the elevator as I can. I look down to see Amy blissfully asleep and decide to take Layla upstairs first.

When I open the door to her, Layla gives me a smile and her little arms go out for me to lift her up. Her smile has my heart expanding until I wonder if it will burst out of my chest. She cuddles into me just like her mama, burying her face in my neck. Damn, there's that twisting in my chest.

I tell her everything that's going to happen, how I'm taking her upstairs, then I'll come downstairs to get her momma. Once I have Momma settled into bed, I'll get her a bottle. When the elevator moves, she startles and clings tighter, yet she doesn't cry.

"Mama." She nods.

"Yes, I'm going to get Momma. Once, I have you in your crib where you can't escape. Then I'll make you a bottle."

33

"Baba. Baba." The words are adamant.

She might be small in terms of growth, but her ability to speak so clearly and with understanding places her months ahead in her development. "Yes, I'll get you a baba."

Once the elevator doors open into the foyer, I have to unlock a door into the condo.

"We're home."

A little eyebrow goes up at the statement. She looks around curiously as I close the door behind me. Her sigh is small as she lays her head on my shoulder. The trust she has in me humbles me. That trust sends me into my office.

I scan the resumes I tucked into the corner in case the people I hired didn't work out. They were all sent to me through a health-care staffing company that already screened them as having good references and passing drug tests. I find the resume I want.

It's for a physician assistant, Sasha Herndon. She answers with surprise clear in her voice. Her happiness with the pay isn't something she hides.

Every member of staff in the clinic earns twenty-five percent more than the average annual salary for the Dallas-Fort Worth area. They also have sixty days of PTO per year that I want them to use, plus their medical insurance is excellent and paid for by me. I want people happy to come to work and benefits are as important as salary.

She hesitates when I tell her I need her to start Monday full-time. I'm not leaving Amy on her own. Just when I think she's about to turn me down, she accepts. I'll call Cleo and have her work Sasha in to cover for me.

Hanging up, I look down at the baby in my arms. "It's easy to be home when there's something worth being here for."

I get her settled into the crib, wincing when I see there aren't any sheets on the mattress. I'll make it up once I get Amy into the guest bedroom. At least those sheets were changed a week ago. A former colleague from Baltimore was in town for a job interview at a hospital here in Dallas.

Layla frowns when I tell her that I'll be right back. I'm grateful there are no tears as I walk away. She's a really good baby.

In the guest room, I pull back the covers so I can easily put Amy in bed.

Getting her out of the car isn't as easy as getting her in. There's no way around it—I need to wake her up.

"Amy, we're here."

Nothing.

Remembering how she wakes and sharpens each time I mention Layla, I try again. "Amy, I have Layla upstairs."

Works like a charm. Warmth floods me. I might not know nearly enough about her, but I know she's a good mom. She hadn't wanted to depend on anyone else. Until I reminded her it wasn't just about her—Layla's needs superseded her pride.

She blinks up at me and pushes herself up from the seat. Looking around the car, she sighs. "Layla? Where's Layla?"

"Layla is upstairs waiting impatiently for her bottle. Once I have you in bed, I'll see to her." I promise.

Sighing, she nods. Her feet go down to the concrete of the garage.

She pushes up and out of the car. I'm right beside her and catch her as her legs go out from under her.

It happens all over again. Everything in me is rioting for more—to hold her tight, to taste her sweet mouth. Chocolate eyes are big and afraid. The fear is a fist to my chest. I never want to see it again. To cover the chaos inside me, I say the first thing I would to any other patient. Because she is, and this is all so wrong to feel when she's ill.

"You really waited until the last minute." I sigh as I lift her and close the car door with my hip.

"I was sure it would get better on its own." She croaks out as she allows her head to fall onto my chest.

I shake my head. "You could have wound up with rheumatic fever or harmed your kidneys."

She flinches at my admonishment. Big pools of melting chocolate are on me. "I'm sorry." It's nothing more than a whisper.

The words pierce deep into my chest. "Hey, it's okay. I'm sorry. I wasn't trying to make you feel bad. It's the doctor in me worried about the damage you could have done to yourself. All that matters is you got the treatment you need and you'll be better soon."

Her eyes slide closed. "Thank you."

I'm thankful her eyes are closed so she can't see what it does to me when she allows her head to fall against my chest. It's wrong, so fucking wrong, to want her this badly as I'm taking her into my home.

It doesn't help when she snuggles into me. I can't take my eyes off her. With her in my arms, it isn't simply emotion I'm feeling—it's a sense of peace I don't believe I've ever felt. Amy is in my arms where she belongs.

I can do this. I can take care of her without losing control of my base instincts. I will treat her like the patient she is until she's healthy enough for me to move beyond a doctor-patient relationship. And no matter what she decides, I will respect it.

In her bedroom, I lower her down on the bed. The moment she's out of my arms, they feel empty—I feel empty. Inhaling deep, I force air into starving lungs. Babbling interspersed with vocalizing that's coming closer and closer to crying warns me to move, or Layla is going to start howling.

I take off Amy's shoes. An urge to throw them away wells up inside me. She's not going to wear anything like them again. The same goes for her clothes—cotton, linen, and silk are what she deserves. No more holes or clothes that don't fit her. Layla too, she'll never wear something stained and second-hand ever again.

Leaving the door ajar a few inches, I go across the hall to the baby's bedroom. When she sees me, she gives a little cry of happiness. "You've been such a good baby girl, Layla. Thank you. Let's get you your baba."

Her little cry of recognition, followed by her reaching for me, hits me square in the chest. Cuddling her close, I'm overwhelmed by the way she clutches at me and babbles happily.

It takes a few minutes to make the bottle one-handed. Once she has the bottle in her mouth, she sucks greedily. I sit with her on the long leather sofa. I'm worried about how quickly she's drinking it.

Every time I try to pull the bottle out to burp her, she gets pissed.

Considering how long it took for me to get her the bottle, and she didn't scream for it, I can't bring myself to take it away.

She finally slows as she gets to six out of the eight ounces. Finishing the bottle, she's happy and smiling. I lay her on my legs, putting my feet up on the coffee table to bring her up more to see me. My cell phone rings in my pocket. I snag it and sigh at the display warning me it's my mother.

Fuck.

CHAPTER 4

$\mathcal{M}$atteo

"Yes, Mom."

"Matthew, I have brought you dinner. Are you at home or the clinic?" Despite being born and raised in Dallas, her voice is ever the crisp northeastern accent of a Connecticut debutant.

It's her nanny's accent. A nanny hired because she previously nannied for the Vanderbilt family. The nanny raised my mother and her brothers and sisters. Her parents barely made an appearance in her life.

Shit, now I feel bad. She brought me dinner again. Because she's aware that I don't eat properly. I run on protein shakes, scrambled eggs, and delivery. Although I'm not ready yet to share Layla or Amy with anyone—let alone my mom—I sure as hell am not going to hide them. "I'm home. You can come on up."

"Wonderful, dear. Five minutes or so."

The front desk called before allowing visitors up—except anyone we had on a list. Family had their own cards to scan in the elevators to come up to the condo. Mom learned to call before simply knocking on my door. I didn't like to wear much more than my boxers at home. She found out the hard way by coming up without calling when I answered the door without thinking.

Opening the door with Layla on my hip, I'm an ass for finding her reaction amusing. Wide green eyes go to Layla, and her mouth falls open. She looks to me, then back to Layla. She blinks a few times.

"Mathew, darling, is that your daughter?" I can't tell if she's happy or not.

To everyone but my mother, I'm Matteo. The difference is that my mother wanted to name me Matthew after her beloved brother, who died a few years before I was born.

My father wanted his children to have names that honored our Latin roots. While my mother was recovering from her cesarian surgery, he filled out the birth certificate with the name Matteo instead of Matthew. Despite previously agreeing to Matthew—she never forgave him for it.

I remember the way Javier found out he had a daughter. I laugh. "Kind of sort of. This is Layla. Layla, say hello to your Gigi. Her mother is in bed. She came into the clinic today with a bad case of strep throat. Once she's feeling better, I'm going to marry her."

Her hand goes up to the base of her throat. "Matthew, my sweet, beautiful child. You know I love you, right?"

I shrug and nod. While I grew up resenting the revolving door nannies we had in place of her as an actual mother. Her explanation of it was how she was raised, so she believed it was how things were supposed to be was understandable. Once she realized how her lack of a presence in our lives hurt me and my brothers, she apologized and attempted to make amends.

Also, she stepped in against my grandfather. In an attempt to manipulate me not to become a doctor, he refused to pay for college or give me any access to the family trust fund. Up until that point, my mother never went against my grandfather—even when she wanted to. His word was law in our family.

My mother never said a word to my grandfather—that I was aware of. She told me if I wanted to be a doctor, all I needed to worry about was getting into school. She would take care of everything else. And she did.

She paid my tuition, gave me a monthly allowance and a credit card in case of emergencies, bought a condo in New York for me to live in for my undergrad, and then a home in Baltimore for medical school. She was there when I needed her in every way.

"Have you lost your mind? You cannot meet a woman and decide you are going to marry her the same day. What does she think about this plan of yours? Does she know you are a Castillo? Or maybe she saw a white coat and—"

"Mother, Amy is unaware I'm wealthy. She might have seen the white coat and stethoscope, but she has no idea I plan on making her my wife. We've barely managed to speak thirty words to each other—"

"Jesus fucking christ, Matteo Alphonso Castillo." I hold Layla close and wonder if I should put her in her crib.

My mother has never sworn in my presence. Her repeated remark of people who swore are not simply uncouth but unintelligent to rely on such words is something I've heard often. She also hasn't said all three of my names at once since I was ten years old and trapped Javier in the dryer and had him go around a few times. He wanted to go in. So, I thought being grounded wasn't a fair punishment.

"Give me that baby right now. I am calling my housekeeper to prepare a room for the poor woman. She can recover in my home, where she and the baby are well taken care of. And not at the mercy of a man who has clearly lost his mind and should be seeking the care of a therapist." She holds out her hands for Layla.

Layla leans into me and babbles something around the fingers she's sucking on. Hmm, she's probably teething. I run a hand over her head and kiss her to reassure her.

"Amy and Layla aren't going anywhere. I'm already going to make an appointment with the therapist Rafe found me. I'll send an email to her today. Since I'm going to make changes in my life to give them the time and attention they deserve—the first of which is cutting my working hours from eighty to only forty. It's going to take some adjusting. I will need outside input to ensure I don't indirectly take anything out on Layla or Amy—"

"Wait, you are cutting your hours down?" She's frowning as much as the Botox will allow. She barely looks ten years older than me instead of the twenty-three years she is due to years of Botox and peels.

"Of course. I already hired the person who will take my hours to keep me from going over forty. Now that I'm thinking of it, I should also have someone who can do part time and is willing to be on call as needed. I'm sure there are going to be times Amy or Layla need me, and I won't be able to go in to work."

A hand goes flat in the middle of her chest. "You already hired someone? And now you are thinking of hiring another person..." She sits down on the leather sofa, her hands clenched in her lap. "I am going to need you to explain, very slowly, why you believe you are going to marry someone you have barely spoken thirty words to."

Hearing her say it, I understand the question. She's not going to like my answer. I sit down in the oversized chair next to the sofa. Layla snuggles into me on my lap, kicking her feet out with a grin.

"I just know." My hand comes up to stop her arguing with me. "I'm aware of how crazy it sounds. Do not fear I didn't wonder if it's a sane statement to make. There is Layla's father to contend with. The bastard broke her car seat base so Amy couldn't leave him. So that promises to be an issue. Amy is very clearly on her last hope and prayer as she was living at a truly atrocious motel. And from what I can tell, barely enough money for her and Layla to survive on."

My mother sighs and pinches the bridge of her elegant nose. Sometimes, I think my mother is overwhelmed by her sons and their unwillingness to fit into the public persona of a billionaire family in Dallas society.

"All of that will cause Amy to be wary of me. I have no doubt it will take time and patience to get her to trust in me. At the same time, I'm hopeful the connection we have is going to help her trust there's something between us she cannot walk away from. She refused to come home with me initially. It wasn't until I told her she could have all the pride she wanted except when it came to what was right for Layla. She folded immediately with regret she couldn't tell me no."

My mother is clearly surprised.

"That speaks to a woman with pride who also loves her daughter deeply and will do what's right for her—despite it being against what she wants."

43

She exhales slowly. "If she wants to leave, you will let her go?"

Those lines are trying to make an appearance on her forehead as I consider the question.

My honest answer is no. But I think she knows that already. "I'm going to do everything I can to ensure she doesn't want to leave. I need your help. Since I don't want to leave them here alone. Could you please shop for what they will need? Layla only has a few things I got from the donation room. And Amy has nothing at all except what she's wearing."

My mother's sigh is from the depths of her soul. "Fine. We have exceptional lawyers who can keep you out of prison."

I can't help laughing. It startles Layla, and she laughs, too. "Thank you, Mom. Say, thank you, Gigi." I tell Layla.

We're both shocked when Layla gurgles the word. "Gigi." Seeing our surprise, she laughs and repeats it. This time more clearly and with pride. "Gigi."

"Oh, my darling, yes. I am your Gigi." She reaches for Layla. This time, Layla happily goes into her arms.

I let go when it's clear my mother has a good grip on her. Odd, my arms feel empty the same way they did when I put Amy down. The sensation leaves me stunned for a moment.

Her eyes are on me with concern. "Matthew? Are you all right, dear?"

Unsettled, I nod as I force a smile. "Yes, you've got my girl, and I'm already attached to her. While you have her, could I make a quick call? I want to offer the job to the person I'm hoping will be part-time and back up before it's too late tonight."

"Yes, go on. Leave me to get to know my newest grandchild." My mother waves me away. Layla laughs and waves, too. Seeing them together, a sense of relief wells up inside me. She might not truly get it, but she's going to support me. And it's why I've never regretted forgiving her for my childhood.

It takes some digging to find the resume. The idea of someone who preferred not only part-time or on-call left me concerned they weren't committed and responsible. Especially when the notes are she has a social media presence that's important to her— that has to be accepted or she won't take the position. The staffing agency reviewed it and felt the videos she posted were unoffensive since they were only make-up reviews and tutorials.

By the time I'm off the phone with her I'm sure she will work out. Once again, the level of relief running through me surprises me. I wonder where it comes from, considering I worked long and hard to make the center happen. Will I regret it in a week or two from now?

I shoot an email to the therapist requesting a session as soon as possible with my reasons for not only seeing her but why an immediate session is necessary. As I write the email, I begin to understand why there's only relief I will no longer devote all my time and energy to the clinic. The center was to give me a place to serve my penance for being rich, the way oncology was before.

Except now that Layla and Amy need me, I'm done. I can finally see there's no need to pay a penance. I've spent fourteen years doing everything I could to save the patients I treated. I served my time. I more than earned the right to be happy, to live a life for myself and not others.

I find my mother completely engrossed in Layla. "We are going to get you the best of everything. You let your Gigi take care of it. Do you like pink, or should we get you a rainbow of colors? I believe we should go with some warm colors with your lovely skin tone. Is your mommy native, or is it your daddy? If it's Mommy, maybe we can go see a pow-wow. They are so much fun. The fry bread is so yummy. I must not have the whole thing. Will you share with your Gigi?"

Hearing my mother refer to another man as Layla's father has bile bubbling up to the back of my throat. Would I have to share her with another man? Send her off on the weekends, wondering if he's taking good care of her. It had to have been bad for Amy to leave him when she clearly was struggling on her own. I make a decision I'm aware could come back to bite me in the ass.

Back in the office, I grab Amy's wallet and open it. I'd left her purse in my office to put in the safe later. The number is in my phone, put there by Rafe when it comes to staffing. He told me to have the staffing agency run everyone through a private security company run by Taylor Hunt and Sam King. They were able to delve into the very minutia of a person's life.

I needed to know everything. The better to be prepared when I faced him with the news that I wanted Layla as my own. That's it—that's all I want out of the call—the means to make him fold on leaving our lives completely and totally.

When I walk into the living room this time, my mother is cuddling a sleeping Layla.

"How did you get her to sleep? She's been out for hours already. I was sure I had another hour or two to keep her occupied."

My mother's smile could split open her face. "She needed a burping session. Poor thing. She was out like a light two minutes after letting out the biggest burp. I'll put her in her crib."

"I need to put clean sheets on the mattress. I'm not sure if they left any." I'm ahead of her. The linen closet in the bathroom attached to the bedroom holds several fitted sheets for the crib and a few extra soft baby towels and washcloths.

The moment Layla is laid down in the crib, my mother is into everything. I have no idea where the pen and small notepad came from she's writing in. "Hm, so I will be doing an afternoon of shopping for them. And do take down the decoration on the wall for Ava. Javier said it would come off easily. We can put something up for Layla soon enough. Do you plan on making the condo your home?"

"Not for the long term. Layla will need a backyard to run and play in. I'll leave it up to Amy to decide the home when it's time."

"What were you thinking for Amy? And do you have her size?" My mother turns the page in her notepad.

"She's an eighteen. And she's only five-three, so keep petite in mind for length. Her shoe size is seven. I want several pairs of shoes for her. She is wearing leggings and a T-shirt. Since it could be all she can afford, could you get her a selection of clothes fit for this chaotic weather of almost January in Texas?"

My mother chuckles. "Yes, it can be difficult to go from a coat and gloves one day to a light jacket the next. I'll buy her basics. She can shop for what she would like once she's feeling better."

I'm nodding, hoping Amy doesn't resent my mother picking out her clothes. My mother has impeccable style. It's timeless in that what she wears can fit in easily almost anywhere. Her clothes were never flashy despite all of them having designer labels.

"Come along, dear. We want to let Layla sleep. You're going to enjoy your dinner right where I can see you."

I roll my eyes as I follow my mother out of the room, careful to leave it open slightly to hear Layla. Once, I got caught up in planning after she brought me dinner and didn't finish eating. When she brought me lunch the next day and found the half-eaten dinner, she was displeased—to say the least. Ever since then she sits with me while I eat to ensure I finish whatever she brings me.

She hands over her notebook. "Is there anything else you can think of?"

Sitting down at the dinner table, I go through it and add a few more things. Once I'm done, I hand her my credit card.

I open the container of food and find one of my favorites, chicken fried chicken with smothered potatoes and green beans. "You're going to make me fat."

She chuckles. "I think you're underweight. Too many muscles and not an ounce of fat."

I'm inhaling my food. Her housekeeper is an amazing cook. I don't bother arguing with her since she's not wrong. My main outlet for stress is working out. I'm heavy on weights and use a rowing machine. I only climb onto the treadmill once a week for a mile. Considering how much I work out, I should be eating more than once a day and chugging protein shakes. But food isn't a priority for me.

Only now with Layla and Amy in the condo, that will need to change. "I'm going to have to fill the refrigerator, but I'm not even sure what to do as far as…"

My mother rolls her eyes and holds her hand out for my phone. She downloads an app and fills the cart. "It's too late for today. So I put an order in for delivery tomorrow afternoon. Most of this is precooked, so you simply need to warm it up. The rest is prepared.

All you need to do is put it into the oven to cook. Since there is no telling as far as allergies go, I have been careful to keep it to mainly non-gluten items and minimal dairy items."

"Thanks, Mom. I appreciate it." I really do. I shouldn't be this clueless as a man at almost forty about ordering groceries. Except I have no idea what grocery stores are in Dallas or where they are. My extent of shopping for groceries was buying bread, eggs, and cheese from a nearby convenience store. In Baltimore, I had a housekeeper who dealt with all of this.

"You are welcome, dear. All right, see me out." She taps her cheek for a kiss.

Closing the door behind her, I wonder how soon before she spills to my brothers, and they come running to tell me this will be a disaster.

CHAPTER 5

*A*my

My bladder pushes me up out of the black. Blinking a few times to clear sleep so I can pick my way over the questionable patches on the motel carpet floor, I'm wondering where the ugly ceiling light went. Huh?

Wrapping my hands around the sheet and comforter, I'm startled to find it's not the thin hotel sheet and abrasive bedspread. My bladder sends me out of bed at a run to the open bathroom door.

My eyes won't take the overhead light, but it's not needed as I can see easily to move around the large bathroom. A nightlight plugged in near the vanity is given more strength from the mirror near it.

As I make my way on unsteady legs to the vanity to wash my hands, brief flashes come back to me. The doctor, Matteo Castillo, with the soft golden eyes. Golden eyes that felt like they saw into my soul and recognized me—even though I've never seen him before. At least, I don't think I have. Or maybe I had. I don't remember how I made it from the motel to the room.

The recognition scared me. Did he know Danny? Was Danny looking for me after all? Only it couldn't be. He's a doctor. I came to the clinic because of the pain in my throat. He wasn't going to hurt me—I knew it instinctively. Then, his gentle touch and concern confirmed it. I felt safe with him, so safe I longed to touch him to find out if he was real. He urged me to think of Layla...

Oh my god, Layla.

I'm back in the room looking for her. "Layla!" Damn it, it's a croak.

A croak that brings him running. The overhead light is flicked on, burning my eyes. "It's okay. Layla is right across the hall. She's sleeping. Come see for yourself."

He's only wearing silky black pajama bottoms. His wide, muscled chest covered in dark hair is on full display. There's a tattoo of a castle peeking through the hair. The oddest desire to trace the lines of the tattoo hits me—what?

I'm pulled out of the odd thought when he opens the bedroom door to the room directly across the hall from mine. The door was open already, only a few inches—enough for her cries to be heard.

When he notices I hesitate to go into the room, he opens the door wider and steps further back. Between the light in the hallway and a nightlight in the bedroom, it's easy to see the white crib with the sides up against the wall. Standing over the crib, I see Layla on her back with her arms spread out.

My sigh of relief is almost painful. The lingering pain from the... he said it was strep throat. Him, Dr. Castillo. I turn to find him watching me closely from the hallway.

"Do you want to get back to bed, or are you ready for something to eat?" He isn't whispering, but his voice is low enough not to disturb Layla.

I shake my head. I want to stay with Layla, but the only other thing in the room is a changing table and an empty bookcase. There's no bed or even a rocking chair.

Beneath the bright light in the hallway, he's somehow bigger, with muscles bulging. After the last year of Danny's abuse, fear is a reflex. I edge into the hall and step back from him. Yet I don't go back into the room I was sleeping in.

He notices my fear. "I'm not going to hurt you or Layla. You need a place to recover and help with Layla while you're doing it—that's all."

"Why?" I push the word out.

In the harsh light of day, all I can do is trust what is before me. Going on feel could end in a painful lesson. I never thought Danny would hurt me.

I don't trust the way he hesitates before shrugging. "You needed help, and I'm here."

"Why?" I press him.

His head goes down for a heartbeat. "I think I needed to take care of someone the way I wish someone took care of me." My chest hurts from the raw honesty in his words. "And Layla," he chuckles. "How could anyone look at her and not want to give her everything she needs?"

Something eases in me. He cared about Layla. It's coming back to me, him saying he took other patients home with him before. That had to be why I felt safe with him—especially with how large and muscle-bound he is.

Oh my god, he *did* carry me. As if I were nothing, and I felt so safe in his arms. It's enough for me to go back into the room I was sleeping in. I have no idea why, despite sleeping for what my body tells me is a long time, all I want is to sleep again.

"Rest. You let yourself get run down. It's going to take a few days of sleep before you feel better." Did he read my mind?

I'm climbing into bed with a yawn when he turns the light off. I don't even have to tell him to leave the door ajar.

This is an amazing dream. A man as stunning as Matteo Castillo could only be made in dreams. He wasn't perfect. His broad fore-head had deep furrows that matched the wrinkles around his golden eyes and wide mouth. While his nose is big, it fits his face. I don't trust his jawline and cheekbones are real. They had to be taken from those comic books I read when I was a kid. All of those hard and sharp features weren't anything I dreamed of before...so is he real?

My last thought is wondering how I'm going to go back to the motel after sleeping in a bed that feels like a cloud beneath silky soft sheets and a comforter. As I fall asleep, it's to the memory of the doctor carrying me. His strong arms were gentle and made me feel so protected and safe...the last thing I thought a man could make me feel after Danny.

MATTEO

I linger outside the room in case Amy needs me for anything else. Once I hear her soft snores, I exhale.

Closing my eyes, I swear long and low. The bastard hurt her. I make it to the office. Pulling up my email, I search for a response from the security contracting company. A report is already waiting.

I glance at my watch. It's a little after six in the morning, and the report hit my email twenty minutes ago. Opening it, I begin reading and almost wish I hadn't. I knew from the way she reacted to me someone abused her—that doesn't make it any easier to read.

Her husband. The word stops me. She hasn't divorced him. My jaw clenches. She will. **Soon**.

The fucker, Daniel Richards, tried to file a police report for her stealing his truck. Except she was the owner of record on it. He got belligerent when a neighbor told the police he heard Richards beating on Amy *again*. Were the cops finally going to do something about it?

He'd gotten pissed at the neighbor and took a swing at him in front of the police. What a fucking moron. When the cops stepped in, he took a swing at an officer. His award for the biggest dumbass in Waco was a night in jail and further charges he wasn't going to be able to get off on, considering he had previous convictions of assault.

Fuck. His family has money, if not a very good reputation. It's not as much as I have, but it's enough to hire a good lawyer. They also throw their weight around the small town of Temple. While they didn't think highly of their third son. He's back in Temple and listing their address as his current one. So, they could still be a factor.

I wince at Amy's childhood, or lack thereof. I'm telling myself to stop reading. The report was only to find out about him. This is what I want Amy to share willingly. Except I can't. And once again, I wish I hadn't. To go from such an awful childhood to that fucker. My heart aches for her.

There isn't much more to the file. I reply to the email thanking them for their quick turnaround and inform them that I have more work for them.

* * *

AMY

My bladder kicks me out of bed again. The moment I throw the covers off me, my stomach begins growling. Ugh, my throat hurts badly enough I'm not looking forward to food. It's not as bad as it was when I went to the clinic, but it still aches to swallow.

Holy crap with this bathroom. There's a soaking tub with jets and a separate shower large enough for four people. Everything is white marble, porcelain, and gleaming silver.

Out of the bathroom, I see another door open to a walk-in closet— filled with clothes. I wonder whose room I'm in. There's a note on the island.

My dear Amy,

I hope you approve of the clothes I selected for you. If anything is not to your liking, have no concern. It can be returned despite being dry cleaned for your immediate wear. We can exchange it for something else that would better suit you.

Bitsy

I blink several times as I wonder if I'm still dreaming. The closet is full. This closet isn't small. Take everything out of it, and it could be a bedroom large enough to fit at least a queen bed with plenty of space to spare. Although hangers are carefully spaced from each other like something in a store, it's freaking full. There's a map of where things are in the drawers of the island. Panties are in one drawer, bras in another, and leggings. Holy freaking crap.

All of this is for me?

Freaked out, I go in search of the man who can answer my questions.

Out of the room, I look to the left to see only one door at the end of the hall. I turn right toward the sound of him talking to Layla. It's an open kitchen, dining, and living room area. There is a large flat-screen television. The furniture is brown leather, with a long roll-arm couch and matching oversized chairs on each side. The area is anchored by a silk rug on the dark, wide-plank hardwood floor.

The table separating the living area from the kitchen seats eight and looks like it's made of one long piece of driftwood. Dark wood floors run throughout the space as far as I can see. I'm surprised the cabinets are a shiny slick red with bronze handles when everything else is in white and brown. Marble countertops add to the white color scheme. The appliances are stainless steel and massive. A double refrigerator large enough for a family of ten matches the six-burner stove with a side-by-side double oven.

I'm fighting not to be overwhelmed by the clear luxury of every-thing when my eyes finally fall on him, Matteo—Dr. Castillo. He's feeding Layla, who is in a brand new highchair with a bright yellow bib covering a pretty sky-blue dress. They both turn to look at me. Their smiles are oddly the same.

"Mama." Layla gives me a little wave before returning her attention to the spoon covered in baby food.

Matteo's eyes remain on me. "How are you feeling?"

I have no idea why I'm suddenly warm. My stomach twists in anxiety watching it happen. "Oh, Layla, no baby."

She was impatient and managed to grab the spoon and smear her face with the bright purple baby food she was trying to get into her mouth. Too late Matteo doesn't manage to grab her hand before she gets it on the pretty dress.

"I'm sorry." I apologize as I rush to grab Layla's hand before she can spread the purple goo anywhere else. Afraid he'll be angry at her and me for not raising her better. "I hope it doesn't stain."

He chuckles as he runs a wet washcloth he already had waiting over her hand. His large hands are gentle with her small one. "It's okay. She's a baby, messes are going to happen. Right, sweetie?"

Layla grins up at him. Her grin is so wide I can't help smiling too. He isn't angry or yelling at her for making a mess.

Relief allows me to exhale air from the bottom of my tight lungs. When he sees me staring, trying to figure out if it's only a hallway or another room past the living room, he nods his head toward it. "How are you feeling? Want to take a tour?"

Suddenly, I'm shy, and why is it so hot in here? Maybe I still have a fever. Since I'm actually able to speak without pain, it's definitely better. "Better, I think. Yes, please."

"Good. I'll show you the place." He unstraps Layla from the high-chair and picks her up.

There is another living room on the other side of the wall. This one is more formal in boring beiges. A white couch is in a stiff fabric with two matching chairs on each side of the couch. Another ottoman is used in place of a coffee table in beige, the same color as the plush large carpet in the middle of the room. The only splash of color in the room is a Christmas tree decorated in reds and greens with clear white lights. It's topped by a regal Santa Claus in bright red velvet. Oddly, though, it's missing a tree skirt.

He's moving down the hallway. There are more rooms down this hallway than the other one. A large full bath with a combined shower and garden tub, an enormous library with a shiny black baby grand piano, an office in the corner with light filling the room, and a game room filled with a pool table, arcade games, and a white screen with a projector pointed toward it.

"This place is huge," I mutter.

He shrugs. "It's not mine. This is my brother's place he built for himself. I needed somewhere while I figured out where I wanted to live. Did you find the clothes?"

"About that..." I follow him into the dining area where he puts Layla back into the highchair. He picks right back up, feeding her as though he's been doing it forever.

"You hate them? I'm sorry. We can go shopping—"

"No, I like them." I rush to reassure him. Actually, I hadn't looked closely. But I hate thinking of him so disappointed. "I'm, um, I mean...why? Why did Bitsy buy me all those clothes? And who is Bitsy?"

"Because you need them." He rolls his eyes. "Bitsy is my mother, and her given name, and what she will also answer to is Elizabeth. I'm not good at buying women's clothing, so I asked for her help. She also got Ms. Layla here all kitted out. Didn't she? Yeah, you liked the pretty dresses."

Layla laughs, kicking her little feet out the way she does when she's happiest. I'm stunned at the way Layla is so comfortable with him. She was afraid of Danny the few times he paid her any attention. Since he only did it to yell at her to shut up—it's no surprise.

"All done. Good girl, eating your food." He cleans her easily and efficiently.

"But there are so many clothes, too many clothes." I'm embarrassed when my stomach growls.

"I can get you something to eat. The fridge is full. You need clothes, so you got what you needed." He gets up, shaking out baby puff cereal onto the tray of the highchair for Layla. She scoops up one and gums it enthusiastically.

"No. I need to take a shower and get out of these clothes." I back away from him. Unbelieving of him getting up to make me something to eat.

"Okay. While you're taking a shower, I'll make you something. What sounds good?"

I'm so freaking hungry. "Everything." Flies out of my mouth. Oh god, kill me now.

His chuckle shimmers up my tummy. "Then it's a good thing my mother filled the refrigerator to its maximum capacity. She went heavy on soups for your throat. There's some I've never even heard of—"

"Soup. Yes, soup, please." All the soup sounds good. A dimple appears. This man is truly stunning. I turn to flee but am stopped before I make it back to the room.

"Amy?" He doesn't need to raise his voice to stop me in my tracks.

"Um, yes?" My eyes find him at the refrigerator.

"What kind of soup would you like?" The question is soft.

"Chicken noodle?"

"Okay, and would you like a grilled cheese with it or some other sandwich? I can make a grilled cheese without burning it. There's chicken, turkey, and two kinds of ham lunch meat."

"I would love a grilled cheese. But I don't think my throat could take the crispy bread. A turkey sandwich sounds good, thank you." I edge back down the hallway.

"Mayo, mustard?" He asks as he opens the refrigerator.

"Mayo only, thanks."

"All right. It will be ready for you. Take your time." He urges me before turning his attention back to the inside of the refrigerator.

My feet won't move at the chance to study him while he's unaware. Wow, he's so freaking stunning. Bent over, his ass is hard and perfectly round. I'm no better than a man. I tell myself to move, but I'm frozen—until he turns back to find me ogling him. Now, I'm practically running away, too embarrassed to say a word.

I fight not to slam the bedroom door. Leaning against it, I'm annoyed that I'm breathing heavily after exerting such a small amount of energy. Truly awake now, I study the large room.

It's twice the size of the motel room I'd been in for too long. There's a small seating area with an oversized chair and a large flat-screen television mounted on the wall. In the corner is a small white desk with an upholstered blue velvet chair.

I hear Layla banging on her highchair. The noise gets me moving to take the shower I'm longing for. I'm grateful as hell to take off my clothes with the promise of new ones to wear. It takes a few minutes to figure out the hot and cold in the shower.

Standing beneath the waterfall showerhead, after weeks of water pressure so weak it felt like being spit on—I fight not to sob with relief. For a long time, I simply close my eyes and enjoy the hot water running over me. When I'm worried I'll use all the hot water I open my eyes and hope to find shampoo in here.

A large cubbyhole is filled with not only white, fluffy washcloths but also body wash, shampoo, and conditioner. It's all brand new. Bitsy again.

The woman has expensive taste. I don't want to even guess what she spent on my clothes. Then I remember designers don't have fat women's sizes—that meant it couldn't be as bad as I fear.

Rinsing off the conditioner, my hair feels like freaking silk. Considering the cheap shampoo and conditioner I've been using left my hair feeling like straw, the expensive stuff is worth it.

I take my time drying off using one of the enormous towels on a heated rack and use a hand towel to dry my hair. There's a plush toweling robe on the back of the bathroom door. Wrapping myself in it, I sigh at how good it feels against my skin. On the vanity is an electric toothbrush with the head of the toothbrush covered in plastic packaging beside a bottle of body lotion. They weren't there last night.

I'm embarrassed at sleeping through her putting all this stuff away and the clothes in the walk-in closet. The bedside clock tells me it's almost two in the afternoon. I can't believe how much I slept. And if I slept that much, why do I still feel like I could sleep another ten hours?

In the walk-in closet, I'm once again stunned by the amount of clothes. My hand catches a long-sleeved, cotton candy pink shirt dress that would probably go down to my shin. It's so freaking soft. Is it silk? Curiosity has me pulling it down. Holy fucking shit, it's not only silk it's totally my size. How did she know?

It's beautiful. I long to wear it, but I'm too worried I'll ruin it or something.

I open the drawer Bitsy labeled as my panties. The drawer is filled with an enormous selection of silky panties. There are so many styles, some I've never seen before. Silk, they aren't silky. These gorgeous panties are all silk. It isn't until I get to the very bottom that I find three lone pairs of cotton briefs.

Opening the bras, they can't be... Oh my god, these are my size. I'm a 42D—a size I only became in the last few weeks. I was on the tightest of the three rungs on my tired nursing bras. Nursing bras because I couldn't afford to buy new bras even though I dried up months ago. How the heck could Bitsy know that?

The question spins in my mind as I go through the bras. They are so freaking beautiful—silk, gorgeous tulle, and chiffon. I don't want to guess how expensive these are. Oh, okay. Beneath the more than two dozen bras in 42D are another dozen in 44D bras. I'm not sure if this is better or not. Bitsy spent money on things that wouldn't be worn.

There are even multiple pairs of shoes. Casual slip-on sneakers, one in black and another in white, a pair of tan leather sandals with a chunky heel, basic black leather ballet flats, black and tan flip-flops made of leather, and even a pair of comfy pink slippers for around the house. Everything is in my size.

Why did Bitsy spend all this money on me and Layla? Thinking of the dress Layla was wearing and the gleaming new highchair, something tells me there are as many new things for Layla as there are for me. What was the point in spending all this money on me and Layla when we won't be here for longer than a few days?

A dozen more questions are tumbling around my mind. I'm urged into moving by the gust of hot air hitting me from the vent for the central air above me. I grab the first bra my hand finds and melt a little at how disgustingly pretty it is. It doesn't go with my plain white cotton briefs, but I shrug it off. It's not like my bra and panties usually match.

In the drawer for leggings, I'm once again astonished. There is no way these smooth, well-made leggings are something I could ever afford. It's not any better when I focus on the t-shirts hanging up. Even though all of them are plain and basic, they're all made of fine cotton so soft they almost feel like silk.

Dressed, my hand is pressing against my stomach in an attempt to still rioting butterflies. There's only one way to find out what the hell is going on.

CHAPTER 6

*A*my

All my fire dies when I find Matteo on his hands and knees with Layla also on her hands and knees. What I thought was a dress is merely a top and Layla is wearing matching pants.

"Come on, Layla, you can do it. You can crawl. You're such a big girl. Give me a little crawl." Layla is chuckling at him as she rocks on her hands and knees.

"She won't do it. It's my fault. I didn't put her down enough because I was too afraid at home. We were pretty much stuck in the bedroom, with Danny hating to see her in the living room. The babysitter who watched her thought she would crawl before I left Danny. But then we were stuck in the gross motel, and I didn't want her on the floor—even on top of a blanket." I sigh.

He goes to his knees, his insanely hard and round ass on his heels. "Hey, it's okay. She has space here to learn and she will before long. Don't beat yourself up over it." Lifting her up into his arms, he gets close. "Your soup is on the stove. I'll get it for you. It should be nice and warm. Your sandwich is ready on the table."

Layla laughs as she cuddles into him. I fight the clench in my chest when she doesn't reach for me. How long have I been asleep? "It's okay. I can get my own soup."

"Yes, but you want to hold Layla. I was going to hold her so you could eat your sandwich with both hands. But you can start with the soup. You can eat one-handed without too much of a mess." He offers me Layla, who gives me the biggest smile as she wraps her arms around my neck.

Oh, my girl. I inhale her baby scent deep into my lungs. She cuddles into my neck. How embarrassing. I'm blinking back tears. I sway and don't realize it until a firm hand is at my back, holding me up.

Instantly, I flash to when he touched me in the clinic. I was sure it was the fever and some weird dream—a crazy shock of electricity running all the way to my fingertips and toes. What the hell is that? My eyes find his glinting gold down at me. Wait, does he feel it, too?

"Why don't you sit down? I'll get your soup." A corner of his mouth tips up. It flashes again. He has dimples in both cheeks. And I'm going crazy. Of course, he doesn't feel it.

Embarrassed, I nod and move toward the table. The poor guy. He's just being nice and—wait. "What the hell with all the clothes and the baby stuff?"

There's a baby swing, a baby activity center in the corner where she can jump and play with the four inset toys, a half dozen baby toys are scattered around the living room and all of it looks brand new. Seriously, what the hell is going on?

An eyebrow is up as he brings me a bowl of chicken noodle soup, setting it next to a plate with an enormous croissant turkey and cheese sandwich. "Why don't you have a seat, and we'll talk about it?"

Warily, I sit at the table. My wariness doesn't compute to Layla. She giggles and reaches for the man with two dimples and the kind of ass women swoon over. My stupid stomach doesn't help either when it growls. I give in at the same time I hand over my daughter —the traitor.

He takes her with a smile, cuddling her close. I'm not sure who I'm jealous of. I can't ignore my stomach a minute more and begin to eat the soup. Damn, this is good soup. I'm a little embarrassed at how quickly I eat. Especially considering my throat is still tight with every swallow.

They don't seem interested in me. They're occupied with a toy where she can twist a mirror, letters, and numbers he's trying to teach her.

The soup and the sandwich are good. I managed to eat almost half of both. Once I'm done, I open my mouth to ask him what's going on.

He speaks before I can. "I'm sorry. I forgot to get you something to drink. What sounds good? There's orange juice, apple juice, pomegranate juice, sweet tea—"

"Does your mother do anything by halves?" I ask, in admiration and fear.

His laughter is bass and mellow and warms me more than the hot shower did. "Nope, it's a Castillo trait. Even though she married into the family, she's one of us through and through."

"Okay, I've had a shower. I'm dressed, and I've eaten. Can you please explain why you bought all this stuff?" I'm wary again and reach for Layla.

Handing her over, he nods. "I called the motel and spoke with the owner. In case he knew of any emergency contact. He told me there wasn't one. I was informed since you wouldn't be in to pay rent today or clean that your room would be rented. He would only hold your things for three days before disposing of it all."

I gasp at the heartlessness of the man. While I hadn't thought we were friends or anything, I thought he'd be a little more under-standing. Although it's a few days past Christmas, isn't it still the Christmas season—supposedly filled with compassion?

"Don't worry. All your things are here in storage."

Embarrassed he saw my pitiful two suitcases and Layla's lack of toys. I cringe inside.

"I'm aware losing the job as the housekeeper there and a room seems like a bad thing. But I think in the end, it's better for you and me. I'm in desperate need of a housekeeper. I inherited my brother's cleaner. Since he moved out a while ago, she took on other clients and didn't really have room in her schedule for me. I'm a pity client because I hate having people in my space I don't know. She only cleans the bathroom, kitchen, and my bedroom. And I need more than just cleaning."

"It looked clean to me."

The eyebrow goes up again. "You didn't look closely then. My mother was not happy about your closet and bathroom. She brought her own housekeeper over this morning to clean your room and bathroom as well as Layla's. It's not just about keeping

67

the place clean. I need a housekeeper. Of all the food in the refrigerator, only a half carton of eggs was there before my mother shopped."

His mom doing his shopping isn't a regular thing?

"Right now, I have an unhealthy dependence on a food delivery app and protein shakes. I'm looking forward to food in the fridge and meals a few days a week—not every day is necessary. Your salary would be fifty thousand a year, paid twice a month. It's only that low because it will be live-in. Since you and Layla don't have anywhere to live and I have the room. It seems like a waste for you not to live here."

My eyes bug out when he tells me the salary. That's low? Live-in? I can clean up after one person to earn that much. Except it doesn't feel like that's all there is to the clothes and toys. "What else is there? Because you didn't do all this for a housekeeper."

His dimples flash again. "You'd be surprised."

I shake my head. I'm not falling for those dimples—although it's not easy to ignore what they're doing to those butterflies.

Sighing, "I didn't even think of anyone helping me with this problem until my mom made an assumption about you and Layla. She thought I was hiding you as my girlfriend. So I figure, why not give her what she thinks you're doing here? I need your help to get her off my back by pretending to be my girlfriend."

"You big fat fucking liar." The words explode out of my mouth.

I startle Layla, him, and me. I have no idea where the words came from.

He double blinks. "I'm not lying."

"Yeah, no. You had me until you said you needed someone to pretend to be your girlfriend. Men who look as hot as you don't need a pretend girlfriend. Did too many people see you carry me out of the clinic, and it's too soon to sell me and Layla, or is it just Layla?"

He's laughing, not mad or stuttering, and interrupting me to argue.

I'm wondering if he's telling the truth after all. "Are you gay and need someone to beard for you? That I would buy."

Shaking his head, he smiles. "Thank you for the compliment. You're not so bad yourself."

I blush so hard my head swims. He takes his phone out of his pocket, works it for a minute, and then offers it to me.

"Read through it. You can see clearly it says Mom. Yep, keep scrolling. They're all about women she wants to set me up with. I've been back in Dallas less than six months."

"Where were you living before then?" I'm curious how far his mom's reach went. Damn, he wasn't kidding. They start with a woman's name and her stats are given like she's up for sale or something. I lose count after a dozen in the last three months.

"Baltimore, Maryland."

"Holy crap, your mom does not give up." I'm impressed and very scared of this Bitsy person. I hand him back his phone. Not only do I believe him now, I feel bad for him.

He shrugs. "I knew it would probably get worse once I came back to Dallas, but I wasn't truly prepared for it. Now it's not just her. My sister-in-law is in on it. And she's confident she has a better pool of women I should meet."

The sun catches the silver in his thick, dark hair. "How old are you?"

"I turned thirty-nine earlier this year."

Huh, I see his age now in the deep lines on his face. Yet he also seems younger when he's smiling at me and Layla. "Why did you come back to Dallas?"

A large hand runs over his face. Suddenly, he's every one of his years and a dozen more. Those frown lines are deeper than the Grand Canyon and his golden eyes are a flat brown. I have no idea why I want to reach out and touch him in an effort to allay the pain in him.

"I lost a patient. It's something I should have gotten used to—considering my specialty. But I never did."

Good. I don't say it, though. "What was your specialty?"

"I was an oncologist. Which means I treated cancer patients, specifically a pediatric oncologist."

Horror runs through me at anyone becoming used to losing a child patient. I hold Layla tighter to me.

"I don't know what happened exactly. I… I couldn't do it anymore. I didn't know where to go. So, I came back to Dallas since my family is here. And I don't know…" he chuckles.

It's a sad chuckle, and my heart goes out to the large, beautiful man who seems incredibly lost. The need to touch him is so strong I flex my hands to keep from doing it.

"I've been saying *I don't know* a lot lately. Anyway, all I've heard was how many women my sister-in-law thought would be great for me. She had better friends than the women my mother is trying to shove down my throat." He shakes his head, frustration clear on his beautiful face.

It's clear he isn't lying. "It's just ridiculous someone like you would pick someone like me."

He frowns. "What?"

Uncomfortable now, I search for the right words. "I'm fat. I graduated from high school at nineteen and from a community college when I was twenty-five. Because I have dyslexia and am poor and couldn't afford many classes while I was waitressing."

I flinch from thinking of Danny, but I can't hide from it—him. "And I'm married. To a man who…"

"What did he do?"

"He was very abusive, and I… I don't want to think of him. I can't pretend to be your girlfriend when I'm married. It's wrong. And it's wrong to lie. Just be firm with your family."

His sigh is heavy. "You're right. I'll figure something else out. Will you at least agree to be my housekeeper? I'm tired of eating delivery and protein shakes." I want to say yes. He sees it. "Let me show you something."

I follow him into a huge pantry with a washer and dryer on one side and multiple shelves with food on the other. There have to be more than forty different protein shakes. They're stacked twelve to a small pallet. "You weren't kidding."

"I could show you my spend on takeout from the delivery app, except it's too embarrassing."

I notice there's a little area of the large pantry on the food side filled with baby food, formula, snacks, bottles, plates, and bowels—

more than she could eat or use in weeks or even months. He cared about Layla.

His mom might have bought the things at his order, but he cared enough to order them. And I don't think I'll be able to forget the way he was on his hands and knees trying to get her to crawl. The way he was gentle as he cleaned her while laughing at her making a mess.

"So, what do you say? Will you save me from those protein shakes?" Both eyebrows are up.

Sighing, I give in. It's not like I really have many options. This place is a huge step up from the motel. Honesty compels me to warn him. "Okay. I'm not the best cook, though."

His smile of relief hits me in the tummy, causing it to tumble a dozen times in a second. "You couldn't be worse than me unless you burn the place down..."

Suddenly, his beautiful face goes tight. "I'm sorry. I should have given you more of a choice. You don't have anywhere to go. If you want to go to a shelter or even if you want to rent an apartment. The pay would be sixty-five thousand a year and I'm good to give you a month up front. My mother is another option. Since her home has seven bedrooms with only her there, there's plenty of room for you and Layla. And she loves Layla already."

The words come out of him, tortured and clipped. Hearing it and watching how he's having a hard time getting them out allows me not to burst into tears from fear he wants Layla and me out. Any other time, I would be twisting in agony that, once again, I wasn't wanted. Except the grip he has on Layla's little hand is tight.

Only I have to know for sure. "Do you want us to leave?"

He shakes his head fast. "No. But the right thing to do is give you all the options you deserve to have. I don't want you here because you feel it's your only choice."

Matteo, echoing my thoughts of only minutes ago, is why I'm staying...that's a lie. *He* is the reason why I'm staying. I feel safe with him. It started when I opened my eyes to find him looking down at me with concern at the clinic. Even though it's a dim, fuzzy memory, I knew he would help me, not hurt me.

His admission when I woke up this morning was raw with honesty. He wanted to take care of us the way he wished someone took care of him. His smile as he talked about Layla and now seeing him with her is another reason.

The way he didn't do anything but chuckle when she made a mess. The way he didn't flinch at the idea of bringing me here to take care of me. Or how, although his feelings were hurt by my fear of him—he didn't take offense or tell me that I shouldn't be afraid of him. Even with his offer of me leaving, he's giving me the room I need while making it clear he's here if I need him.

I would never go to a shelter. A waitress I worked with told me about a shelter after Danny gave me a black eye. She encouraged me to take my own pillows because her sister's daughter caught a bad case of lice while she was there. I don't want Layla in that environment.

An apartment should be appealing, except it's not. All alone in an apartment sounds scary. What if Danny finds us?

As awesome as his mother sounds, having her attention focused on me and Layla is as scary as being alone. What if I make a mess or drop something? While this condo screams money from how large and nice everything is, Matteo has made it clear he isn't bothered by the mess. That and here it's comfy and cozy to me. It feels safe here.

Matteo deserves to know. "I want to stay. Is it bad because I'm hiding behind you? Danny's family has connections. If they find me before I file for divorce, they and Danny could make my life hell. I do want a divorce as soon as I can afford it. But he..."

My stomach twists just saying the words. "He told me if I left him, he would file for full custody of Layla. But he doesn't want her. It's only to hurt me."

He exhales slowly. "I promise you, no matter what, he will never get close enough to hurt you and Layla ever again. As far as him getting custody, I won't let that happen. His family connections will never be better than my family's. Does that change your mind about staying with me?"

I believe him. This man would put himself between Danny and me and Layla. Except he didn't need to. He had the kind of money to build a wall between Danny and us. Yet, that's not the reason I shake my head. I don't want to leave here—him. I'm not sure why I feel so safe with him. Maybe it's the memory of him carrying me. Maybe I still have a fever. All I know is I'm not ready to leave this place or Matteo.

Something happens low in my tummy at the relief on his face. "Good. Now give me her so you can get back to bed." It's an order as he holds out his hands for Layla.

"I'm fine." I try to argue. Layla, the traitor, goes right to him.

He exhales what's almost a laugh. "Yeah, right. You look like you're about to fall over. Just a nap for an hour or two."

I'm ushered down the hall, right up to the door. I want to argue. Except I ruin it by yawning.

"Tell Momma, night night." He waves to me. Layla laughs as she waves.

Annoyed with them both, I close my door harder than I have to. He's bossy as hell. Then again, he probably has to be as a doctor. I yawn again as I climb back into bed. This is ridiculous. I'm not going to sleep for another hour or two again after all the hours I already slept.

I'm so grateful he didn't blink at my admission of hiding behind him. Behind his hard ass and his strong, broad chest—*stop thinking that way.* That will only lead to embarrassment because a man as gorgeous as he is doesn't want someone like me. No matter what he said.

It's too bad I couldn't bring myself to agree to pretend to be his girlfriend. That's as close as I would have gotten to being the girl-friend of a man like him. Pretending would be bad for me. I have a feeling he would make me want things I can't have.

As darkness takes me over, I sigh at what might have been.

MATTEO

I'm holding Layla long after she's fallen asleep. Holding her is more for me than for her. Amy called me a liar. How she knew I was lying when she barely knew me shocked both of us.

It was fucking spooky. She told me she didn't believe me because I was hot. I smile at the way she said exactly what she thought of me. Only I knew it wasn't why. Her knowledge came from the same crazy connection telling me that she's mine.

In the left brain—the part that rules logic—every neuron is screaming to abort fucking mission. This is all insane. Except it's not even the right brain ruling right now. It's something I laughed at before I laid eyes on Amy. It's kismet, fate, all that stuff that exists in the ether somewhere not ruled by anything other than feeling. It can't be denied. It won't be denied.

She felt it, too. That's why she chose to stay with me when I offered her other options. Every word hurt to say, but it didn't feel right *not* to give her choices. After everything she's been through, Amy deserved the right to have a choice of what her safe space would be.

I was certain she would choose her own apartment. It didn't matter that I had no idea where the apartment would be. As I said it, I imagined her in a cozy two-bedroom nearby. I felt compelled to offer up my mother's home, as my mother had wanted to take her home. There was no doubt Mom would happily accept Amy and Layla staying with her.

The moment she said she wanted to stay, I wondered if I was only hearing what I wanted. It was the moment Layla laid her head on my shoulder all over again. Just like then, I wondered where the twisting came from in my chest.

The small, hopeful smile affirmed her choice. She might have said she was hiding behind me, but I'm aware that's not the only reason. The only question I have is, is she also aware?

A twinge of guilt hits me for lying to her when she clearly had a distaste for lies. Her ex had done more than hit her body. He hit her soul and her trust in men. Yet she felt the connection between us—the desire simmering beneath the surface. If she pretended to be my girlfriend, it would give us both the freedom to explore the desire.

Except she wasn't ready to even pretend. She needs time to heal, not simply from her illness but from what he put her through. I don't mind waiting. For her and Layla, I'll wait as long as she needs.

Then again, maybe she won't need an excuse. She looked sad when she said no.

CHAPTER 7

*A*my

I'm seriously annoyed to find I didn't sleep for an hour or two. I slept for four hours. Four freaking hours. Matteo, with his bossy, hot ass, better not be one of those people who gloats when they're right.

This time, I find him asleep on the couch with Layla on his chest. Layla is awake, chewing on her fingers. Lord, his chest is so wide. He's wearing a long-sleeved plain cotton shirt in black to match his black sweats. It's seriously unfair how gorgeous he is. How could a man like him possibly need a fake girlfriend?

Layla sees me and gives a happy giggle and reaches for me. "Mama."

I melt at how happy she is to see me. I get my hands under her, but Matteo's arms tighten around her, not letting her go. He's awake, and brown eyes find me. Once his eyes meet mine, his arms fall away from Layla.

"Hey, how are you feeling?" He asks as he sits up.

Now I feel bad for thinking he'd rub in being right. I shrug. "I got four more hours. I feel better than when I woke up earlier. My throat only feels like I'm trying to swallow a small marble now instead of one that didn't want to go down at all like it did before I took a nap."

His eyes widen. "Why didn't you say something? I could have given you something for the pain. The reason I gave you a shot over pills was due to how much quicker the shot is supposed to work. However, I should have thought there could still be lingering after-effects. I apologize."

Pushing up from the sofa, he towers over me. It sends me a step back, wary of his size and strength. Eyes down, he gives me a wide berth as he moves around me. "I can grab it now. It's lidocaine. So it tastes like crap—"

My hand goes out to his arm to stop him without thinking. I should have thought of it first because I'm not going to get used to that crazy sizzle running through every cell in my body. He does feel it. His big body goes tense at my touch. I would have thought it was a bad thing, yet his sigh is deep and of relief—almost like he was glad it happened.

Tearing my hand away, too much of a coward to try to figure out what it means. "I'm good. Please, it's okay. I would have asked you for something if I needed it."

An eyebrow goes up. "That's a load of crap. You would have suffered in silence. For some reason, you think you deserve pain—to suffer—which is bullshit. You don't deserve it, and if I can relieve it, then I will. I'll be right back."

His words sting more than a blow. How could he say that? How could he *know* that? I sink down on the couch, still warm from his big body.

Layla claps, happy and content in my arms. Running my hand over her soft, round head. I press a kiss to her temple. If she were hurting, I'd do whatever it took to relieve her pain. Yet, I wouldn't even consider it for myself.

"Amy?" Matteo is back and offers me a small spray bottle. It's labeled clearly as lidocaine, but there's nothing to indicate it's a prescription.

I take it. "Is it yours? Do you need it?"

His smile is soft, like his eyes. "I've had it by my bed because my throat dried out so badly with this weird weather it felt like I had a paper cut. I bought a humidifier and haven't needed it since. Hold it in your throat as long as you can by gargling, then spit it out. It's not awful if you swallow it, but it's not great either."

"Thank you." I hand him Layla and take it into my room to use it. Oh, that is nasty. Once I spit it out, I brush my teeth.

When I come out of my room again, he's got Layla on his lap, sitting on the chair beside the couch. "Thank you. It works—I can't feel a thing. Is the weather in Dallas hugely different from Baltimore?"

He exhales what might be a laugh. "It's fifty-six degrees here with light winds. There's snow on the ground in Baltimore. It's been there for a week, and it's thirty-four degrees. East Coast weather took a lot of getting used to after growing up in Texas."

"How long did you live there?" I'm curious about him.

"I spent twenty years on the East Coast. I wanted my specialty to be child cancer, and Johns Hopkins was the best med school for it. My hope was to do my undergrad and med school there. But I didn't make it in for my undergrad. It didn't matter I got into several top-notch Ivy League schools—I wanted Johns Hopkins."

Again, I wonder how he could really think I would be a good choice for a fake girlfriend. He had his choice of Ivy League schools, and I went to a tiny community college. The mere idea of having to answer where I got my pathetic associate's degree has me cringing deep inside.

"As disappointed as I was, I accepted at Columbia in New York. Then I worked my ass off to become good enough for when it came time to apply for med school. I applied again and got into Johns Hopkins. I made it clear to my professors that it was where I wanted to do my internship and practice. Thankfully, it all worked out."

He's so driven. It hits me. "Who made you want to be a child oncologist?"

Those golden eyes darken to brown as they fall from mine. He pulls out a worn leather wallet from his pocket. Opening it, he takes out a picture and offers it to me. It's a faded school picture of a little girl with a mischievous smile. She's black with her hair in braids with brightly colored beads at the end.

"She's the reason, Susan Cartwright. I met her when I was eight and told her and anyone who would listen that I was going to marry her one day. Her leukemia appeared when she was eleven. She was dead before she turned fourteen."

Oh my god. "I'm sorry." I offer him the picture back.

He takes it and nods. "Me too. She was what kept me going during those years when I wondered if I could make it through medical school. When my first patient died..."

"And when your last one died? When you decided to quit and come back to Dallas." I prompt him when he trails off, lost in a distant memory.

Shaking his head, he sighs. "When Lucy died—my patient. Not even Susan could keep me going. I did everything right, and she died. It shouldn't have happened. I've lost so few patients over the years because I fit the treatment to the patient, not the treatment for the cancer. The way many of my colleagues did. Cancer treatment is..."

A large hand covers his mouth as though he doesn't want to let the words out. "It's not easy on the patient. You're bringing them to the edge of death to kill the cancer. Sometimes, the treatment doesn't just kill the cancer. After all these years, I had it down. Two plus two equals four. There are laws that—"

"Three plus one also equals four. Albert Einstein said: As far as the laws of mathematics refer to reality, they are not certain; and as far as they are certain, they do not refer to reality."

A bemused smile appears as an eyebrow lifts. "And you think I would be ashamed to have you as a girlfriend? No woman I've been with has ever quoted Einstein to me. By the way, my nephew has dyslexia. There's nothing to be ashamed of in being dyslexic. He didn't start university until he was twenty. He's a lawyer now."

I can't hide my surprise. "I'm impressed. It was torture just to get an associate's degree."

He shakes his head. "Santos had the best in study aids, tutors, and professors who made allowances for his dyslexia. He still called me in the middle of the night, complaining about the same feeling of torture. You should be proud of your degree. No one in my family, or me, would ever see your dyslexia as a negative."

I'm not sure why I'm close to tears. "Things were so hard for me. It became easier to memorize things. Danny laughed at me, studying at night. And rolled his eyes at how happy I was earning a B on a paper. When I finally graduated, he said they gave it to me because they were tired of seeing me at the school."

His jaw clenches. "It wasn't true, not a word. He was breaking you down, so you'd be grateful for him, which is complete bullshit. You are a woman anyone would be proud to have by their side. You're stubborn, intelligent, and street-smart. You also have the kind of integrity that's getting harder to find. A good mother who cares more for her daughter's safety and health than your own. You aren't perfect, none of us are. You need to learn not to diminish your accomplishments and yourself. Be proud of who you are—how Layla would be proud of you if she had a say."

I blink back tears. Layla is concerned and reaches for me. I take her from Matteo, and she buries her face in my breasts. "You don't know me. I met you a day ago, and I've been asleep for most of it—"

"While you were running a fever and barely able to stand, you told me that you could take care of yourself. You gave in to letting someone help you only when it became clear you could not take care of your daughter. You weren't willing to hand over your problems and let someone else handle them the way so many would, and frankly, there's no shame in doing so. The way you aren't willing to lie to my family when it would benefit you and Layla, I know enough." He's firm.

I'm blushing at the way he talks about me. No one has ever said anything like it before. "What do you mean when you said lying would benefit me and Layla?"

"As my girlfriend, the vehicle I'll buy you would be much nicer than the safe and serviceable SUV or minivan you'll use to run errands in. Also, you'd go shopping for nicer clothes for you and Layla. I'd also be making calls to find the best nanny for Layla. Now, I'll only be looking at getting her in with the nursery school—"

"You're buying me a car? And more shopping, are you nuts? Why in the world would you hire me a nanny?" It finally hits me, nicer clothes than what I have now—which were already some of the nicest I've ever had. "You're rich. Like rich, rich."

The exhale thing that's almost a laugh. He nods. "I'm rich, rich. My grandfather founded a construction company in Mexico City. Once he emigrated to the United States, he opened an office in Dallas. It took off. He shut down his other offices to focus on growing it. Within a decade, he became a citizen and a multimillionaire with offices in Austin, El Paso, and Houston. That was more than forty years ago. Now, the Castillo Company is in Los Angeles and Phoenix. They recently shut down their Miami and New Orleans offices because my older brother was tired of working sixty hours a week. He wanted to devote more time to his family."

He shrugs like it's not a huge fucking deal. "There were some issues when my father and his brother took over after my grandfather retired. My father and uncle fucked up big time, and the company was in freefall. My older brother Rafe walked out of high school and into board rooms. Rafe and my grandfather managed to right the ship, and now the company is worth billions."

"Billions?" I can barely get the word out.

"Yes. While I have nothing to do with the company, the earnings from it gave me the means to make my own money. The monthly allowance I received while I was in college was more than I needed, so I used the remaining money to invest in the market, medical technology, and companies that needed money they couldn't always get through typical investors. I rarely lost any—I usually made it back overwhelmingly. Once I started receiving money from the family trust, I could invest more and get a higher return.

I hold Layla tighter to me, needing her against me because I feel like I'm in a dream. This can't be real. I'm sitting in the home of a billionaire who asked me to be his housekeeper and pretend to be his girlfriend to keep his family from throwing women at him. "You wanted me to pretend to be the girlfriend of a billionaire? Me? I'm no one—nothing compared to you."

His jaw goes hard, and the air around him has me sitting up straighter, preparing for something I can't define. "I'm aware your soon-to-be ex-husband said horrible things to you in order to keep you from believing in yourself enough to think you could do better than him. However, I'm going to warn you that I do not like, nor will I stand to hear you say such things about yourself. You are **not** nothing. You are not no one. Everyone has an intrinsic value to the world and others all their own. You are worth far more..."

I watch as his hand covers his mouth. I want desperately to know what he was going to say. He shakes his head. "Please. If not for yourself, then for Layla. Do not put yourself down that way. Do you think Layla is nothing?"

The question is painful as she gives me kisses in the wet way she does with her whole mouth open on my jaw. I fight not to squeeze her to me. All I can do is shake my head.

"You don't know me." It comes out of me in a tight whisper—not because my throat hurts, but because the words hurt.

"I know all I need to know. But I would love it if you told me more." It's a gentle invitation.

Once I do, he'll understand and…agree? I shake my head to clear it. "My father used to beat my mother, me, and my two older brothers the same way Danny did to me. To escape any way she could, Mom got addicted to drugs. She overdosed when I was fourteen. I promised myself that I would never be with someone like that. But I did the exact same thing, down to a man who would hit a baby. The day I left him, he was going to hit her. It's why I left with barely any money and no plan."

"That was brave of you. I wondered what led you to be all alone with a baby. You got out before she experienced what you did. And she'll never know that because of you. It must have been hard to lose your mother so young when you needed her most. She must have been in a lot of pain. My hope is you'll tell me your father suffered for the pain he caused everyone."

My chest twists at the sincere sympathy in his eyes as they meet mine. There's not an ounce of disgust—how Danny reacted when I told him. "I don't know if he did later. He just walked out after they took her away in the ambulance and never came back. My older brothers left, too. They didn't even tell me goodbye. I'm not sure where they are. I went into a group home."

I cringe at the memories of that place. "When I was eighteen, I left. Even though I hadn't graduated high school yet and could stay until I did. I found a roommate desperate for my rent money."

Her kindness was something I badly needed. When she married and moved to Florida three years ago, I missed her and still do.

"Danny was a regular at the restaurant I waitressed at. I was twenty-three and had no interest in men. All I heard from them was that I was too fat to be appealing. Most men looked through me as if they were afraid treating me like a human being would cause me to fall in love with them and become some sort of stalker or something. So, I avoided men entirely. My focus was on school and trying to find a way out of waitressing. Danny was persistent. I was flattered. He was forty-two, had a good job he'd been at for years, and owned his own house. While he was no cover model or anything, he wasn't ugly. And more than a few times, he said he didn't usually like women who were as big as I was. But there was something different about me. It made me feel like I was special to him."

"Nineteen years older than you?" He hisses the words in barely contained anger. "The fucker was too old for you. He counted on your youth and inexperience. As far as your weight, that's complete bullshit. I can't answer for other men, but you are *extremely* attractive."

I blush when he says I'm attractive while my stomach flips a dozen times. He's just being nice...right? *Stop it. Focus.* He doesn't need to worry about some lovesick idiot in his house.

"He lied a lot. It turned out he didn't own the house, he rented it. Stupidly, I was flattered by the lie—thinking it was because he wanted to impress me. Almost a year after our first date, I got pregnant. Then I had a miscarriage. I'd only known for two weeks and was only ten weeks in, but I was torn up over it."

"I'm sorry." The words are hushed.

"Thanks," I mumble. Even now, a pang of sadness hits me. "It was the first time he yelled at me. I needed to shut up and stop crying. I didn't take it in, not really. In the moment, I welcomed it. I didn't want to keep crying. He said he was sorry. Then he promised we would have another baby when the time was right."

"You didn't deserve it." Is muttered low between gritted teeth. "Promising to have another baby to replace the one you lost is bullshit. There is no replacing what was lost. Not in your heart or in your mind. You are allowed to feel your pain and express it the way you need to."

I swallow a lump at his understanding. "Then my roommate told me she was moving out of state. Danny figured I might as well move in with him. I was on the pill by his demand. For over a year, things were great. Well, now I can see it wasn't really. He put me down a lot and would say it was a joke. If I said anything, he told me that I was too sensitive. Then he would say he loved me like it was supposed to make it all better."

Looking back now, the number of red flags is almost overwhelming. How could I have not seen them? Layla waves her hand as gibberish comes out of her. Almost like she's speaking for me.

"I didn't love him." I'm waiting to see disgust in Matteo's eyes. Or at least judgment, except there's none. "I wanted to. After he told me he did, I said it. Kind of like if I said it then it would make it true. Any day, I told myself, it will happen. Only it never did."

"You aren't the first person to think the same thing. It's probably more common than people actually being in love. And sometimes, it does grow into love. Sometimes it doesn't. Whether it does or not, it's bullshit to hurt a person because they figure out there isn't love there."

Running a hand over Layla's head, I fight tears at his gentle assurance. Am I telling him all of this for him to understand it didn't start with Danny hitting me? It felt like any normal couple I saw around me... That's not true. I saw better relationships. I just didn't think I deserved what they had.

"As soon as I got my associate's degree and started interviewing for a new job, Danny told me we were moving to Waco. There was a position I was perfect for, and I was positive they were going to hire me. They even assured me they had no problem with my dyslexia—another person who worked there had it, too. So, there were already things in place to accommodate me. Except they never called me back. He said it was a sign to move. He'd get a better job, so I wouldn't have to work at all since he was ready for a baby."

Matteo shakes his head. "He was making you dependent on him. With you in a new city, you would feel like you couldn't go back. That you had to make it work. You also didn't have friends or support there to help you see how bad things were."

My stomach twists at how stupid I was for being happy I didn't have to work. Hearing Matteo say it, I can finally see how right he is. Not working kept me trapped. "I didn't see it then. I wish I had. Instead, I agreed with him that my job would be staying home with our kids. Three months later, I was pregnant. We got married, so his insurance would cover me and the baby. I was sad it was only a courthouse ceremony."

I'm embarrassed to admit how sad I was. It was silly to be sad. I should have simply been happy I was getting married.

"Everything changed when we found out I was having a girl. He didn't hide his disappointment. Instead, he made me promise the next one would be a boy—as if I had control over that. He got meaner and stopped saying he was joking. Then he slapped me. Immediately, he apologized on his knees. He'd gotten hurt and was drinking and on pain pills. I convinced myself it wasn't him." Closing my eyes, I fight back the tears. "I'm so dumb. I should have left then."

Suddenly, Matteo is beside me. He takes my hand, and the sharp zing of electricity running through me sends my eyes up to his.

"You *weren't* dumb. Men like him are looking for sweet, kind, women like you to accept them the way they are. They don't want to change for the better—the way you deserve. He didn't start by thinking he was going to hit you. There was no plan for that. But deep down, he resented you. You didn't want him or need him. So he contorted himself and you until you did. Until you were afraid, he would leave you. Once you needed him, he won."

"He resented me from the beginning? Why move me in with him or be excited about me being pregnant?" It doesn't make sense.

"We all want to be needed, to be cared for, to be loved. When you met him, you didn't need any of it. He resented you for not wanting any of those things from him—he had to work to get you. In his eyes, it meant you had more power in the relationship. Once he had you, you were a trophy he won. Until things got real with the pregnancy and miscarriage. At his age, he probably figured, why not be with you? Until you didn't give him what he wanted. Then he began to resent you again."

Oh my god, I see everything from the beginning with new eyes. "I was so stupid to fall for all of his bullshit."

"No, you weren't. It's not on you for taking him at face value. He's the one who lied and manipulated you. Men like him go after younger women because they've experienced less heartache, dealt with fewer assholes, so it's easier to get what they want from you. If you had agreed to jump into something with him, he would have used you for a few weeks or months and moved on to the next woman."

I shake my head. "I think deep down I knew he would move on if I gave in. It's the reason why I was so resistant to getting involved with him. I didn't believe he wanted the same thing I did—a relationship. But you're giving me attributes I don't know if I can live up to."

That exhale laugh thing. "I'm calling it as I see it. Hopefully, in time, you'll see it for yourself. Thank you for telling me about what you endured. You didn't have to."

"You need to know who you have living in your home."

His sigh is heavy. "Thank you. And I have to tell you in full disclosure that I had you investigated... Because I needed to know who I had in my home."

It doesn't really surprise me, especially with the whole billionaire thing. It also doesn't bother me. "You are crazy bringing home some woman and her baby. What if you woke up to all your stuff gone?"

"Since it's not my stuff, I'm not attached to anything. Even if it was all mine, I wouldn't mind. Because I know you would be doing it for Layla, not you. You can have anything for Layla. She deserves the world. So do you. You just don't believe it yet." He squeezes my hand gently before letting me go.

The moment he lets me go, I long for his touch again. I shake my head. "You are crazy."

I say the words to him, but also to myself. *Stop wanting what you can't have. It will hurt so much worse when it's all over.*

"Maybe." The words don't offend him. "I'm starting therapy tomorrow. I have to admit I'm not looking forward to it." Standing, he smiles down at me. "How about some dinner? I'm getting hungry."

CHAPTER 8

*M*atteo

I walk away from her. Because if I don't, I'll take her into my arms. She's not ready for that. The last thing in the world I want to do is move too fast for her.

She follows me into the kitchen with Layla on her hip.

"Let me see what all my mom bought. She made sure to get most of the food options we only need to warm up, although there are a few things we need to cook. No, you sit." I order her as I try to focus on the inside of the refrigerator. Instead of the way her shirt is pulled tightly over her breasts by having Layla on her hip.

"I feel like that's my job." She sighs.

I shake my head. "Not until you're recovered. Let's give it a few more days. Okay, our options for food we only need to warm up are chicken fettuccine, chicken and cheese green chili enchiladas, salmon with rice, and the last thing is meatloaf with mashed potatoes and green beans. The stuff to cook is pot roast with baby potatoes and carrots, stuffed peppers, stuffed flounder, and stuffed chicken, so basically stuffed things. What sounds good to you?"

"The chicken fettuccine, please. Layla loves pasta. She loves she can eat what I'm eating. Since pasta is soft, I've given her some." Layla perks up at the sound of her name, hooting for attention. Damn, she's adorable.

"Chicken fettuccine it is."

There's a plastic outer container, and inside it's a thin metal tray to go into the oven for twenty minutes at 350 degrees. I like that it's not supposed to go in the microwave. Bypassing the oven, I go to my crutch appliance in the kitchen.

"What is that?" Amy asks.

"It's a toaster oven and air fryer in one. I might have lied. If you took this, I'd be upset. I use it in place of a microwave. Food tastes a thousand times better in it. Especially takeout I reheat. It's almost as good as when they deliver it. I'm going with the oven setting. It doesn't take forever to preheat or make the room hot like a regular oven. When it comes to being single and not a great cook, this helps."

"I guess I would have thought someone as accomplished as you could cook. My cooking is pretty basic." She warns me again.

At least I'm completely honest in the need for a housekeeper. "While I learned a few things from my grandfather as a kid, in college and med school, I didn't have the time to cook. I lived off things that took minutes to cook in the microwave—cheap ramen, sandwiches, and scrambled eggs. I finally gave up ramen noodles when I got older. But once I got the time and tried to cook, I managed to forget most of what he taught us. After I set off the fire alarm for the fifth or sixth time, I gave up."

I'm not going to tell her if it weren't for the high sodium in the cheap ramen, I'd probably still be eating it. "I don't care if you can cook. I'm content if you order these meals. It saves me from being bad with too many hamburgers and fries—my red meat intake needs to come down, along with my grease. No amount of time lifting weights will save my heart from trans fats."

I love her smile and shake of her head. She doesn't smile nearly enough. I'm going to do my best to give her every reason to smile.

"I'm not picky and will eat most things. My main problem is I forget to eat when I'm busy. I also have a hard time deciding what to eat, and it's easier to swallow a shake and go back to work. Do you have any dishes you like to make?"

"My mom raised us on a meat and potato-heavy diet. The things I can do to a potato are what I'm most proud of. When I lived with my roommate, she taught me about spices and how cheap chicken was to cook. I wish I could say I have a bunch of recipes featuring chicken—I don't. It's mainly different variations of chicken seasoned differently and rice." She shrugs self-consciously.

"That doesn't sound bad to me. Although it's probably a good idea to add more veggies. Even though I honestly hate eating vegetables." I admit.

"My housekeeper in Baltimore loaded my freezer with vegetable sides I only needed to toss in the toaster oven. Half of them were covered in cheese. There were some in sauces I liked. I'm not expecting you to whip up a Michelin-rated dinner or five courses. My previous housekeeper was a lot like you. She would cook grilled chicken to go with the frozen sides, so there was always something to eat in the fridge. I'm good with that." I try to reassure her.

"How did you go so long without one here?" She catches her bottom lip with her teeth.

I fight not to groan at the way it's wet and full, wondering what she tastes like. Shit. My cock is stirring. I turn my attention to how much time is left on the food.

"Like I said, an unhealthy dependence on takeout. The current cleaner will be relieved when I inform her that I no longer need her. If I hadn't told my mother that you agreed to be my house-keeper she would have had someone in here before the end of the day. She was upset at the amount of dust on the baseboards. I didn't—and still don't care about baseboards. I needed the kitchen and bathrooms clean."

"Today? She couldn't really hire a housekeeper on a Sunday, could she?" Her chocolate eyes widen.

I've never been into chocolate, yet I have a sudden, desperate craving for the sweet treat.

"Your mother sounds scary."

"She isn't as bad as she sounds. It was her assumption I was using the housekeeper thing as a cover for our dating that made me think of asking you to pretend to be my girlfriend. She's fallen in love with Layla and has Layla calling her Gigi already. My mother has a habit of collecting children and deeming herself their Gigi."

She looks warily down at Layla. I'm not sure if it's good or bad when Layla pipes up with a happy "Gigi."

* * *

AMY

I can't help going tense at his mother thinking we were a couple and at the idea of her calling herself Layla's grandmother. Layla's happiness is a punch to the gut. Although Layla was always a happy baby, it was almost like she was happy to please me—as if she believed she had to be happy to be loved—the way I grew up.

Only now she's genuinely happy. It's like she went from a 60-watt lightbulb to a 100-watt. I'm glad she's happy, yet deep down, all I can think is—how much it will hurt her when we move on?

One thing I've learned is that good things don't last. What will our lives look like when Layla is ten and knows what a Gigi is, and Bitsy has moved on to her real grandchildren?

"Hey," it's soft, almost a whisper. "It's all going to work out. I promise."

How can he read me so well? "How can you be sure of that?"

Both dimples flash. "Because I said so."

I shake my head in wonder. "Because you're a billionaire, and things always work out for you."

He exhales a laugh. "My grandfather told me once that you don't get what you deserve. You get what you're willing to fight for. I didn't get into the undergrad I wanted—I had to work my ass off for it. In medical school, no one gave a shit how much money my family had. You have to pass every test and treat any patient the same way someone who doesn't have a dime next to you has to. When it comes to losing a patient, money doesn't protect you from the pain."

"I'm sorry, that was rude." I'm ashamed.

"It's fine. I got it a lot when colleagues found out about my family." He says it's fine, except I can tell it isn't. Feeling guilty all over again, I accept when he changes the subject. "If my mother makes you uncomfortable in any way, let me know. She doesn't get a free pass because she's my mother."

"I guess... I don't want her to think I'm taking advantage or something with all the things she's bought for me and Layla. Especially when I no longer feel so guilty about not being able to give her anything for Christmas. Or that she spent her first Christmas in a crappy motel room."

Matteo shakes his head. "She won't remember her first Christmas. You did the best thing for her. It wasn't easy to leave, but you did it to protect her. That is what she'll remember."

I get lost in the swirling gold of his eyes. I'm not sure why I can't catch my breath and why it feels so warm. It must be because the fever hasn't left completely.

The toaster oven goes off with a high-pitched ding, startling me. I blink and find him using oven mitts to pull out the tray. "The directions said to let it sit for five minutes. Let me get some oatmeal made up for Layla."

"I can do that—"

"No, you can't. I'm forbidding it for tonight." He smiles down at Layla. "Yeah, you know we're talking about you. You're so smart."

His eyes meet mine. "You've done an amazing job with her. The way she already can talk. She recognized the alphabet and got excited when I said it. Then she did her baby talk like she was trying to repeat what I was saying."

I blush. "I worried I was being too... I don't want anyone calling her dumb the way they did to me. That's not fair to her either, though—"

"Hey, it's okay. You're a good mom. She knows she's loved. It's rare for a baby who has lived through the environment she did to still be happy and smiling. She's like that because of you. And please remember, not all babies or children meet every milestone at the same time."

Tears sting my eyes at him calling me a good mom. All I've wanted since the moment they placed her in my arms was to be the best mom I could be. I was going to give her the childhood I longed for. One where she felt safe and loved and never worried about not having food in the refrigerator or if the electricity would be shut off when she woke up—the way I did.

Watching him move around the kitchen making formula and carefully adding oatmeal until it was what he deemed the perfect consistency. I can't help but be impressed. The words fly out of my mouth without thought. "You're good at all of this. How many kids do you want?"

He goes still. Soft gold meets mine. "I never gave it much thought. More than two would be nice. Having built-in friends and someone to learn from is something I'm grateful for in growing up with my brothers. What about you? Growing up, what was your dream for the life you wanted?"

I'm not sure why it's so hot in here. I want to be flippant, to make a joke. Only with those golden eyes so intent on me, I can't.

I've never once spoken it aloud—too afraid it would never come true if I did. Since Matteo has been so honest, it feels wrong not to return it. "I dreamed of four children, two boys and two girls. The boys would be older and take care of their little sisters the way I wished my older brothers would for me. It felt like I lived alone even before my mom got lost in drugs."

Remembering the silly dream, I blush from embarrassment. "To be an artist, to paint and my work would sell steadily. No huge shows or fanfare, just a few people who loved what I put on canvas. That they found it...worthy of their money."

"And your husband? What did you dream he would be?" How does a man so large speak so softly without whispering?

"I didn't see him in my mind. It always felt like it was just me and my children." I shrug. How did I never see a man? The children had to come from somewhere. A man never even crossed my mind.

He grabs a bib, and the second Layla sees it, she gets excited. Taking the small bowl, spoon, and bib to the highchair he sets them on the tray. "Do you want to feed her, or can I?"

The way he asks, as though he *wants* to feed her—take care of her. Despite the mess that's feeding her. It steals the air from my lungs. All I can do is nod as I strap her into the highchair.

While I was getting her bib on, Matteo managed to dish out the chicken fettuccine and place both our plates on the table. He also has a glass of sweet tea and the orange juice he insisted I drink.

Sitting down across from him, I watch as he cajoles Layla into eating the cereal with the promise of some pasta if she finishes her bowl. I'm not sure she understands him, but she eats the cereal begrudgingly. Finally, he gives in and puts a noodle he's cut into tiny pieces on her spoon. She's hilarious with how excited she is, opening her mouth so wide I wonder if it hurts.

I laugh when she slurps down the noodle while she kicks her feet and her hands ball into fists.

"Yeah, this is some good noodles. Good job eating all your cereal like a big girl." Matteo chuckles.

Her mouth opens wide like a baby bird begging for more. He sighs and begins cutting up another noodle for her. "It's a good thing you're strapped in because you're kicking your feet enough to take off into space."

"I'm glad she likes this because I've never made fettuccine before. I'll probably order more of this. It's better than what I've had in restaurants."

He nods. "Yeah, this is great. Calling it a grocery store is a bit of an understatement. You can order whatever you want or think is necessary. Your phone is going to be delivered tomorrow. I'll get all the apps to order from there and everywhere else you might need loaded with my card."

"I have a phone."

An eyebrow goes up. "A phone you have to load with minutes. The phone is all yours and is paid for. For the next five years—even if you walked away next week. I pay all my bills in lump sums or auto-pay. Because of the question of whether you would stay, I wanted to ensure you would always have a reliable phone. There is a location tracker on it. You don't have to turn it on. My hope is you will, not because I'm going to watch your every movement. It's just so I know you and Layla are safe. It will be the same with your vehicle."

"You weren't kidding about the car. You're getting me a car?" He really is crazy.

His chuckle skims up my tummy. Those dimples are flashing at me. Layla laughs when she sees him do it. "Yes, you're getting a vehicle. For when you need to run errands and get around the city."

"I have the truck."

"The truck doesn't seem dependable or safe for you and Layla. It's in the parking garage. However, I would rather you sold it and kept the money for emergencies."

I can't believe he's so nonchalant about me selling the truck and keeping the money—not even giving him that to pay him back for buying me a car.

"I was told it didn't have air conditioning. Driving around in the Texas heat without air conditioning will make you sick. It's not a big deal. I bought a vehicle for my last housekeeper. While, yes, it wasn't until hers broke down, not allowing her to do all I needed her to do. It was necessary then, and it's necessary now." He shrugs.

I finally understand. He bought his last housekeeper a car, so he doesn't see it as a big deal to buy me one. Rich, rich is one thing in theory, another in action. "It just seems like such a waste."

A frown appears, and Layla, who is staring at him intensely, also frowns. It's adorable. "It isn't to me. I want to ensure you're driving something that isn't going to leave you and Layla stranded or isn't safe if you were in an accident. If you're running around doing things for me, then you'll get a vehicle to do said running around in."

He pauses, "I have a vehicle my mother bought me that I haven't been driving. Since it's a BMW SUV, I didn't think it was a good look for me to drive it to the clinic every day. So, I bought a non-luxury SUV almost as safe. I'm happy for you to drive the BMW as it's one of the safest vehicles on the road. And I'll buy a new one for myself—in case I need to drive Layla, or you need to use my vehicle."

"Why can't I have the non-luxury one? Then you won't have to buy anything."

"Because the BMW is safer. I'm going to donate the other one to a local charity."

"You're still buying a new vehicle in the end, though." I melt a little inside at his concern enough to purchase the same thing for him to drive on the off chance he'll need to drive Layla. His concern for our safety isn't something I can argue against. "Okay, I give up."

"Good." I like he isn't smug. "Now, if you're not going to help me with my family, how about helping me figure out what I'm supposed to do now that I'm not working eighty hours a week. Tell me, is there anything you did or wish you could do for fun? Give me some ideas."

Embarrassed, I sigh. "I haven't had time to myself in years, even before I had Layla."

"There wasn't anything you liked to do or wish you had time for? You're about to get more time for yourself soon. I hope I'm not messy enough for you to spend more than forty hours a week cleaning and cooking. Even if you do have Layla to take care of at the same time. You mentioned painting."

"It's been years." I sigh. "I used to love drawing and painting."

"I have to admit I don't know much about art. I've heard mentions of oil, watercolor, and acrylic. Was there one you preferred over the other?"

"Well, watercolors were the least expensive. I like working with them. Acrylic was cheaper than oils and you could build them to create more dimension. I got some super cheap oils when I first started dating Danny. He made me feel like shit for spending the money—even though it was mine. I wished I could afford to paint with them after I ran out. For years, I kept to sketching and drawing. Maybe I'll get a new sketchbook and some pencils."

I'm excited and looking forward to it. Worried I'm talking too much, I turn the question around on him. "You don't have any hobbies at all? Not even when you were a kid?"

He shrugs. "I like Legos because my grandfather bought them for us as—I think—a step toward the construction business. Aside from working out, I didn't allow anything to take my attention from studying and work. My sister-in-law joked about teaching me to cook. I'm not against it. I simply want to enjoy my time without there being an end result I'm working towards." For the first time, he's self-conscious. "Sorry, that's probably a very rich person thing to say."

"No, I get it. Doing something without a goal feels self-indulgent. But it shouldn't be. Why does everything have to be a form of work with a goal in mind? Why can't it be just because you want to?" I shrug when he gives me a wry smile that causes flips inside my tummy. "You mentioned your brothers. How many brothers and sisters do you have?"

His smile is wide. "I don't have any sisters. My mother tried. She stopped when she got her fourth son."

"Four boys? Your poor mom. That sounds like pure chaos."

The smile slips. "My mother was hands-off. We were raised by nannies."

"I'm sorry." It's clear it's not a great memory.

One shoulder lifts. "While I resented it growing up, I came to understand since it was how she was raised, she didn't know better. She was married off at eighteen for money to save her family. By the time she was sixteen, they were living on credit provided by their name alone. My grandfather had it with my father's antics and thought marriage would settle him. It didn't. He kept sleeping around and getting into trouble long after they were married."

"Wait, her parents basically sold her into marriage? And he cheated on your mom, and they didn't divorce?" Holy crap.

Nodding, he sighs. "Marriage among those with money is rarely about love. It's more commonly about consolidating money and power. My mother was raised to accept it. My father's family had money but no name, and her family had a name but no money. It was a perfect match for everyone but my mother. Divorce wasn't done in her family or in their social circle."

"How sad." No wonder his mom is so fierce. She had to be to survive.

He shrugs. "She doesn't regret their marriage, which surprises me. As far as she's concerned, having us was worth it to her. Even with the pain she endured when my oldest brother died of an overdose at seventeen. I think it's why she was so intent on gaining custody of his son—almost like a replacement for the son she lost."

"Oh, Matteo, I'm sorry. Were you close?"

"Sadly, no. Manuel was the oldest, and my dad spoiled the hell out of him. He was a bully, and I hated him. My mother blamed drugs on him overdosing. It was the means, but he was the cause. He drove too fast and drunk, more times than he drove sober. Thankfully, Santos is nothing like his father. He's my nephew, yet we were raised like brothers."

"Does Santos live here in Dallas? What about your other brothers?" I want to know everything about Matteo.

Matteo might have been born rich, but that didn't mean he grew up with a lot of love—the same way I didn't. Oddly, it makes me feel better that money wouldn't necessarily have made a difference in my parent's love for me the way I was so sure it would have.

"Hm, no. He's in our Los Angeles office. Rafe is my older brother and heads the family company in our corporate office here in Dallas. Javier is younger than me and is the head counsel for the company, and he's also here."

Layla squeals to get attention, startling us both. "What? You're not getting any more noodles."

Her eyes go wide, and she blows a raspberry.

We both laugh.

I yawn.

"Go to bed. I'll take care of her." He urges me.

Sighing, I don't bother arguing. "Fine. Goodnight, baby. I love you. Be good for Matteo." I kiss her cheek, and she chuckles at me. "Night."

"Night." He nods at me.

CHAPTER 9

Amy

Consciousness is sudden and complete. I can't hide from it the way I wish I could. I don't understand why I feel worse than I did yesterday. My head feels like it's filled with sand, and all I want to do is sleep. Only the thought of Layla gets me out of bed and into the shower.

I hoped the shower would help me feel better, but it doesn't. Unlike yesterday, there's no joy for all the pretty clothes. I grab another pair of black leggings and a matching black t-shirt to go over the cotton panties and first bra I touch. My head feels so heavy my neck can barely hold it up. I find Layla's room empty and a clock telling me it's almost noon. Crap.

In the living area Matteo is sitting on a baby blanket on the floor with Layla's hands in his, her standing the way she loves. She's bouncing up and down, laughing as he goes through the ABCs. He is seriously adorable with her.

Layla spots me and cries out. "Mama."

Matteo turns and my knees threaten to buckle at the way his beautiful face glows with happiness when our eyes meet. Gold. They're gold when he's happy. "Hey, how are you feeling?"

Taking Layla when he offers her to me, I cuddle her close. "Not good. I feel worse than I did yesterday. My throat doesn't hurt as bad, but I'm so tired, and my head is…"

"It will get a little worse before it gets better. You slept through the worst part. How about you get back to bed? I can get the television working in there. I'm also good to set you up with snacks and drinks. I'll get Layla's monitor to keep an ear out for you. You can let me know when you want dinner or anything else."

His offer is so thoroughly sincere. He *wants* me to spend all day in bed, and he *wants* to take care of me. Suddenly, I'm overwhelmed with gratitude and… I don't even know. The tears trickle out of me. Then I blink, and they're pouring out of me.

"I'm, I…" I'm stuttering and my throat is thick with an emotion I've never felt before. I don't understand why I'm crying.

"It's okay, sweetheart. You don't feel good. Even with the infection dead, you let it go on for too long. Which means it's taking a minute for your whole body to heal and you feel better." It's the soft voice he uses with Layla. Is he not talking to Layla? I sway, and in an instant, I'm in his arms.

A sigh of relief escapes me. His arms are the best place in the world. Here, it's safe even with the crazy electricity. I'm not just safe in his arms—I feel whole again. As if a part of me I was missing is found with him. Is that what the electricity means, like when metal is heated and fused back together?

"Okay, let's get you to bed." He drops a light kiss on the top of my head. I can't stop from snuggling into him, loving how he carries me with Layla as if it were no big deal.

Too soon, we're back in my bedroom. He settles me on top of the wide queen bed I made up. I hate when he puts me down. "I'm going to grab some more pillows and a throw so you can get all cozy. I have it on good authority, from a multitude of my young lady patients, that naps with throws are always better than under the covers."

I can't help smiling, thinking of him with the little girls he treated. I love how he listened without dismissing their emotions, concerns, or declarations. Who he is with me is who he was with those patients—I have no doubt in my mind.

When he straightens from putting me down, Layla reaches for him across my stomach. "Just a minute, sweetie. I'll be right back. I have to make sure Mommy is settled."

A twinge of pain hits my chest. Matteo is just being nice. Like he was with his patients. He's simply a good man—person. I have to stop seeing things that aren't there. The poor guy, I bet he has a dozen women thinking they're in love with him.

"All right, we have this soft throw blanket I got for Christmas. I've taken a nap with it already, and I must admit it was a pretty good nap. Here are two more pillows for you. Let me take Layla while you get all comfy." We trade, and Layla goes to him eagerly.

"While you're getting sorted, I'll get you something to eat. What sounds good? For soup, there's more chicken noodle, potato soup, tomato basil, a very tasty butternut squash—"

Hm. "Butternut squash?"

He nods. "It's kind of like sweet potato but lighter."

I hesitate. "It sounds good. Can I get soft bread with it?"

His smile makes me glad I'm lying down because my knees couldn't take it. "We have just the bread. It's a good thing my mother bought it in a two-pack. She warned me it was addictive, and she was right. I had half a loaf with goat cheese. I'll get some cut up for you. Do you want it warmed and butter on it?"

"That sounds good, thank you." I snuggle down into the cloud of the already soft mattress and all the pillows around and under me.

Matteo sets Layla down on her hands and knees at the foot of the bed. "Want to show Mommy what you did today?"

She laughs as she crawls to me.

"Layla, my big girl. You're crawling?" I sweep her into my arms.

"There was a toy she wanted, and she wasn't willing to wait for me to give it to her. I managed to catch it on video." Matteo offers me his phone.

My heart expands and then sinks as I watch the video. I'm glad he captured it on video, yet sad I wasn't there when it happened. She's getting so big. I look up to find him gone.

I'm surprised he left me with his phone. Danny got upset if I even looked at his. He never set it down—it was always in his hand or pocket. When he bought me a new one and added me to his plan, I thought it was a sweet gesture. Only later did he admit it was so he could see my location and all my calls and texts. It's why I left it behind after sending all my photos of Layla to my email address as a way to back them up.

Danny constantly accused me of cheating. Especially after I tried to read some spicy books to be better in bed. It was only because he told me often I was bad in bed. When I explained why I did it, he laughed at me. It was a mean laugh. From then on, I just laid beneath him and prayed he finished quickly—which he usually did.

Holding Matteo's phone I have no doubt I could go through it and find he is exactly who he said he is.

Matteo is back carrying a tray and a small lunch box. He sets it down out of reach of the curious Layla.

"Okay, we have the butternut squash. The big bowl is because even when it's cold, it's good. We have a half dozen slices of bread, three with butter for the soup and three to try with the goat cheese I have in the cooler. In this dish are cucumbers and strips of red pepper to go with the goat cheese or the hummus in the cooler." He points them out in a glass dish.

His grin leaves me breathless. I'll eat everything for another grin with both dimples.

"The cooler is so you have a choice at all times. Since you have a hard time asking for things, I thought this might help. If there is anything you want more of or if you want something not on the tray or in the cooler, I want you to ask me for what you need." His eyes catch mine and refuse to let go until I nod.

"All right. Let me go get some toys for Ms. Layla. How about I get your activity center?" He's talking to Layla.

I swear she nods like she understands him.

"Be right back, sweetie." He tells her.

I get the tray settled over me, then remove the extra bread and put it on the nightstand. There's plenty of room. It only holds a lamp, tissue in a marble dispenser, an alarm clock, and the lidocaine.

Matteo is back with a basket full of toys. Curious, Layla is instantly in the basket. She gives a little cry of joy at seeing her toys. "This should buy you at least a half hour. Now let me get this television on for you."

The huge flat-screen television is swivel-mounted on the wall. He works the remote and enters a code. A selection of streaming services appears on the screen—there's even two for music.

He's beside me without me noticing. "It's easy. There's only a code to bring this up. You can get into any streaming you want, and you can also do cable. I believe you now have access to a hundred different series and a thousand movies. Hopefully, something catches your attention."

His phone rings. It's beside my leg. "Layla has been changed and fed. But if you also want some alone time or to take a nap—let me know. I can take her. It's the clinic so I better answer. I'll be right back."

The clinic... Wait, it's Monday. Shouldn't he be at work? Did he take the day off because of me? What if it's causing problems at the clinic? I need to tell him that I can take care of myself and Layla— he doesn't have to stay. Except a few minutes stretch to ten, and my stomach begins growling. I give in and eat. As soon as he comes back I'll tell him.

Layla is content with the toy she and Matteo had at the dinner table and isn't trying to eat my food with me. It's an interesting toy, almost like an activity center in a ball.

I'm poking around the streaming services out of curiosity. A cute fuzzy series about a preteen girl and figuring out the world has me settling into the pillows. Matteo wasn't kidding about the bread—I could eat a whole loaf of it.

I've never had goat cheese before. I use a small piece of bread and take the smallest taste. Hm, salty and creamy. It's yummy. All three pieces and the goat cheese are gone along with half of the bowl of soup. Careful, I put the tray at the bottom of the bed, breathing a sigh of relief it doesn't jostle or anything.

Layla is gumming a teething ring attached to her purple dress. "Are you teething, baby?"

Her answer is a smile and a trail of drool. Chuckling, I clean her up with one of the two linen napkins from the tray. Happy, she cuddles into me. It isn't long before she falls asleep in my arms.

Once I'm sure she's asleep, I shift her onto her side with a pillow propping her up.

Two episodes into the series, heat hits me—pulling my eyes to the open door. Matteo is leaning against the frame. I'm guessing he worked out and showered because his hair is damp, and he's changed. Although he's in black sweats again, instead of the long-sleeved black shirt he was wearing, he's now in a plain white t-shirt. The shirt is too thick to see through, yet his muscles are clearly defined. I wish the shirt was as wet as I am at the sight of him.

Oh my god, where the hell did that thought come from? And how am I not afraid of him when he's big and strong?

"How are you feeling?"

Words won't come. I'm supposed to tell him to go to work. Except I don't want him to. All I want is to ask him to hold me again.

He moves slowly until he's right beside me. Down on his haunches, we're eye to eye. Concern is in every inch of him. "What is it? Talk to me, sweetheart."

"You should be at work?" The words feel creaky.

Tilting his head to the side, he studies me. "No. You need me. Here is where I should be. The clinic can run without me. You're stuck with me for the next few days. I took today and tomorrow off. I'm off Wednesday for the New Year holiday. Since we're only open for six hours, the clinic is operating on a skeleton crew. I didn't dare put myself on the schedule. My staff begged for the time and a half hours."

I laugh at the mock horror on his face.

"My brother's nanny will be here in the afternoon to help you with Layla on Thursday. If you're not okay with the nanny, I'll cancel her and stay here with you. You let me know what you need."

Everything eases inside me until he tells me a nanny will be here. I want to argue against a nanny, except my throat is too tight to let more than a few words out. "Thank you." Is little more than a whisper.

His face is soft with something I can't read. "No thanks are necessary. I'm happy to be here with you and Layla. I'll let you enjoy your show."

"Please don't go." I rush to stop him. Oh god, how embarrassing. I can't look at him. I'm being all needy and pathetic.

From the corner of my eye, I watch Matteo drag the chair from the desk close to the bed. He sits down and leans back. "I've heard a lot about this show. How is it so far?"

I'm stunned, unable to answer his question.

A dimple appears. "You need me. So, I'm here. Whether it's at home or beside you watching television. I see you finished off the goat cheese. If you liked it, there's an herbs and chives one I had to force myself to stop eating."

"I can't wait to try it. I've never had goat cheese before. I was afraid I wouldn't like it."

During the episode we chat about our favorite snacks as we both become engrossed in the show. My hair is driving me crazy. It's in its usual braid that's becoming so loose I need to undo it and braid it again. I get frustrated and undo it.

"Are you okay? Do you want me to grab a brush for you?"

I sigh. "I need to brush it out and braid it again, except I'm not in the mood to deal with it."

"I can do it. If you're okay with me…"

"You can braid hair?" I'm shocked.

He does that exhale laugh thing. "I can. Many of my patients were girls with long hair. Their moms weren't always there. And they needed someone to braid it…" The smile slips. "Before they lost it to chemo."

My chest does a weird twisting thing because I know he would have been as sad as the girls who lost their hair.

A clearing of his throat tells me I'm not wrong. "I can do a French braid or a simple braid. Whichever one you want."

"Yes, please."

"Where's your brush?"

"The bathroom on the vanity." I'm sitting up, wondering how he can do it.

The chair he's in is close, but I would have to hang off the edge of the bed for him to reach easily. I look behind me. With all the pillows he added for me to lay on there's a lot of room between me and the headboard. If they were removed, he would be able to fit behind me. I begin trying to remove them without waking Layla.

"Here, let me help." He grabs the remaining pillows and places them at the foot of the bed. A hand on the headboard helps him get his leg on the outside of mine on the bed.

I'm embarrassed and don't know what to say as he begins brushing it. "Every other time I brush it out I tell myself I'm going to cut it." I mutter.

"I hope like hell it never happens. It's beautiful." A beat passes. "However, I do understand long hair can be difficult to take care of as well as time-consuming. If there are any hair tools or products you want to buy to help you, add them to the household purchases. Does it sound like I'm telling you not to cut it? I don't mean it that way. It would simply be a tragedy if you do."

I fight laughter. "Thank you, that's very sweet. I'm only thinking a few inches—to the middle of my back. It's been more than a year since I cut it. At the very least, I want to get rid of the split ends."

His slow, gentle brushing is almost hypnotic it's so soothing. "It's like silk."

"Thanks to the shampoo and conditioner your mother bought. The stuff I was using had it feeling like straw. I just wish I could do more than put it in a braid. Leaving it loose with Layla's tendency to grab and pull isn't an option."

"That's too bad. I wondered why you kept it in a braid." He begins separating it into three pieces. "Do you want it high or low?"

"Low, please, at my nape." I'm glad he asked. I do my best to ignore the way his long fingers continually brush my neck. Except every touch causes heat to build low—where it shouldn't.

After brushing the individual sections, he begins braiding the sections together.

"I can't stop thinking of you braiding your patient's hair. And the pain the girls went through when they lost their hair." I wince as I wonder if I should have said anything.

"It was sad." Another clearing of his throat tells me the word doesn't cover it in the least. "Many parents couldn't put their work or caring for their other kids on hold to be there for their sick child. And the few who could, often couldn't bring their other children with them. It's why I housed several families at my home. There's a charity built into the hospital intake that helps with housing. Unfortunately, they didn't always have accommodation for large families. I had two bedrooms on the main floor and another two in the basement for them to use."

"How awful to not be able to stay with their child while they went through that." I sigh.

"It wasn't easy to see. That's why I set up a charity to pay for housing as long as they needed to stay in the area. A portion of my trust goes into it every month."

This man, sitting with cancer patients, braiding their hair, housing families in his own home. I would wonder if he were real if someone told me about him. I remember the question I had when he mentioned it. "When did you get your trust? I thought those things were an eighteen or twenty-one thing."

His exhale laugh thing sends air over my neck. Oh my god, it's a good thing I'm sitting. It's stronger than the first time he did it, and I can't stop the shiver it sends through me.

"No, my grandfather was certain he gave my father and uncle too much money too soon. I think he judged them by what he would have done at the same age. Except there were too many differences between how their life was growing up and his. They had whatever they wanted by merely asking. My grandfather had to work three jobs to help feed his brothers and sisters when he was a kid himself. If I were married and had children, I would have gotten access to my share of the trust sooner. Since I had neither, I didn't get anything until I turned thirty."

"You mentioned he didn't pay for your school. Did the trust pay for it?" I meant to ask him last night.

"It was supposed to. My grandfather first created the trust to pay for our education—both private school as children and university as adults. Then he changed it to ensure we had the quality of life he worked so hard to give his kids. But he got angry when I said I was going to school to be a doctor. Since he was the trustee, he refused to release the funds to pay for college."

"That's crap. You wanted to be a doctor. It's not like you were planning on becoming an actor or musician or something." What an asshole. "How were you able to go to school and get the allowance you mentioned?"

His chuckle holds no humor. "I understand now why he did it. The more of us in the company, the more the work would have been spread out. I've worried for years about how hard Rafe was working. Javier gave up the immigration law he did on the side because it was either that or have no life. Seeing it now, I forgave my grandfather when he apologized for what he did."

He's better than me because I don't think I could have. But I don't dare say it out loud.

"It was my mother who covered tuition and gave me my monthly allowance. She also bought a condo in New York and my house in Baltimore. Like I mentioned the other day, most of the money I've made is from the leftover allowance. I lived below my means in school—I was too embarrassed by how hard everyone around me stressed about money to spend my full allowance."

"That's awesome of your mom." I exhale in wonder. "But your grandfather sounds like a control freak. I don't know if I would have been able to forgive him." Darn it. I wasn't supposed to say that last thing.

"Yeah, my mom has her moments. Control freak fits him perfectly. He changed the rules of the trust when I told him I would accept it when I turned thirty. It's now written that no more than fifty percent of what's received can be given away, or we get cut off from it permanently. It could be refused outright the way Javier did. Javier didn't need it after making his own billion. At Yale, he met a lot of students who couldn't find investors—typically because they were too young or women. It's what gave me the idea to invest beyond the market. I couldn't refuse my trust when it could go to help others. I take my percentage and put it away for retirement."

"Since you have so much money, why don't you retire?" I'm curious.

"I don't think my guilt over being born rich will let me. I'm sure I'll be doing something in some capacity to give back until I'm incapacitated or dead." His tone is one of acceptance.

"Is that what drove you? The guilt from being rich?" I'm understanding him more.

"Pretty much. Guilt played a factor in so much of what I've done. I think guilt is a part of the reason I did my best to keep Susan's memory alive for so long. I thought it should hurt more to lose the person you wanted to spend your life with." His voice is low as he confesses.

I shake my head. "You were a kid. I was certain I was going to marry the lead singer of my favorite boy group. Now, if you were to hand him to me on a platter, I wouldn't want him. It turns out he also has no problem ending an argument with anyone—girl-friend or paparazzi—with his fists. Things can change. It's no one's fault when you grow out of love. I think you said that yourself yesterday."

He's quiet for a long minute. I hope like hell I didn't make him angry. His hand runs down from the top of the braid to the bottom, giving me the lightest tug. "All done. Where were you when I was fifteen and needed to hear it?"

"In diapers, I think." I bend my head back to look up at him. He's laughing, really laughing. It's the best sound in the world. When he looks down at me, he shakes his head. I let my head fall back against his chest.

A crashing sound comes from the television, and we both look to it. The main character made a huge mess. We groan in unison at what it means to the girl. Since I don't have to sit up straight, my back brushes against Matteo's chest. "She's never going to live it down with her mom."

When his arms wrap around me to bring me more in contact with his wide chest, air stutters out of my tight lungs. Closing my eyes, I let myself relax against him.

"This is a good show. Usually, when they're dealing with someone as young as she is, the messages feel overly heavy and silly." He muses.

"Hm, true. I didn't like watching television geared toward kids when I was one." In his arms is the best place in the world. I think I become engrossed in the show, but I slip into sleep without realizing it.

The next thing I know, yummy smells are teasing me awake. I check the clock on the bedside table to find I was asleep for more than two hours. Layla is gone. I'm sad I missed out on more time in Matteo's arms.

No, stop it. He doesn't need you getting clingy. Matteo is just an extremely nice guy who cares about all people. Remember, he offered to move you into an apartment or his mother's house... But when I asked if he wanted me to leave, everything about his answer screamed he was honest when he said no.

Out of the restroom, I go into the kitchen to find Matteo at the table. Layla is in the highchair next to him. He's eating while Layla gums banana squeezed out between her fingers. I'm shy, worried I messed up when I fell asleep on him.

"Hi," Matteo greets me with a smile. His eyes are gold.

"Hi, is she actually getting any of that in her mouth?" I chuckle.

"It's more or less her dessert. She got half of the banana in her oatmeal. You liked your oatmeal, didn't you?" Layla pounds her tray with enthusiasm and laughs. "There are green chili chicken enchiladas on the tray. Or I can make you something else."

"It smells delicious. I'll have some of this." I open the cabinet where I saw him take our plates from yesterday. Six enchiladas remain on the foil tray. I scoop two onto my plate.

"There are beans on the stove," He points to a small pot.

"No thanks, I'm not really a beans person." I shake my head as I join him at the table. "These enchiladas are delicious."

His eyes run over me with concern. "Feeling better?"

So we're not going to talk about me falling asleep in his arms? Okay, because simply thinking about it has me blushing. "My head doesn't feel as bad. I still feel like I could sleep for another ten hours, though."

Lines appear in his forehead. "Any fever or chills? Head pounding like a migraine?"

Sighing, I shake my head. "It's just me. It's always taken longer for me to get better than most."

"You might have developed rheumatic fever or even damaged your kidneys. Are you peeing, okay?"

I consider the question. "I think so. It doesn't feel like it's too often or not enough."

"You'll tell me if you feel worse. If you're not feeling better by Wednesday, I'll take you to work and run some other tests."

It's an order. I fight not to laugh and nod. "You didn't get anything to drink, you want something while I'm up?"

"Ice water would be good, please." Layla becomes interested in my plate the second Matteo is up. "No, baby. Eat your banana. It looks yummy." I encourage her. She slams her hand down with the banana in fury.

Before she can cry, Matteo is back. The moment she sees him, her outrage disappears. Now, she's interested in what he is eating.

Matteo hands me the glass of water. He has a bowl of ice cream. "That looks good. What flavor is it?"

"It's cookies and cream, and it's very good. I'm sorry. I forgot all about the ice cream. There are as many different ice cream containers in the freezer as soups. Besides this one, there's chocolate chip cookie dough, plain chocolate, plain vanilla, something called Death by Chocolate, and caramel with sea salt."

"She just does not do anything by halves." I'm once again impressed and slightly fearful of her.

"Yeah, she is." He sighs. "She might have gone overboard again. It's going to be up to you. Whatever you want to do, I'll agree with."

Unease fills me. "What did she do?"

His sigh is heavy. "We talked last night about you feeling guilty about Layla and her first Christmas in a motel. It's my own fault because I was asking her to do more shopping for you. I promise it was just going to be some sketchbooks and pencils, and she... I'll have to show you."

CHAPTER 10

Amy

He looks so worried. Bitsy—Elizabeth—in yet another shopping escapade, has gone overboard. And he's worried it will upset me. Now *I* feel guilty. It's only me feeling that I don't deserve all the nice things he and his mother have done for me. Like I have to worry about paying him back because nothing comes without a price.

Yet Matteo has repeatedly made it clear that he doesn't expect something back. I finally understand. Bitsy and Matteo have so much money that the toys, clothes, phone, and even the car are pocket change to them. It's needed, so why not?

"I'd like to see." I push up from the table.

Sighing, he unstraps Layla from her highchair. She hooks an arm around his neck and lays her head on his shoulder. Seeing them together, Layla happy and content in a way she was never with her own father has me blinking back tears.

He leads the way, stopping in the second living room—or would it be called a sitting room? Oh my gosh, it looks like Christmas exploded in here.

Layla lets loose a squeal of happiness as she reaches for the tree. The tree was previously decorated in a muted kind of way. With pretty yet kind of boring green and red metallic balls interspersed with a few in silver.

Now, it's an explosion of color with gorgeous ornaments. There are snowmen, cartoon characters in Christmas settings, penguins covered in glitter, and Santa Claus going down a chimney, eating cookies, and reading a long list. In between those new ornaments is garland in red, green, and silver, along with bright, multicolored lights. Below it all is a gorgeous quilted red velvet tree skirt covered in presents.

A faux fireplace with a mantel is now in the corner of the room. Above it is a large wreath with not just holly but bright red, green, and gold ornaments. On the mantel are white candles among faux tree garland wrapped in ribbon and white lights. Hanging from the mantel are bright red stockings trimmed in lace with our names on them. There's one for me, Layla, and Matteo—all bulging with candy coming out of the top.

I'm awestruck. Unable to find words, I turn to Matteo, who looks as though he's prepared for me to yell or something.

"This isn't all of it." He murmurs low.

"How could there be more?"

Sighing, "Follow me."

I do so in a daze. The room used to be his office. It's a corner room with large windows covered in thick, bright white curtains that are open. The desk, chairs, and filing cabinet are gone. Only two book-cases along the wall remain. In the corner, where the large windows are, is an easel and a large wooden workbench with multiple drawers. Along one of the walls are a dozen blank canvases in various sizes.

"This was a thought, but I didn't want you to feel overwhelmed by all of this. It was just supposed—"

This man wanted to give me exactly what I dreamed of, yet he also wanted to wait until I was ready to receive it. Without thought, I lay a hand on his arm. That spark is there again, only it doesn't scare me as much as it did yesterday.

"Thank you. I love it." I give into the need surging through me and go up on tiptoe to kiss his cheek. It isn't merely a spark, it's so intense it wakes up every cell in my body for more. I want to find out what his lips feel like against mine.

No. Stop it. Enjoy this moment for what it is, and don't hope for more when it wouldn't be fair to him. "Really, thank you for everything."

Oh my god, is he blushing? How is he real? "Well, it was technically my mom who did all the shopping and…"

"Yes, but it was because it was what you wanted. To give me and Layla a Christmas, even if it's a few days late." I squeeze his arm lightly before letting go.

Layla reaches for me. I take her and cuddle her close. "Want to go open presents? Yeah, let's go tear some stuff up."

* * *

MATTEO

When she lets go of my arm, everything in me longs for more of her touch. Carrying her to bed earlier today was heaven and hell. Heaven at having her in my arms, and hell when I had to put her down.

I resented the fuck out of the call from the clinic, taking me away from her. Except it was a good thing. It kept me from opening my mouth and telling her everything.

It was far too soon for that. Even if I was certain she felt something for me, too. Amy might feel it, but it also scared her. She was afraid of trusting in anything—not just me.

That fucker really hurt her. Not simply her body but her mind. While she left him more than two months ago, she was simply surviving. There was no time for her to truly recover. To learn to trust in others and herself. That she wouldn't find herself in the same place again, or worse, for trusting in the wrong person.

I had my first therapy session this morning with Hillary. I'm grateful she's willing to do them by phone since I didn't want to leave Amy and Layla alone. And in the future it's more convenient for my schedule. Today was mainly an introduction.

She wasn't happy I spent most of the time talking about Amy and asking what I could do for her and how best to handle my attraction while balancing her need to heal. But she gave in when I explained everything Amy had been through. The shit she told me is still fucking with my head. Amy's possible PTSD, trauma responses, anxiety, and all the ways I could screw up left me in a cold sweat.

What it boiled down to was that Amy needed time. Since I wasn't sure I could keep my mouth shut, I hid from her. After the call from the clinic, I put the finishing touches on the presents and

Amy's studio—wondering the whole time if it would be a good thing or blow up in my face.

Then, I worked out until my muscles burned. Even as I did it, I was annoyed for needing to jerk off in the shower. But I was glad I did. If I hadn't, when I was braiding Amy's hair, I would have probably come in my damn sweats. Hearing her little gasps and shaky breathing when my fingers brushed against the back of her neck almost completely undid me. The only reason I managed to keep my cock limp was to remember she'd jump and run if she felt what she did to me.

It's so fucking adorable watching Layla and Amy opening presents. They're down on the floor together. Layla is chewing the paper. Amy is showing her everything they got. It could be the morning of Christmas with us as a family.

"Matteo, this one is for you." Amy offers me the small box. "Come open it."

Because I couldn't deny her a thing, I go down to the floor with her. I open the present. Amy is curious, so I show her the two silk ties.

Her eyebrows go up. "You wear suits?"

"Yes, I usually take off the jacket once I get to work and put the white coat on. My grandfather had a thing against casual clothing in business settings. He considers it a respect thing for the business and the other person. I also like the ease of suits. No worrying about shopping. I call my tailor who has my measurements, my clothes get made, and can be picked up a week or two later."

"You have your suits made for you? Wait, clothes? As in more than suits," Her eyes are wide.

Layla looks from her to me and widens her own eyes. It's so fucking cute I can't keep from chuckling. Layla isn't sure if she likes me laughing at her.

"When you consider how long quality suits last, it's not like it's an outrageous expense. And it makes sense for them to make my other clothes if they have my measurements for the suits." I shrug.

"What else do they make?"

"Everything," I admit. "From my boxers to my polos."

"Wow. Rich, rich." She giggles, and it's the cutest fucking thing I've ever heard. "Now I get why rich men always get ties and cufflinks for gifts."

"When we had Christmas together, I got ties and cufflinks."

"That's all you got?" Her smile turns sad.

"Christmas for us isn't about giving gifts. It's about being together. When we could buy whatever we want for ourselves, it's not really easy to get a gift for each other." I assure her.

Her smile is back. "Your mom is really sweet to make sure you have something to open also. These sketchbooks are perfect. Two different sizes and both fit in these gorgeous leather portfolios. I used to imagine having something exactly like this growing up."

Ah fuck. Her smile could split her face. She leans over and kisses me on the cheek again. "Thank you."

Layla pats me on the other cheek. My two girls. So freaking beautiful and happy. I don't think there's a better gift in the whole damn world.

She goes back to opening presents with Layla. Layla is positive the wrapping paper is more important than the toys Amy is trying to show her.

"Another one for you, Matteo. I want to know what it is." She waits expectantly after handing it to me.

To please her, I open it.

It's clear she's not sure why it's a good gift. "Huh, a razor. It looks wicked. No, Layla, don't touch."

"My mother saw me admiring Rafe's. I considered buying one, then forgot all about it by the time I got home."

"Hmm," she tilts her head as she studies the razor. "I'm not as afraid to meet your mom as I was yesterday."

Her confidence has me wondering. "Why?"

"Because she cares about your happiness. And if you say I'm good, she will, too. No warning me off that I don't belong in your world like a bad soap opera or something."

She isn't wrong.

"Oh, Matteo, all the colors. These are gorgeous. Thank you. And they come with a box. I love them." She's sighing with happiness as she runs a hand over the tubes of oil paint.

Layla is trying to taste one of the tubes. "No, baby, let's see. There's another gift for you."

Grumpy at not getting a tube, Layla blows a raspberry at her mother. She slaps at the baby doll Amy was trying to get her to play with earlier. Stormy brown eyes find me, and she reaches out to me. I take her from Amy, who sighs at her daughter's antics.

I cuddle Layla close. She needs a nap.

"Another one for you, Matteo." Amy hands me the box and waits for me to open it. "A watch? Patek Philippe. Never heard of it. I thought it would be a Rolex or something." She shrugs and returns to opening the gifts.

Sighing, I put the watch back into the box. My mother, I swear sometimes. Yes, the watch is not flashy. It's actually one I looked at myself. However, the watch costs about a hundred and fifty thousand dollars. I didn't think it was a good idea to wear it at the clinic around low-income patients.

"Matteo, this is big, and it has your name and mine." Amy pulls it out from under the tree where it's tucked away.

"How did I miss her putting it under the tree?" I shake my head. "She is too devious. I don't doubt one of the twins brought it up when I was laying into her about the whole art studio."

CHAPTER 11

*M*atteo

Amy giggles. "Your mom played you like a violin." Tearing off the paper, it's a wooden chest. Carved into the top of the chest: Matteo and Amy's Adventures

My heart pounds so loud I wonder if she can hear it. Our names together—like we're a couple. I watch as she traces over the inscription. Does she know or understand what it means?

"I'm officially in love with your mom." Her eyes are glowing. Opening the top drawer, she finds a card on top. With a big smile, she reads it: "Keep your hands busy." Ooh, knitting needles and a bunch of crochet needles. What pretty yarn."

I exhale in relief. "I told her I asked you what you liked to do so I could get gift ideas for you. She must have thought we both needed to find new hobbies."

She pulls out two boxes. One is a car, and the other is an intricate castle. "Model building. Yeah, these are for you. I'm not interested in building models. Jigsaw puzzles, ooh, pretty scenes. Pottery class, this is for both of us. This would be so much fun. I've always wanted to try this. Can we please go?"

Her eyes are wide in pleading. Fuck me. If she ever finds out what her saying *please* does to my cock, I'm screwed all to hell. Pottery class doesn't interest me, making her happy does.

I nod and hope like hell it isn't as bad as I always thought it would be.

"Yay, thank you. Okay, next drawer. Holy crap, do you know how much this camera costs? And this is put in here as something you or I *might* be interested in. Rich, rich."

She shakes her head. "For the record, I would love to use this. Please? To take pictures of things I could maybe paint."

"It's yours." I look in the drawer. "A folding fishing rod and reel? Nope, not interested in that either. A cooking class? This sounds like fun."

She takes the card from me. "This is cool. We can pick what to make. It's just us, so we don't have a group of people. And it ends with us eating it as a night or afternoon out. I like that. Can we do it?"

"Sure. You tell me when, and we'll do it." Her sheer happiness is making my cock hard. She's so beautiful I could simply stare at her for hours.

Opening the next drawer, her eyes go big. She chuckles. "Get moving. Twelve yoga classes, private again. I could do this. I took a few classes with my roommate and liked it. But I always worried about being fat in front of other people."

"Hey, don't say that. Please." I work to keep my voice even. "We talked about it."

Her face falls. "I'm sorry. I...I don't like thinking of myself like that. It's just what I've heard for so many years." She shrugs sadly. "I'll try."

Catching her chin, I bring her face up to mine. "I'm sorry. Internalizing the outside is common. It's not easy to ignore if you hear it from the media and people around you treating you differently or calling you that. But it's bullshit. You're a *beautiful* woman. Whether you're a size eighteen, bigger or smaller. I don't like hearing anyone, including you, put you down in any way. Okay?"

She nods as she blinks back tears. "Thank you."

"I don't deserve any thanks, but you're welcome." All I want is to take her into my arms, to show her I find her absolutely stunning. Except she's not ready for it, so I let her go.

Layla squeals for attention. "Hey, sweetie, I think someone is tired and needs a nap."

"Okay, but not yet. We have to finish finding out what is in here." She turns back to the chest.

"Some golf balls." I shrug. "I could get out on the green with my brothers. They don't hate it. I've only ever gone to a miniature golf course a few times when I was a teenager with my brothers."

"A calligraphy book and different types of nibs. These are cool quill pens. Hmm, scrapbook making stuff, no thank you. Dance classes—this is so cool. Matteo, we have to do this. Pretty please. It's also private, just you and me learning to dance. I've always wanted to do something like this."

Holy shit, my cock jumps at the idea of holding her close in a dance class. I should be saying no for that reason alone. Instead, I'm nodding. I think I'm mouthing the right words. I'm not sure because my brain seems to have short-circuited.

Amy yawns so wide she almost falls back. Damn it, I'm not taking care of her. My cock goes limp at what might have happened if she fell into the tree. She barely caught herself.

"Come on, you both need a nap."

Pouting, she gets up slowly. "I already took a nap. And it wasn't a short one."

"Okay, you don't have to take a nap. Why don't you grab your sketchbook and spend some more time in bed?" I cajole her. I'm certain she needs more time doing nothing more stressful than switching positions for her nap.

"I will if you let me draw you." I'm getting lost in her melting chocolate eyes.

"I'd love to." She doesn't have to ask twice for me to be close to her.

It takes almost twenty minutes to change Layla out of her banana-covered dress and into a new diaper. She needs a bottle. I fix this one with a little oatmeal cereal, hoping it will help her sleep longer. I'm impressed by how quickly she finishes her bottle. I wonder if I made the hole in the nipple too large to allow for the thickening of it with oatmeal. After a burp that startles us both, she's out like a light.

I'm working to keep my cock down as I go into Amy's room, only to find she's also asleep. She's adorable with her sketchbook clutched to her chest and a smile on her face.

Sighing, I gently take the sketchbook from her and set it and the pencils on the bedside table. Then I cover her with the throw blanket. Turning out the light, I make sure the door is left open a little.

Like a fucking pervert, I fast walk my ass into my bedroom to jack off—for the third time today.

Christ. I haven't needed to do this in forever. Sex was something I viewed as necessary. At the same time, I didn't need it often. Once or twice a month was enough for me. Would I have liked it more? Some weeks, yes, but most weeks, no. My low libido seemed about right, considering how depressing my work was.

If I needed sex, my only requirements were the woman understood it wouldn't lead to a relationship, she didn't work on my floor, and she wasn't married.

My longest relationship was with a nurse in cardiology. We were on and off for almost four years. It ended when she became a travel nurse.

For the most part, I had no-strings relationships lasting around a year. The moment they wanted to get serious, I ended things. It was just sex I wanted from them.

With Amy, it isn't just sex I want. I want every day and night until I take my final breath. I brace a hand against the cool wall of marble. Remembering her in my arms, she fit me *just* right. The smell of her skin drove me to distraction. I wanted so badly to taste her, to discover what made her moan, whimper, and plead for more.

The way she melted into me in her sleep—my cock jerks in my hand. Soft and delicate, her curves had my cock raging for her. Thank fuck she was asleep because there was no way I could have hidden how badly I wanted her.

Shit, it takes minutes before I'm coming hard. This is the most embarrassing part of it all. I could fuck for hours. It was important to me my partner was always satisfied—and I needed to ensure the woman was positively soaking wet in order to take my cock. Yet the mere thought of Amy has me coming in minutes.

Out of the shower, I throw on clean clothes that are basically the same thing I was wearing—hoping like hell she won't realize I changed if she wakes up again.

Back in the formal living room, I shake my head at the amount of discarded wrapping paper. My mom and the twins outdid themselves. I'd worried the twins would spill to Rafe and Carrie about Amy and Layla. They promised they wouldn't. Even though I know it's wrong to ask them to keep any secret from their parents, they knew how wary Rafe was of anyone new to the family. His protective streak would have Amy on edge far more than my mother ever could.

Once I'm done cleaning everything, I study the wooden chest. Running my hand over mine and Amy's name in the wood. I'm not sure why it feels so momentous to see our names together—as a couple.

I take the chest into Amy's studio. It fits on one of the shelves of the bookshelf. Remembering Amy's interest, I grab a jigsaw puzzle of one of Monet's paintings. This might be fun.

AMY

I wake up cranky because I fell asleep. Rolling over, I snuggle into the throw Matteo covered me with. I sigh deeply as I remember opening all the presents. Not only were there things for painting and sketching, but beautiful things for my hair, tote bags, and two beautiful designer handbags that cost more than I've made so far in my life.

As much as I loved the handbags, it's the amazing studio that gives me goosebumps. Matteo told her he wanted to give it to me. Yet he was listening when I told him that I wanted to get more comfortable with art by just getting a sketchbook and pencils first. He couldn't have known it was about me being over-whelmed by the idea of creating art again after not doing any for so long.

Danny had shaken his head when he saw me with my sketchbook. He laughed and agreed when I shrugged once, saying I knew it wasn't as though I'd ever be an artist. After he laughed, I never again pulled out my sketchbook when he was around. Gradually, I stopped opening it altogether.

Yet Matteo encouraged me to draw and paint. He didn't give me effusive encouragement, telling me that I could be a successful artist. There is only support for me to do something I love.

A wail of pain gets me out of bed so quickly that I almost fall. I'm in Layla's room fast. Matteo is right behind me. Layla's little face is mottled in red as she chews on her hand. She's in my arms. I turn to find Matteo in her bathroom closet and returning with baby Orajel.

Uncapping it, he's at my side. "I know, sweetie. That tooth is finally breaking through, isn't it?" He squeezes a pea-sized amount onto a finger. "Please open for me. It will help, I promise."

Layla is fighting him, not wanting to open her mouth. Firmly, one hand grips her chin, and the other pries her mouth open enough where he can coat her bottom gums with it. She wails and tries to spit it out.

I rock her. "It tastes awful, but it will help. Just give it a minute, sweetie."

Matteo watches, his face miserable as she glares at him with betrayed eyes. "I'm sorry, baby girl. Please stop looking at me like that. I'll give you all the noodles you want."

Running a hand down her back to try and soothe her, I shake my head. "Don't go promising her things while you're suffering now. She'll play you so hard. It does suck when she's crying, though. God, it just kills me to hear her sobbing."

"Yes, especially when she's normally such a happy baby." He runs a hand through his hair.

Finally, her little sobs subside. We watch as her head comes up from my shoulder. She's rubbing her gums together, clearly trying to figure out where the pain went. When she gives us a hesitant smile, we both sigh at the same time. Our eyes meet, and I smile. "Thanks, she can't say it, so I will."

He shakes his head. "I'm just glad I thought to add it to the list. I was kind of surprised she didn't already have at least two teeth already."

"Is it bad she didn't have teeth until now?" I worried about it for weeks in the motel.

"No, not necessarily. Remember, not all babies meet milestones at the same time. Although, I would like to take her and do a workup on her to ensure there isn't anything hiding. She seems so small for her age." His eyes run over her with concern.

Relief fills me. "I'd really like that."

The smoke alarm goes off.

"Crap," Matteo disappears.

I follow him to find a plume of black smoke coming out of his beloved toaster oven. He unplugs it, turns on the vent hood to pull smoke out of the kitchen, and using oven mitts, takes it off the counter.

"Can you get the French doors to the rooftop, please?" He asks.

The black phone beside the French doors begins to ring. He sets the toaster oven on the counter. "Hello? Yes, sorry. It's a cooking fiasco. Everything is fine. Thanks for checking."

"Who was that? Oh wow. How could you not tell me this was out here? How many floors high are we up?" A gust of cold wind hits me, sending me back inside with Layla.

Matteo laughs. "That's why, and the phone is for the front desk. We're on the fifth floor." He's only a few feet behind me. Using a towel, he waves it in front of the smoke alarm. It finally stops going off. "I'm sorry, sweetie. That was loud, huh?"

Layla nods and reaches for him. I let her go, and he cuddles her close. "Okay, the bad alarm is done."

"Front desk?"

"Yes, now your question about how many floors up reminds me. You were completely out of it when I brought you here. We're on the fifth floor, without a floor above us. Let me take you on a tour of the place." He gestures to the door.

I look down at the leggings and shirt I'm wearing. "Um..."

"You can throw on some shoes. Don't worry about changing. We aren't leaving the building." He reassures me.

I run back to my room and grab the comfy-looking leather flip-flops. Matteo is waiting with Layla. He opens the door of the condo, and we're in another entryway.

"Damn, I almost forgot the keycard. I'll be right back."

He holds up a gold card. "I'm going to ensure the desk gives me another one of these for you."

The elevator opens, and we get on. Layla looks around and clings to him when it goes down.

"It's okay. You remember this, don't you?" Her wide eyes say she doesn't.

"You don't need your keycard to go downstairs, but it only goes to the ground floor. No other floors can be selected without scanning your keycard. But if you want the elevator to open to the parking garage, scan your keycard and press the ground floor button. It will open at the back of the elevator directly into the garage."

"That's neat."

When the elevator opens, we go down a long hallway to doors marked exit.

He opens the door, but we don't go outside. There is a pool, fire pit, barbeque, and a green space larger than the closest city park. "The pool is heated if you're brave enough to try it. Do you see the green space past the pool? It's for residents to do what they want with their small plots. However, none of the owners have chosen to do anything with it. No one even has a dog to walk on the grass. So, if there are days when Layla is driving you crazy, and you need to get outside, you can come out here."

Scanning the card against a pad, I hear a lock release, and he opens the door.

"This is the mail room. Packages can be left at the desk if you let them know to tell the carriers, and they can sign for them. But there's an option for privacy. You could pop out of the elevators to get your mail without running into the people at the front desk."

It's a large room for so few boxes. "That's it for a five-story building?"

"Yep, my brother bought this building and spent almost a year overseeing the rehab of it. He kept it small, only two condos per floor."

He opens the door to a twenty-person theater with a projection screen. It's like an actual movie theater but nicer, with large recliners.

"We can use this anytime. Just tell the front desk to reserve it." We cross the hallway. "The same with the owner's lounge. This will hold a hundred people." Only a few more feet down the hallway brings us into a huge lobby like something out of a fancy hotel. "Speaking of the front desk. Jeanie, hi, this is Amy. She's moved in. And this is Layla."

"Hi, Layla. Ma'am."

"Amy, please." I'm not sure why I'm embarrassed.

"Jeannie, could you please get us another card made for Amy? We're finishing up the tour of the place."

"Yes, sir. I'll have it ready."

He opens the door to a large gym for such a small number of people. "This has a sauna and a jacuzzi. There's also a jacuzzi upstairs on the roof, so you don't have to worry about coming down here. I forgot to mention the desk is open twenty-four hours a day."

We're back at the front desk. Jeannie offers a keycard to Matteo. He thanks her and guides me back to the elevator.

"You can press the button for the elevator, and it will open. However, as you can see, none of the buttons will light up to get it moving until you scan your card."

"Wow, rich, rich." I murmur.

His chuckle slides up my spine. "Yes."

Somehow, it doesn't make me as tense as the last time he confirmed it. That wealth shields me from Danny and gave Layla and me a Christmas unlike anything I've ever experienced.

Dinner is the stuffed peppers, which we both feel could have more spice. After dinner, we're all yawning, and Layla gets another dose of Orajel on her gums as she tries to chew the frozen baby wash-cloth Matteo made for her in two.

"Go on, put her to bed. I'll clean up in here." Matteo is firm.

He's gone long before I'm done putting Layla to bed.

In my own bed, I marvel at how lucky I am. I was certain getting sick was the worst thing that could happen to me. Instead, it was the best thing ever. Because Matteo was the doctor who saw me. It's funny how life has a way of giving not what you want but what you need.

CHAPTER 12

𝒶 my

I wake up too late for a mom. It feels late. Turning my head, the clock tells me it's a little after ten in the morning. I never heard Layla cry, even though my door was open wide—not simply ajar by a few inches.

Matteo and the darn monitor. He kept the video monitor for Layla with him because he said I would hear if she needed me. Since he was further away, he needed the monitor. He's all of ten feet further away from her. It was so I could sleep longer.

I'm cranky, and I'm not sure why. The more I think about it, I figure it out. It's been nice having someone take care of me. No one has ever done it before. There are no memories of my mom doing much for me. She was deep into her addiction by the time I was eight. I don't remember much before that.

All of that is at an end now. I feel better. Okay, not one hundred percent, but a solid eighty percent. Finally.

If I'm fine, there's no need for Matteo to take care of me. It's my turn to repay him for all he's done.

It's New Year's Eve today. I wonder what his plans are. Will he go out tonight? Maybe he has a date... I refuse to acknowledge the way my stomach twists at the thought of him on a date with another woman. The time of it being just me, Matteo, and Layla is almost over. He's going to go to work. I'll be here cooking and cleaning for him. Because I'm the housekeeper, that's all I am.

Out of the shower, I get dressed in my usual leggings and a long-sleeved shirt.

In the dining room, Layla is offering Matteo some of the banana squished between her fingers.

He opens his mouth, pretending to eat it. "Yummy, thank you. Your turn. You eat it now."

She laughs and sucks her fingers into her mouth.

"Mama," her cry, loud and happy, fills me full of love.

"Good morning, baby. Look at you being a big girl eating your oatmeal. Oh, that banana looks yummy." I kiss her cheek and get covered in banana and oatmeal.

Matteo chuckles and offers me a wet baby washcloth. "Here you go. Sorry."

I wipe my mouth. "It's all right. I've gotten worse from her. I'm sorry I slept so long. Thank you for taking care of her."

"Don't apologize. I took care of her so you could sleep. I love taking care of her. She's really a good baby, even teething. Don't worry about making breakfast. I ordered it in. Since I wasn't sure what you would want, I got a few things."

"Holy crap, you ordered three breakfasts?" I study the boxes waiting on the counter. "You really do have an addiction to ordering food."

He shrugs, "It's so easy. And I couldn't order eggs Benedict for me without ordering it for you too. This is chicken and waffles. And this is egg, bacon, and cheese on a croissant with country potatoes. A few minutes in the slightly smoky air fryer will make it taste like it's fresh off the stove."

Shaking my head, I laugh. "That eggs Benedict looks delicious. I'd like that one, please."

"Good, it's been forever since I had their chicken and waffles."

I can't take my eyes off how deftly his hands move. I'm remembering how nimble his fingers were as he braided my hair.

"That's a relief. How long will it take? Because it looks good." I stare at the toaster oven, willing it to be done.

"It will take a few minutes. Sit down, and I'll bring it to you. What do you want to drink? How about some orange juice?"

Sighing, I go back to the table where Layla is banging her spoon on the highchair tray to a beat she likes. "God, I love seeing her happy. She can make as much noise as she wants, and I won't get hit for it."

Matteo appears in front of me. "He hit you when she made a noise?"

I jerk my eyes to his in horror. "I said it out loud?" Too late, I slap my hand across my mouth. My head drops in embarrassment.

"Amy, please look at me. The shame isn't yours, it's his. None of what happened was your fault. Not a single thing."

My hand falls from my mouth and goes to my stomach to still the rioting there. "I think he hated her. She couldn't cry or make any noise. He would get angry just looking at her. I didn't understand it. Sometimes I think she knew, and she didn't make much noise... if he was there."

Tears fall, and seconds later, I'm wrapped in Matteo's arms. I hold him tight, desperate for his strength, his warmth after what feels like too long cold, and alone.

He's murmuring low in his chest. What he's saying beyond, "It's going to be okay. I promise." I have no idea—it's the vibration running from his chest to mine that calms me.

In his arms, I believe him. It was going to be okay. In the end, it would all work out. I'll work for Matteo and live with him and Layla in this beautiful condo until I'm able to stand more firmly on my feet. One day, I'll move us to a little house with grass and trees where she can run around and play. It will be a good life with us safe at last.

His large hand gently cradles my head. I go still. For a moment, the memory of Danny grabbing my head and squeezing me when he was angry flashes. Except it's not Danny. There's no scent of tobacco, sweat, and beer. I inhale deeply taking the scent of him into my lungs. His scent is leather, something green, the slightest hint of rich vanilla, and something all Matteo—it's deeper, richer, and intoxicating.

"Mama," Layla calls to me. "Mama. Mama. Mama." It's on a loop, and it's not going to stop. I pull away to answer her. For the first time, I wish like hell I didn't have to.

Matteo's arms slide down to my waist. "Hey, sweetie. You want Mama's attention?"

147

I find her grinning wide, her hand in her mouth with drool running down her arm. It's only when Matteo lets me go that I go to her.

"What—oh my, someone needs her diaper changed." Unhooking her from the chair, I can't avoid her banana-covered hand. "Come on, let's go get you changed."

Flashing Matteo a grateful smile, I carry a babbling Layla to her room. After changing her stinky diaper, I clean Layla of the last remnants of banana clinging to her baby fingers. She's also managed to get banana on the pink dress she's wearing.

"Let's get you into a clean dress. What do you think? Do you want to pick it out?" I ask her as I carry her to the walk-in closet.

I'm once again overwhelmed by all the new pretty dresses, rompers, and the two-piece sets of long tops with pants and some with shorts. There's no way she could wear all these clothes before she grows out of them. She reaches for a bright red dress.

As I dress her, she's all smiles clutching at it across her tummy. It hits me, as young as she is—she loved the pretty dress. I blink back tears. She was aware of the differences between her old clothes and her new ones. New clothes I would never have bought. Even if I had the money, because I thought she wasn't aware.

I'm forever grateful to Matteo for these new, prettier things. It's because of Matteo and Bitsy that she's wearing a smile and loving her red dress.

Her eyes are wide, her breath catches, and she loses her smile. Oh crap, I wipe my tears and force a smile to reassure her. I worked hard to never cry in front of her—when I had control over it. The last thing I want is for her to see me crying. Especially when I left the reason for tears in Waco.

"Wanna go help me eat breakfast with Matteo?" I ask her with a wide smile. Does she laugh and nod because it's a baby response, or is it because I said Matteo? I'm almost positive her eyes lit up when I said Matteo.

Matteo is at the table where a plate of eggs Benedict and a glass of orange juice are waiting.

"It looks good." I let go of Layla as she reaches for him. He laughs at how excited she gets when she sees him.

"It is. This is the only place I order it from."

He cuts a strip of his waffle off and gives it to Layla. While she's munching on it, he gets her back into her highchair and strapped in again. She likes it—a lot. His pour of syrup over a fried chicken breast atop a large waffle is light.

Crap. "You're eating lunch, and this is my breakfast."

Shaking his head. "We just did this. It's not a big deal. I wanted you to sleep. How are you feeling, by the way?"

I give up on arguing with him. "Better, actually. I don't feel tired, the way I have the last few days. Oh my god, this is good."

He chuckles. "I told you."

We eat in silence, broken only by Layla's babbling requests for more waffle. I think she eats almost half of it.

"How do you feel about Nancy coming Thursday to help you with Layla? She's an excellent nanny. My sister-in-law loves her." He sees my hesitation. "If you would prefer, I can stay home again. She doesn't have to come. That's why I'm asking now. To let her know or have the clinic schedule me off."

Guilt hits me. "I don't need anyone. I'll be fine. I can take care of Layla by myself."

"No, I'm not comfortable leaving you home alone all day with Layla. I don't trust you will rest with her. You'll try cleaning and doing too much and set your recovery back." He's shaking his head. "I'll call in—"

"Okay, okay." I hate how well he knows me. "She can come. I'll behave." I sigh.

His sigh is slow. "It's not about getting you to behave."

I nod. "I get it. I do."

"If you get it, do you also get I want you to speak to my therapist for you and not for any other reason?"

* * *

MATTEO

Chocolate eyes go wide with hurt. "I don't need—"

"Really? Because I do. I have in the past when I first started in pediatric oncology due to it seriously fucking with my head. And I continued for more than four years until my therapist moved to another city. I'm going again, and I haven't gone through half of what you have." Her beautiful face softens. "Do you think less of me for seeing a therapist?"

She's quick to shake her head.

"You can be honest." I invite her. "I want you to be honest."

Layla, sensitive to her mother's upset, is swinging her eyes between me and her mom. I put another small bite of waffle on her tray, and she gobbles it up.

Amy's head goes down, unable to hold my eyes.

"It's no different from a physical ailment. Take, for instance, a broken leg. Could you get by without a doctor? Maybe. However, nine times out of ten, it won't heal correctly without a doctor resetting it. You'll likely walk with a limp for the rest of your life. It can be painful to go through, but there's going to be pain you're carrying that will hurt new relationships and yourself. I'm not saying you have to have therapy to heal from what happened to you. I do think it would help you be the best version of yourself."

She fidgets with her fork. "What, no using Layla against me?"

I shrug. "No. I figure I only get to make that argument sparingly. I think you're a good mom who knows it's better not just for her but for you too."

"You were so close." Sighing heavily, her eyes meet mine. "How many times do I have to go?"

I swallow a sigh at her not getting it. "You don't *have* to do anything. If you're going to go into it with the end in sight, then I don't think you should do it at all."

She's hurt again.

"Fine." Pushing up from the table, she almost makes a dignified exit—until she remembers Layla. Then she's back, refusing to look at me as she unhooks Layla from her highchair and goes back to her room. Her door slams shut loudly enough I could have heard it if I were on the other side of the condo.

I sit wondering if there was another way I could have handled it. After giving myself a headache, I decide I couldn't have. Talking with Hillary, I agreed Amy likely has PTSD. How could she not after what she went through? Despite what I said, I don't believe she'll fully recover from what she went through without therapy.

Either she hates my guts now or later. Because I'll always do not only what she wants but what she needs. And she needs therapy. I'll give her time to reconcile herself to that.

Since there isn't much I can do until she admits it, I decide to take a nap. Layla was up too damn early this morning.

* * *

MATTEO

While I was tired, I thought I would get an hour or two, I'm surprised by the more than three hours of sleep I get.

I find Amy's door open and her sobbing. "Amy, what's the matter? Are you okay?"

Her eyes are swollen from crying. "You left."

Fuck. I'm down on my knees at her feet. "No, sweetheart. I was taking a nap. I didn't leave. I would never leave you."

Throwing herself into my arms, she squeezes my neck tight. "I'm sorry. I'll go to therapy. Please don't be mad at me."

"I'm not mad. I promise I'm not. It doesn't matter. You don't have to go. Forget I said anything. It's all right. Don't cry. I could take anything but your tears." I beg her. It is seriously fucking with my chest to hear her deep, ragged sobs.

I don't move until she attempts to pull away.

When I feel it, I get up—taking her with me. Sitting down on the edge of her bed, I put her in my lap. She buries her face into my chest.

I lean over and grab several handfuls of tissues from the bedside table. I offer them to her. It's a few minutes before she finishes cleaning up. I'm a wimp leaving her to it—seeing her beautiful face swollen from tears is more than I can endure twice in one day.

Finally, I find my voice. "We're going to put a pin in discussing therapy until you tell me it's something you want to do. Beyond that, it's none of my business."

Her hand goes to my chest, using it as leverage to push away and look up at me. "I'm sorry. I was going to tell you that I'll go. Only I looked everywhere and couldn't find you."

"I want you to do it for you. Not me, not even Layla—"

"You're not listening to me. I want to go, for me. The reason I hesitated over the nanny coming tomorrow was because I was afraid. Afraid of someone new, of someone breaking the feeling of it being safe with no one invading this space. It's felt like a comfortable cocoon of you, me, and Layla. And I didn't want someone to come into it and end that feeling. I'm tired of being afraid. Okay, maybe some of it is for Layla. I've lived life afraid since she was born. I want to be brave for her." Tears fill her eyes again.

"Okay, it's whatever you want. Only what you want." I assure her.

How is she still beautiful with her eyes and nose red? Giving into need, I rub my thumb over her cheek. Her chocolate eyes meet mine. I watch as her teeth catch her bottom lip. Wet and full, I long to soothe it with my tongue.

"I will never leave you and Layla. I'm not going anywhere. Nothing is more important to me than you. Do you understand?" Shit, I could be fucking this all up. It's too soon to make proclamations, but I *need* her to know.

Chocolate disappears as her pupils dilate. Her breath catches. At last, she gives a small nod. It's not enough for me. I need her to say the words. My thumb moves over her lips, "I need you to say it, sweetheart. Do you understand?"

She melts into me. "I understand, Matteo."

Jesus, Amy saying my name with need and desire turns me to stone. "Say it again."

Can she feel my hard cock beneath her? My entire body is hard and tight for her. No other woman has ever done this to me— made me desperate to touch them, taste them.

No. She's not ready for everything I want from her. *Get it together, Matteo, before you fuck this up and scare the hell out of her.*

Her small, pink tongue slowly slides along her bottom lip, almost touching my thumb. Fucking hell, I want to beg her for the feel of her tongue against my skin. "I understand, Matteo."

How I don't come, I have no fucking idea. Amy is my woman, and she *wants* to be my woman. In agony, I set her back on the bed. Letting go of her is like letting go of my dreams finally come true. Soon—but not yet. "Good."

"I'm going to change my shirt," I mutter as I walk away. Before I give in to the need, clawing at my gut, I get as far away from her as I can.

I make it into the shower without stopping to even undress. With a flick of my wrist, the water is on a temp I don't care about. Tearing my clothes off, this time I'm a two-pump chump, coming hard— almost violently.

Christ. My hair isn't even wet.

Damn, my head goes down. I should be embarrassed, and I am. But I'm also fucking exhilarated. Amy understood I wanted her, and she wasn't pushing me away. Not only was she not pushing me away, she wanted me too.

Thank fuck.

My happiness lasts for the ten minutes it takes me to dry off and get dressed again.

Amy is wide-eyed in the kitchen as I walk toward her. She's hesitant. "Are you going anywhere tonight?"

I'm confused by the question. "No, why?"

"It's New Year's Eve. You don't have any plans at all?"

Did she really think I would be anywhere but here with her? "No, my brother asked if I wanted to go to his place at Christmas. I wanted to turn him down then. Another night spent going over the available women in a fifty-mile radius isn't how I want to ring in the new year. I texted him yesterday with the excuse of being worried I was coming down with something. Told him about all the strep going around at work. He might have wondered if I was lying. However, he decided not to push it."

"I'm surprised your brother is good with loaning you his nanny."

"He's not loaning me his nanny. His nanny is nice enough to work on her day off. And she's nice enough not to mention it to Rafe. I'm not ready for him asking me if I've gotten your background checked and verified for himself that you have no ulterior motives."

Chocolate eyes go wide with hurt. After considering my words, the hurt dissipates, and she nods. "I get it. It's just being on the receiving end of the mindset is...odd. When you know you aren't. I wish I had done a background check on Danny. He had a previous charge for domestic violence and another for assault. Maybe I wouldn't have said yes when he asked me out."

I open my mouth to agree, only to catch myself. "I hate you suffering at his hands. But to wish you were never with him would be to unwish Layla. I couldn't do that."

Shaking her head, her smile lights up her beautiful face. "How do you always know the right thing to say?"

"Practice. Talking to families going through literal hell as they watch their child...I couldn't *not* say anything. But what can be said? Fourteen years of practice."

She loses her smile. "I'm glad they had you as their doctor. And I bet they were, too."

"You're too kind." I clear my throat. "Since we're not going out, how about our own version of celebrating? Every New Year's Eve, our nanny would let us go nuts with all the bad stuff she never let us have during the year."

For the first time, she's scared. "Like what kind of bad stuff?"

"I don't know, maybe a cake, some candy. Is there any ice cream my mom left on the shelf?" I rush to explain. "What are you thinking?"

The tension goes out of her. Why was she scared? Her shoulders lift, clearly embarrassed. "Danny drank every day. At first, it was just on the weekends. He said he was just celebrating the end of the week. In the few New Year's Eve parties I've been to, there was liquor everywhere. I assumed...sorry—"

"Hey, don't apologize. Like I said before, you went through so much I couldn't imagine. There's no switch that flips that makes you no longer wary of something bad happening or certain the other shoe is about to drop because it can't stay good. It's a trauma response. It keeps you safe. Don't be sorry for protecting yourself and Layla. For the record, I'm not much of a drinker. Since I considered myself always on call for my patients, I rarely drank. When I'm with my brothers, I'll maybe have two fingers of scotch. It's not often, though—especially if I'm driving later."

She blinks and shakes her head as she wipes away tears. Turning away from me, shaky air comes out of her. I'm aware she's trying to get herself together. I hate she feels the need to hide from me as she does it.

"Please stop making me cry. You summed it up so perfectly. I finally stopped wondering if I'm going to wake up from the best dream ever. But now I'm—" Another shake of her head. "Okay, I'm definitely calling your therapist."

I force a chuckle I'm far from feeling. "I'll make sure she knows your call is coming. So, is that a yes or a no on creating a delivery order that will have the shopper wondering if a kid got ahold of their mom's phone?"

Laughing, she nods. "That sounds like a lot of fun."

And it is. I find she loves sour candy and isn't a huge fan of chocolate. She's never had salt and vinegar chips and has an addiction to spicy chips. My mom also left a few flavors of ice cream on the shelf—we ordered three more.

We settled onto the couch while we waited for the order, and I put on the series we watched while I braided her hair. She did want to do the jigsaw puzzle. As we sorted through the pieces, I found out her favorite color is cobalt violet, not purple or blue, but something in between the two.

She's a Taylor Swift fan and loves Pink. Her mom played blues in the house. So she loves Stevie Ray Vaughan, Muddy Waters, B.B. King, and Eric Clapton. And yes, Layla is named after the song. Her mother used to play Layla on repeat, wishing she had someone who loved her the way Clapton loved Layla.

I discovered that she loves rainy days so much that she opens the windows to let the scent of rain in. She also likes tea and **loves** coffee. Her sad sigh as she talks about not having her favorite coffee in months makes me want to run to the store this second to get it for her. I checked the app for the Moka pot she used to make the espresso. Except the stores have all closed early for the holiday.

As a doctor, I depend on coffee, but I don't love it nearly as much as she does. I encourage her to buy the pot and espresso she loves, and if she needs a grinder, all of it. I can't wait to try this coffee. The way her face dropped at my lack of brand knowledge or even a preference has me laughing.

While she likes rainy days, she hates being cold. She's always loved Christmas—admitting she once had her tree up until February. I tell her to leave everything up for as long as she wants. When she's ready for it to come down, let me know, and I'll help her. The way her eyes light up at the idea of leaving the tree up is every fucking thing. I don't understand why she loses the light seconds later.

"I'm feeling guilty about all the Christmas gifts and shopping done for Layla. You were right, she was too young to appreciate it. It was a waste." Her forehead knots.

"Hey, don't do that. It wasn't a waste. I think one of the great things about kids is seeing the world through their eyes. It reminded me of when I was younger and used to be excited by Christmas. I'm glad we did it." I assure her.

She's back to smiling. I can barely hear her telling me about her favorite Christmas gifts above the pounding of my heartbeat in my ears. One gift she left behind when she went into the group home was the family dog. Walter was a poodle and Maltese mix and her best friend. She wanted a dog, but Danny told her no.

Chocolate eyes big, she asks if I like dogs. I tell her that I love dogs. I simply never had the time they deserved. I see a dog in my future, and I can't wait.

I want all the family things I told myself I didn't want for years. It wasn't that I didn't want them. I believed I didn't deserve them. Since I was born with the biggest blessing in the world, money, I didn't get to have all the other things people wanted in life. I needed to pay for my wealth in other ways. Devoting myself to helping others is what I needed to do to even the scales.

Fuck those scales. Fourteen years of complete devotion to saving lives gave me the satisfaction of saving those lives. It also gave me severe fucking depression. I earned this—her.

I'm going to spend the rest of my life devoted to her and Layla. Hopefully, more children will follow. I can't wait to see Layla as a big sister. Our family will be the most important thing to me, and they will never be in doubt about that.

I'm going to give Amy everything she deserves. It's a good thing I have a private jet at my disposal since she dreams of standing in front of the masters of art.

She longs to go to the Art Institute in Chicago or the National Gallery of Art in D.C. and see the art in the Louvre. I'm aware there are a few other places art lovers long to see, like the Prado in Madrid and the Uffizi in Florence. I'm going to need to renew my passport and get her and Layla one.

I note all her favorite foods, some are my favorites as well. Her second favorite holiday is New Year's Eve. She loves the idea of beginning again, hopeful that it's true. And she loves how it all ends in fireworks.

We tune into New Year's Eve celebrations around the world and watch the fireworks. Her wide eyes and gasps have me more entranced than the fireworks. Dinner is the salmon and rice to balance out all the candy and chips. Dessert is ice cream because it's still a celebration. Layla is put to bed at her normal bedtime of seven.

Amy falls asleep a little after ten. I have everything cleaned up and am in bed by eleven myself. It's the best damn New Year's Eve I've ever had.

CHAPTER 13

$\mathcal{A}$my

Sleep is slipping far away when I hear Layla laughing, followed by Matteo's deep voice. I roll over to find it's a little after ten in the morning. Sighing, I'm so damn grateful for him letting me sleep in. Of everything, I really am the most grateful for the rest I've gotten.

Although I had more time to sleep in the motel room, I've spent the time stressed out about finding a job.

I'm finally feeling better. Not just in body...as corny as it sounds, in spirit. It's not only from sleep. It's also because of Matteo. How he helped with Layla and seemed to love her as much as I do. The way he understood things about me even I didn't.

When I first opened my eyes to him, if I had been told what would happen over the last few days I wouldn't have believed it. Power radiates from him, not because of his muscles and width. It's almost like it's a part of who he is. Yet he is nothing like what that power would normally mean—something to be feared, to be wary of crossing.

I blush, thinking of how gently he held me while he was on his knees. He was being nice. I'm sure he didn't even remember what he said to calm down a nearly hysterical woman.

Except Matteo doesn't say things he doesn't mean. It might be less than a full week, but I know it the same way I know my name. He didn't just say it, he made me repeat it. For a moment, when he told me to say it again... I press my legs tightly closed against the heat pooling at the core of me.

Stop it. Don't make him hurt you by telling you he doesn't want you the same way you want him.

In the shower, despite what I told myself, it won't stop running through my mind. Matteo's hand gently cupped my chin as his thumb ran over my cheek so slowly I could feel every ridge of his fingerprint. The electricity from his touch wakening every cell in my body. His promise to never leave me and Layla. How he would always be here for us—no matter what.

It was a promise that I have no doubt in my mind he would do everything he could to keep. Yet...how could he know what will happen five or ten years from now? I'm just the housekeeper, right?

The questions swirling in my head are giving me a headache—enough. It won't be answered now, so focus on what I can control.

In my closet, I don't know what has me reaching for it. It's a beautiful silky sundress in lilac with floating tendrils of teal. I barely notice the way I'm biting my lip until I pull it down and hold it against me. I wonder if it really will fit. I'm slipping it on with my eyes closed, certain it will be too small. Except it's not. It fits perfectly.

I don't recognize the woman in the mirror. The lilac against her skin gives her a glow I've never seen before.

Matteo has the nipple of Layla's bottle between his lips as he attempts to fix a bottle one-handed because he has Layla on his hip. When he sees me, his mouth falls open, losing the nipple. He blinks a few times.

His eyes are gold. "Good god. I mean, morning. Good morning. Beautiful, you look beautiful."

Layla cries out, "Mama."

I'm blushing and don't dare meet his eyes. I focus on Layla. "Good morning, my sweet girl. Come here."

I try to take her, but his arm is still tight around her. "Sorry. I, um, yeah. Okay. I'm going to make a bottle. I was making a bottle."

He lets her go and I cuddle her close. My stomach growls.

"I'm starving." I open the fridge. "What sounds good for breakfast this morning?"

Motioning to the toaster oven. "I've been up since seven this morning. I ordered in. You mentioned liking that fast-food chain's biscuit breakfast so there's one in the toaster oven to stay warm for you."

"Seven in the morning? Did Layla wake you?" My tummy is warm at him remembering my favorite breakfast.

"No, I just woke up and couldn't get back to sleep. I've got a ton of paperwork I need to do on a daily basis. I was backed up on it. I've worked my ass off to get it done. My eyes feel like they're about to cross, but it's almost done." He sighs as he finishes the bottle and takes Layla from me when I begin trying to reheat the breakfast one-handed.

Her cry of delight at the bottle he offers has both of us laughing.

"Wow, that is a lot of paperwork." I do a double take at several piles of paper spread out along the long dining table.

"Yeah, sorry. I'm almost done. If you could just slide that pile over." I do as he asks. "Thanks. No, Layla. Mommy can't share that with you. Drink your bottle."

Layla pouts around the nipple in her mouth. "I'm going to get a glass of orange juice. Do you want something while I'm up?"

"I'm good, thanks."

Filling the glass, it comes out of the container faster than I thought it would. I'm worried about spilling some when I carry it to the table and take a sip.

I'm proud I didn't spill on my walk from the kitchen. When I set it down on the table, some of it sloshes over the rim of the glass.

"Careful, please." Matteo murmurs.

I don't know what comes over me. His words were his usual quiet. There wasn't even a warning to them. What happens when I don't do what he wants? When I mess up. The back of my hand sends the glass on its side with a light clink of glass to wood. The moment I do it, my stomach falls to my feet. "I'm sorry. I'm sorry. I'm so sorry."

"It's all right, Amy. Don't worry about it. Take Layla, and I'll clean this up." There's a twinge of defeat, nothing else. I hear it, but I don't. Why isn't he angry? When will he hit me for messing up?

I was wrong. I messed up hours of work. He spent all morning on it, and I ruined it. But he's not yelling. He's telling me that he's going to clean it up.

What? No. I *have* to clean this up. I have to clean the mess I made. I'm moving fast, trying to save the paper from the orange juice. I swipe the orange juice to the floor, better the floor than the papers. Then I'm on the floor to clean up the orange juice. Only I have nothing to clean it up with. I use the skirt of my dress to try to soak it up. Except it's silk and not soaking up anything.

Matteo is on his knees with me. He takes the dress from my hands. "It's okay, Amy. It's okay. Stop saying you're sorry. It doesn't matter. None of it matters. It's all right. I'm not mad. It was an accident. It's okay. I won't hurt you. I will **never** hurt you."

What does he mean I'm still saying *I'm sorry*? Oh, I am. I can't stop saying it. I mean it. I need him to know I mean it. I'm sorry I ruined all his hours of work. I'm sorry I did it on purpose. I'm sorry that I am going to wreck this because I wreck everything. He's going to figure it out any day...

I'm in his arms, his hand at the back of my head, pressing me into his neck. Inhaling him, the words finally stop. He's rocking me like I do with Layla. One large hand is cradling my head, the other is running up and down my back.

Vaguely, I hear Layla speaking gibberish to herself. Still, Matteo doesn't let me go. I realize I'm clinging to him so tightly my hands hurt. His breath is coming in deep and out slow. I find I mimic him when the deep breath centers me. I allow one hand to unclench his shirt, then the other. But I can't bring myself to even think of unwrapping my arms from around him.

"I shouldn't have done that. I did it on purpose and—"

"Nothing you do will ever make me mad at you enough for me to hit you—hurt you. Not today, tomorrow, or any day of the week. Do not apologize for doing what you needed to do to feel safe with me. It's another trauma response. And it's nothing a hundred hours of therapy would fix because you had to know. There was no other way than to do what you did. I'll give up three hours, three days, three weeks of work if it helps you feel safe with me."

How does he always know the right thing to say? The only thing he said was for me to take Layla. Matteo was going to clean up the mess I made. I'm positive he didn't know I did it on purpose. It wasn't until I lost my shit like some kind of psycho and told him that he knew.

Except Matteo didn't think I was psycho. Once he figured out why I was waiting for a blow—the math I thought was calculus—he figured out like it was simple addition and subtraction.

Matteo wasn't mad. Not about the hours he lost to boring paper-work and not about me testing him. He understood, and he wasn't angry.

"Please tell me you have a weird thing. You can't be this perfect all the time. Do you have a secret stash of clown paintings or weird old puppets? Please." I mutter, only half-joking.

His laugh is everything. "No, I'm sorry."

He's quiet for a minute. "There is one thing I've never told anyone. I mean, my brothers kind of know… I don't want to say bad because I don't think it's bad. I know some people would think—I'm a Star Wars fan. It would be considered geek-level. I have the dialogue of the first three movies memorized. I've seen every movie at least twenty times because I have to start from the beginning when a new movie comes out. Since we're baring our souls here, you deserve to know."

Another long pause. "Please don't tell anyone. Especially my brothers. They'll never leave me alone about it. I'll be teased mercilessly until the day I die."

* * *

MATTEO

It starts low, almost like when the old cars needed to warm up from the cold. The motor would barely hum, then grow louder and louder. That's how Amy's laugh begins. At first, I wondered if she was crying again.

When she pulls back, I hate letting her go, but I love the way she's laughing so hard she's crying again. Her hand goes to her chest as she tries to stop the great bellows of air she's taking in.

Hearing her laughter soothes my soul after the heart-wrenching past few minutes. When the glass tipped over, I kissed an early night away. Shit happens. It wasn't a big deal. Until I saw the abject terror flash on Amy's face.

It was as if someone reached into my chest and pulled out my heart to show it to me. I wasn't sure how I stayed standing. Every time she said she was sorry, it sent another lash of pain from a whip across my chest. I didn't dare get close—standing over her might cause even more fear.

I put Layla on the floor with her favorite toy and prayed she wouldn't pick today to become mobile. Then I went back to Amy who was on her knees wiping at the orange juice with the skirt of her dress.

The dress she was so happy in only minutes before. I went down on my knees with her. Although I hated the cold juice soaking into my pants, I didn't give a fuck about anything until I got Amy in my arms.

I'm not one hundred percent certain anything I said made sense. It was all about reassuring her that it was okay. I wasn't mad. I wasn't going to hurt her over something so small that was an accident.

When she admitted she did it on purpose, my heart broke. My poor baby, she was afraid. Her fear needed to know for certain she was safe with me. That I wouldn't hurt her or Layla if something angered me.

Like her previous trauma response, I was a little surprised it didn't come earlier. Until I realized she was finally feeling strong again. It was because of that strength the trauma response kicked in. If she had done it before she was feeling strong, she wouldn't have been able to deal with being wrong.

If I failed the test while she was still unable to take care of herself let alone Layla, she wouldn't have seen a way out. God, I'm a bastard.

Once she stops laughing, I meet her chocolate eyes. "You should stay with my mother."

All of her glow disappears. "I said I was sorry. I'll be better. I won't do it again—"

I press a finger to her lips, hating the agony in her words. "I don't *want* you to go to my mother's. I know it's crazy since it's only been a week, but it's like you've always been here. And I couldn't imagine how empty the condo, and I will feel with you and Layla gone. However, I see now I didn't really give you a choice. Since you were already here and felt safe, you didn't want to leave. Which makes total sense—"

She wraps her hand around the wrist of the finger I have against her lips. "You're wrong. I wanted to stay with *you*. Please, don't make me leave."

The relief is so massive that I exhale from my toes. "As long as you stop apologizing. About anything. You don't need to apologize for taking up space, for being you. Do you understand?"

Tears glisten in her eyes as she nods.

"Good, go get cleaned up while I take care of this mess. Once you're done, it will be my turn."

She shakes her head. "I made this mess. I need to clean it up."

"This isn't just any mess, it's your confirmation you and Layla are safe with me. I would clean this up a thousand times with a smile on my face while I do it. Now go on. Any minute, Layla is going to get upset at not being in the middle of the action." I grasp her at her waist and lift her to her feet.

Eyes wide, one hand goes down to the table to steady herself. "I keep forgetting how strong you are." There's something I can't define in her words as a smile plays on her sweet, pouting lips. "I'll be right back."

Watching her walk away, my heart is back together, shiny, and feeling new at how her spine is straight and her shoulders back. She's never walked so confidently before. I don't have to take her and Layla to my mother's. Amy is here, and she's not leaving.

Thank fuck.

* * *

AMY

Shedding the orange juice-covered dress into the hamper, I don't feel like the same person I was when I put it on. Maybe it's because I feel like a woman, not a scared little girl fumbling my way to adulthood.

I had a baby. I'm a twenty-seven-year-old woman. Only I often didn't feel it, even less so as Matteo took care of me and Layla.

It wasn't that Matteo turned me into a woman. It's that he tore away the myth I believed in—I had to achieve a milestone or pass some test society set for me. Only then would I get my badge of womanhood.

Except it wasn't true. I wasn't a girl, weak and without any control over my life. I was always a woman with the power to effect change. It didn't get any more powerful than taking control of my life and leaving the group home before I had to, going to school and making my own money, or making a home with my roommate.

For fucks sake, I was the mother of the most amazing baby girl who was already talking at only nine months old. I'd earned the badge of a woman. I didn't need anyone to give it to me.

Matteo tore away my own self-doubting fears. Just because my lack of self-esteem didn't let me see it didn't mean it wasn't there. I stared the unknown down of what Matteo would do to me, prepared for the worst-case scenario and had the resolve to do it. Because I had to know if we were really safe with him.

It didn't matter that the aftermath was me a sobbing wreck. While this time it was Matteo who put me back together. I've been the one to do it before and if I have to, I can do it again.

CHAPTER 14

$\mathscr{A}$my

My alarm goes off too early. Why is my alarm going off? Oh yeah, I have to make breakfast and pack a lunch for Matteo. I'm up and out of bed with a bounce to my step.

Is it weird that I'm looking forward to cooking for Matteo—not just cooking for him but also cleaning for him?

Is someone going to come and take my feminism card? It isn't about cooking and cleaning for him. I want to take care of him to repay him for the way he has taken care of me and Layla. It isn't fair for Matteo to always take. It's my turn to give back to him.

I understand now what the homemaker title means. I want to make a place where he didn't just sleep and eat. Somewhere, he looked forward to coming home to every night. Because he wanted to, not because he had to. The way he admitted he was never here made it clear he didn't really consider this big, beautiful condo his home.

Maybe it's because it's his brother's. He's only staying here until he finds something else. Except he didn't seem to be in any rush to find somewhere else to live.

With the kind of money he has, he could have bought something or even rented ninety percent of what's on the market within a week or two. Yet he's been in the condo for almost six months.

Yesterday, after I showered and got dressed again, I found Matteo had cleaned everything and was playing with a happy Layla. His smile told me all was well, and I believed him. He handed me Layla and went to get cleaned up himself.

The rest of the day passed easily, with us playing with Layla, watching television, and working on a new jigsaw puzzle together. It was the kind of day some might call mundane—maybe even boring. I wouldn't have it any other way. I've never wanted anything more than a simple, quiet life. Yesterday was perfect to me.

I don't hear anything from Matteo's room as I go into the kitchen. Is he in the shower? The thought kicks over a hive of bees I didn't know were in my tummy—the butterflies are gone—replaced by frantic, buzzing bees at the idea of Matteo naked with water running down his body.

Stop thinking like that. Don't wish for things you can't have, and put more on Matteo than he can give.

Forcing the thoughts down, I try to figure out what to do for breakfast. He mentioned he liked the ease of breakfast burritos. In Texas, they're called breakfast tacos. When I told him, he laughed and said he'd been told that every single time he made the mistake of calling them burritos.

Whatever you call them, tacos are one of my favorite and easiest breakfast dishes. We have everything for good tacos: eggs, potatoes, bacon, and cheese.

I decide to go with a croissant sandwich for his lunch and carrots with a Greek yogurt dip. For his afternoon snack, I give him goat cheese and some of the soft, yummy bread. There aren't many containers to pack everything in. I don't think anything as prosaic as Tupperware would dare appear in the cupboards. I add a glass storage set to the list, along with two different lunch boxes, because this cooler thing is pretty small.

His lunch is packed, and breakfast is ready when Matteo appears. God, he is so freaking hot it's not fair. Those bees are back and have escaped my tummy, leaving hot, sticky honey in their wake. They buzz frantically at my fingertips, longing to touch him.

My mouth goes dry then wet. He could be a freaking model or something. His dove gray suit fits him like a glove. A light blue shirt and a striped vest with a silver tie tucked into the vest barely contain the muscle rippling beneath the silk.

Simple bar cufflinks glint in the light. Those aren't sterling silver— I have no doubt they are solid silver. In all the ways he attempts to downplay his wealth, it screams money in a way none of the flashy stuff did.

"Good morning. How are you feeling?" Light brown runs over me in concern.

The concern causes the bees to disappear in a blink of an eye. Matteo is simply being nice. He's a doctor worried about a patient he brought home. *Stop it before you embarrass yourself and him.*

"I'm good. I have breakfast ready for you. You need to write down all your favorite things to eat so I can plan better."

He nods. "I'll do it today." A large, slick, black phone is handed to me. "This is your phone. I apologize. I meant to give it to you yesterday. I've loaded all the apps for shopping and delivery. They're connected to my credit card for you to buy whatever you need."

Despite the order I gave myself only minutes ago, Matteo mere inches from me at my side, is causing havoc inside me. I inhale his cologne, and it sends thick honey through my veins. I'm trying to focus on what he's showing me on the phone, but it's not easy. I don't see what he's doing on the phone. All I can think of is his hands on me, his fingers—

"Sherry was the housekeeper. She's coming by in an hour or so to give you the lay of the land, so to speak."

I snap out of my reverie, praying he's unaware of what he's doing to me. "Is she really going to be okay with me taking her job?"

"She's very happy you're taking over. It's the first time I've heard her laugh since I met her. The nanny is Nancy, and she'll be here at eleven. She will stay to watch Layla for us. They're delivering my new vehicle sometime today, along with the paperwork we need to transfer the vehicle I already have to your name. It's a courtesy— since they have several copies in their office. We'll fill it out and go to the county tax office to transfer it. The office closes at 4:30, so I'll leave work by 3:00 since I'd rather we get it all taken care of today."

My stomach knots. "You're serious about this car thing?"

An exhale that might be a laugh. "I don't joke about anything important to me. Ensuring you and Layla are safe is extremely important to me. No more arguing when it comes to what I want to give you."

Sighing, I give in. "Okay, fine. No more arguing when it comes to what you want to give me."

"Good girl." His voice has dropped an octave, and those golden eyes shimmer with heat.

Those words cause a red-hot burning coal to slide down from my stomach to my core. With a wink, he hands me the phone. The smile playing on his lips is one I've never seen there before. I don't know why but I have the oddest desire to taste them to find out what it means.

He knows what he did to me. I swear he does. He takes his plate to the table without a look back at me, like he didn't just rock my world. There's coffee waiting for him on the table. Since I didn't know how he took it, I also put the sugar and half and half beside it.

"Coffee tastes great. It's the perfect strength for me."

The words get me moving again. I'm a little resentful at how unaffected he is. I could be wrong, and this is all in my messed-up head.

We'd thrown in two drip coffees in the order yesterday. The one I made today is the one we both thought would be the tastiest. "I'm glad. It's the one with pecan flavoring to it."

"It works for me. I'm only in it for the caffeine."

"Duly noted. Do you have a microwave at work to heat what I send with you for lunch?" I ask as I set the small cooler on the table.

He blinks a few times. "You made me lunch?"

I shrug. I'm not sure why it feels like something momentous for me to do for him. "Yes, of course. I thought that's what you wanted —for me to make your three meals a day. Do you not want me to?"

"No, I mean, yes. Thank you. My housekeeper in Baltimore didn't. I did have the hospital cafeteria, a half dozen fast food, as well as a handful of sit-down options around the hospital. There aren't many places near the clinic. I often ordered delivery. Also, yes, there's a microwave at work. I made sure there's a toaster oven, too."

I can't help laughing. "Okay, if I clean you out, I promise I'll leave the toaster oven behind."

His smile has my stomach flipping a dozen times. "Everything but the toaster oven."

Layla can be heard babbling. "I better go get her."

"Can I see her before I go?" He stands, hesitant.

"She'd love it."

Opening the door wider to Layla's room, I feel Matteo a few feet behind me.

"Hello, gorgeous." He whispers to her.

She's on her back eating her fingers and swings her head to us. Seeing us through the bars of the crib, she lets loose a happy cry. "Mama. Dada. Dada. Dada." Rolling over, she keeps saying it until she's on her feet. One chubby hand is holding the top of the rail. The other is reaching out to Matteo. "Dada."

"Oh my God. I'm so sorry. I didn't teach her that. I've only said 'dada' to her maybe a dozen times her whole life." I'm mortified. Also, why is she saying it now when she didn't once all day yesterday?

He chuckles, scooping Layla out of the crib. "There's no need to apologize. I love it." His dimples are deep in his cheeks. "I'm so proud of you for learning a new word. We were watching some baby shows the other day while you were resting. She loved them. Dada is so proud of you."

Giving her kisses on her neck, making her giggle he's as happy as she is. An alarm goes off on his phone. "Damn, I need to get going." He hands her to me and takes the alarming phone out of his pocket. Clearing it, he sighs. "Okay. I'll see you around three. If you need anything, call me. The number for my cell and the clinic is in your phone."

"I will," I promise him.

"Okay, bye, baby girl. Be good for Mommy." He kisses her on the cheek. We're so close that for a moment, I wonder if he'll kiss me. But he only smiles. "See you later."

"Bye," I whisper. I'm holding Layla tight, unable to move. Did I want him to kiss me goodbye?

"Mama." Layla pats my cheek. Did I seriously forget my daughter when she was in my arms? I'm losing it.

Knock it off, you're the housekeeper, and that's it. Don't go dreaming of things that will never happen.

* * *

AMY

Sherry arrives exactly when Matteo says she would. And is so freaking nice. She's also more grateful than Matteo for me taking over for her. I was given the dry-cleaning phone number and told they pick up and drop off. She sent everything he owned off because she didn't have time to do laundry and advised me to do the same with my clothes.

I'm given an array of cleaning products because I'm shocked to find she's right—there's only dishwashing soap and laundry detergent in the condo. She also gives me a few recipes to get out stains and walks me through how to clean things like the tubs with the jets. And how to use the washer and dryer, just in case.

Once she's gone, I have breakfast with Layla. Layla says 'dada' about a hundred times, leaving me cursing those shows he let her watch. I'm not sure if it's a good thing or not she keeps looking for Matteo. He's only been gone a few hours and she already misses him.

I deep clean the kitchen and the dining room, not missing the baseboards.

The black phone rings, scaring the shit out of me. "Hello?"

"Ms. Goff, you have a guest—Ms. Nancy Calder. Should I let her up?" the man asks.

I'm surprised he called me by my maiden name. I never got around to changing it legally, but I used Danny's last name daily. "Um, yes, please."

As I wait for her, I'm tortured by thoughts of the need to file for divorce. Fear has me flinching at dealing with Danny at all. I'm grateful as fuck I never changed my last name, but Layla has his name, and I hate it. I don't want her to have anything to do with him.

I don't know all the legalities of how to do it. I also have no doubt he'll sign away his parental rights if I give up child support. Once he does that, I can stop being afraid he will try to take her from me. His threat of filing for custody and how he would get custody because of his family still eats at me. He promised I would never see her again if I left him.

But Matteo promised me it wouldn't happen. That his family is mightier than Danny's, and I believe him. Except does he really want to get involved with a divorce and custody case? Layla, feeling my turmoil, lays her head on my shoulder and babbles softly.

I'm grateful for the knock on the door, pulling me away from my thoughts. She's older than I thought she would be. I'm guessing she's in her early forties, with a few streaks of gray throughout her dark hair. "Hello, thanks for coming. I appreciate it. I'm Amy."

She smiles and waves at Layla. Layla smiles and waves back. "Hi, I'm Nancy. I can never say no to Elizabeth. She's such a sweetheart. And who are you?"

Layla buries her face in my neck. "This is Layla. She can be a little shy with strangers."

Well, she was until Matteo. Then again, I wasn't awake for how their first meeting went.

"Hi, Layla. You're so pretty." Her voice is lower.

The minute Layla hears that, she peeks out at Nancy. "She loves to hear how pretty she is. Can I get you anything to drink? I can put on more coffee."

"Oh no, thank you. I've had my max on caffeine today." She lifts a tumbler. "This is the eight thousandth attempt to drink more water. I've been promised this is what will help me get my eight glasses of water in a day."

I laugh. "I've never been good at it either. If I get more than three glasses, I'm proud of myself."

"Me too. It's a little easier on the days when I'm working because I keep to a schedule. That is another reason I didn't mind working

179

today. I'm also never going to say no to more money. I love this family. They're so giving. Which is shockingly rare among the wealthy. I once had a family say I had refrigerator privileges. Then would deduct everything I ate from my pay at the end of the week. They charged me two dollars for a pickle." She shakes her head. "Never mind, she'd spend thousands of dollars on clothes she never wore. Rafe and Carrie are so down-to-earth and sane. I love them."

"Wow, I can't imagine working for people who did something like that. Thank you for your help today. I would never have asked for a nanny myself—Matteo was insistent."

"I'm happy to help. I get so bored on my days off with the weather a question of what it's going to be on a given day. I'm not okay driving when it's raining out. So, I can't make plans. I end up staying in my room, vegging in front of the television. Elizabeth paying me for a day and a half helps."

I'm stunned. "A day and a half? I keep thinking I won't be surprised, but I am every time I find out what Bitsy spends—I mean Elizabeth."

Her eyes go wide. "You got Bitsy already? She really does like you."

"I'm confused. Why is it a big deal she referred to herself as Bitsy?"

She chuckles. "Because in rich people's land, it means you're in the inner circle. She gave you permission to call her Bitsy in public—which is the only place you'll call her that. At home, in private, you'll call her Elizabeth. Only someone who is a good friend would dare call someone Bitsy in public."

"Huh. I wondered why Matteo rolled his eyes when he referred to her as Bitsy."

"Are you looking for a nanny? I have a friend who isn't happy where she's at. If you are, she's also a native Spanish speaker—the way the Castillo family wants their nannies to be."

I shake my head. "No, this is only for today. Matteo was adamant I have someone help me with Layla because I'm recovering from a bad bout of strep throat."

Her disappointment is clear. "Okay, if anything changes, let me know. Hi Layla, do you want to come with me? I hear you love walking. Matteo says you need to crawl better first."

Layla goes to her but gives me a long stare to make sure I don't go anywhere. Nancy gets down on the baby blanket I spread out where we played after breakfast.

With Layla keeping an eye out for me, I sit down at the dinner table where she can see me and go over the things to order that aren't groceries. I flinch when I see the total. Remembering it's not my money, and he wants me to spend it, I close my eyes and hit buy.

Once I see Layla laughing and happy with Nancy, I decide it's time to take the plunge on cleaning Matteo's bedroom and bathroom.

A massive four-poster bed so large I would need a step stool to get on it dominates the room. Dark brown bedside tables are on each side of the bed, with sleek black lamps on both. The hardwood flooring runs into this bedroom, too. A light brown shaggy carpet attempts to soften the hard lines in the room—it doesn't work.

There is a sitting area with a long leather sofa in front of a flat-screen television. I'm drawn to the—what has to be more than a dozen—Star Wars models. Oh my god, he is a geek. I can't hold in my laughter. This is what he does in his free time.

I can't believe this. I never would have thought it for a second. It's taking everything in me not to touch anything. I'm terrified I'll break or mess something up. This is it, his one thing that's...he said negative. I can't see it as a negative. I think it makes him more human.

I wish like hell I understood what Star Wars is. I never watched the movies. Once, there was one on the local channel. Since I was desperate for something to watch without cable or streaming, I decided to leave it on. I missed the first twenty minutes and was completely confused. In the end, I used it as background noise as I sketched.

As I take in all the models, I wonder if he wanted me to dust them or something. Until he tells me to, I'm not touching them—too afraid I'll break something.

An accent wall behind the bed is a light gray. The rest of the walls are boring white without any art or anything personal on them—it could be a hotel room or something. Only the models tell me this is Matteo's space. He hasn't made this place home.

Sighing, I shake my head as I realize how long I've been in here without doing anything. The sheets on his bed are light blue, matching the navy blue duvet cover. I find two extra sheet sets, one in white and another in gray. I go with the gray to match the dark gray duvet cover while the other is also being washed. It feels oddly intimate to decide what sheets go on his bed.

I wonder if other women have slept in the bed with him. What did they look like? The memory of him without a shirt, only in the pajama pants flashes. Did one of them trace the tattoo on his chest with their finger—the way I wanted to?

Oh god, knock it off. It's none of your business.

His walk-in closet is larger than mine. There are more than twenty suits, half of which are wool and the other silk. His casual clothing consists mainly of khaki pants and polo shirts.

I'm right about his cufflinks. All of them are silver and gold. Many of them are plain, but there are also diamonds, onyx, sapphire, and mother of pearl. There are more than thirty for him to choose from—rich, rich. His tie collection is massive. I run my hand over the silk ties in awe.

I don't mean to linger over cleaning his space, but I take twice as long as I did the kitchen and living room. I'm embarrassed to find Layla is down for her nap and Nancy is watching over her while reading on her phone.

Nancy eats a late lunch with me. We discuss Layla's progress. Nancy is a former kindergarten teacher and was impressed with how advanced she is. She urges me to enroll her in a nursery school. I thank her for her thoughts without telling her that I'm not sending Layla to school when she's not even two years old.

After I eat, I resent needing a nap myself. Nancy urges me to lie down before Layla wakes up.

In bed, the thought of Matteo shirtless haunts me again. What would it be like to touch him? For his arms to trap me against his hard body. I have no doubt he wouldn't be simply a good lover—he would be amazing.

The way he was gentle yet firm with both me and Layla screamed that he would be the same with a woman. I don't think I'll ever forget how it felt for him to hold me after he braided my hair. Every inch of him against my back was hard, burning into me, so I'll forever feel him.

It's a shock to me the way my body responds to the memory. I can't remember the last time my nipples were hard or my core was so wet—no. *Stop, don't think of him like that. It will only end in heartache.*

CHAPTER 15

$\mathcal{M}$atteo

On the way to work, all I want is to turn around and go home to them. When Amy said it felt like we were in a cocoon of just us, I didn't quite understand what she meant. Yet the further away from her I get, I do, and long for it back.

This morning felt like a dream. Amy made me breakfast and had coffee ready—like something out of a sitcom. Then, when I went into Layla's room the joy on her face at seeing me had me wondering if my heart could be contained in my chest. Her big smile as she said 'Dada' had me feeling ten feet tall and bulletproof.

Despite it being the excuse to keep Amy close, I hated leaving her home to clean. It felt wrong. I take care of her and Layla in everything. Her cleaning up after me and preparing dinner, even if she only sticks something in the toaster oven, aggravates the hell out of me.

My day is busy, as usual. Yet I find myself constantly thinking of Amy. How is she doing? Did she rest? Did Layla get a long enough nap? Is Nancy good to Layla? Was Layla afraid of Nancy? It drives me to such distraction I break down and call Amy to check on her.

"Hello, Amy's phone. This is Nancy." A woman answers.

"Where is Amy? Is she all right?" I demand. What is she doing answering Amy's phone?

"She's sleeping, sir. I only answered because I saw it was you and didn't want you to worry or anything. Both Layla and Amy are taking naps."

Relief hits me so strongly I'm glad I'm sitting at my desk. "How did they do today? Was Layla teething? Did Amy work too hard?"

"Layla did love the frozen baby washcloth, which is a very good trick. She didn't seem to be in real pain or anything. We did some walking, with me holding her hands. Amy was cleaning a bedroom, I believe. I gave Layla a bottle when she got a little cranky, and I could tell she needed a nap. She sucked it down. After a burp session, she was out like a light. I put her down in her crib. I'm not sure if Amy worked too hard, but she clearly needed a nap as well. I urged her to take one after we ate a late lunch." Nancy summarizes.

"Good, thank you. I'm still planning on leaving at three. The dealership delivered my vehicle already. I was able to make an appointment online for the tax office. Hopefully, it will all go smoothly, and we'll be home no later than five."

"No worries, sir. I'm in no rush to get home."

A brief knock on my open office door brings my eyes up to find Cleo in the doorway. "Thank you. I need to go."

The issue is a delay of delivery for the antibiotics that still haven't arrived. We're now running low on the penicillin shot. Damn it.

* * *

MATTEO

After placing a new order with a competitor of the antibiotic supplier, we'll receive the shipment in two days—in a bid to become our new supplier. I give the okay for our team to write for a different antibiotic that's stronger than what we're running low on since we have a good stock of it in our pharmacy.

I stuff the remaining time-sensitive paperwork into my briefcase to work on at home. I scan the remaining paperwork and calculate it will take another two or three days at least. All this paperwork means I can't see patients. I need more staff.

It doesn't matter how well-paid my people are. I was the one who was content to work fifty hours a week—not them. Even with hiring someone on call, after me being out of the office for less than a week, everyone is nearing their stress point. As the person running this, it is unacceptable for me to let them get stressed out.

With that thought in mind, the last thing I do before leaving is hire another doctor to ease the workload. Bonita Gutierrez is new to Dallas from Houston after a divorce and is looking for a more balanced day than joining a practice. She needs a few days to establish care for her children and can start Monday.

Before I leave for the day, I send an email to let the other staff know. Cleo, I inform in person.

"Do me a favor and close my door. Have a seat."

Her eyebrows go up as she does. "What's up?"

"I hired another doctor who will take my place seeing patients. She starts on Monday. I'm going to be a backup only. The on-call I hired will need to be scheduled until then."

Cleo's smile is knowing. "Thank goodness. You had me worried about you. The miracles a good woman can perform. Who is she? Did your mother finally get her way?"

I shake my head. It still bothers me that I met her because she was a patient.

Head tilting to the side, she studies me. "It's the pretty woman with the baby."

My chest twists, wondering if she'll report my ass to the board—the way she should.

"Hey, I'm not going to say a word. You are one of the straightest arrows I've ever met. We can't control love. It's going to happen—or not—and we either deal with it or hurt ourselves trying to fight it."

The words flow out of me. "I didn't intend for it to happen. I'm aware it's wrong. But I couldn't...." I shake my head. "There are some issues, though. So, I'm taking it slow. For now, Amy is my housekeeper. Once she's stronger, I will let her know how I feel."

"Well, I'm happy for you both. It wasn't healthy the way you were working. You have done amazing things with this clinic. The community is grateful as hell. There's nothing wrong with leaving the patients to others and focusing on the running of the place. It's just as important as seeing patients." She assures me.

Hearing her say it allows me to exhale. Even though I told myself that there was nothing wrong with stepping back on seeing patients, a small part of me wondered if it was just me rationalizing things to allow me not to feel guilty. Cleo is a straight shooter who says exactly what she thinks without pulling punches.

I stand. "Thanks, and on that note, I need to leave to get home."

"You have a good night."

Opening the door, I find Amy and Layla on the floor, playing on the blanket spread out. Nancy is making a cup of tea.

Layla cries out happily, "Dada."

The same way it did this morning—it absolutely wrecks me in the best fucking way possible. I don't miss the way Amy's beautiful face lights up when she sees me, then falls when Layla says it and reaches for me.

"Hi, how are you feeling?" I swing Layla into my arms. She's happy and hugs me tight.

"Good…um, I'm sorry she's calling you that—"

I shake my head. "I'm honored by it. It also makes sense with me being the only man in her young life who takes care of her."

Sighing, she pushes up off the floor to sit on the couch. "It feels wrong. I mean…"

"Hey, everything is going to work out. Trust me. Now, how are you feeling?"

Another sigh. "I feel better, nearly one hundred percent. Which is why it surprised me when I slept through the alarm I set for my nap."

"Because you pushed yourself too hard today. Your body will remind you it needs rest, whether you want to give it or not." Layla kisses me open mouth on my cheek. "Thank you for your kisses. I missed you today, too. How was your day, my sweet girl?" I sit down on the chair beside the couch with her on my lap. She babbles at me and does a lot of pointing to her basket full of toys.

"You want one of your toys?" I ask, taking her to the basket. She points at the ball activity one. I give it to her, and she's happy when I sit down again.

"I'm going to change real quick. Do we have time?"

"Of course. It looks nice outside, but it's cold. So dress warm. My mom did get you both a jacket and a coat. If you wear long sleeves, you should be able to wear the jacket. If not, then you'll want the coat." I warn her.

Her face falls. "I was hoping it was warmer with the sun out. I'll be right back."

Nancy waves at me. "Hello, would you like a cup of tea?"

"No, thank you. How are you? You're good to stay?"

"Oh yeah, Layla is a sweetie. I'm going to take her into her room, though, so she doesn't see you guys leave. It will cut down on her getting upset." She holds out her hands to Layla.

Layla shakes her head and buries her face in my neck.

Damn. There's that clenching in my chest again. "I'm sorry, baby girl. I missed you too. How about we go change your diaper?"

I motion for Nancy to follow me. She understands and is only a few feet behind me.

Settling Layla down on her changing table. I give her kisses on her neck. She's giggling as she clutches at my face. I step back, and Nancy steps forward. Layla looks for me until Nancy takes off her diaper and talks to her. And Layla's attention is on her.

I exit the room as quietly as I can.

"She's going to cry when we're gone, isn't she?" Amy murmurs. "Maybe we should wait..."

"I'm trying hard not to think of her crying while we're gone. However, we won't be gone long. It's not a bad thing to get used to you not being with her twenty-four-seven. She didn't cry when I took care of her, except for when she woke up hungry once." I'm not sure if I'm trying to reassure her or myself.

Amy sighs. "Okay, you're right. Let's get this over with."

* * *

MATTEO

I offer her the keys down in the garage. "This is going to be your vehicle. Do you want to drive us to the office?"

"This?" Her eyes are big. "A BMW...it's just—what if I scratch it or wreck it or something?"

"Then I buy you another one."

She shakes her head. "I can't believe—"

"Did we not already discuss how much money I have? It's fine. The only thing I'll be worried about is if you're all right or not. It's metal, wood, and leather. You're more important than all of that."

I open the passenger door for her after she shakes her head when I offer her the keys again. Once she's inside, I close it gently.

During the short drive to the office, she's quiet. I don't press her.

It's not until she answers the questions of the woman at the office that she says anything. When I pay the taxes, the woman raises her eyebrows. However, neither woman says a word.

Back in the garage, I hand her the keys. She takes them and stares down at them. I'm not sure if she's upset or not. She blinks, and tears fall.

"Amy, sweetheart, do you want to talk to me?" I loathe when her eyes are filled with tears—it seriously stresses me the fuck out.

Sniffling, she wipes her tears away. "Thank you. Really, it's such a huge gift. I keep wondering if I'm still asleep in the clinic and never woke up. Because since I met you, every day has been better than the day before it."

I can tell she's embarrassed by her tears. "I'm glad. How about we order in for dinner? I don't want you cooking."

Upstairs, Layla lets loose a squeal at the sight of us, then promptly bursts into tears. Amy takes her and attempts to soothe her.

"How did she do?" I brace myself for the worst.

Nancy shrugs. "She was fine. I will admit to bribing her with a teething biscuit."

Amy is walking her around the room as I give Nancy some cash. I insist when she tries to wave it away, telling me my mother already paid her.

I'm on the couch looking through the delivery app. Amy gets close, and Layla reaches for me. I take her. Her tears mess with me as much as Amy's. Finally, she begins to settle.

We pick a seafood place and wait for delivery.

Amy picks up my briefcase from beside the chair and sets it on the dinner table. We only sit on the inside of it, where the island ends from the kitchen, so the other side is kind of a catchall spot. "Where's your lunch box cooler?"

"I forgot it. I'm sorry. I'll bring it home tomorrow." I'm giving Layla her bottle before bed.

"Did you like the sandwich?"

Shit. I go still. "It wasn't bad."

Her eyes narrow on me. "Really, another turkey sandwich for tomorrow is okay?"

"Sounds good."

"You big fat fucking liar. I sent you with a ham and cheese sandwich." She's annoyed.

"I'm sorry. I got busy." I'm sincere in my apology. I feel bad for not eating what she took time to make.

Exasperated, she shakes her head. "You weren't lying—you forget to eat."

I nod. "I get busy, and it never crosses my mind."

"Do you not get a scheduled lunch or something?" Her arms are crossed over her chest.

"I do, but I usually end up working through it."

"Should I call you to remind you? What time is it?" She takes out her phone and types something.

"It's at one. You don't need to call me. I'll set an alarm."

Her eyes tell me she doesn't believe me. "Whatever. I'm going to the restroom before our food gets here."

After Layla burps, I put her down in her crib. She waves as I tell her goodnight. I swear she's so fucking cute my heart aches in a way I never thought was possible.

When the delivery arrives, I go down to get it from the front desk. Back upstairs, Amy is waiting with drinks ready.

During dinner she asks me questions about the clinic and my plans for it. I give her the number for my therapist, at her request and tell her to let me know if she needs me to arrange a sitter for Layla. Since I'm full on talking about work, I ask how she and Layla liked Nancy.

It's barely nine, and she's yawning, so I tell her to go to bed. I'll clean up after us. With a smile she thanks me and goes.

CHAPTER 16

*a*my

The morning is a repeat of yesterday, complete with Matteo going in with me to get a smiling Layla who said 'dada' about twenty times before Matteo left for the day.

Since everything is cleaner from yesterday, it doesn't take as long to clean today. I check the weather and get Layla dressed in an adorable purple jogger set. She hates the coat I try to put on her, so I wrap her up in a blanket and then another one over her car seat when I take her downstairs.

It's almost twenty minutes past the time I thought I would leave. I check the clock in the dashboard to see it's almost fifteen past one as I pull up outside the clinic. Getting Layla, her diaper bag, and lunch through the front door of the clinic takes a minute.

When I walk through the doors, there is a wide desk with two women. One of them, an older woman with long hair in thick braids, is on the phone.

The other is younger with bright blue hair. She's concerned. "Oh, my goodness, you look so much better. Are you sick again?"

Confused, I shake my head. "Um, no. I'm sorry. Do I know you?"

"I'm Willow. I was here when you came in." The smile is back.

"I apologize. I don't remember much from that day."

She nods. "No worries. You seemed bad off. I'm glad you're not sick again. How can I help you?"

Now I'm embarrassed. This seemed like a good idea before I got here. I wonder if he'll think I'm crossing a line or something. "I'm here to have lunch with Dr. Castillo."

Her brown eyes go wide. "That's great. He never said anything about it. But he can forget sometimes when he's busy. And goodness, is he busy with paperwork. Let me ask Cleo to come get you and escort you to him."

Picking up a phone, she dials and a moment later tells the woman what I said. "Okay, give her a few minutes. She'll be right here."

She said a few minutes, but it's more like twenty seconds. I barely have time to put down the bags and Layla on an empty seat when a woman appears. An older woman, heavy-set and wearing glasses, comes through the doors. Her concern is clear. "Amy, is everything all right?"

I nod. "Hi, I'm hoping to have lunch with Matteo. So he'll actually eat."

A smile lights up her whole face. "Thank goodness. I've worried about him and the way he overworks himself and forgets to eat. I'm glad you're here. Let me grab a bag for you. Follow me."

Grateful for the offer, I give her Layla's bulky diaper bag. As we pass through the doors, it's busy but not hectic.

Cleo stops outside an office with the door open. "Dr. Castillo, you have a visitor."

I hear a soft curse from inside the room. "Come in. It's my mother, isn't it?"

"No, it's not your mother. I hope it's okay to come have lunch with you." The look of shock on his face has me laughing. Then his smile is bigger than Layla's after getting her way.

"Yes, please. Cleo, can you do me a favor and close my door? Thanks." He takes Layla's car seat from me and leads me to the long, low, tan leather sofa in a corner of the large room.

"This is a wonderful surprise. I hate to admit you know me well. I set my alarm for lunch, then got caught on a long phone call and completely forgot. Let me grab the cooler you packed."

I shake my head. "Don't bother. I only packed you some string cheese because I knew you'd forget."

Opening the bag, I packed our lunches in I grab two glass dishes full of the chicken fettuccine I added broccoli to. I'm glad everything is still warm from me making it before I left. I hand him one, putting mine on the low table in front of me.

He unwraps Layla, who chuckles with happiness at seeing him. I take out another dish, this one filled half with goat cheese and the other half with hummus. I packed as much of the bread he loves as would fit without getting smushed.

Unfastening Layla from the car seat, he puts the car seat on the floor beside him and settles Layla onto the couch. She's interested in what we have until I give her a bottle. Since she can hold up her bottle on her own, she's preoccupied while Matteo and I get sorted.

"This looks good. I'm not a huge fan of broccoli; this is one of the few ways I'll eat it—in something."

"You didn't get me the list of what you like and don't like. I'm not leaving here today until we get it written out." I warn him.

He sighs. "You're right. My apologies."

"It's all good. I wasn't sure beyond a few of the dinners we've had that you seemed to like."

I ask him about his day so far, and he explains that he has a backlog of paperwork to get through. Then he shifts the conversation back to me and how my morning has gone.

Once we're finished with lunch, we work on his list. I take down not only what he likes but also what he doesn't like. I can't hold back a chuckle over how much a doctor doesn't like vegetables. He admits they usually need to be covered in some kind of sauce. It takes us a few minutes to find the frozen vegetables in a sauce his previous housekeeper bought that he liked. I add a half dozen to the order I'm working on.

Layla finishes her bottle and crawls all over Matteo.

I notice his lunch hour is almost up. "Now, am I going to need to do this again tomorrow, or will you stop and eat your lunch?"

Chuckling, he shrugs. "I can't make any promises. My mother diagnosed ADD might kick in again. It's not my intention to go without eating."

I sigh. "Fine. I'll make sure to bring more toys for her, so she doesn't use you as one." Layla has her hands buried in his hair and is gnawing at his ear. "Come on, sweetie. It's time to go home. We have to let Matteo get back to work."

When Matteo puts her in her car seat, she begins crying loudly and screeching, "Dada."

"Damn, she needs her nap." Matteo picks her up again and begins walking her around the room to soothe her.

"Matteo, it's okay. She'll cry it out and fall asleep on the way home."

He shakes his head. "I'm not letting her cry. It's better to get her to sleep now. The drive home is so short you'll wake her up again when you try to get her out of the car to take her upstairs, and that will really piss her off."

Layla is in a temper and fighting his soothing while at the same time clinging to him tightly. "It's okay, sweetheart. I'm sorry. I know. I hate leaving you, too. I do. I wish I could stay home all day and play with you."

I have everything packed and can only sit and watch Matteo walk her around the room, gently rocking her and speaking low. It takes more than twenty minutes before she calms down. In all that time, Matteo never checks the time or betrays any annoyance for the, at times, screeching and crying baby in his arms.

Once the crying has stopped, she babbles to him. He nods repeatedly as though he understands her and talks right back. At last, she puts her head down on his shoulder and sighs deeply—something she does when she's given up fighting sleep. Maybe five minutes later, her eyes close. Matteo continues to walk her for another fifteen minutes, talking to her softly.

I'm a little embarrassed. It's almost an hour after his lunch was supposed to be over. "I'm sorry. I don't think this is a good idea after all. We took up so much time—"

"Hey, no. I loved it. Even this part." He runs a large, gentle hand up and down Layla's back. "This is one of the perks of being the boss. No one is telling me to get back on the clock. With me trying to get through my backlog of paperwork, our on-call person agreed to come in today and tomorrow. And I hired someone who will start next Monday."

Lifting one of Layla's hands up to his mouth, he kisses it. I'm grateful as hell his eyes are on her because there's no way I can hide what it does to me. It's like he reached inside my chest and squeezed my heart with his bare hand.

The good thing about Layla is once she's in a deep sleep, she won't wake up in the middle of a thunderstorm or earthquake. Matteo gently puts her into the car seat. He watches her before he buckles her in.

I can't identify the smile on his face as he looks up at me.

"She is mighty in her fury. I'm not as worried about her health as I was. Let me grab my stethoscope to listen to her. When you come in tomorrow, is it all right if I take blood for the workup I mentioned?"

I nod. "I would appreciate it. I'm a little worried since it's been so long since she saw a doctor."

A few steps take him back to his desk. His movements are fluid as he grabs it and wraps it around his neck. He sits down in front of the car seat. Pressing the stethoscope to her chest, he's gentle. I see the doctor in him. Everything screams he's done it a thousand times.

For fourteen years, he treated kids and lost some of them. I have no idea how he lasted as long as he did. I'm glad he isn't doing it now. This is a man who feels deeply. Even the kids he didn't lose made him ache at watching them suffer through his treatment—I have no doubt in my mind.

I'm so lost in thought I miss him saying my name.

"Are you all right?"

"What? Yes, I'm fine. Sorry. I'm thinking about whether to go shopping now or later. How does she sound?"

"She sounds excellent. The labs I run will take a few days. Once I have the results back and everything looks good, I'll be happy."

His smile is turning my brain to mush. Am I staring at him? "Great, okay. Well, I better get going. Don't work too late."

"I won't. Let me carry Layla outside since you have so many things."

I follow him out of the clinic. Willow waves as we pass her. I wave back with a smile.

"Matteo, you should have grabbed your jacket." It's cold today. I have the plain fleece jacket over the long-sleeve pink top I'm wearing. Since I was just coming to the clinic, I went with thicker leggings.

He laughs as he opens the back door to put Layla inside. "After so many years in Baltimore, this is nice weather."

Once he has her inside, he pulls the blanket over Layla down to her chest—so it isn't covering her face. He holds his hands out for the bags. I hand them to him. Settling them down on the floor, he closes the door.

"Thanks for coming. I appreciate it. I'm feeling better. Before you came, I was getting another headache. Now, no headache. Even after Layla got upset." He's glowing with happiness.

Dear god, he's so gorgeous I can't breathe. Does he see my longing? His head tilts in question.

"Good, I'll see you at home tonight." I force out the words from my tight chest, unable to meet his eyes. Getting in the car, I close the door.

Matteo's eyes narrow on me as I put on my seatbelt. I don't miss that he stands in the cold, staring at the car until I'm out of sight.

* * *

AMY

I worry it will be weird when he gets home. Except it's as if it were any day. Layla cries out in happiness to see him. He picks her up and cuddles her close. After we eat dinner, he gives her a bottle and puts her to bed.

Once he's back, we sit down and do the jigsaw puzzle together with the television on. We talk about his day, but not for long. He wants to know how I'm doing and more about me. I tease him about setting a time for us to do the things from the Christmas chest. I tell him I want to do the pottery first.

He doesn't flinch from it, "I'm good for any day during the week after five. Now that I have hired another doctor, after this Saturday, I'll have Saturdays free. Don't forget, I have brunch at Rafe's on Sundays. It's at ten, and I'm usually there for around two hours. The offer is still on the table for you to save me from my mother and sister-in-law."

I force a laugh at the last bit. He might think my past and how poor I am is no big deal. But sometimes, when you're too close to something, you miss the bigger picture. "I'm sure you're strong enough to endure."

"I'll do my best."

We go back to the puzzle. But I find it hard to focus. What if his mother did manage to set him up with someone? Would she be okay with me and Layla here? How soon before this came to an end? I make an excuse and flee to my room.

Stop it, Amy. You can't have him. You're just the housekeeper—nothing more. If you don't get it together, you'll ruin this.

Yet as I lay in bed restless and unable to sleep, all I can think of is Matteo with the kind of woman he belongs with. She would be a fancy college graduate with perfect blonde hair and legs up to her neck. He adores her, and he leaves me and Layla behind while she cries for her dada.

Oh god, shut up. Focus on one damn day and get through it until you get to the next.

* * *

AMY

Friday and Saturday are like Thursday, except Layla doesn't have a screaming fit. Matteo feeds her the cereal with formula while we eat, and then he walks with her until she falls asleep.

When he leaves on Sunday Layla is taking her nap. And I'm hiding in my room pretending to nap too.

Once he's gone, I can't settle—roaming every inch of the condo, including the very cold rooftop deck. Until_the weather sends me back inside.

I grab my notebook and go into Layla's room to sketch her. The sketch is supposed to be her sleeping in her crib. Instead, it's a sketch of Matteo holding her while she's asleep.

It isn't until I'm shading his insanely hot ass I realize what I've sketched. Red with embarrassment, I flip the page and try again. Except this one is him and Layla at the dining table with him feeding her.

My nerves are shot by the time he comes home. His mother pushed hard on him until he broke. He agreed to help out a woman desperate for a date on Saturday for some work thing.

It's my fear from last night. He's going to go on a date with a beautiful woman who belongs in his world.

Oh god.

CHAPTER 17

$\mathcal{M}$atteo

The next week is a little bit of heaven mixed with hell. Heaven, because Amy brings Layla and has lunch with me every day. I discover Amy's sarcastic sense of humor matches my own. And per her request, I share more about growing up and becoming a doctor. Although I want her to do all the talking so I can simply hear her voice.

I deserve the hell. It's of my own making for upsetting Amy with the whole date thing. No matter how many times I try to explain, the woman isn't looking for anything; she needs an escort to a work event. It was nothing—the woman was nothing to me.

Amy nods yet remains anxious and tense.

"I can't do it." I call my mom Friday after Amy asked multiple anxious questions about the woman during lunch. "Tell Melissa it isn't happening."

Her sigh is heavy. "Matthew, you must stick with the plan."

"Fuck the plan—"

"Language, Matthew." Mom is stern. "Explain why you think it's a good idea to deviate from the plan."

Rolling my eyes, "I'm not okay with upsetting Amy. This date thing is upsetting her. She's miserable."

Another sigh. "Which is the entire point. Amy is understandably wary of becoming involved with anyone. It does not matter how many times you reassure her that she is acceptable as a potential partner. Her low self-esteem will not allow her to believe it until she sees we will take her as she is. Once she accepts it, she will also accept her own feelings for you."

I'm shaking my head. "I can't hurt her like this."

"Matthew, it is a shot. It stings, but the end is worth it." My mother throws back a saying I've used too damn often.

I want to argue. Only she's already hung up.

Fuck.

Melissa Hodge is a woman from old money. At thirty-two, she has heard her biological clock is ticking from her mother, father, big sister, younger sister, and even her family's cook.

The issue is she's a lesbian and doesn't want kids. She isn't going to come out to her parents because it would ruin their image. My mother found her escorts to work events to keep her family's hopes up and give her breathing room. Since I felt for the woman, and she understood it would only be a one-time thing, I agreed to escort her.

I was told it was for a company event. Too late, I realize I was lied to. It's something on the old money social calendar, which means cameras. She plays coy when the people behind the cameras ask questions. I play bored.

Exactly one hour after we walk through the door, we walk out. I'm pissed. I would never have done it if I knew there would be cameras. Melissa isn't happy. I don't give a fuck.

I drop a sullen Melissa at her home without escorting her to the door of her condo—something I've never done before.

I'm in a shit mood when I get home. Without thinking, I slam the door closed. I think we're both surprised to see each other. Amy is on the couch with a carton of ice cream, eating out of it with a spoon.

"Are you all right?" Amy asks with a frown across her brow. I hate the sight of it. Her lines are too damn deep there.

Sighing, I nod. I know it's not wise, except I need to be near her. I sit down heavily on the couch beside her. There's only maybe three or four inches between us. A small part of me exhales with relief when she covers those inches with concern as she presses against me. At that moment, all the frustration I'm feeling vanishes.

"My mother is a master manipulator. She said it was a work event. It wasn't. It was an old-money social calendar thing. If I'd known that, I wouldn't have agreed to it." I shake my head.

"Did you run into your mother there? How did she think you wouldn't be mad?" Amy is as surprised as I was.

"No, we only stayed for an hour. My mom hasn't been doing many old-money social things lately. The damage is done. Us together at an event like that meant serious. It's either a ring to follow or cohabitating. Since she's from an old family, it would have to be a ring. Since no ring will follow, I'll be labeled the asshole." As angry as I am, I don't feel comfortable telling Amy that Melissa is a lesbian. It's not my secret to tell.

"That's insane. I can't believe your mom did that to you. You weren't kidding when you said she's relentless." She takes a spoonful of ice cream. "I think I'm back to being afraid of her."

I nod. "She has her moments. I told you. Every brunch, or time I spend longer than twenty minutes with her, it's the same thing. Can I have some of that?" I nod at the ice cream.

"Sure," she hands me the carton and the spoon.

My cock goes hard at the idea of sharing a spoon with her.

"So your mom wants you with anyone—she doesn't care who it is? She would really be okay if it were me. If I agreed to..."

I go still. I don't dare let her see what the prospect of her playing a part that I want her to be for real and the rest of our lives does to me. "Despite her money, my mother isn't a snob. She cares more about a person's character than where they came from or the amount of money in their bank account. As I told you before, she was extremely hopeful you were my girlfriend. The only concern she expressed was how quickly our relationship moved."

She's pensive. I offer her the ice cream back. She takes it and the spoon. Spooning out another bite, she sucks on the spoon before giving it back to me. Sighing, she nods. "Okay, I'll pretend to be your girlfriend."

My cock jerks. I scoop a spoonful of ice cream and feed it to her. She blinks and accepts the ice cream. "Thank you. I understand it's not something you want to do. I appreciate it. I'll do my best to limit the time playing the role in front of my family. Nothing happens you feel uncomfortable with."

She sags into me with relief. "You make me feel safe. I never doubted it for a minute. It wasn't because of you…"

"I'm glad. I think it's a good idea to discuss what you are okay with ahead of time."

I offer another spoonful of ice cream. She accepts it with a smile and a small shrug. "What are you thinking?"

"Can I put my arm around you?" I hold my breath as I wait for her answer.

Her nod is hesitant. I slowly slide my arm around her, settling my hand on her shoulder. Everything in me screams in agony when she sinks into me. She takes the carton of ice cream and takes another spoonful. Once she's done, she scoops out some and holds it out to me. My whole body is hard for her.

"My brothers aren't overly affectionate with their wives but there are times when they kiss, nothing more than a press of the lips to a cheek or brow. Would that be okay?" I hold my breath.

She considers it for a moment that feels like an eternity. A moment in which she feeds me another spoonful. I take it. It might as well be dust until I know her answer.

Finally, she nods.

Air rushes into my desperate body. I steel myself—just one kiss. She's not ready for more. I press my lips to her pink cheek. She blushes easily. When she's really embarrassed, the pink goes all the way to her ears, like now. It's longer than it should be. Yet not as long as I wish it was before I pull away.

A breathy little moan escapes her—skittering down from my chest to my cock. I let my forehead fall against hers. Not daring to let her see how such a simple kiss is sweeter than every dream I've had of this moment, I close my eyes and simply savor the moment. A sigh chases away the dark. I open my eyes to find Amy fighting back a yawn.

"It's your bedtime," I whisper to her.

She shakes her head. "Five more minutes."

"Five more minutes. I want more ice cream."

Eyes glinting a soft chocolate, she gives me another spoonful of ice cream. We both sigh and close our eyes. And that's how we fall asleep.

I come awake when I feel something wet on my side. What the hell? I'm lying on the couch with my feet hanging off the end. Amy is in my arms on top of me, her head on my chest. The wet is from the remaining ice cream spilling onto me from the carton.

I'm able to snag the carton and place it on the floor. Shit, I hope it doesn't ruin the carpet.

I should get up and carry her to her own bed. If not for her, then my back. Except I don't want to. Amy is asleep in my arms, and I'm not giving that up. I'm going to savor this moment.

Worry hits me she'll be cold. I manage to pull off the throw blanket from the back of the couch and spread it out over her. When she begins to move, I go still. Only when she doesn't wake up do I give in, wrapping my arms around her. I want to hold on to this moment for as long as I can but I'm asleep in minutes.

* * *

AMY

A beeping urges me awake from the best dream of my life. My bed moves. What?

I'm on top of Matteo. Oh my god. I meet golden eyes watching me in bemusement.

"Morning. Sorry about my alarm." He's apologizing to *me*?

"I'm sorry. I'm so sorry." I try to push off him and almost fall.

He catches me. Slowly and carefully, he sits up. The moment he lets go of me, I scramble off his lap to the corner of the couch. "Hey, don't say you're sorry. I should be apologizing. Sometime in the night, I woke up. I should have carried you to bed then. I was worried I couldn't manage to get you to bed without waking you up and messing with your sleep, so I didn't."

"There's ice cream on your shirt. Oh shit. Will it come out? Ah crap, it's on the rug." I fell asleep holding the ice cream carton.

Last night comes rushing back to me. For a split second after he slammed the door when he came home, I was scared. Then he saw me, and his whole face changed—the very air around him changed. And he was back to being the gentle and sweet Matteo.

When he sat down on the couch close enough to touch those bees swarmed me all over again. They were angry, desperate for him. If I touched him, they would calm—I knew they would. So I allowed the honey flowing in my bloodstream to allow me to melt away those few inches that separated us and sunk into his hard body. Nothing had ever felt as right as Matteo's body against mine.

When he explained why he was upset, I couldn't believe what his mom did to him. She was going to keep pushing until he gave in. What if he fell in love with the next one? Fear of losing Matteo had the words coming out of me—I would pretend to be his girlfriend.

There was something in his golden eyes that stilled the rioting bees. That made me want to admit I didn't want to pretend. Only my tongue was tied up in knots.

He fed me ice cream. I fed him ice cream. He asked if he could put his arm around me. Everything in me screamed yes, but all I could do was nod. Then he did it and I sunk into him like there were no bones in my body. He asked me if he could kiss me, just small kisses—the kind he would only give me in front of his family.

I wondered if he could hear my heart pounding because it was all I heard in my ears when I said yes. He kissed me. It was only the press of his lips to my cheek, but that simple touch changed me on a cellular level.

He's rewritten my DNA with only his lips pressing to my cheek. Okay, maybe it wasn't my DNA. At the very least, it's everything I believed was possible. All those times I thought I was crazy, his thumb on my lips, him brushing my hair then holding me after, the good girl moment. I wasn't crazy—Matteo *wanted* me.

It doesn't matter I'm a former foster kid with a druggie mother who overdosed. The fact I didn't graduate high school until I was almost twenty didn't matter to him. My community college associate's degree I didn't get until I was twenty-five. He wanted me despite all the reasons why he shouldn't.

I can't believe it. He's beyond out of my league. What could he want with me? Now that I'm thinking of it—I'm not sure. His mom played him. Maybe I'm wrong, and he doesn't want me.

What if it's only about sex—because I'm here? There's no way he could really want me for more. I'm someone to keep his mom off his back. Except for the kiss... Fuck, I'm getting a headache.

"Amy, I'm sorry. I didn't mean to upset you. I'm—"

Oh shit, he's genuinely remorseful. I need to know. I have to know. I'm unable to hold it in a second longer. I blurt out the question. "Can I get the number for the housekeeper you had in Baltimore?"

Matteo freezes. "Denise? Why?"

It takes a minute to think of a good reason. Forcing a shrug, "I meant to ask before. There were a few questions I had about housekeeping in general."

The frown on his forehead is deep and then gone. "Sure. I'll text you her number."

"Thanks. I'm going to jump in the shower and get dressed before Layla wakes up to go to your family brunch." I force myself not to run for my room. My phone pings with a text before I close the door.

I call the woman. My stomach is twisting with knots as I wait for her to answer.

"Hello?" Her voice is deep. It sounds like she's older.

"Hi, my name is Amy Goff. I'm Matteo Castillo's new housekeeper. I was hoping to ask you a few questions. If it's okay with you?"

She's quiet for what feels like forever before she finally laughs. "Matteo, god I miss him. How is he doing? Best damn boss you'll ever have. A real sweetheart. The man gives a shit—too much, I thought sometimes. I'll be happy to answer any questions you have."

"Did he really buy you a car? How did that..."

Another laugh. "He sure as hell did. I was running myself ragged after my minivan died on me. Since I was only working for him about a year, I was scared he'd fire me for not having my own vehicle no more. I was still working part-time as a CNA and going

213

to school to get my nursing degree. He was the easiest part of my day. It wasn't nothing to shop for him and clean up after him since he was never home. And the pay was damn good for it."

I sag onto the bed in relief.

"Public transportation in Baltimore is better than most cities. It's also a pain in the ass. Finally had to admit to him I didn't have a car no more when he asked me to get something on the other side of the city. It would've taken half the day to get up there and back."

Thank fucking god.

"Anyway, he gets all mad at me. He leaves the hospital in the middle of the day and orders me to be at his house. I'm thinking he's gonna fire my ass, and he wanted his keys. I get there and tells me to get in his car. Doesn't say nothing the whole drive. I'm too scared to ask questions. We roll up on a dealership for Honda. I tried to tell him I'd be good with a Chevy or something, but he told me no. He'd read reports the Honda Odyssey was safer. To think of my boys."

I press my hand to my chest. It's so Matteo that I can practically hear him saying it.

"As happy as I was at getting a new car, I was worried. How was I gonna pay him back? He gets all offended. It was a part of the job for me to run his errands and handle his business. The same way he provides the vacuum to clean up, he's going to get me a vehicle. He doesn't want to hear nothing about me paying him back. There wouldn't be a bonus at Christmas time like he did before. He gave me five grand in cash at the beginning of December because there were five people in my house to buy gifts for. My mother lives with me, so me, her, and my three boys. I said I was good with that."

I've heard everything I need to hear, but I let her keep talking.

"He tells them we're there to get a new minivan for me. Since he's paying cash, he doesn't want no bullshit haggling. They showed us what they had in stock. And he paid for it then and there. When I finished signing all the paperwork, he told me to get back to work. I tried to thank him again, but he didn't want to hear it. He's a good man. A real good man. Saved me from my dick of an ex-husband too." She sighs heavily.

I freeze. "How did he save you?"

Another sigh. "We was married, but I kicked him out going on five years. I didn't have the money for no divorce. Then the bastard went and stole my tax return. Seven thousand dollars, if he'd been in front of me—I'd be in jail right now. I finally said that's it. I was going to divorce him and put his ass on child support. I didn't expect nothing from child support. I wanted him hurting the way he hurt me and his kids. Anyway, I asked Matteo if he knew any good lawyers to go to. Two months later, I'm divorced, and he's on child support. Matteo never let me pay or worry about nothing."

The knots in my stomach unfurl. I was terrified that the car and clothes and taking care of me and Layla came with a price after all.

"Was there anything else you wanna know?" The question pulls me away from my head.

"No, thank you. I appreciate you taking the time. Great person to work for, got it. Thanks."

"He sure is. All right now. You have a good day and tell him I miss him."

"I will," I promise.

I end the call and stare at the phone. She was a lot like me. A woman with kids who needed help. Matteo gave it to her without asking for anything back. I'm even more confused than I was before I called her. He hadn't done a thing for me he hadn't done for her—I mean, he didn't bring her into his home. But he did it for others often, so it wasn't special for me.

He wasn't going to use the things he bought or did as a means to get me to be with him. There was bound to be some kind of attraction when two people were in close proximity to each other. I mean, I want him too—when I thought I'd never want another man again.

Do I want him because he's here or... I shake my head. For me, it's not because he's available. It's the crazy electricity every time we touch. The way his eyes go gold when he looks at me. It's how gentle and thoughtful he is with me and Layla. There are so many things I can't list them all out—it would take hours, and I would be hoarse.

Squeezing my eyes closed, shame hits me hard. I'm a bad person. I knew he woke up in the middle of the night. Because I did, too.

I woke up and wondered if I was dreaming again, having the best damn dream in the world. Only I realized I wasn't when his breathing changed. I should have gotten off him right then. Except I didn't. I lay there while he covered me with the throw blanket. Then fell right back asleep with the sound of his heart pounding beneath my ear.

It was wrong of me not to get off him when I woke up. Or maybe this is one of those few times where two wrongs—both of us not getting up—make an amazing right? Is it so bad if neither one of us...

Through my door, I hear Matteo greeting Layla. I back away from the door, terrified he'll somehow hear my thoughts. No, that's the guilt. The guilt of not admitting I woke up too. Because I'm afraid he'll figure out I want him...wait. If he wants me and I want him, how is it a bad thing?

I don't have the strength to love him and lose him. If it's only because I'm convenient, I couldn't do it. I'm not built for just sex. The pretending is going to be bad enough. I said yes, hoping it could become real. Maybe he would really want me as his girl-friend and then maybe one day for forever.

What if I gave in? Could wanting grow to love?

Hearing Layla laughing gets me moving. I don't have time for this. I'll figure it out later.

I speed through my shower. Once I'm out, I use a hair dryer brush I found online as an amazing tool to dry long hair. I've used it once already and love it. I look like I actually know what I'm doing with my hair.

In the walk-in closet, I find a long-sleeve, maroon shirt dress that goes to just below my knees. I love how it's fine cotton throughout the body and silk along the hem and the collar. The only shoes I think go with it are the black ballet flats. In the mirror, I sigh. I barely recognize the woman in the mirror—in the best way possible.

I find Matteo putting together Layla's diaper bag. Layla is in her high chair, playing with a toy. When Matteo sees me, he straightens.

His eyes widen and go gold. "Hi, you're...beautiful."

"Thank you." I blush at his sincerity. No one has ever called me beautiful before.

Layla sees me, and she waves. "Mama."

"Hi, baby. That's hilarious. You cut out the middle of a kitchen towel?"

"I was worried about her getting her dress dirty. Of course, it's the first morning when she doesn't get messy." His eyes narrow on me. "Did you talk to Denise?"

My stomach twists as I nod. "Yes, she said to tell you that she misses you."

He's waiting as though he expects me to say more. Sighing, he nods. "I'll hand her off. She had oatmeal and ate it all. I have a bottle of water and some formula in her bag in case she needs a bottle while we're gone. Anything else you think she'll need feel free to add."

"Okay."

I'm wrong for watching his ass as he walks away.

He takes a lot less time than I did. Damn, he's gorgeous in black slacks and a dark gray, thin cashmere sweater. When I was in his closet collecting the clothes from the hamper, I couldn't stop from checking out his clothes. The sweaters he has were hung oddly. Out of curiosity, I checked them out. They are all either cashmere or cotton—most were cashmere. Rich, rich.

"I'll get her if you'll take the diaper bag."

"Okay," I take the bag from him.

"Do you want to drive, and we'll take your vehicle? Or do you want me to drive my car?" He asks.

I'm surprised he gives me an option. I do love that he made sure there was a car seat in his car. "Yours and you drive, please."

CHAPTER 18

*A*my

My stomach flips a thousand times during the drive. "Okay, so who is who?"

"We're going to Rafael and his wife Carrie's home. They're parents to twins Elliott and Riley and baby girls Elena and Stella. The twins are Carrie's little brothers that she raised. They're the reason Carrie and Rafe met when they tore up one of his construction sites."

"Oh my god."

"Yeah, not sure how they managed to wreck the CAT on site, but it turned out to be more than three hundred thousand in damages. Rafe got a little more than pissed and was going to press charges. Carrie went to him to try and talk him out of it. It all worked out in the end." He shrugs with a half-smile.

"Javier and his wife Hope will also be there. Hope used to be the nanny he needed after his daughter, Eva, was dropped off on him.

Her grandmother decided she didn't want to take care of Eva after Eva's mother died."

"Oh my god." I shake my head. "I know more words than that. But damn, your family doesn't have normal beginnings to their relationships. No meeting on a dating app or anything."

His laugh fills the car. "Something like that." But there's something about the way he says it that has me studying him. "My mother and my grandfather, Luis, will also be there. While my mother is all for talking, my grandfather is not. Don't take it personally if he doesn't say much. It's just how he is."

The neighborhood of homes are actual mansions. Rich, rich. When he pulls into a mansion the size of my old apartment building, I fight the urge to ask if I can stay in the car. It's ridiculous, I know, but—

A gentle hand comes down on mine that I didn't realize was in a fist. "Hey, it's going to be okay. They're going to love you. My family is excited to meet you, so they might be a little over-enthusiastic. If someone says anything to you that upsets you, you let me know. I'll take care of it."

His calm assurance, with the slightest edge that appears when he says to tell him if anyone upsets me, eases the twisting in my stomach. And starts a fizzing through my blood. With a gentle squeeze of my hand, he lets it go.

We're at the door. Matteo is at my side with a babbling Layla in his arms.

He holds out his hand, "Can I hold your hand?"

The question calms me in a way nothing else could. I nod and take his. Those bees are back, awakening every cell in my body to prepare for more of his touch.

Suddenly, the door opens. Two teenagers tower over me. They're obviously brothers. Despite Matteo mentioning they are twins, they don't look alike. One has dark brown hair and freckles over his cheeks and nose. The other has dirty blond hair and doesn't have a single freckle I can see.

"Hi, I'm Elliott." The dirty blond says with a welcoming smile.

"I'm Riley. Did you like the box?" Blue eyes are curious and eager.

"I loved it. I'm planning on the pottery class first. Thank you. It was so unique."

They're nodding in unison without even realizing it. Looking at each other, they high-five. Riley is proud of himself. "Yeah, Gigi was just going to gift card you. We were like, nah. It's gotta be fun."

"I loved all of it, especially the box. Thank you for thinking of it."

Riley nods and points to his brother. "That was Elliott. Him and Abuelo made it together. They make a lot of things. If Elliott didn't find ways to give stuff away, he couldn't walk around in his room."

"Riley, Elliott, you have to let them in. Come on, back it up." The deep voice is from behind them. The door opens wider. A man who is definitely Matteo's brother is there. His thick hair is darker than Matteo's, and he's maybe two inches taller than Matteo's six foot two.

"Rafe, this is Amy. Amy, my older brother Rafe." Matteo speaks to me, but his eyes are on Rafe.

The smile playing on Rafe's mouth is something I can't pin down, maybe teasing, maybe knowing. I take the hand he offers willingly. His eyes are on my other hand, still in Matteo's.

"Please come in." He steps back his hands go on the shoulder of each twin. "Elena is fighting a nap. Do you two mind taking her upstairs and—"

Both take off running at high speed before he even finishes speaking.

Rafe chuckles. "To think we were worried they would resent her before she got here. Now, she owns them. Well, hello, you're a gorgeous girl. Hi, sweetie." Rafe is talking to a beaming Layla, who is waving at him.

Matteo says proudly. "This is Layla. She's teething a bit today."

"I can grab Elena's old pack-and-play. I pulled it out of storage last week for Stella's impending need. It's been wiped out and is ready to go." Rafe offers.

I look at Matteo, and our eyes meet. As if Layla knows we're talking about her, she clings to Matteo's neck. "Dada. Dada."

Rafe's eyes widen and he looks from me to Matteo. Matteo is looking down at Layla. "It's okay, sweetie. I'll hang onto you. No jail time for you. I don't think she's ready yet for me to put her down."

"Why are you in the foyer? Come in. Come in. Amy, hello, my dear. I'm so happy to finally meet you."

The woman is exactly as I envisioned: tall, blonde, beautiful, elegant, with enough charisma to turn a room of doubters into believers. Although it's clear from having her sons standing next to her she's gone to lengths to preserve her beauty, it doesn't appear unnatural.

She takes my free hand and squeezes lightly. "Beautiful, as your daughter indicated. Hello, sweet girl. Come to your Gigi."

I watch in astonishment as Layla practically flings herself at Elizabeth and clings tight, babbling the whole time as Elizabeth walks away.

We're walking deeper into the home, past open doorways leading to formal sitting rooms, a library, and a music room with a grand piano and several instruments lining the wall.

The family living area is more relaxed than any of the rooms we walked past. It's open to a chef's dream kitchen.

The man and woman on the couch look up from the baby in her lap and the toddler girl who is clinging to her father. I'm introduced to Javier, his wife Hope, and their daughter Ava. Joaquin is their son and only a few months old.

Rafe's wife appears and greets me with a hug. "Sorry, I'm a hugger."

I return it, oddly touched. "It's okay."

An older man with gray hair appears from the kitchen and is introduced as Luis—Matteo's grandfather. He simply nods at me.

While it's clear everyone is curious, no one says a word until Matteo does. "Everyone, this is Amy. We met at the clinic where she came in ill. I was instantly smitten. As her doctor, I didn't dare say a word about it. We got to talking about how she was a housekeeper at a hotel and didn't love it there. You all are aware of how badly I needed a housekeeper, so I asked if she would be willing to be mine."

He squeezes my hand gently. "When I found out she hated where she was living. I offered her the rooms in the condo for her and Layla. Don't be a lawyer, Javier, and tell me how many ways she could sue me for letting her know I was interested in her. If she sues me for harassment later, I'm good with it. She can have everything she wants."

I'm grateful he doesn't tell them the truth about me being basically homeless. He could have made himself sound so much better for saving me from myself when I was sick and even more so from the horrible motel. It almost sounds normal...not exactly, but almost.

"Except the toaster oven," I remind him.

His laughter fills me full. "Everything but the toaster oven."

I have a feeling both his brothers are aware it isn't quite the truth. Yet, they and their wives are welcoming.

"I'm so glad to see Matteo is finally smiling. He used to say Rafe was wound so tight he worried he'd have a heart attack before fifty. I thought the only reason he said it was from personal experience. I'll admit I had a friend I was trying to set him up with." Carrie giggles.

"No worries, I'm glad he found someone. No hard feelings about my friend—she wouldn't have put up with how bossy he is. I keep telling her it's not as bad as she thinks it is. I love my bossy husband." She smiles at Rafe, who meets her eyes across the room.

"I wondered the same thing about him overworking." Hope sighs. "He worried me. Javier said there was no talking to him. Matteo was dealing with a lot of guilt for giving up oncology. Today, he seems like a whole new person from last week—at least ten years younger and happier. It's adorable how sweet he is with your daughter. I'm glad he met you."

We look to where the men and Elizabeth are sitting on the large sectional sofa holding the babies, who appear to be trying to talk to each other and very excited to see each other. I blush. "Thank you, I'm glad too."

"So, are you from Dallas? It feels like lately everyone I meet is from

California or New York. I'm originally from Houston, then I moved to Austin, then Dallas." Carrie is curious.

"No. I grew up in Temple." I don't want to talk about Danny and the painful two years in Waco. "I moved to Dallas hoping for a better job. It wasn't much better than what I left behind, though. I'm grateful for Matteo's job offer. Even though I feel awful, I barely know how to cook. He keeps saying he's fine with the premade stuff from the fancy grocery store. I started watching videos to try and learn..."

"I feel you on that. I'm grateful for our housekeeper and Elliott. All I had down were the basics. I've learned so much from Elliott."

"I'd love to teach you how to cook. Javier rarely lets me cook anymore—unless it's a special reason. You would think I'm in jeopardy of burning myself to a crisp or something. I'm not really complaining. It's adorable the way he refuses to let me do anything around the house. I hated giving in on getting a nanny to help. It's annoying how right he was, though. Two babies under two is hard. It would be awesome to have company during the day."

Her enthusiasm has me agreeing, even as I worry I'll mess up and give away I'm not *really* Matteo's girlfriend.

A little while later, I'm in the kitchen making Layla a bottle when Elizabeth approaches me.

"I love that dress on you, my dear. I have excellent taste." Elizabeth says without an ounce of humor.

"I wanted to wear it the moment I saw it, thank you. The clothes are beautiful." I'm careful to ensure no one is near us.

"No worries, my dear. Eventually, it will all come out. My other sons have no reason at all to judge. Their own love stories are not quite conventional. I am simply glad you learned to trust in

Matteo. He is utterly besotted with you, and he absolutely adores your daughter." She sighs.

"I am so very grateful you came into his life when you did. I was sure he would become so wrapped up in his work that he would not look up and enjoy life. The moment he told me he hired someone to take up his slack in order to be there for you and Layla as a partner—I knew it was real. The Matteo who first arrived back in Dallas would have wanted you to fit into his world. He would have wanted you grateful for the hour or two a day he would spend with you." Looking down at Layla, she gives her a kiss on her forehead.

"Then he changed his mind about finally seeing the therapist Rafe found for him. Except it wasn't for him, it was for you and Layla. In case he felt resentment for changing his hours for you and Layla. He didn't want to put any of it on you two." She shakes her head. "Thank you for loving my son."

Tears sting my eyes, and I can't swallow against the words threatening to spill out of me. I want to admit I loved him, but this is all a lie. Did she think he could come to love me?

Matteo mentioned he was going to talk to a therapist on Monday. We met on Saturday—he had to have scheduled the appointment before he met me. I don't deserve her gratitude.

"If you want to go, I would love to go with you." Elizabeth smiles down at me.

"I'm sorry. I was thinking of something else. Go where?" I blush to admit I wasn't listening.

She doesn't seem to mind at all. "To a pow-wow. I would love to go with you and Layla. Matteo probably would, too."

I'm shocked. "You've been to a pow-wow?"

"Oh yes, it was a lovely experience. One of the nannies we had was from the Cherokee Nation. She asked if she could take the boys. I wanted to go first to see what it was all about. It was a marvelous experience. I agreed to the boys going. They went to a few before she moved on to a position in Oklahoma—to be closer to her family. Would you like to go, my gorgeous girl?" She kisses Layla.

Layla takes her bottle with a grateful smile at Elizabeth.

Elizabeth cuddles her close. "I am so glad to have more babies in our family. To see my boys happy with their wives is all I have wanted for years. My last one is Santos. I will need to work on getting him from our California office home to Dallas."

Poor Santos, I wonder if I should tell Matteo so he can warn him that Elizabeth is working on a plan. "Matteo mentioned him briefly. Why is he in Los Angeles when everyone is here in Dallas?"

"Such a good boy he can be. He heard Javier moaning one too many times about our office in Los Angeles. Since he and his girl-friend were having issues, they thought it would be a way of solving those issues by moving from Boston to our office there."

She rolls her eyes. "It only took all of three months before they realized their issues had nothing to do with geography. Thankfully, they have parted ways for the hundredth and last time. I did not like her. She treated him as though he was lucky to have her due to his dyslexia. I almost bit my tongue clean off every time I spent more than ten minutes in her company."

Anger flares through me. "Dyslexia doesn't mean dumb, what a bitch." Oh no, she doesn't seem like the type to curse. "I apologize. Years of dealing with…I have dyslexia as well."

Her smile is serene. "She was indeed a bitch. I agree with you.

However, I did not dare say it loudly. Santos would not have welcomed my opinion."

"Mother, you can't keep her all to yourself." Matteo appears at my side. His eyes are on a sleeping Layla. "Carrie would like to eat. I'll take Layla and put her in the pack-and-play after all while we eat."

I'm a little confused. Nothing is on in the kitchen. I follow Elizabeth to the dining room hesitantly.

The table is groaning with food. I see through the French doors was cooked in the outside kitchen. An outside kitchen, rich, rich.

Matteo is back. Taking my hand, he guides me to a place at the table right beside him. His grandfather is at the head of the table on Matteo's other side. Rafe is at the other head of the table.

There's a breakfast casserole with hash browns, gravy, sausage, and eggs; a pizza with eggs and bacon. As well as several large bowls scattered throughout the table filled with bacon, scrambled eggs, sausage gravy, biscuits, and croissants.

I'm not an adventurous eater. I stick with scrambled eggs, biscuits, and bacon. Matteo pours me a glass of orange juice without me asking.

His grandfather asks Matteo about his work and expanding the clinic. The conversation lasts for several minutes while I talk to Elliott, who is on the other side of me, about how he loves cooking. He was the cook and planned the menu.

During a small lull in the conversation, Luis smiles at me and asks. "When will you be divorcing your husband?"

The question stuns me. Matteo lays a hand on my own. "I am dealing with it. He is a violent man. The lawyer is working to ensure Amy and Layla are as safe as possible."

I look to Matteo. He's working on it? He hired a lawyer? Relief and annoyance battle within me. Matteo feels it, and his eyes meet mine. The message is clear—we'll discuss it later.

"Good." Luis nods at Matteo. He turns to Riley, who is on his other side. "You got into helping your brother and added nutmeg again, didn't you?"

Just like that, Luis is done with me.

It's another two hours before we leave with a still-sleeping Layla. Everyone waves goodbye with genuine smiles...except Luis.

* * *

MATTEO

The moment we're in the car, Amy asks the question she's been holding in. "Why didn't you tell me about the lawyer?"

"Because it's not a simple or straightforward process. Once I was sure it wouldn't upset you, I would have. It had to start with getting you an address here in Dallas County. There are a bunch of requirements around divorce in Texas I had no fucking idea of. One of them is you have to live in a county for ninety days before filing there—"

"Ninety days?" Her words drip with fear.

"Hey, it's going to be all right. This is why I didn't want to tell you ahead of time. Your old boss, the hotel owner, was willing to provide the video of the day you came in, showing you had obviously been beaten. We also have a statement from the neighbor who your ex tried to attack. He heard him beating you. The lawyer is hoping we can use that to get around the ninety-day thing to serve him with divorce papers within the week." I want to pull over and hold her, except we're only five minutes from home.

"I've purchased a small house to set as your place of residence through a shell company unrelated to me and hired a rental company for it. It's less than a mile from us—close but not too close. The lawyer already filed an emergency protective order with that address. It was approved. Although it's only good for twenty days, there's more than enough evidence for it to keep being approved. She's already drawn up divorce papers and paperwork for him to sign away his parental rights to Layla."

"How can you be so sure he'll sign?" Amy clearly wants to believe me.

I exhale a laugh. "Money will get him to do it."

She shakes her head. "If he knows you're a billionaire, he'll demand more than he deserves. I don't want him making any money for all he's put us through."

"He won't know I'm a billionaire. He'll know I'm a doctor, and that's enough. Enough for him not to question where the money I offer him comes from. Not enough for him to think I'll be able to give him more. As for him making money, he won't have it for long. Once he's signed everything, I'll put the worker's comp insurance company onto the fact he's not as hurt as he says he is. They will sue him for the money they've paid him—"

"Wait, he got money? When did he get money?" She's pissed.

"He received his first check a week before Layla was born. Since it included back pay, it was almost five thousand dollars."

"That son of a bitch. He had five thousand dollars but no money for diapers for Layla." She closes her eyes. "He's on drugs. He spent that money on drugs and the women he was cheating with."

Relief fills me. She knew he was cheating on her. "Yes, OxyContin and cocaine. He's got a few girlfriends. One of them is his best friend's wife, who lived in the same apartment complex you did."

Her sigh is heavy. "Can you please keep me informed of this whole thing going forward?"

I'm grateful when I pull into the garage and can give her all my focus. "Yes, I will," I promise her. When she doesn't say anything, I press. "What else is upsetting you?"

A frown appears. "Your grandfather... I didn't get the feeling he liked me."

I shrug. "I don't give a fuck if my grandfather likes you. We still don't have the best relationship after the whole refusing to pay my tuition bullshit. I understand why he did what he did. While he's apologized, we both said things we regret. Our relationship has never truly recovered. I'm sure me living on the other side of the country all these years hasn't helped either."

"I give a fuck." She whispers.

Taking her hand that's balled up on her lap, I squeeze gently. "He doesn't know you yet. It was one afternoon. In time, he'll see everything I do and lo—like you too."

She sighs. "It doesn't feel all right. But if you say so..."

"I do." As badly as I want to, I don't tell her if the choice was between her and my grandfather that I won't hesitate to choose her. She's still not ready.

I can't go upstairs and pretend nothing has changed when it feels like everything has. "How about we go check out the art museum?"

Her eyes go wide. "I'd love that."

CHAPTER 19

*A*my

The next day, I'm cleaning the kitchen after breakfast when there's a knock at the door.

I open it to find Hope holding two large cloth grocery bags. "Hi, I'm here to teach you to cook. I was talking with Elizabeth, and she mentioned you take lunch to Matteo every day. Javier comes home for lunch. I figured we could make something to feed them."

"Oh, yeah, okay." I totally planned to come up with an excuse to avoid her. Only she's so happy. I step back to allow her into the condo. "Thank you. I didn't expect you to take time out of your day."

"I don't mind at all. Although I did have to do some begging for Javier to let me come over. He was worried about me going into the grocery store to shop. I had to put an order in. He didn't want me wandering around the store by myself." Her giggle is adorable.

"It's wrong to love how possessive he is. Blah, blah, blah, toxic masculinity. Whatever, I guess I'm a toxic woman because I'm just as possessive over him as he is about me. I can't stand the sight of him even smiling at other women—so there you go."

Glad I can be honest in one thing, I admit. "I hated the idea of Matteo out with Melissa. All week long, I was worried he'd fall in love with her or something."

"Elizabeth." Her chuckle is knowing. "She's as ruthless as her sons when it comes to getting what she wants. I'm positive the date she set up for Matteo with Melissa was totally to get you two together." She begins removing the items from the grocery bags.

"Really? I did wonder why she did something that made Matteo so mad."

Layla squeals from the activity center that she's bouncing in. "Hello, cutie pie. I left my kiddos with the nanny. It's nice to unplug from being a mom for a little while. I adore my kids, but sometimes it's nice to be me—not mom. Just for a few hours."

I nod in understanding. "I think we all need that sometimes. As soon as I had Layla, people at work only talked to me about her— it's like I didn't exist."

Hope takes out a large pan and sets it on the stove. "Same. I gave in to Javier on the nanny for help. At the same time, it's been nice to get out of the house and get my nails done or hair done and not worry about rushing back to meet their schedule. Except for having to pump, of course."

I'm surprised by the amount of seasonings she's taking out of one of the bags. I'm about to mention one of the cabinets is full of the same seasonings when she opens the cabinet and begins throwing them away.

"These have been in here since before we moved out. Seasonings take your cooking from okay to awesome. Most are good for at least six months to a year. People are going to bitch they're better for longer than that—I don't care. As far as I'm concerned, anything longer than a year, toss it."

I don't dare argue and study the spices, half of them I've never heard of let alone cooked with.

"Today, we're going to make enchiladas. There's a long way of boiling the chilis to rehydrate them and blending them. Then there's the spices method and tomato sauce. These things are going to be staples you always keep in the pantry so you can easily throw all kinds of meals together." Her hand is over half the items she has on the counter.

Over the next two hours, Hope is the sweetest teacher ever. She's patient and thorough. We make chicken and ground beef enchiladas. I learn how to chop, julienne, and slice. I'm also shown how to use all the tools in the cupboards that overwhelmed me before. I also learn which spices do what and go together and which don't.

I discovered how easy it is to make tortillas, and flour goes everywhere—including on Layla.

It's the way I always imagined having a sister would be. I'm grateful I didn't get a chance to turn her down.

"These are so freaking good." I moan as I take a bite of one. "But I do think the ones with the rehydrated chilis are better."

She shrugs. "Me too. Except sometimes it's not always something you have time for, or you forget to buy them. This is another way of having what you want using what you have. It's how they talk about the whole formula versus breastfeeding—fed is best, it's not breast is best."

I nod, surprised by her vehemence.

"Sorry, I just talked to a friend I made during Lamaze class. The poor thing is having the hardest time breastfeeding. People are making her feel awful about giving up and using formula, including her shitty husband."

"Poor woman. I never realized how hard breastfeeding was until I had Layla. Everyone makes it seem like it's this natural, magical thing that just happens. If I hadn't been in the hospital with an infection and had the lactation specialist come in every day for a week, I wouldn't have been able to do it." I cringe at the memory of feeling like a failure.

"Exactly. My mom had a bunch of kids, and I never saw her struggle with breastfeeding. Only because she learned before I was old enough to see it. And no one wants to talk about struggling because then you're made to feel like you're the problem and a defective woman. It's bullshit."

Hope is holding Layla. Layla's eyes are big and her mouth is open wide as she stares up at Hope.

"I'm sorry, sweetie. Am I getting too cranky for you? I don't mean it." She looks up to me. "It's funny how sensitive babies are to the adults around them. I'm not upset with you. No, I'm not." Hope kisses Layla over her face and into her neck.

Layla laughs loudly.

An alarm goes off on her phone. "Okay, I need to get going. Javier will be home soon for lunch."

We split the enchiladas we've made. So she can take some home to Javier.

"Let's do this again next week. This was fun." Hope says as she gives me a hug goodbye.

"I'd like that. Thank you so much." And I really mean it.

* * *

AMY

"This is the first appointment. It's simply to meet and assess—for both of you. You don't have to come back, and you can leave at any time." Matteo reassures me for the third time today.

I do that exhale laugh thing I thought was all his. I'm so glad he ignored me when I told him I could come on my own. He arranged for Elizabeth to take care of Layla at the condo. Since this is during her longest nap of the day, I'm hoping she will sleep through the time I'm gone.

A door opens, and a woman fills the doorway. She's small, with graying hair and large blue eyes that take over her face.

"Hillary Swift." She holds out her hand.

I take it for a brief handshake. "Amy Goff. Amy, please."

She nods as she sits down in a smaller chair that fits her perfectly and gestures to an oversized chair in front of her own. "Tell me, Amy. Are you here because you want to be or because Matteo pressured you?"

"Wow, going straight for the insults." I thought there would be a little more of a progression.

Her smile is brief. "It isn't an insult." She studies me. "Before we begin, I want to verify you are coming to me based on your desire to do the work. It is a great deal of work, considering what Matteo told me. It will simply save us time."

"I'm here because I want to be. I didn't want to come at first. Until Matteo helped me understand therapy is like going to any normal doctor. There are some people who are lucky and always healthy enough they don't go to the doctor often."

I sigh. "Some people have a major accident like what Danny did to me. Sometimes, it's like my childhood dealing with my mom and dad, and it will take a long time to fix. It can hurt, but it's important and will help in the end."

"Good." She nods. "I'm glad you understand it's going to hurt. Not just the EMDR with Danny. The roughest EMDR will be dealing with your childhood. We are going to have to dig up the foundation you're standing on and tear it out piece by piece. That foundation was built by abuse and neglect. It enabled Danny to lead you to believe you deserved what he did to you—when you sure as fuck didn't. You left one cycle of abuse to go into another. The work to figure out what to lay down as your new foundation can also be difficult if you aren't here for you. That's why I asked if you're here for you or Matteo."

Closing my eyes against the pain that she promises is ahead of me, I imagine getting up and walking out. Matteo said I could. He would accept it. He wouldn't like it, but he wouldn't argue with me.

"Are you ready to begin?"

Exhaling slowly, I nod.

* * *

MATTEO

I'd gotten the warning Rafe was coming to join me for lunch at noon. His secretary called to confirm my lunch time with Cleo this morning. Cleo put the woman on hold and called me, asking what I wanted her to tell the woman. I told her to confirm the time.

I'm surprised he waited until today. It's now Friday—almost a week since I brought Amy to the house for brunch.

Hope showed up Monday for a first lesson to teach Amy how to cook. I'm grateful as hell for Hope. Amy has been smiling and talking about it all week. She even got the courage to cook a few times. It wasn't bad. One of the meals wasn't great—she left out salt. But I didn't dare admit it. The other things she cooked were good, though. I love how her confidence is growing every day.

I'm not worried about Rafe's visit. Once he understands Amy and Layla are the only things in this world that will make me happy, he'll lay down the concerned big brother mantle.

Once we settle this, I won't have to worry about him giving Amy a hard time. I don't want her upset, especially after everything has been going so well over the last week. It felt like Amy was growing more comfortable in her skin. She's laughed and teased me often over the last week. Last night, she let me help her in the kitchen. We had fun to the point I couldn't have cared what the food tasted like.

The appointment with Hillary was the only cloud in the sunshine of this last week. She came right into my arms out of Hillary's office. I held her for a while before I felt good enough to drive us home.

She hadn't been ready to talk about it. I assured her she never had to be. What happened in therapy was always between her and Hillary. I never wanted her to feel as if she needed to talk to me about it because she didn't.

Over the last week, I have found myself leaving work earlier and earlier. I'm leaving today at three again. With Layla going to bed at seven, I wanted more time with her, and I don't feel guilty in the slightest about it.

Rafe nods at me in greeting as he sets down a bag from one of my favorite Italian restaurants. I've got two favorites for lunch. If he got me a sub sandwich, he's spoiling me. If he got me the chopped salad, he's being Dad Rafe.

"Thanks, I'm starving." I take the bag and set it on the table in front of the couch, where I usually have lunch with Amy.

Two chopped salads are inside, with the same no onions marked on each box. I roll my eyes as I hand him one and motion to the couch as I sit down on one side.

He takes the box and sits down. Putting down the box without opening it, he turns his attention to me. "I'm concerned."

I exhale a laugh. "I was surprised it took you until now to make an appearance. Or is it because you're rescinding your open invitation to brunch on Sunday?"

"I would never do that. You are always welcome. So are Amy and Layla. If they are family to you, then they're family to us. I'm simply concerned you've—"

"I'm the one who taught Layla to call me 'dada.' She is my daughter. As soon as Amy is ready, she will be my wife. I'm aware I need to get rid of her current husband, and I will. If you've done all your digging, you saw she was abused by the fucker."

Rafe sighs and nods.

"I'm not exactly happy that security company of yours handed over her file so easily," I mutter.

"They didn't want to. And only did after I told them if they didn't, I'd find another security company that would find out everything I wanted to know." He defends them. "Remember, they've been my go-to for the last six years."

"Whatever, it's fine. I have a lawyer working on it. Amy signed off on the petition for divorce. Everything should be good to go to protect Amy and Layla within about two weeks. By that time, it will be the ninety days since she established residency here in Dallas necessary to file for a divorce in this county. Since the lawyer thinks it's best to keep the number of special allowances to a minimum, he'll be served divorce papers two days after the day— as well as a demand he terminates custodial rights. I'll give him a week and demand a meeting for his signature on both. If need be, I'll have a cashier's check waiting. It's nice when a judge up for re-election and needs a large donation is also a former victim of domestic violence. No better win-win than that. No need to wait sixty days for it to be finalized by the judge. The judge is also willing to waive the thirty days after the divorce is final before we can get married."

He tilts his head to study me. "I never thought you'd be one to pay off a judge."

"I never thought I would be either. Until the moment Amy was a sobbing wreck in my arms—not from the fear I would hit her— because she was relieved that I *wouldn't*. When it comes to severing the last tie to that time and keeping Amy and Layla safe, there isn't much I wouldn't do."

Wincing, he nods. "You're certain Amy is with you for the right reasons?"

I send an eyebrow up at him. "I wouldn't care if she was with me for the wrong reasons. Once the divorce is finalized and she's ready, Amy will be my wife, and Layla will be my daughter. As far as I'm concerned, they are already. A piece of paper doesn't mean a thing when it comes to them."

"Okay, okay, I get it. All I want is to ensure you've thought things through. I care about you and what might come after. Please, simply give some thought to a prenup."

Shaking my head, "I'm not interested in one. Besides, I'm sure you and Mom will sic lawyers on her the moment I screw up, and she kicks me out."

He exhales a laugh.

"You good now? Got your big brother's due diligence out of the way? Can we eat, please?"

Rolling his eyes, he opens his own box. "When did you become such a know-it-all jackass?"

"Come on, I'm no Javier with a law degree. I'm worse, a doctor. You just missed out on it because I barely came back for the last twenty years. It's only been two-minute phone calls for me to diagnose and tell you what to do." I fork some romaine lettuce with some mozzarella and salami in my mouth. Damn, that's good. I look up to find Rafe staring into his salad. "What's wrong?"

Finally, his eyes meet mine. "I'm sorry for letting that be the extent of our relationship. Mom went out to see you. I didn't even think of it. I should—"

"Rafe, you called me once a week to check on me during those first years of college when I needed it, and you were busy as hell while doing it. Yeah, sometimes we only talked for five minutes. There were far more times when we talked for hours. Then I thought I was supposed to be a man and didn't need you. That is on me. I could have picked up the phone." I refuse to let him blame himself.

"Yeah, but..." His jaw is hard.

"No. Don't do that. I get it's taken some time to repair your relationship with Mom, but I had her. If I needed someone to talk to, she was the one I called. She answered every time. We can't undo what's happened. We can simply do better now."

He nods. "Fine. You're right. When the hell did you become so...smart?"

Laughing, I shrug. "It was all that time in college and med school. Is it okay if I use the jet tomorrow to take Amy to Denver? She's an artist. And I want to show her as much art as I can. I'm also looking at a three-day trip in a few weeks to Chicago. For her to agree to it, I'll have to call it a belated birthday. I'm considering two weeks in Europe to see art there for our honeymoon. Mom recommended someone to help me plan everything, and we're still working out the best way to see the most art."

"I love the ask, then the tell. There's no need to ask. I told you when you got here. Check with the office to confirm no one in the company is using it. If not, the jet has your last name on it. You have every right to use it. But you're the one paying for the fuel, and it isn't pocket change."

I nod at his warning. Talking with the coordinator at the hangar where the jet is parked yesterday, he gave me some figures. As far as I'm concerned, it's worth it to make Amy happy.

* * *

AMY

"Why are we up early on a Saturday, Matteo?" I yawn as I head straight for my Moka pot for caffeine.

His chuckle is annoying before coffee. "Only you would find nine in the morning early."

I give him the stink eye.

"I'm sorry. It *is* earlier than you're used to on a Saturday. However, I think you'll forgive me when you find out what the surprise is. The small issue is you're going to want to change. As we're leaving the condo."

It's a dreary day today. Exactly the kind of day to be lazy and hide in the warmth of central heat. "Do I have to?"

"You're going to make me tell you the surprise before we leave, aren't you?"

The caffeine hasn't hit my veins yet because the Moka pot hasn't released its life-saving brew. So, I'm not sure how it feels like I'm winning already. Back to the counter, I lean against it and cross my arms. Blearily, I stare down Matteo. He's looking, per usual, gorgeous in black slacks and a cashmere sweater—this one thick and in navy.

"I mean, Layla isn't even up yet. There's something out there about sleeping when she sleeps. I think I earned finding out what this surprise is."

An eyebrow goes up. He prowls toward me. Those bees are awake and buzzing at the look in his eyes. Heat hits me everywhere, and my lungs are tight, making it hard to breathe deep. The bees are pissed with the need for air. I finally figured out it was never a temperature I was running those first few days—it was all Matteo.

Oh my, they're turning gold. His hands come down on either side of me, caging me in. I don't feel trapped—I feel protected with his body all around. His heat warming me from the inside out. A smile is playing on his beautiful lips. Will I *finally* find out what those lips feel like on mine?

"You are feeling better. This is a different Amy, mouthy in the morning. I like it. Although I think I'll ensure I have your coffee waiting before I wake you next time." His voice is low and washes over my skin, turning it hot and tight in anticipation of his touch.

I hate that while he might be close, it's not close enough—since no part of him is touching me. As much as I hate it, it's probably the only reason I can form words. "It would go a long way to me not feeling stabby."

An exhale of air, almost a laugh. "Oh no, not stabby. Considering we're in the kitchen near knives, I'll tell you the surprise to save myself from stitches. The jet is getting gassed up as we speak. We're taking a day trip to Denver to see the art museum there. It's not the National Gallery of Art or even the Art Institute of Chicago. However, they have a lot more impressive art than the museum in Houston or here in Dallas. Once they close, we'll grab an early dinner—"

I close my eyes against the tears threatening to spill over. But I'm too late.

His lips are near my ear. Hot air washes over me, causing a shiver I can't hide. "Why are you crying?"

"Because you keep making me." I try to defend myself. My neck is weak, and my head falls to his chest.

Sighing, his arms go around me and hold me loosely. "You deserve every good thing in this life. Eventually, you won't cry when something good happens."

"Promise?" I mumble. I'm annoyed with myself for the tears. How is he going to want to kiss me if I'm crying? I might be in his arms, except it's not the way I was hoping.

"I promise. Now, your Moka pot is filling and I do believe I hear Layla. You get some coffee. I'll get Layla." He lets me go and steps back.

"Okay, I'll get dressed after I have coffee."

"Dress warm. It will barely kiss forty degrees. I'll be layering Layla." Is said over his shoulder.

CHAPTER 20

*a*my

I'm grateful for Hope coming today to keep me out of my head. Things have felt off from Matteo since Denver. The moment in the kitchen when heat shimmered between us thrilled me. I was certain he would make a move or...something during the trip.

We had the best day. On the plane there, we watched the first Star Wars movie, and I actually liked it a lot. Over the long four hours we spent in the museum, he was patient and had a smile on his face the whole time. Dinner was at a nearby noodle place where we laughed at Layla in heaven at all the noodles she got to eat. It felt like we were a family.

But by the time we were in the car on the way back to the plane, he began growing distant. Once we were in the air with a sleeping Layla secured in her car seat, I hoped I could draw him out again. Despite my telling him I wanted to watch another movie, he shook his head and demanded to know what art I liked the most that we saw that day.

We talked the whole way back—well, I talked and he listened. I kept trying to draw him out but the distance remained. The night ended with a smile and a nod of goodnight at my door.

I hoped it was him tired or something. At his family's brunch yesterday, while he held my hand and kissed my cheek, the warmth behind his touch was gone. It was like we were room-mates, and Layla was our only connection. I'm trying not to freak out, but it's not easy.

Today, we're making a chicken pot pie so she can teach me how to make a roux and pie crust. Both were a lot easier than I thought they would be.

We're doing individual pot pies, so once again, she can take hers home to Javier, and I can take ours to Matteo. The moment they're in the oven, she urges me to sit down and makes us a cup of tea.

Once she sits down with her tea, she sighs. "You keep saying you're fine. But you are a horrible actress. Talk to me. I won't tell anyone, not even Javier."

I give Layla some more puff snacks. Finally, I give in. "I don't know what I did. Matteo has gone kind of cool on me. I'm confused. We had the best time in Denver…and then—nothing."

She sighs. "I did notice the way his smile didn't quite reach his eyes yesterday. It also seemed like you weren't happy either. Is that why you were…"

I nod. "I was hurt. But I didn't feel like I had a right to be. I mean, I don't understand what's the matter with him. Maybe I did do something wrong."

"I don't know. The way he looked at you, it didn't seem like you could do any wrong. Every time you weren't looking at him, he was looking at you. Maybe it's time to just talk to him. Communication is key, the good and the bad. As much as it feels like he can read your mind at times, they can't always. And it's not really fair to assume he can." She's gentle.

This is where lying sucks. I can't admit to her the truth about this being a fake relationship. A part of me wishes I could tell her, and she would be able to give me advice on what to do.

"You're right. I'll talk to him." Even though I won't. I'm too afraid of him figuring out I'm in love with him. I couldn't stand to hear Matteo let me down gently.

Her smile is one of relief.

The pot pie tastes better than anything I've ever had before.

"You are an amazing cook. Javier must really love you not to let you cook." I sigh.

She laughs. "Yep, he admitted he's looking forward to lunch today though."

* * *

AMY

Although I hate that Matteo had to work today, I'm excited by the surprise I have for him. The steaming braised beef soup noodle smells amazing. My order is for dumplings. I was worried the soup looked too similar to ramen to order my own bowl since I don't like ramen. I'm regretting it.

I set the bags on the table while I wait for Matteo to finish with a patient.

"Beef soup noodle, my favorite. Thank you."

Shaking my head, I laugh. "How did you know what it is? I kept messing up and calling it noodle soup. The lady was annoyed at me."

"Because this place was in my top three of delivery."

"I still feel bad you never told me you like this. I liked the place we tried in Denver. I'm willing to try new places."

He shakes his head. "I keep telling you, it's not a big deal. I'm really not a picky eater."

Layla exclaims. "Dada. Dada up."

We both go still, and our eyes meet. "Where the heck did she learn that?"

I'm as shocked as he is. "I have no idea."

"Oh, my goodness. You're getting so big. That's my girl. You're so smart. Up? Okay. I'll pick you up." Matteo is smiling almost as big as she is. She's kicking her feet at his praise.

Her arms go around his neck, and she hugs him tight. "I'm sorry. I missed you this morning, too. You slept too late for me. I was going to be late for work."

Sinking onto the couch beside me, he grins. "Now that the tests came back saying she's healthy, I'm relieved. I guess she just takes after her mama and is going to be on the small side."

I roll my eyes. It's on the tip of my tongue to say I'm far from small because of my weight. Except as I see how happy she is in Matteo's arms, it dies. I don't want Layla growing up hearing me say stuff like it. And I don't want her thinking it about herself.

I'm trying to coax her out of Matteo's lap with bites of dumpling so he can eat, but she's not having it. "Your dada is trying to eat his soup. Come on, I'll give you a whole dumpling all to yourself, and you can use your two new teeth on it."

Her eyes are wide at the offer of a dumpling, but she shakes her head and leans back against Matteo.

"It's okay." He assures me. "I got a bite. It's enough for now. Hand over some of those beef rice dumplings."

I offer him the container. "I mean, we do say we're picking her up. But I didn't think we said it that often."

He chuckles. "More than enough for her to learn the word, obviously. I'll ensure the nanny has experience working with toddler teaching."

"What do you mean, a nanny? I can take care of her."

His sigh annoys the fuck out of me. "Layla is a sweetheart. She's also demanding. You need time for yourself to do your art. Then there's my mom watching her on Wednesday for your therapy appointment—"

"If it's bothering Elizabeth, then I won't go. I don't need a nanny. I'm fine. I don't care if I don't have time to do my art."

"I do. She would, too, if she knew the choice was between having another person who would be under her spell and her mom being happy and fulfilled. Ever since you've spent time working on your art, you are much happier. You're smiling all the time. And you finally lost that line in your forehead I thought was permanent. It doesn't have to be a full-time nanny. Just twenty to twenty-five hours a week." Matteo doesn't raise his voice, yet even Layla picks up on the steel in it.

Her eyes swing between Matteo and me. She's concerned, and I hate it because it feels like it's been forever since I saw it.

Unable to hold his eyes, afraid he'll see the truth, I study Layla. While I loved spending time in my studio, and I felt inspired after our trip to Denver—it's not why I'm so happy. Only I can't tell him that he's the reason I'm happy and smiling.

I'm too afraid if I do I'll break down and tell him that I love him. It will ruin everything.

I hoped maybe I was being too sensitive about last Sunday when I talked to Hope on Monday, yet as the week has gone on it's only gotten worse. He smiled, only it never reached his eyes unless he was looking at Layla.

I'm so pathetic I'm counting down the hours until tomorrow. Hoping for something—anything from him.

"Hey, it's okay. If it's going to upset you, we can shelve this for later."

Ashamed that I can't meet his eyes. "Please."

He catches me around the back of my neck. It shocks me. I'm not afraid of the touch. It's the way every cell in my body activates in preparedness for more of his touch.

Brown turns to gold. His teeth come out to catch his bottom lip. Bringing me to within inches, I pray I'm not panting the way I think I am. Is this it? Will he finally kiss me? "You understand everything I do is for you, right? To make you happy."

Oh god, how embarrassing. I'm drooling at the way heat is hitting me everywhere. I can only nod. Any second…

"Good." He lets me go, and I go cold.

"Dada," Layla is patting his chest.

"What, baby girl?"

She opens her mouth and leans into him.

"Ah, you want to give me kisses?" He leans down for her to reach him. "Thank you."

After she gives him kisses, she sticks her fingers in her mouth and chews on them.

"She's ready for her bottle." I rush to cover my rioting body.

The water I boiled for her bottle is now only warm. I add the formula and shake it. She opens her small hand for it. Chuckling, I hand it to her. She takes it and cuddles into Matteo.

"I'm sorry. I'd take her, but I don't think she'd come to me. I didn't think it would be a big deal for her to wake up to you gone. She asked for you when she woke up. I told her you were at work; she seemed down. By the time breakfast was over, she was fine." Her eyes are on him even as she's falling asleep.

"Well, I'm a bad dad because I love it. I didn't expect it to be an issue either. As soon as you leave, I'm going to get on the phone and hire another, at least, PA, if not a doctor. I thought I had enough people, but with one person out of town on vacation and another sick with strep—it appears I was wrong. At least their vacation is over come Monday. Once we're back to fully staffed, it will open more appointments to see patients and establish care. Which is better for patients. Being seen regularly will allow us to get in front of issues, cutting down on emergencies."

"I was wondering if seeing patients today would make you want to go back to the floor instead of focusing on paperwork." I share the fear I had when he got the call from Cleo last night when a PA went home sick.

His chuckle is low as he runs a large hand over Layla's head. "I wondered the same thing. If anything, it confirmed I made the right choice. I don't regret my time as a doctor—not even my specialty. At the same time, it's something that can consume you if you let it. I don't want to be consumed by it anymore. There is no better time in my day than seeing Layla first thing in the morning, and she's excited to see me. Coming home…"

I look up to find his eyes on me. Gold.

"Actually, coming home might be the best thing." He murmurs low.

Am I moving, or is he? His tongue slides out over his lips—

A knock on the closed door startles us both. "Doctor? I was hoping to take my lunch."

"Shit." Matteo looks at the clock. "Sorry, two minutes." He calls out.

"I'm sorry. I didn't even look at the clock." I'm up covering the food. "I'm going to leave this here. Please eat your soup. Go on. I'll clean this up."

Nodding, he grabs his white coat and stethoscope. Before I look up again, he's closing the door behind him.

AMY

I'm thrown by a knock on the door less than an hour after Matteo leaves for work on Monday. Hope called earlier today to tell me she wasn't feeling well, and we decided to skip cooking lessons for the week.

I set down my palette on the dining table, hoping I don't get oil paint on it. I've worked more in front of the French doors to the rooftop deck than in my studio. It was easier to bring my things in here to keep an eye on Layla in her playpen or activity center than to drag her things in and out of my studio.

All I want to do is hide the painting I'm working on. Except it's too freaking big to move while it's this wet. It's a three-foot by four-foot canvas. The man in my favorite art supply store gave me a discount because the original buyer never came to pick it up. I'd wanted to try a larger canvas but was too worried it would seem egotistical that I thought I had art good enough to use this much space.

Removing the apron I'm wearing to prevent paint from splattering on my dress. I make my way to the door.

Layla is content in her activity center, bouncing as high as it will allow while she chews on her favorite toy.

I'm shocked to find Rafe. His serious expression sends my stomach twisting. "Is Matteo all right?"

An eyebrow goes up as he studies me. "Yes, he's fine—for the most part. It's why I'm here."

Confused by the cryptic words, I step back and motion for him to come in.

"Have a seat," he invites as he stands behind a chair at the dining table.

His eyes go to my canvas. My stomach twists even tighter. Matteo mentioned that Rafe is into art. He's the reason why a Degas and Picasso are in the art museum in Dallas. A nod is all he gives the painting before returning his eyes to me.

My legs all but go out from under me. The man is imposing as hell —especially when he remains standing—towering over me. Odd how I'm only now seeing how strongly he reminds me of Matteo. "What's the matter?"

"Is it money you are seeking from my brother? Because I can give it to you. I have no problem putting five million at your disposal today. It would allow you to go as far away from your ex-husband as possible and provide for you and your daughter for years."

Outraged. "How dare you—"

"I dare a whole hell of a lot when it comes to my brother and his happiness. I was willing to let this go on as long as I believed he was happy with you. Even if you didn't love him, his love would be enough to carry your relationship—he believed. I resolved not to get involved. Yet, for the second weekend in a row, I have to watch you rebuff his love and affection at every turn."

"What are you talking about? Matteo doesn't love me." I shake my head. Wanting isn't love. And wanting simply because I was in the same space as him isn't enough for me—not when I have Layla to worry about. I'm not going to let myself and her get attached when it's purely physical.

"He doesn't. Okay, don't be mad. He came up with me being his fake girlfriend to get your mom off his back. I love him, but I can't because this is all fake. He's being nice to me."

"Fake? *Nice?* He's so in love with you that he went from working eighty hours a week to barely thirty hours a week to be with you. Matteo is a good man. However, even he isn't nice enough to go so far as to plan—" He clamps his mouth shut and shakes his head.

"Plan, what? What is he planning?" His outrage couldn't be faked. Rafe wouldn't be here if he didn't believe every word he said. Maybe Matteo told him to keep the fake thing going, or maybe... Matteo loves me.

"Oh my god, he loves me? Like, really loves me?" Now I'm up pacing the kitchen.

His eyes narrow on me. "It would appear I got it wrong. And you. I apologize."

"Oh, shut up." I throw at him as I keep pacing. "You and your sanctimonious bullshit. The only reason I'm not throwing you out is because I need answers." I stare him down. "Did he love me *all* this time?"

One shoulder goes up, then down. "I don't know. I was unaware of this fake girlfriend thing."

Annoyed at him all over again. "When did you find out he loved me?"

His eyes drop from mine. "You should talk to—"

I make it back to the dining room table. "What is Matteo planning?"

"I don't know what you're talking about."

"Bullshit. I'm tired of being lied to."

That eyebrow goes up again. "Then you should talk to Matteo and demand the truth." His eyes flick to the painting. "Are you willing to sell it?"

Is he serious? I'm not one hundred percent certain how I feel about the man, but Matteo loves him. And he did come over here because he loves Matteo, so…fine. "Yes?"

"Will you take a hundred for it?"

What the hell? I got a slight discount because the owner wanted it gone, but any other day the canvas itself is a hundred dollars.

Whatever, I need this weird moment to be done so I can go back to freaking out. "Okay."

A final nod to me, then he's gone.

I want to scream it out loud. Matteo loves me. I wince at how dumb I was not to see it sooner. I mean, for fuck's sake, he did everything short of saying it. Even then... I flashback to two days ago when he caught me by the back of the neck and what he said. He did say he loved me—I just didn't *hear* it.

My alarm goes off. It's time to get ready to take lunch to Matteo. Except I can't. I can't see him now that I know. It's the same way I was weird with Matteo yesterday. My longing for him felt so raw. I was certain if Matteo looked at me for thirty seconds, he would see it.

If I go to see him at work, I won't be able to keep my mouth shut. And his office at work is not the place for us to talk about it.

Turning off the alarm on my phone. I chicken out and text Matteo.

Hey, I'm not feeling great. Is it all right if I skip bringing your lunch today?

The time it takes for him to text back is agony.

Are you running a fever? Feeling achy? I can come home.

I don't know what to type because I want him to come home. I need him here now. Before I figure out what to type, another text comes through.

I'm on my way.

Thank god, is all I can think.

I've cleaned up and put all my paints and canvas in my studio. Layla is lights out in her crib after a bottle heavy with oatmeal.

FIONA MURPHY

I hear the elevator and wonder if this is going to be really good or really bad.

CHAPTER 21

$\mathcal{M}$atteo

The whole way home, I'm running through what could be wrong. She was fine when I left this morning. What if it's the flu? I should have had her get a flu shot. Especially if she's going to be walking through the clinic. This is all my fault. She's not going to the clinic anymore. Damn it. I hope like hell Layla doesn't catch it.

I open the door to find Amy sitting on the couch. Her arms are crossed as she stares at the television that isn't on.

"Amy, are you all right?"

Chocolate meets mine. "You lied to me."

Fuck. There's only one thing I've ever lied to her about. How she suddenly knows when she didn't before I left this morning is the only question I have. I'm done lying.

I nod.

"You love me." The words are a whisper.

"Yes." Denying her words would only be another lie. Although I wish like hell I could tell if she was happy, sad, or—something.

"When were you going to tell me?"

"Once I made you fall in love with me," I admit.

I make it to the sofa and sit down on the edge. I'm relieved when I take her hand, and she doesn't fight me. Except her eyes won't meet mine.

I'm dying here. She hasn't said a word. "Amy?"

Her eyes come back to me. "What?"

"Are you mad or…"

She shakes her head. "I'm just worried about your skills of detection. Because I think I loved you since the moment you pulled up the chair beside my bed to watch television with me."

It's Layla calling me 'dada' all over again—Amy loves me. I want to hear it a thousand more times until she's hoarse from saying it. "You love me?"

Her smile is everything. "Yes, I love you, Matteo Castillo—"

I catch her around the back of her neck and pull her into my arms. She laughs and throws her arms around me as I settle her on my lap. "Say it again."

"I love you. If you were a *little* more open, I might have said it the day I woke up on top of you. The reason I called Denise was to find out if you really bought her a car."

My joy dies a little. "You thought I lied about the car?"

"Yes, because I figured out you wanted me. But I only thought you wanted me. I didn't dare think you were in love with me. A part of me was wondering if you did everything because of that or… Everything got confusing in my mind. Did you expect something in return?" Her sigh is heavy.

"Unfortunately, the call to Denise made things worse. Aside from bringing me and Layla home with you, you did all the things for her that you were doing for me. It felt like confirmation you just wanted me physically. Like it was only due to us being in the same space. As badly as I wanted you—loved you. I was too afraid it would end badly if you didn't love me. Then Rafe…"

I shake my head, astonished she couldn't tell. And not sure I won't kick Rafe's ass later because he probably only told her as a way of trying to scare her away or something. "I wondered what happened for you to know. Did he do something stupid like try to pay you off or something?"

Her shrug says it all.

"I'm going to kick his ass."

A small hand goes to my chest, pressing softly. "No, don't. If he hadn't told me, I wouldn't have figured it out. He only did it because he loves you. I'm not mad at him. I'm very grateful."

Laying my hand on top of hers, I nod. "I guess I should be glad he outed me. It would have taken a lot more time for me to feel free to admit it to you. When we were in Denver, I came so close to saying something. Until you said something about being relieved we were friends. It felt like you were hinting that you weren't ready for more."

Her mouth drops. "Are you serious? That's what made you pull away? I was babbling because I thought you caught me staring at your ass when you bent over the stroller to pick up Layla."

Now, my mouth is the one that drops.

The blush goes right up to her ears. "You have an amazing ass. I've been kind of unable to stop staring at it every time you bend over."

I can't stop laughing.

She shakes her head. "I can't believe my stupid mouth had us wasting more time. When we came back from Denver, I missed you. It felt like you were beside me...yet not."

"I was battling hard, baby. You were finally growing stronger, and I thought we could try. I hoped like hell I could do everything right and make you fall for me. There's that spark, that crazy connection every time we touch. Only there was no guarantee. I was willing to wait for as long as it took for you to be ready. I thought you needed time to heal from your ex."

Opening her mouth to argue, she sighs and nods. "I think I did need some time to get used to what I felt for you. When Rafe spilled, I was angry at you for not telling me. All I could think was, we've wasted so much time. Then I realized it's only been a month."

Hearing her say it, I'm as surprised as she is. How could it have only been such a short time when it felt like I was waiting forever to admit my love for her?

"It's weird how it feels like I've always loved you. At the same time, I think if you told me that first week, I would have been too scared by... I don't know—everything. Thank you for giving me time to let my heart become ready to let you in."

Her admission pulls my own out of me. "I left oncology because I lost all feeling. Every single one: anger, frustration, sadness, happiness. All of it. I couldn't do what I did without feeling anything. I was sure it would come back, only it never did. Weeks, then months, went by. In the back of my mind, I knew something was wrong. But I was too worried about what it might mean to search for answers. It was all this gray nothing. Until I looked into your eyes—I swear I felt every emotion I should have felt and didn't for months in one moment. I knew you were special. I couldn't let you go."

"I'm glad. I don't want you to let us go."

"No chance," I promise her.

A small, soft hand runs over my cheek. "I want you, this. I'm just—I don't know how to do this...with you."

"Hey, it's okay. There's no rush. We have all the time in the world—"

She presses her lips to mine. I'm stunned and open my mouth to her tongue darting inside. I attempt to deepen the kiss. Except I can't, all I taste is fear.

I cup her beneath her chin to hold her still. I'm inches from her, our breath mingling. "Talk to me, Amy. We can take this as slow as you need. But if there's something else, did he rape you?"

Eyes wide. "No, he didn't rape me..." Realization hits her. "Not like that. I get now he did in the way he would harass me until I gave in. Or several times when I woke up to him trying to—" Her eyes squeeze closed. "I thought because it didn't really hurt, or he didn't hold me down."

She shakes her head. "I don't want to think of him now. He doesn't get to take this away from us. I'll talk to Hillary about it later. I

FIONA MURPHY

don't want to take this slow. I'm also not so delicate I'm going to break. The only thing I'm afraid of is being enough for you. I'm bad at this. So bad I had to read books to try to be better and was still bad."

I stop her words with a press of my lips to hers, then pull back. "He was your first."

Shyly, she nods.

Working to contain my rage at the bastard, the shimmering concern in her eyes pulls me out of it. She's right. He doesn't get to take this moment away from us.

Focusing on her, I shake my head. "It's **all** his fault. It was another way of keeping you under his thumb. Of making you afraid to try with another man. Another way to trap you with him and keep you from searching out pleasure. When you deserve all the pleasure in the world."

Her smile is cock-achingly sexy. "Right now, the only pleasure I want is you."

I take a deep breath and fight for control. "It feels like I've waited for you forever. All the twists and turns in my life were to get me to you. I want to go slow so I don't overwhelm you. You get close, and I don't recognize what you turn me into for you. The last thing I want in this world is to scare you or hurt you in any way. I never want to cause you pain or fear of me. Do you understand?"

* * *

AMY

This gorgeous man, how could he think I would fear him? Espe-

264

cially when he says such beautiful things. In his arms, with him all around me—I'm back where I belong.

Those bees are also back. Buzzing angrily beneath my skin, turning it hot, tight, and aching. They're determined to break free to get to him. "Matteo, I don't fear you. I never have. The only thing I'm afraid of is waking up and finding this is all a dream. Again."

A large hand cradles my cheek, running his thumb over my lips. "I dreamed of you every night and woke up hard and aching for you."

Finally, his lips brush against mine. Too light, it's not enough. I open my mouth to him. He sweeps inside, at first delicate tasting, teasing, learning every inch of me. His kiss is the first sip of coffee made perfectly—sweet and bold and shooting straight into my bloodstream. It cuts me free of everything holding me down, sending me soaring off the edge of the world and plunging headlong into him. I want to slip from my skin into his, to crawl inside and get lost in him.

It doesn't matter that my lungs are burning for air. When he lifts his mouth from mine, it feels like he's tearing me in two.

"Tell me you're mine." He demands.

I don't hesitate. "Always, I've always belonged to you."

My reward is his touching deep into my soul and claiming me as his, the same way he gives himself up to me. He tastes of sunlight bright and bold, and every secret wish I ever had come true. All around us, the world is burning. I open my eyes to find it's not the world burning—it's only us. That heat sets us both on fire so that we can melt back together and become one.

Suddenly, we're moving. I wrap my legs around his waist and cling to him as he carries me down the hall to his room. Thank god.

I'm lying on his big bed. I want to cry when he steps back. Until he takes off his jacket and begins tugging down his tie.

I sit up and unzip my dress. Peeling it off, I find he's torn off his own shirt. He's only in a thin, plain white shirt clinging to his wide, muscled chest. Those muscles flex and move impressively as he breathes deep. Gold touches me everywhere.

For two seconds, I'm worried about what he thinks of my body. His jaw is tight as he squeezes his eyes shut. Suddenly, they're open and find mine. If I weren't already on my ass, my legs would give out from under me at the way melting gold turns my bones to dust.

"You are so beautiful. Every dream I had doesn't compare with the real thing." The words are a whisper. He shakes his head. "Every night and half a dozen times during the day, I was hard for you. I've jacked off more since I met you than I did the entire year before. In my mind, I've bent you over everything from the couch to the kitchen sink. You have no idea how many times I wished my dinner was your pussy. My cock ached as I imagined eating you until your pussy drenched the table beneath you."

Sweet and so dirty, I blush at how wet his confession makes me. This stunningly gorgeous man wants me, not only dreamed of me, he touched himself to *me*. I undo my bra with pride.

Watching his throat work as his hands fist at his side pulls the words from me. "Don't you want to touch—not just look?"

"Are you protected?" Is ground out of him.

I'm not sure why the question twists me up. I shake my head. The words aren't planned, but I mean them. "No, I don't need protection from you. I want all of you. I want your baby."

The awe on his face fills me full of happiness. "You want my baby?"

"Please."

He tears off his shirt and tosses it behind him as two steps bring him to the edge of the bed. "I'm never letting you go. Even if you beg."

It's a warning. That brings a smile to my face. "I don't want you to. I want all of you forever."

I give into need and lay my hand on his chest. The thick hair on his chest is softer than I thought it would be. Muscles ripple and strain beneath my touch. His skin is hot silk over what feels like corrugated metal.

"Forever is a long time, but not long enough when it comes to you." A strong hand catches the back of my neck and brings my mouth to his.

CHAPTER 22

*A*my

The hair I thought was soft sends a hiss out of me at the sensation of it tangling with my tender, aching nipples as he slides down my body. Hot, so hot. His tongue teases an already tight nipple, then blows my mind as he continues toying with it as he sucks deep. *Oh god.*

Stronger and stronger, he sucks before allowing my tortured flesh to fall from his mouth. I didn't even realize I was lying on the bed until a knee is between my legs, opening me wide for him. His mouth is back, sucking deep, oh so deep.

Yes, more, please. Teeth graze my nipple and tug as he allows it to fall from his mouth.

I'm on the verge of begging for more when his mouth finds my other breast. It isn't the same as he did before—the pressure is stronger, verging on pain—both him suckling and his tongue. And it's driving me out of my mind. My hands are in his hair to keep him there. I love it. *God, I love it so much.*

His mouth is back on my other breast that velvet tongue tracing every ridge and valley. I send my hands down his back, desperate for more—for all of him.

He grasps both hands in one of his own and lays them above my head. I try to leave them there but can't, I *need* to touch him.

"Bad girl, your hands on me are going to have me coming before I'm inside you." He growls seconds before a rough hand smacks my ass. The sound stuns me. It's not just the sound, it's how wet it makes me. Matteo shoots off the bed before I blink.

Anguish is all over his beautiful face. He's so still I don't even think he's breathing. The words spill out of me. "I'm sorry. I'll be a good girl. *Your* good girl."

A shuddering breath escapes him. He shakes his head.

I'm off the bed in front of him. My hand is on his chest. "I'm not afraid of you. I've never been afraid of your strength. Those books I read. I liked when he spanked her, when his hand went around her throat to control her, even the times she was forced onto her knees to swallow his cock. They were fantasies I never thought I would let come true because I never believed I would be with someone I trust as much as I trust you. In the same way, I don't want you to hold back in your strength—I don't want you to hold back from all the ways you make love. I want all of you in every way."

A hand goes into my hair to pull my face up to his. "I've never made love until you."

This man. "I like that we're each other's first when it comes to this. But I'm also glad you've had much more experience."

His lips graze mine. Gold meets mine and holds. The heat in them is burning me from the inside out. "I'm not trying to scare you, but

269

I'm big. It's going to take some work for me to be as deep inside you as we both want. Simply thinking of you makes me hard. Seeing you—I still don't know how I didn't come. If I'm going to last long enough to ensure you're so limp and boneless that you won't fight my cock, I need you to not touch me. Do you understand?"

I can't speak. I can only nod.

He picks me up and puts me back on the bed. But surprises me when he leans down and grabs his tie off the floor.

"You can say no to anything at any time. We'll also go by common safe words. Red means stop, and it all stops. Yellow means I can continue, but be prepared to stop if you need me to. Another thing, just because we do something once doesn't mean we have to do it again. Everything I do to your body is for your pleasure alone. However, if you don't love it, if it doesn't feel good to you, or leaves you feeling uncomfortable afterward—then we won't do it." He's firm.

I'm a little confused. "What do you mean, it's for pleasure, but it doesn't feel good after?"

"There are many things that might feel pleasurable at the time but afterward leaves you feeling bad about yourself. When you are high on what your lover is doing to you with an orgasm just out of reach, you will give away everything, not say your safe word, and plead for things you don't want to get it. I've never had a woman regret what happened—I'm not into too many kinks beyond a few taps to add to pleasure in anal play, and I need to be in control. Since you have had so little experience, you might want to try it and even enjoy it, but it doesn't mean you have to do it again."

"But I want to make you happy."

He shakes his head. "Baby, I'm never going to be happy or feel satisfied if I know you're only doing something for me. You happy, makes me happy. If you only do something for my pleasure, I'll spank you a lot harder than what I just did."

"I love you, Matteo Castillo. And I need you too much not to touch you." I offer him my hands for the tie.

One eyebrow goes up. "Good girl." The words send a hot rush of wet heat to my core. "Lay back and put your hands above your head. One hand holding the other, not palm to palm."

Without hesitation, I follow his instruction. He moves around the bed. His fingers, nimble yet gentle, secure my hands together at my wrists.

"If you want out, tell me. Be careful not to fight it too much because it will tighten, and silk is unforgiving." When he's done, he rounds the bed again to stare down at me.

He licks his lips, and I open my legs for his eyes. The pretty yellow panties are silk and clinging to me where I'm soaking wet for him. Two fingers on each hip slip beneath the waistband. Slowly, his hands roam over my ass, squeezing each cheek. My lungs shudder as I remember him saying he's into anal. It appeals even as it scares me. Those large hands slide down my legs, caressing my thighs— trailing down so slowly he's driving me out of my mind.

I forget it's to take my panties off until he has them in one hand and tosses them over his shoulder.

"So damn sexy. I love your curls." He murmurs low.

One thick finger slides over my lower lips. I want to be embarrassed by how wet I am, but the satisfaction as he coats his finger in it won't let me. He brings his finger up to his mouth and sucks on it, his eyes close.

"*Delicious.*" Is a moan from his chest.

Pride fills me at the pleasure on his beautiful face.

Gold meets my eyes, and I melt at what I see there—feel as if he reached out and touched me. "If this is a dream, I pray I never wake up."

"No dream," I assure him.

With firm hands, he parts my legs and holds me open. He inhales deeply before hot air sweeps over me. His velvet tongue runs over the slit of me, up so slowly, before traveling down again. Once, twice, I'm desperate for more than simple tasting.

He groans as though he's in pain, and the vibration sends a shudder through me. "Sweeter than candy, I could eat you for hours and never be satisfied."

That velvet tongue sharpens as it opens me, sinking into me by barely a fraction of an inch. I plead for more, and he gives it to me. He's deeper, his tongue grazing over my swollen clitoris. *Please more.* But he's already moving down again.

His tongue goes deeper, and I sigh in relief. Except it's not nearly enough. Gentle, soft, he learns me the same way he learned my mouth. That velvet tongue is a lash of fire everywhere but where I want it most. He sucks deep on my inner lips as his tongue fucks into me in a preview of what's to come.

More, please, more. I'm close to the edge. I swear I could reach out and touch it. *No.*

He stops, and if there were air in my lungs, I would scream. His tongue roams down to where the wet heat of me is pooling low. I'm wondering if I'll pass out from the shame filling me at the sound of him slurping at me echoing around us. Until his moans of pleasure at how good I taste, how much he loves how wet I am for him has the shame disappearing in a poof of smoke.

Oh, his tongue is moving again, slow, *so damn slow*. Matteo drives me out of my mind. Teasing, tasting, he sucks my outer lips at the same time his tongue runs over the tortured flesh. I can't breathe. Dear god, I can't. Finally, he lets them fall from his hot mouth.

Two fingers open me wide, and he's sucking on my inner lips again. At first, he's soft, almost gentle, but gradually, the suction is stronger and deeper, and—ye*s. Oh god, yes.*

He stops **again**. I sob at the loss. Up his tongue moves, swirling over my swollen lips before teasing the tight bundle of nerves. It's the lightest of touches, yet it sends me soaring over the edge of the world. Down, down, I splash into the waves and float in silky pleasure all around me.

Only he's far from done. It doesn't matter that all of me is still swollen and tender. Two thick fingers sink into me, finding their way to my channel. Thick and hard, they fuck me in a steady rhythm pulling me out of the waves and up into the stunning bright light. The sun is too strong, burning every inch of my sensitive skin. *It's too much. I can't.*

His mouth is back on a tight nipple, sucking deep, balancing me on the knife's edge of pleasure and pain as his teeth graze me. Oh god, it feels **so fucking good**.

My hips rise to meet those fingers, wanting more, needing more. With a loud pop, he releases the tortured nipple that misses his mouth the moment it's gone.

He's at my other breast. His fingers go deeper at the same time he sucks harder than he did before. The combined attention of both his fingers and his mouth is shooting me close to the sun. I need to tear my skin from my body—it's burning me alive. Too hot, I can't take it anymore.

"Matteo, please," I'm begging incoherently.

"That's it, baby, come for me. I need you to come. I need to be inside you. Come for me." He growls against my breast.

I'm so close, almost there. *Please. So fucking close.* His thumb slides up over that swollen bundle of nerves. Another press over my clitoris, harder—**fuck yes.**

It's no gentle splash into the waves. I shatter into a million pieces— coming so hard it's almost painful. Those fingers don't stop, driving me to tears.

"You are so beautiful, breaking apart for me. It's like looking directly into the sun." He murmurs as he presses his lips to mine.

All my bones are mush. I can barely breathe as small tremors continue running through me. From far away, I feel him slip off the bed. I can barely turn my head to find him.

Undoing his belt, he slides it from around his waist. I blink, and he's pushing down his pants with his boxers in one push.

"Oh my god." I moan. From fear or anticipation, I'm not sure. I think it's both.

"I warned you. It's why I made sure you were so weak your body couldn't fight me. I'll fit. You can take me. You're mine. Every inch of you was made for me."

Fear sends my hand up to his chest. Capturing my hand, he presses his lips to the center of my palm. "Matteo."

"All right, my love. This once, you're in control. You control how deep I go." He murmurs as he moves. Suddenly, I'm over him—he's lifted me onto him. I'm on his stomach, his hard cock burning against my ass.

The fear had hardened the mush ever so slightly, but I'm still weak. Only my hands down on his chest keep me from falling on him.

Strong hands are at my hips, lifting me up. "Open for me, baby, spread your lips for my cock."

Because I need him, I do. I gasp, losing all the air from my lungs at the feel of the thick, wet head of his cock pushing into me. Hot, so very hot.

"So hot. It's like you're burning me." I moan.

"It's to brand your pussy as mine. No man will ever fit you the way I do. You're going to mold to fit me alone." He grits out as he slowly impales me on him.

My arms go weak as I lower my mouth to his. Against his lips, I whisper. "You branded yourself into my very soul. If I can't have you—I don't want anyone."

A hand goes into my hair and another around my throat. His kiss is fierce, commanding, demanding everything, and I give him all I am.

Oh god, my body melts into him—unable to stop sinking onto his thick, long cock. He is silk over steel, forcing my body to allow him inside. Deeper, I can't take any more—I can't. I feel every ridge, bump, and vein searing into me.

"Just a little more, baby. You can take me. I'm so proud of you." He croons low.

I want to argue, to tell him that I can't. But his thumb finds my clit —oh god. My legs give out from trying to hold myself up, and we're skin to skin, and it's utter perfection.

"That's my good girl. You took every inch. I told you, you were made for me. Your pussy fits me perfectly."

Pride at taking him sends my hands down on his chest and me up. Grinding on his cock, I shiver at how amazing he feels.

"You're so damn beautiful." Is a growl from low in his chest. A large hand reaches up to cup my breast. "I can't wait until I see our baby here."

The words send me in motion on him, desperate for him to come inside me and give me his baby. "I need you."

"I'm right here, my love." A hard thumb teases an aching nipple.

"I need you to take over. I love it when you do." The words are barely a whimper.

Gold blasts me. "Then I'll give you everything you ask for." It's a promise.

His hands are back on my hips, holding me in place. Oh god. He's moving now. How am I on top, and he is in such complete control? Harder and harder, he's answering my pleas to fuck me as hard as I need.

Yes, *just* like that. I can't hold myself up and collapse on his hard, wide chest. He holds me tight and fucks me like a man possessed.

So close. So close. It's right there. I hit my climax, and once again, I'm falling from the heavens into him. Matteo catches me and holds me safe in his arms. With a groan, he comes too, filling me full of wet heat. Oh god, oh god, it sends me spinning into another small orgasm so tender and sweet.

The pounding of his heart under my ear and inside me sends me into the darkness with a smile. I know this isn't a dream because no dream I have ever had in my life has ever been this amazing.

* * *

MATTEO

I feel Amy slip into sleep. But I'm unwilling to even blink for too long. A part of me is terrified this is still somehow a dream. That when I awaken, I'll be alone in my bed again.

Except, when I dreamed of her before, the taste of her sweet pussy wasn't coating my tongue. The scent of her skin and hair didn't sink into my lungs with every breath. Her pussy didn't cling to my cock as if she didn't dare let me go. This isn't a dream because it's better than any dream I've had of this moment.

I won't kick Rafe's ass. Hell, I don't know if there's a gift good enough to thank him for giving me Amy here in my bed—my arms. Nothing about the moment I admitted I loved her went the way I thought it would. And I wouldn't have it any other way. Hearing her say it, my arms tighten around her without thought. I will never get tired of those words on her lips. The way her eyes melted as she looked into mine.

Finally, Amy is aware she's mine forever and wants to be. The same way I want to be hers. I want to scream it from the rooftops. I want to tell everyone I have ever met in my life that this beautiful, sweet, intelligent woman loved me. *I* won her heart, and I'm never letting her go.

There are a hundred things I want to do: call a wedding planner, buy a house yesterday, call work, and tell them I'm never coming back—change everything in my life to make this woman happy. Yet those would take me away from the now of me buried in her body with her in my arms. And the only place I want to be is here.

CHAPTER 23

Matteo

We were pulled out of bed and the tangle of our bodies by a demanding Layla only a few hours after we made love.

I had to send Amy in to take a shower while I was feeding Layla because the sight of her all glowing and soft and wearing my shirt was keeping my cock so hard it fucking hurt. She thought it was funny. I promised her a spanking later for laughing at my pain. Then she turned my cock to stone when she blushed and told me she was looking forward to it.

If Layla weren't in my arms, I would have followed her into the bathroom and given her delicious round ass the spanking she wanted. Something she wanted that I never planned on giving her. When I realized the bastard hit her, I decided I would never spank her. I never want her to fear me.

In the past, I've spanked women to add to the pleasure of taking them from behind and during anal. I enjoyed it, but it wasn't necessary for me to come. Although I did it so often, I didn't even think of it when I was with Amy. And I'm a bastard for the relief I felt when she asked for me to spank her again.

While I always did my best to ensure a woman was soaking wet to take my cock, one woman—a cardiologist who worked in the hospital—told me she didn't need it. After our first time together, she asked me to spank her and fuck her without concern she wasn't as wet as I always tried to ensure she was. I did as she requested. She came quickly and so hard it shocked me.

She explained she enjoyed a small measure of pain that happened with spanking and rough sex since I had to work harder to get my cock deep into her. Afterward, she told me she was into BDSM. I had heard of it. However, I had no plans to learn anything about it.

Up until her, I was extremely vanilla, almost boring. Sex was strictly in a comfortable bed, missionary, and a few times from behind. At the time, I wasn't even into anal. With my size, I didn't want to ask for more than a woman seemed comfortable with. Rafe had the talk with me before I went to college to always keep a woman's pleasure as the priority and to ensure she came several times before I did.

I learned a lot about the lifestyle and what appealed to her. And the longer we discussed it, the harder my dick got.

Control was the one thing I always had to have—in everything. She noticed. As a submissive, she hoped I was already in the lifestyle so I could be her dominant. We already had the talk about me not looking for anything lasting. I was concerned about committing to something that would require a level of trust I believed she would need.

She shrugged and said she knew me well enough. All she needed was someone who was clean to tie her up and treat her like a whore for a few hours. She also wanted someone to tell her what to do so she didn't have to think. The relationship lasted for almost three years before she met someone who matched her in every way and was interested in a long-term relationship.

Once our relationship ended, I didn't seek out another in the lifestyle. While I enjoyed it, I preferred to keep things simple. I've found many women, especially women who had to be seen as in control and strong, longed to give up control in bed with a partner they trusted. A hand around their throat, their orgasm withheld if they didn't follow instructions—being given instructions—was welcomed and made them wet. If a woman didn't welcome it, I had no problem leashing it at the moment. But I never saw them again.

I'm grateful as hell that Amy welcomes it. I can't wait to find out what else made her wet while she read. That is going to be fun.

Layla wasn't the only one who needed to eat. We're sitting down to dinner after I put Layla down for bed.

And we're having an argument that I don't want to have. I wanted her to be more accepting of this. But she's only digging in her heels.

"I don't want Layla to be a tablet kid or plopped in front of the television. If she's with a nanny who is here in the condo with you at the same time, the nanny can engage her more and keep her occupied. It's important to me that you have time for you."

Her cute mouth opens to argue with me.

I hold up a hand to let me finish. "I don't want you to wake up ten or twenty years from now resentful of me or Layla and wonder what if—for anything. But especially the art that gives you so much joy. I'll take care of her when I'm home. I also want to have time with you. There's no getting away from the fact that as the wife and mother, so much is going to be on you. I want you..."

"Matteo."

I'm worried she's annoyed with me, but her smile is indulgent and happy.

"You win." The words are soft. "Also, I don't think tablets are evil. I think they're like televisions. If people are using them to watch the kids, so they don't have to? Then yes, it's bad. The same way I don't want a nanny to raise our kids. I don't want a tablet or television to watch our kids either."

"You said you wanted me to knock you up." She blushes all the way to her ears. I love it. "How many do you want? Three more for the four you wanted?"

"Yes, please. Is that all right? Are four too many?"

I shake my head. "There is nothing in this world I would rather do than fill you with our children. I think Layla will be an awesome big sister. Our children won't need to be worried about being protected. We'll do that."

"Now that she's asleep, let's work on giving her a little brother or sister."

She sighs. "I still need to finish cleaning up dinner. Five minutes."

Shaking my head, I exhale. "I don't like you cooking and cleaning. I hate you taking care of me."

Her eyes go wide. "What?"

"I'm aware I should. For a minute when you told me you made me lunch that first day, I did. But I don't like it. It makes my skin itch. I take care of you in everything. All those men who want their women to make them a sandwich turn my stomach even more now. I don't even like when you bring my food to the table. I can only get through you bringing me lunch because I get to see you and Layla."

Her head goes down. When she lifts her face to mine, tears are running down her face. It's a kick to my chest. I'm out of my chair, and she's in my arms.

She sighs. "If nothing else, hopefully, therapy will help me stop being such a crybaby."

I pull back to look down on her. "Hey, I don't want to hear you put yourself down like that. From your childhood alone, you went through tough shit. Then you had someone beat you so badly that you thought it was safer to run with a baby than to continue living in that environment. Now you're waking up to all the ways he mentally and emotionally manipulated and abused you. If you didn't cry over it, I would think something was wrong with you."

"Every day, you have me falling deeper and deeper in love with you. Thank you for loving me and Layla." Her love is glowing in her chocolate eyes. I swear my heart is going to burst outside my chest. "For years, all I've heard is that my worth was based on what I could be and do for a man. I felt like I needed to pay you back for...I don't know being with me, loving me. Here you are, giving me a car, the art, the nanny. How can I pay you back for all of that?"

"You *do* pay me back—by loving me too. Your happiness makes me happy. It's not about you cooking me dinner or making me lunch. And it sure as hell isn't about you cleaning our home. Just you, it's all you."

Her small hand runs down my chest as one eyebrow goes up. "Are you sure there isn't something else I could be doing to pay you back? Like you bending me over the island the way you fantasized —and I did more than a few times."

I catch her hand and send my other hand into her hair. Pulling her back to meet my eyes, I shake my head. "I want nothing more than to bend you over right here right now. But I refuse to even joke about us making love as some sort of currency. There will be times when you aren't up to making love, whether it's because you're tired, or once you're pregnant and you don't feel comfortable, or when you are on your period and don't want to be touched. I never want there to be a time when it's sex to satisfy me—not making love for the connection we both need."

She glows like the sun. "I'm an idiot for never seeing how clearly you've loved me from that first day."

"No, sweetheart, you were understandably slow to trust in what you saw. Say it. I need to hear it again."

"I love you, Matteo Castillo. Will you please bend me over the island to fulfill the erotic fantasies I've had of you doing it?"

Capturing her mouth I taste her words on her lips. Her kiss is chocolate sweet and scotch neat, intoxicating as it sets fire to my veins. I finally understand addiction in a way I never did before. I'm addicted to this woman's mouth, the smell of her, her little moans and whimpers, her soft body against mine, her tight pussy around my cock, and the taste of her juice on my tongue.

It takes four seconds to get the sundress she's wearing off. I *need* to see all of her. Fucking hell, I could come just looking at her. "You bad girl, running around without any panties."

She moans. "I didn't want to waste any time."

I undo her bra and spin her around so her back is to me. Cupping her breasts, I weigh their precious weight in my hands. I've never been a breast man, but she makes me one. I love how responsive she is when my mouth is on them.

Fuck. She is soaking wet, her juice running down her inner thighs. I send my fingers into her and find her clit. All it takes is a few swipes of my fingers for her to shatter in my arms.

She's clinging to my arm to hold her up. Now she's ready. The island is too far away. I press her down so that her breasts meet the wood of the dining table.

I undo my pants and free my cock. Just one quick taste. I can't resist. I'm down licking the cream of her come. *So fucking delicious.* Her juice is sweet, like a strawberry to me, with a hint of tartness that only makes me want more. But her come—**fuck**. My cock is leaking as I suck deep to swallow as much as I can.

I'm a bastard for loving how incoherent she is in her begging for me to fuck her. It's exactly how I need her to be to take me. I line up my cock to her weeping pussy and thrust into heaven.

Tight, so fucking tight. Her body is still fighting me. I grip her hips and surge deep until we're skin to skin. Closing my eyes, I muster all my strength to keep from coming.

I suck deep on her neck as I begin moving. Christ. Her already tight pussy clings to me. Pulling back, I smack her ass.

Thank fuck all she does is moan and squeeze me again.

"Don't grip my cock, bad girl." I grit out as I spank her ass again.

"I'm sorry, Matteo. Please don't stop. I'll be good."

What she does to me. I'm so fucking close, but she's not, and that won't do. Gripping her hips tight, I give her everything she's begging for—fucking her hard, fast, and as deep as I can go.

It could be four minutes or four strokes, I have no idea, I'm simply thankful when she comes with a gasp of my name. I follow her into heaven as her pussy milks my cock for every drop of come.

"I love the way it feels when you come inside me." Is a breathy little moan that escapes her.

Pulling out of her has her pouting. "I want you inside me all the time. The better for you to knock me up."

I pick her up and take her into our bedroom. "Don't worry, baby. We're just getting started."

She giggles, and it goes straight to my chest.

* * *

AMY

I answer the delivery with excitement. I'm grateful the store was willing to deliver the enormous canvases since they wouldn't fit in the SUV. After the last week of working on the smaller canvases and feeling limited by their size. With the memory of how free I felt with the three-foot by four-foot canvas, I went into the art supply store and asked for more in the same size.

For once, I followed Matteo's edicts of refusing to think of price and bought everything my heart wanted. They had two of the three-foot by four-foot and offered to deliver them. While I was waiting for them to confirm how long it would take to produce more, I found paints in colors I didn't have and added them to my purchase. I spent a small fortune and didn't feel an ounce of guilt for doing it.

Doris, our nanny and housekeeper, keeps ahold of Layla as I direct the man to my studio. It really feels like a studio now, with several canvases done and drying throughout the room.

Thanking the man for the delivery, I give him a twenty-dollar bill because it's the only cash I have on me and wonder if it was enough to Doris.

"Oh, sweetie, yes. It was just right for what he delivered." Doris reassures me with a pat on my shoulder.

Relief fills me. I'm so grateful we found Doris. None of the applicants the elite agency sent us felt right. Matteo gave in and changed the requirement that the nanny have Spanish as their first language. His wariness was that school-taught Spanish was different from Spanish learned and spoken in Mexico, the way his grandfather spoke and taught them.

As a former middle-school teacher who taught Spanish, Doris understood Matteo's concern about the differences in Spanish. Since she taught in an area with a majority of students whose parents came from not only Mexico but many Central and South American countries, she understood the differences. She spoke Spanish easily with Matteo and assured him she would teach me and Layla the Spanish he spoke.

Matteo liked her willingness to teach me Spanish because he wanted us to speak Spanish with Layla and our children. Doris would be the one who spoke English with them. For now, with Layla, we would speak both languages within our comfort zone.

I loved how Doris also understood my concerns about having a nanny. I liked that she didn't tell me how she was going to nanny Layla—the way the others had when I explained I had never had a nanny before and wasn't sure how it would work.

Matteo butted in to lay down the law of me getting at least two hours a day to myself. I would have time to spend in my studio or doing whatever else I needed. However, I was adamant that it would include my therapy appointment time on Wednesdays.

She chuckled at us and offered her services as a nanny and house-keeper. She'd never been a nanny, but she used to clean houses as a second job to supplement her low teacher's salary. Matteo didn't even want to discuss it and told her she was hired.

I love him, but he drives me crazy sometimes. It's even more annoying how right he was. It's only been a week, and I'm beyond grateful for her. And Layla loves her.

She isn't living in while we're in the condo because Matteo wanted to be able to make love to me anywhere without worrying about her being there. I had the same thought.

Layla squawks. When she sees she's got my attention, she fists her little hands for me. I take her from Doris and cuddle her. Layla is gnawing on my shirt. I decide to get her dressed in something adorable for her daddy.

CHAPTER 24

$\mathcal{M}$atteo

Once Amy sets Layla down on the floor by the couch, Layla yanks her blanket off all on her own. She breaks into happy laughter at the sight of me.

My baby girl. God, I love her so damn much. "I told you to call me when you get here so I can carry Layla in for you."

"She doesn't weigh a ton. I can do it." Amy sighs.

I catch her close with an arm around her waist. "I'm aware you can carry her in. You can do any damn thing you want. I want to be able to lighten your load because I care about you."

My lips are a breath away from hers when Layla lets loose an ear-splitting shriek. Amy jumps away, or she tries, but my arm is firm around her. I sigh as I look down at my grinning daughter. She knows exactly what she's doing. "I'm sorry, *mija*. Since you didn't get enough attention, you're not letting Dad get his kiss, huh?"

Her laughter tells me I'm exactly right. I shake my head, pull Amy tight against me, and sneak a kiss. Letting her go, I focus on Ms. Layla, who is now clapping loudly.

Unplugging her from her car seat takes a minute. While I'm doing that Amy is unpacking our lunch.

I cuddle her close and give her kisses on her neck. "Did you have a good day with Doris? Hmm? Is she taking good care of my girl?"

Her eyes scrunch up with happiness, telling me Doris did good today.

We manage to eat with Layla stealing bites of spaghetti noodles from my spaghetti and meatballs. Amy picked up our lunch from the place where Rafe got our lunch. It's become a favorite for both of us.

It's adorable the way Layla fights sleep. Her eyes are closed while she opens her mouth for more noodles. Amy hands over her bottle and takes my food so I can feed Layla.

Layla manages to get a little more than half of her oatmeal-laced formula before she does the little hum around the nipple of the bottle. It's what she does right as she's falling asleep. I kiss her gently on her cheeks, forehead, and nose. She loves it and lets out soft chuckles before she finally gives up and allows sleep to over-take her.

Rocking her, I give it several minutes before I take the bottle away —if I do it too soon, she's awake again and cranky.

Once I'm sure she's completely out, I settle Layla back into her car seat. Ensuring her neck is up so she doesn't suffocate, I sigh as I sit back on the couch again.

"You're so smart," Amy whispers as a hand runs over my chest. "I'm a bad mom. It never even crossed my mind to have her neck up. I thought it was safe when…"

Pulling her into my lap, I catch her around the back of the neck and stop the words. "I saw it a dozen times in the ER. You have been a mom once for less than a full year. Stop putting yourself down. It makes me crazy."

Her sigh is from the bottom of her lungs. A finger comes up to trace over my lips. "I love you. Have I told you that today?"

I nod. "A few times, the first when I woke you with my cock. Which I sure as hell didn't deserve. Say it again at your own detriment. I'm trying to be professional at work and Layla is two feet away."

Almost two weeks after we first made love, and I'm still greedy and desperate for her on an almost hourly basis. My number one focus is to give her as many orgasms as I can before I enter her, in case I embarrass myself by coming only seconds later. Since my woman demanded I stay inside her long after we both came down from heaven, I was often able to begin slowly all over again—the better to seed her sweet pussy.

The hand on my chest runs down to squeeze my already half-hard cock and turns it to stone. "In all the time I've brought you lunch, we've had one knock on the door. Besides, we're parents. There will be times when our baby is going to be beside the bed in their bassinet and—"

"And you love the idea of us getting caught." I'm proven right when her blush goes to the tips of her ears. Shifting my hand around to the front of her neck, I bring her lips a breath away from mine. "I'll never let it happen. No man will ever see your gorgeous body or hear you begging me to fuck you or even listen to those little whimpers that escape you while I work my cock inside your tight pussy."

Despite the fact that we're firmly in February, this is also Dallas. The chaotic weather is at almost sixty degrees today. Amy is wearing a long black velvet skirt with large red and pink roses on it and a silky black button-down top.

Offering her neck to me, she swings her leg over my lap the way she loves to do. She's moaning as she grinds down on me.

"I love you. I love even more when I fall asleep with your cock inside me. And I fucking adore you when you wake me up with your cock inside me. It's why I told you I love you. The feel of your cock is so hard and hot that you warm me up from the inside out. Fuck me, please. I'll be quiet—they won't hear me begging you to come inside me. When you fill me full of your come, I swear it sends me into another orgasm. Please fuck me. I'll be a good girl, I promise."

"You're being a very bad girl." I yank up the skirt and spank her ass without nearly the heat she deserves for turning me into a fiend who can't keep my hands off her even at work. "Begging me to fuck you and turning me into an animal for your pussy."

Her grin is triumphant as she leans back and rips off the blouse. I undo her bra and capture a hard nipple, sucking deep. Her arms wrap around my neck.

I nip at her delicate skin, not recognizing the utterly feral beast she turns me into every damn time. I'm fumbling with my pants, desperate to free my cock. Good girl that she is, she helps me and tugs her panties to the side. Once I'm out, she works to get me inside her.

She moans. "Suck harder, I love it so much."

Never able to deny her, I suck hard, and she shudders as she sinks down on me. Holding her in place, I fuck up into her until she's sobbing with her orgasm. Thank fucking god, I'm seconds behind her.

It's a long time before I can move, and it's only because she finally lets go of the grip her teeth have on my shoulder. We're both breathing heavily, yanking air into our lungs, starving for it.

"If you kill me, it will make it harder for you to get my money." I sigh.

The witch giggles. "Harder but not impossible."

I run my hand through her hair to pull her away from me. "True. I've shifted money and created trusts for Layla's education and you for whatever you need."

Shaking her head, she kisses my cheek. "I hate talking about if you're not here."

"It's only a just in case. While I do believe Rafe and Javier would ensure you're taken care of, it's not their responsibility—it's mine. Doing it made me feel better."

"Because you liked taking money out of your bank account." She sighs.

I consider her words. "You're right. I've never truly been comfortable with the money, no matter how many hours I worked in a day or kids I saved."

"Is that why the money went into my account today? Or did you forget about my salary being deposited?"

"There was no forgetting. You're going to be getting three times the amount once a month starting next month as your allowance to do with whatever you want." I run a finger over her breast. Damn, I got carried away.

* * *

AMY

It's not easy to focus on what he's saying as he runs his finger over my breast. Except the words don't make sense to me. "An allowance?"

"Yes, an allowance to do with as you want." He's watching me closely, trying to figure out if I'm upset.

I'm more confused than anything. "How am I getting you paying for everything *and* money? Or is that what I'll use to pay for my art supplies?"

"No, I pay for everything you want and need, like your art supplies and clothes. You get it so that it's always there for you." He shrugs. "If it was important enough for my mom to write into a prenup. Then it's important enough for you to have as well. There are also no guarantees in life. When money got tight, and shit hit the fan with my grandfather's company, it was my mom's money she saved and invested that paid for things. Like I said, my mom paid for my school, an apartment in New York City, and my house in Baltimore while I went to med school." Matteo explains.

Rich, rich. He's giving me money just for it to sit an account—just in case.

The phone on his desk rings, reminding us that I'm sitting on his cock, at work.

"Oh crap." I nearly trip trying to get off him. The jerk starts laughing way too loud. "Shh, Matteo." I'm terrified someone is coming through the door.

"I have a standing order not to knock on my door unless it's an emergency." Big hands lift me up and give me a minute to find my footing.

"How is it so late? How do you manage to make me lose so many hours?" I find my bra, get it back on, then go looking for my shirt.

"You're not so bad at that yourself." He's up and checks his phone. "I'm not answering that. They can wait."

I blush at the very large wet spot on his pants. "I'm sorry."

He glances down and shakes his head. "I love it—don't you dare apologize. I have clothes I can change into."

Opening the bottom drawer of his desk, he unrolls a pair of black pants and a black polo. "You have clothes at work?"

"Being a doctor is a messy occupation. If you don't bring your own change of clothes, you will wear scrubs home. I'm too old to wear scrubs home."

I watch with greedy eyes as he gets undressed and then very slowly gets dressed again. "Behave. I only have one change of clothes."

Catching him by his shirt, I bring his mouth to mine. "Spoilsport."

He chuckles and spanks my ass. "Tonight."

It's a promise. I can't wait.

* * *

AMY

I'm so freaking lucky. I sigh as I release the water from the bath-tub. Matteo sent me in to take a nap almost an hour ago while he fed Layla and got her down for her nap.

This morning she woke me up too freaking early for a Saturday. I'd dressed her and fed us breakfast before he woke up. He was embarrassed, but I didn't mind. I liked letting him sleep as late as he needed. That didn't mean it was all right with Matteo. As far as he was concerned, he failed if I was the one to take care of him.

I hop in the shower to rinse off, then wrap myself in a robe.

Out of the bathroom, I find him on top of our bed. I smile wide to find him there. He shakes his head and laughs. "I'm so freaking lucky to have you."

I climb onto the bed beside him. "I was just thinking exactly the same."

A hand runs down from the neckline of the robe before spreading it wide as he cups a breast. "I should be letting you take your nap."

Lowing my lips to his, I shake my head. "I don't want you to."

"Hmm, if you say so." He reminds me of a lazy lion with the way muscle and sinew flex beneath the black t-shirt. "I'm not going to be able to deny you a single thing."

"In that case..." Those eyes of his widen with curiosity. I run a hand over his hard chest, dying to find out if the skin there tastes the same as the skin of his neck. "I want to learn your body the way you have mine."

His eyes go heavenward. "Do you have any idea what you're asking of me?"

"Please, Matteo, you just said you couldn't deny me anything."

I blink, and I'm on my back beneath him. How the hell does he do that? And will it ever not be hot?

Oh, his cock is pressing into my soft stomach. "I think about you and find it hard not to come. I'm not going to be able to lay here with your hands running over me and not embarrass myself."

Matteo makes me downright smug. This gorgeous, sexy man could barely contain himself over my body. "I *never* get to touch you?"

"Never is a long time." A shoulder comes up in a shrug. "Maybe after four kids and twenty years, I'll be able to last long enough for you to get your fill."

I'm laughing exactly the way he intended. A finger slides my hair away from my face. "*Please* let me taste your body with my tongue."

He bites off a curse before flopping down on the bed beside me. "Fine. But I warned you."

Hmm, now that I've gotten my way, I'm not exactly sure how to go about it. Seeing my hesitation, he sits up and takes off his shirt before lying back down. Oh, damn. I'm no better than a man. Because holy hell, is he stunning, and I'm drooling. I'll be more than happy when he grows a spare tire, but for now, the man is perfection on a scale I was not prepared for.

"I might come from the way you're looking at me." The words are a croak of sound.

"You're so very lickable," I mutter.

While the hair over his chest is thick, I can still see an old gothic-style castle tattoo over his heart. I trace the edges of the tattoo with a finger. His muscles flex and jump beneath my touch. I flick my eyes up to find his tightly closed.

Wow, his stomach muscles flex in time with his clenching jaw. The hair over his stomach is thinner. Intrigued, I run my fingers down over his muscles. I'm fascinated with his body because I swear it feels like beneath his skin is corrugated metal—not muscle and sinew. Every inch of him I touch shudders beneath my fingertips.

I barely manage to brush against the waistband of his sweats.

"I'll come in your hand." It's a warning gritted out between his clenched jaw.

Smug, I shake my head. "I have complete faith in your strength of will."

"You might, but I don't. I gave you your chance." A hand grips my wrist.

"Matteo, that was like two minutes." I plead.

"It's not my fault you didn't use your time wisely."

Deciding to take a page out of Layla's book, I stick my bottom lip out, make my eyes big, and plead. "Please."

His sigh is loud. "Fine, you'll get two more minutes as long as you climb on my face and let me eat you until the only thing holding you up is me."

"Two minutes is all?" I can't remember my own name once he begins eating me. I'll forget, and I swear he knows that.

"Three minutes, and that's all I'm willing to do. I don't negotiate with terrorists." He's stern.

I sigh and fight not to smile. I'm not going to point out that he did, in fact, negotiate or that I am positive I've won.

Letting go of my wrist. Big hands go around my middle to lift me over him. "Grab the headboard, *mi amor*, and hold on tight."

297

Oh, I clutch at the headboard. Even from beneath me, Matteo controls me—owns me. I'm so hot I'm burning up, and tearing off my robe provides no relief.

* * *

MATTEO

I spank her ass and watch with satisfaction as a cheek shakes. "What have I told you about giving me all your weight? I want all of you every time."

She widens her legs and sinks further down as desperate fingers roll a tight nipple. "Matteo, I'm trying not to suffocate you. But I swear it's like you're trying to kill me, so it's only fair."

"I'd rather drown in the sweetest juice I've ever tasted than live without it," I assure her. Running my tongue over the pearl of her, I use the sweet juice running down my chin to send two fingers deep.

I'm a bastard for loving the blush sweep down her face to her breasts as I slide my thick middle finger between her ass cheeks. "Matteo?"

"Yes, my love?" I ask as I suckle deep on her clit. Her body isn't fighting me as I press my finger into her tightest hole, stopping once I've reached the knuckle. "You should see how beautiful your ass is spread for me. I'm so proud of what you can take. I can't wait until my cock owns this part of you."

A shiver racks her body. "I've never..."

"You will. The same way I made sure your pussy was ready, I'll make sure your ass is too. You'll come long and repeatedly from my cock in your ass the same way as you do from my cock in your tight pussy." It's a promise I intend to keep.

"Are you sure? You're so big." She gasps as I begin slowly pulling out my finger until I'm almost out before pushing back inside.

"I have to, *mi amor*. I **have** to own all of you the same way you own me."

"Oh, Matteo, it's different." She moans in time with my finger sliding out of her ass. A little gasp is cut off when I pull out to the very tip.

Sucking her clit, I begin fucking her ass slowly, almost out, before pushing back in faster than the time before. Her head goes back as she begins tugging and pinching her tight nipples. "I can take more. I think."

Yes, she can. She's already moving her ass to meet my finger. Relief floods me. I don't have to have anal, but I'm not going to lie and say I don't love it. Except she has to love it too. It doesn't matter how much I like it if she doesn't.

Watching my woman's orgasm build from the finger in her ass, and my tongue in her pussy means this woman is perfect for me in every way. I answer her little gasps with another finger.

"Yes, Matteo, oh yes." She whimpers.

I suck deep on her clit as I send two fingers up her tight pussy at the same time I fuck her ass.

"Oh, god. Oh god. Oh my fucking god."

"You love it, baby? Me filling your pussy and your ass. You do, don't you?" I taunt her.

"Yes, oh my god. Yes. More, Matteo."

299

I'm keeping her full. Fucking in both her ass and her pussy and swirling my tongue around her tight clit. Loving the way her whimpers flow over me as she begs me to fuck her.

Amy hits her climax with a cry so loud I worry she'll wake Layla. Her whole body goes limp. I roll her under me, holding her tight. God, she is so damn stunning. I love every inch of her delectable body. There's nothing better than her body pressed against mine. The way she softens to fit me—it's on another level completely.

She cuddles into me. "Matteo." She sing songs my name.

"Go to sleep," I mutter. "You need your rest."

Her giggle is fucking adorable. "Your cock is still hard and poking into me. There's no way I could sleep through that."

Another giggle floats up to me seconds before she grips my cock. Aw damn, two minutes isn't going to be easy—shit. I promised her three minutes. Why the hell did I agree to three minutes?

I almost jump out of my skin when her tongue teases the tip of my cock. Sonofabitch. Squeezing my eyes shut, I begin counting down. No fucking way am I going to be able to last three minutes. A moan comes out of her and slides down my spine sharper than a scalpel.

Nope, can't do it. I grasp her by her throat and pull her away.

"Hey!" She's outraged. "I still have at least a minute."

"Times up." I'm pretty sure it's not, but I'm going to come all over her without being inside her.

"I love your body, Matteo. Please let me have my minute. I'll suck your cock so well, I promise." I'm stunned at her determination as she opens her mouth and licks the side of my cock. "Hmm, yum."

Taking advantage of my shock, she licks all the way to the head of my cock. With each small lick, her soft little tongue is tearing my skin from my bones. She sucks the first few inches into her hot mouth.

Fuck. Fuck. Fuck. I'm fighting not to come and losing. My brain is trying to work out if it's less embarrassing to come on the comforter or the side of the bed when she goes onto her knees beside me. I roll her under me.

Her gasp of surprise is swallowed by me as I plunge deep into her soaking-wet cunt. In the blink of an eye, she's fucking me back, begging for me to fill her with my come. Thank fuck she comes fast. I follow her right into paradise.

"Matteo, I'm going to get you back for not giving me my full three minutes." Amy sighs.

"We'll try again after four kids and twenty years," I promise her.

"I'm holding you to it." She warns me.

I get us both under the covers. She still needs a nap. "I wouldn't expect anything less from you. Now, take your nap."

A little hand runs along my bicep. "You know, I'm glad you have me seeing Hillary. Before seeing a therapist, I would have driven you and me both crazy, not really believing you meant it about taking care of me and Layla. Like you were just saying it to be nice, to make me love you more."

"I'm glad she's helping you, *mi amor.*"

"I was thinking about something Hillary said. How it wasn't good to have any one identity. What if something happens to you to lose your identity? It reminded me of how lost you seemed when you talked about you giving up on being an oncologist…"

"Before I met you and Layla, I think that would be a valid concern. Now, it's more important for me to ensure you and Layla are taken care of. I thought I was only doing good by seeing patients, the hands-on of doing it. With time, I've come to understand that I'm helping more people—not just patients by hiring more doctors and nurses and paying them well."

Her sigh is happy. "I'm glad. I worried you'd resent not working the way you used to."

"Not in the least. It's more important to me that you and Layla are taken care of than all the other stuff. There's only so much guilt a person can carry around for something I didn't have control over. I was born into a rich family. I've given away as much of my money as I could and done as much good as possible with it." I really am over it.

"Good," she sighs into my mouth.

And that's how we fall asleep. Perfect.

CHAPTER 25

*a*my

We're leaving the art museum again. I'm so damn grateful for Matteo asking if I wanted to come here again and tell him that.

He doesn't say anything until we're both in the car.

He's quiet for a minute, not even putting his key in the ignition. "I'm not a huge fan of art. I could appreciate it when it was in front of me. However, I didn't search it out. I went to the National Gallery of Art in D.C. for a date in the first few years of living in Baltimore—just once. All the amazing art close by, and I only bothered going once. Without you, I wouldn't have cared in the least."

"Is that good?" I'm confused.

"It's very good. And it makes me a little sad. As beautiful as it is, it didn't become that way to me until you."

"Ah, now that makes me sad." It really does.

"It is." He's quiet for a minute. "Thank you. This is something I wouldn't have without you. The way you know things about the painting and tell me about the artist… It adds another layer."

I blush at the compliment. "You're welcome."

He presses a brief kiss to my lips. "What do we want for dinner? Do we want to pick something up on the way home or order something once we get home?"

We decide to pick up some Mexican food. With Layla getting determined to use her now three teeth at every opportunity, I decide to get extra rice and beans. She loves beans, but she's hit or miss on rice.

Between the wait at the restaurant and how long everything takes, Layla wakes up again when we go upstairs. The minute she sees food, she opens her mouth for us to feed her. I feed her a small spoonful of rice. She spits it out. "Layla, gross."

"Ah, Layla, you don't like rice? Are you sure?" Settling her onto his lap, he offers her another spoonful. This time, Layla swallows it down like it's ice cream.

I roll my eyes. "She is a daddy's girl."

His grin could split his beautiful face in two. "There's nothing wrong with that." He assures her as he kisses her cheek and feeds her another spoonful of rice. "No, there isn't."

I'm shaking my head at them both.

Layla is asleep again as I clean up after us. "Are you going to lay her down for her nap?"

"I got her. What do you think about us taking our honeymoon in New York? We could see shows and museums and stay in a hotel or the condo my mom still has there. There's also my place in

Baltimore. I kept it as a place for families to stay in, and it's empty now. We could see the National Gallery of Art. Or would you want to do the Paris thing instead? I think Paris has better art museums. The woman I talked to about planning the honeymoon gave me a comprehensive plan, but I don't know if we're going to be able to get the passports in enough time." Matteo has his eyes glued to his phone.

Out of all the questions, only one makes it out of me. "Married? We're getting married?"

An eyebrow goes up as he tucks his phone away. "Yes, married. What did you think me telling you that you were mine was about?"

"Matteo Castillo, I can't believe you. That's the worst proposal in the world. Those awful jumbotron proposals are a few steps up from that."

He rolls his eyes and reaches for me. I back up. When he sees it, an eyebrow goes up. "I love you, woman. You've given me a life. And a daughter. Why the hell did you think you were going to get away from me?"

I want to melt like a marshmallow at his declaration. But I hold fast. If I buckle, he's always going to get his way. "Nope, try again. I want flowers. I want a ring. I want the question. An actual proposal, Matteo Castillo."

His chuckle slides down my spine. "Fine. You'll get your proposal. It will come. For now, I need your input on where we're going on our honeymoon. We're going to Chicago for the Art Institute for three days as a late birthday present on Wednesday—after your therapy appointment. Going during the week will hopefully mean we get the museum to ourselves."

This man. "For my birthday?"

He nods. "Yes, if Layla gets a do-over for Christmas, then you get one for your birthday. I was told I was crazy for going to Chicago in February. We won't be able to go out on the water for our own personal architecture tour." One shoulder goes up. "That just means we'll go again when it's warmer."

Okay, maybe he doesn't need to propose. "I can't believe it. Thank you."

"You're welcome. Back to the honeymoon. Where would you rather go? I wanted us to go overseas, but I'm not sure we'll be able to get our passports back in time."

"You want to go on our honeymoon based on where the better art museums are?"

"Yes," he shrugs. "If it's important to you, then it's important to me. It's not like you'll never get to go. I'm sure you'll probably have more fun without Layla and me, but I also know it will take forever for you to go by yourself."

"Have I told you how much I love you?"

"It's been a few hours. Show me."

* * *

Matteo

"Why is he being such a prick today? He's only smiling at the babies." We've already eaten brunch and my grandfather is as far away from my mother as he can get while still being in the same house.

Rafe shrugs. "I think they're arguing again."

"I repeat, when is Mom going to divorce Dad?" I'm serious.

"Don't. Let them get to it when they're ready. Speaking of, when are you going to deal with the asshole. I don't want you going alone."

"I'm not going alone. I am not an idiot." I roll my eyes at Rafe. "He won't know I'm alone though. The security contractors will be with me, out of sight. They've had eyes on him since day two. I'll drive down to meet up with him tomorrow. We're meeting in his lawyer's office."

Javier's forehead is a knot of concern. "I should go with you. In case there's any question of law and to watch your back."

"No, you guys are staying here. If you come, he might recognize one or both of you." The last thing I need is for him to realize who I am. "Enough about all of that. I need your ideas. I kind of messed up with not having a romantic enough proposal. Help me out here. Give me something to turn her to mush. I'm already a little worried since it's clear she wants the big wedding. If she wants a big wedding, she'll get it. I just don't want to wait on anything."

"A big wedding? Sucks to be you. I was grateful as hell that Hope wanted a judge and some of her family."

"I liked mine and Alicia's wedding. Something tells me Amy doesn't want as big as what you're thinking. She seems like she doesn't like much attention."

He isn't wrong. "I was surprised. I hadn't thought she would want one. What do you mean?"

"I mean, she wants the wedding, but she doesn't want a hundred guests." Rafe sees I don't get it completely. "If there are more than that, she'd freak with having to be around so many people."

I'm relieved. This won't be so hard after all. "Do you think I should consider churches? I don't know all the rules and all of that. It's going to happen fast when it does. I'm hoping she's pregnant already. I don't care how old-fashioned it sounds. There's no waiting until after she has the baby for me."

Rafe exhales a sigh and shakes his head. "I swear it's like you're trying to give me a heart attack."

Javier laughs. "Whatever, you said yourself, he's been looking less miserable. Who cares if it's in a few months versus a few years?"

"Thanks, I'm feeling less miserable too. I changed all my accounts already and set up new trusts for her, Layla, and any other children we have. She's also in my will."

"Lawyers," Rafe mutters.

"That's how you know it's serious. You know, Matteo and his loathing of lawyers."

Too true. It's good they both understand.

As I watch Amy try to understand my mom's fake smile, I wonder If I should tell her about what's going on. Would it be betraying their privacy, or is it better for Amy to know so she doesn't ask the wrong questions?

"Your mom and your grandfather?" Amy exclaims loudly in the car on our way home.

"I think you woke up, Layla," I mutter as I keep my eyes on Layla. She startled at how loud Amy was.

"Matteo, your mother, and your grandfather are having sex?" Now she's whispering.

I can't help it. I laugh. "Why are you whispering?"

"I don't know, it sounds like something you should whisper. Because, oh my god, your grandfather and your mom..."

"Yeah, well. Apparently, it's been going on for a few years. I hope it means my mom and dad will finally get a divorce."

"Wait, your mom and your dad *still* aren't divorced?" She's back to whispering.

"Nope, supposedly the reason she didn't divorce him was money. While they're married, she gets the payment from the trust that's due to him. She gets the payment, and my dad gets his salary. Maybe it made sense when there were kids she was paying for, but she has to have enough money now. She's getting a hundred thousand a month from the trust—not even she could spend that every month."

"You get a hundred thousand a month from the trust?" She's barely moving her lips.

I nod. "Yes, don't freak out. It will go up with every life-changing event."

"What do you mean it will go up?" She wheezes the words out.

"When we get married, it will go up by a hundred thousand. Once I adopt Layla and with each child we have, it increases by a hundred thousand. It tops out at five hundred thousand per month." We stop at a red light. I'm checking her to ensure she doesn't pass out.

"Holy shit, Matteo. Your grandfather put all of that into a trust, then made it so you couldn't get it because you didn't fall into line with him? That is so shitty."

I bite back a bitter laugh. "Now you understand why I was so pissed off at him, and our relationship never really went back to the way it was before. It's why you're getting the allowance. I'm getting it for your support. As far as I'm concerned, it's yours. But my mom not divorcing my dad for more than twenty years doesn't make sense to me."

"Wow, I can't imagine being someone's wife for so long without loving or even liking him." Amy shakes her head.

"I don't get why she's resistant to the divorce. Or if that's what's going on between her and my grandfather. But I do think they've had an argument, and that's why they were both tense today."

"That's not cool. Your grandfather stressing your mom out like that." Amy frowns.

"Hey, we don't know what's going on. We need to stay out of it unless they ask for our help or input. It's none of our business." I caution her.

Shrugging, she struggles to contain her bottom lip. "It doesn't seem fair."

"How it seems might be different from inside. Don't get involved." I'm firm.

"Fine." She huffs.

CHAPTER 26

$\mathcal{M}$atteo

I know I should tell Amy that I'm meeting with her ex this afternoon, but it never feels like the right time.

She and Layla are only gone for maybe three minutes before I leave, too.

The moment I'm in the car, I hook up my phone to the car's Bluetooth and hit send on a number I've been calling often over the last few days.

"Sir? I'm falling behind you now. The men on him report every move he's making is to plan."

"Thank you, Sean. Hopefully, this is a smooth and simple process." I end the call. Checking my rear-view mirror, I see him behind me as I get on I-35. The drive will be a straight shot on the busy highway. Bringing up the navigation app, I'm informed it will be a solid two hours to get to the lawyer's office in Temple.

I'm not surprised when I arrive to find the asshole is late. Despite prying by the lawyer, I kept my story simple and repeated it often —I'm a doctor in a free clinic where I met Amy. I want to marry Amy and adopt Layla.

Enough of a reason for me to be here with some money, but hopefully, the free clinic part won't have the asshole thinking I can easily come up with more money. I don't want him thinking—he's shown he's not one to do it very often, and I need him to keep it that way.

When I called to set up the appointment with the lawyer, I didn't give him my name. All I said was that I was a friend of Amy's who wanted to get the signed divorce petition. Since Amy was afraid of him, I was acting on her behalf.

Matteo Castillo isn't exactly a unique name in Texas—probably even Dallas. But if they connected it to a doctor and Dallas, the asshole would know I have money and keep pumping me for every dime he thought he could squeeze out of getting him to sign.

The lawyer reviews the paperwork I brought for Richards to sign. It's a copy of everything he was served with two weeks ago because I didn't trust him to have it all. The divorce papers, the NDA, and the paperwork for Layla. In Texas, a parent has to sign an affidavit of voluntary relinquishment of parental rights that the judge needs to approve. The judge in my pocket is ready to sign off on everything once I get it to her. She also confirmed waiving the thirty-day wait period there is supposed to be after the divorce is finalized.

His lawyer might think something is off about my story, but Daniel Richards is greedy and broke. He'll accept the story without digging any deeper.

It's almost a half hour before the asshole finally arrives. He's shaking off his lawyer's admonishment. The sight of the man has me fighting back the urge to vomit. The fucker never deserved Amy and Layla.

Swallowing bile, I force the words out. "Amy doesn't know I'm here. I just want this to be over so we can be married. I'll adopt Layla. You don't have to pay child support or anything."

He eyes me. "Who are you?"

I shrug. "I'm a doctor. I met her when she was sick. She and Layla are fine—if you care to know."

His laugh is bitter. "I don't care about either of them. You warn her if she tries to come after me for child support, then I'm going to go for full custody of the kid. I'll get it, too." He points at his lawyer. "He's got the paperwork waiting to go."

"I said we don't want child support. Sign away your rights. That's what I'm here for—your signature." I point at the paperwork.

Black eyes narrow on me, he's studying what I'm wearing. I have no doubt he thinks he knows how much the clothes I'm in cost— he'd be wrong. "What will you give me for signing all this?"

The man is not surprising in the least. "I have a thirty-thousand-dollar cashier's check for you after you sign everything."

I offer it to him. He snatches it out of my hand. Showing it to his lawyer. "It legal?"

"It's valid. And if it's what you want, yeah." The lawyer shrugs. "Just know if you say anything about Amy, Layla, or even signing the NDA, then it automatically gives him cash and—

"I don't give a fuck. I'm not ever talking about that fat bitch or that

313

kid that's probably going to grow up and be as ugly and fat as she is. Anyone ever asks—I don't know shit about either of 'em."

A secretary is called in as a notary to witness everything.

The lawyer also signs off as a witness. It takes maybe five minutes for everything to be signed. I finally exhale once it's all done.

"Thank you," I mutter as I stand.

"No, man. Thank you. I thought I was going to be stuck with that brat and her fat ass. My parents weren't going to bail me out of it with her."

I'm a doctor, not a violent man by any means. But I am when I look at him. I don't dare do or say anything to betray the way I really feel. He signed. That's all that matters to me.

Before I get back on the road, I see the time and swear. It will be late before I get home. I text Amy and tell her that I got caught up with a patient in an emergency. Now that it's resolved, I'm staying a little later to finish up paperwork.

* * *

AMY

I'm beginning to wonder if something is wrong. Matteo said he'd be late, but I didn't think it would be this late—it's almost six thirty. I should be getting Layla ready for bed.

I startle at the doorbell going off. Layla jumps higher in her little activity center and squeals. She probably thinks it's Matteo.

Opening the door, I find Riley and Elliott.

"Hey, can we talk to Matteo?" Elliott asks with pleading.

"I'm sorry. He's still at work. You can come in and wait if you want." I step back to give them room.

"But he wasn't at work when we went there—" Elliott hits Riley, cutting him off.

"What do you mean he wasn't there?" I can't believe what they're saying.

The elevator opens to Matteo. His eyes meet mine. "What's the matter?"

"Um, we can go." Elliott offers.

Matteo shakes his head. "Come in." He looks to me. "What's the matter?"

"They said they went to see you at the clinic, and you weren't there. Where were you?"

An eyebrow goes up at my question.

Riley moves toward the door. "We're gonna go—"

"No, don't." I can't forget the pleading in Elliott's eyes. "We'll discuss it later."

"We don't want to start a fight." Riley sighs.

"It's fine." I insist. "We'll talk about it later. This is important to you. I can leave if you want me to."

Layla starts yelling, "Dada. Dada. Up Dada."

Matteo makes it to her in three steps. "I'm sorry, baby girl."

She buries her face in his neck and clutches him tight as he sits down in the overstuffed chair with her.

Both teens sigh as they sit on the couch. "It's not that. You can stay, but I just needed to hear what you thought..." Elliott runs a hand through his hair. "Riley thinks you'll know what to do."

I sit in the other chair. Matteo's eyes narrow on me before returning them to the twins.

"I don't want to go to Yale. I'm not sure how to tell Rafe. I get it's an honor he and Abuelo see us as Castillo even though we're...but I don't want to go into the family business. I want to have my own restaurant. Riley wants to focus on pottery and woodworking."

"Like, what will Rafe feel? Not what he'll say. I know he'll say it's okay. But what will he feel about it—about us?" Riley winces as he asks the question.

Matteo considers the question before he shrugs. "He'll say and *mean* that you two need to do whatever makes you happy. If going into the family business is going to be miserable for you, then don't do it. It's important to him that you do what will make you happy. Rafe mentioned he told you both already he and your sister will pay for your schooling, but they won't pay for much beyond that. If you're lucky, Gigi will loan you money to start your restaurant. He will want to ensure you two have thought of that. However, if you go into the family business, you're going to get an extremely large salary. Something to consider."

"They wouldn't help more?" It doesn't seem fair to me. "I mean, your mom helped you."

"Yes, it's why I said Gigi would loan them money. Hell, she might even just give it to them. My mom is much more permissive and grew up with old money, so won't see it as a bad thing. I'm not saying Rafe and Carrie think it's a bad thing, but they would want them to work hard. Everyone is of the mindset that just handing money over isn't the way to raise the kids. We're doing the best we can while preparing them for the real world." Matteo's eyes meet mine.

I agree with him. The last thing I want is to raise spoiled kids who take their lucky lives for granted.

"I don't care. I'll do whatever I need to do to open my own restaurant one day. Spending four years at some Ivy League isn't necessary." Elliott's lower lip juts out.

"You say that now, but who do you want coming to your restaurant? The Ivy League universities aren't about the school pedigree alone. It's about the connections you make and build. Deep pockets have an easier time spending money. Those are the clients you want, people with money to spend on an evening out and who want to be seen—want to impress others that they can afford it." Matteo's eyebrow is up as he looks at Riley. "What *mijo?*"

"I'm not willing to do whatever it takes to become an artist. I love the freedom to create whatever I want in pottery and woodworking—making things with my hands—but I like our current life. If I can keep the same lifestyle by continuing a legacy I want to be a part of, then I'll do it. There were too many nights of wondering if we were going to go into foster care because Carrie couldn't keep us for me to go back to being poor." Riley shrugs self-consciously.

"There's nothing wrong with admitting that," I assure him. "Maybe someday something else that means more will come along, and if it never does, that's okay too."

Seeing the change in Riley, I'm glad he at least found the assurance he needed.

"I'm relieved and a jerk enough to admit it. I was feeling guilty both of us weren't going into the Castillo company when Rafe clearly needs help." Elliott admits.

Riley sighs. "I was worried you would think I was selling out because I'm not willing to give up money for art. It's like I can take it, or I can leave it. I'm also thinking Matteo is right. You should still go to Yale. Make connections and take time to learn all you can for the business side."

He considers his twin's urging. "Maybe. If Rafe is okay with me going and not planning to continue with the Castillo company. I'd feel like I was stealing any other way."

"I think it's more than fair. I also think Rafe will surprise you. What makes you happy is the most important thing to him." Matteo is firm.

Both teens sigh in relief.

* * *

MATTEO

The moment the door is closed behind the twins, the words fly out of Amy, "Where were you?"

This woman is not afraid of me. She's not going to let me get away with anything. Good. Smiling, I pull her to me. Her hands go up to my chest to keep me from squeezing her tightly. Layla clutches at my neck as though she were trying to climb up me.

"I met with your soon-to-be-ex. He signed off on the divorce, his parental rights for Layla, and the NDA. It only cost thirty thousand. Tomorrow my lawyer will be sending evidence to the insurance company paying workers comp. He'll be out that money within a month. I have a judge who will put everything through by Friday. It was supposed to be a part of your birthday present."

Her beautiful face falls. "I can't believe you didn't tell me."

"I didn't want you stressed. There was no need for it. He didn't do or say a single thing that surprised me. I always knew I would come away with his signature, and it was the only thing that mattered. If I told you, you would have asked to be there, and that wasn't going to happen." I'm not going to apologize.

Rolling her eyes, she sighs. "You are such a jerk. I'm annoyed with you being so bossy."

"No, you aren't. You love how bossy and in control I am. I'll always keep you and Layla safe. Since you trust in me, you're simply annoyed you didn't know ahead of time."

She rolls her eyes again. "You really are annoying being such a know-it-all. Fine. I love it, and I would have spent every minute you were gone concerned. There, are you happy now?"

"I am. Very fucking happy. He signed. Tomorrow, you're going wedding dress shopping with Mom, and I leave work a few hours early for the person to meet with us to help us plan the wedding. I'm taking Wednesday off completely and after your therapy appointment at two, we go to Chicago. No work, no phone calls— just you and Layla. How soon before we can confirm you're pregnant?"

Melting into me, she sighs. "We started at the perfect time. We'll know very soon."

My cock hardens until it feels like steel at the idea of her pregnant. "After we come back you and Mom are going house shopping on Monday. I want us settled before the baby comes."

"You want us to move?" Her eyes are wide.

"Yes, I want you to have your own home so you can make it everything you want. Any house you want, however you want it to look, you're getting it." I promise her.

Chocolate is melting up at me. "How very presumptuous of you. There's that proposal you're supposed to be working on."

"Not presumptuous. I know you crave me like I'm your air, the same way I do for you. Marriage, forever without any escape, is all I want, too. Let's get Layla to bed, so we can have our own little celebration of him signing the papers. And make sure we're doing all we can to ensure you're pregnant."

CHAPTER 27

*A*my

"Matteo, that is simply not possible. We cannot plan a wedding she deserves in the time you are proposing. Especially if she wants to have it at the Museum of Art. A custom wedding dress will take weeks. I cannot believe you." Elizabeth sighs.

"The reason I picked this designer is not simply because she's local and makes beautiful clothes for plus size women. She promised she can deliver a dress in eight days. I called the museum, and after a sizable donation, we have a date twelve days from now. I'm not in love with it happening on a Monday and in the afternoon at that. But I checked the weather forecast, and it will be a warmer day. So in the end, it's better."

A custom dress made just for me? We're having the wedding at the Dallas Museum of Art. Oh my god, that's amazing. But all the information flying at me feels overwhelming. Twelve days, we're getting married in only twelve days from now in a big society wedding? My knees go weak, and I sag into the overstuffed chair.

"Amy, my dear, are you all right?" Elizabeth is concerned as she rubs Layla's back to soothe her as Layla reaches for me.

I shake my head. "I'm fine."

I'm picked up and put into Matteo's lap. How do I forget how strong he is? "Talk to me. What's the matter?"

"I love the idea of getting married at the museum, but I'm not sure about all the people," I admit. I'm worried I'm being a pain for being so anxious.

"All what people?"

"You know, all the people your family will want to invite." I gesture to Elizabeth. "I wouldn't want anyone to worry about offending people if they don't get an invitation."

Matteo catches my chin in a firm but gentle grip and brings my face up to his. "This wedding is about you and me. My family won't have any input on our guest list. I'm aware I have to invite my father. Never mind I talk to him twice a year, for a ten-minute conversation consisting of nothing more interesting than the weather and work. My nephew, I'm looking forward to. Other than that, there are maybe three former colleagues I would like added to my guest list. The rest will be up to you."

"Oh." I don't understand why I'm disappointed when I should be happy.

"What's wrong?"

I want to lie, but he knows me too well to even try. "I guess I didn't think I'd be disappointed about…"

"You want a big white wedding."

I'm too embarrassed to say the word, only able to nod.

"I know. I remember you saying you were disappointed with your courthouse wedding. We can have a big wedding without having three hundred guests. It's one of the reasons why we're having it at the museum. We'll fill it with an obnoxious amount of flowers. There is a call out for a string quartet for the ceremony. We can keep them the whole way through or do something else." He assures me.

"How do you know me so well?"

He chuckles as he presses his lips to my cheek. "Because I love you."

"You're planning a wedding better than I ever thought I would have."

"Since it's going to be your last one, it has to be amazing. And there's a lot more to pin down. We have to work with the event coordinator for the museum, but we're also going to have our own planner. They're both going to be here this evening. Once we tell them what we want, we leave it to them to make it happen."

"Have I told you thank you for loving me today?" I sigh and wish like hell Elizabeth wasn't standing nearby with Layla in her arms.

"Not yet, and you better not. I need to get to work, and you need to get your dress." Matteo is very aware of what I'm thinking.

I kiss his cheek before sliding off his lap. "I'll tell you later tonight."

"I'm counting on it. Doris, please take Layla into her room. She's going to get upset when we all leave at once." Matteo's hand is at my back.

* * *

AMY

Once we're in the car. I remember. "We need to stop at my bank so I can deposit a check from Rafe."

Elizabeth's eyes are wide. "Rafe gave you a check?"

"Yes, for one of my paintings. When he asked about buying it, he said one hundred. I thought he meant one hundred dollars. Some guy came to pick up the painting today to ensure it was properly wrapped for transportation. He brought a check for a hundred thousand dollars." I'm still light-headed from all the compliments he gave me while he oversaw the packing of the canvas.

"Thank goodness. You had me worried about Rafe. He can get a little too involved in...things."

I think of the money Rafe offered for me to walk away and chuckle. I'm not mad at him. He only did it because he cared about Matteo. In the end, his coming to me is how I found out Matteo loves me, so it was a good thing.

We're at a small boutique that proclaims it specializes in dressing plus-size women. There's a warning that it will be closed from the beginning of our appointment for three hours.

"She's closing for me?" I gasp.

Elizabeth chuckles. "No, my dear, she's closing for herself. Once it gets out that she made your wedding dress—she's going to be booked solid for brides who will come from all over Texas."

I blush as I open the door.

I'm only one step inside when a woman appears. Relief hits me that she's also plus-size.

"Hi, I'm Rebecca. You must be Amy." She offers her hand.

Hoping my hand isn't as sweaty as I think it is. I take it. "Yes, and this is Elizabeth. Thank you for making my dress."

Elizabeth shakes her hand and looks down at her with concern. "You will really be able to make a dress for her in only eight days?"

"I understand your concern, but I can do it. Your son is paying me enough to cover the expense of an employee going full time instead of only working weekends in order for me to focus on the dress."

Over the next hour, we go over the things I don't like in dresses because it's easier than what I do like. I had to scan a few bridal magazines before things got clearer in my head. Since I hadn't really thought of wedding dresses in a while.

She starts with a sketch and scans it into her computer. It looks like me, using my measurements, which she took after we got the introductions out of the way.

"Oh, I thought the skirt would be different." I'm disappointed.

"That's why I went with this program. I actually started as a seam-stress and made a lot of clothes for women. They would come in with pictures of things they wanted, but once I made it—it didn't look good on them like it did on the model. Sometimes, simple changes like fabric or even moving a hem make a huge difference. This has saved me so much time and clients money. Since I don't have time to get this wrong or do more than a simple alternation, this is going to make it possible to get the dress finished and exactly what you want."

A few more changes, and I finally love how I look in a dress on the screen.

I'm then told we're also here to shop for a dress for an event at city hall. The Castillo Company finished an update there, and it will be the reopening ceremony.

It will be my introduction to the Dallas social scene. Elizabeth will be introducing me as Matteo's fiancé.

"Matteo will be annoyed with me. I wanted to warn you, though, so you'll be prepared."

Under Elizabeth's supervision, I tried on five dresses and three I liked and agreed to. I also found more clothes that I can't put back. Rebecca made most of the clothes, and the ones that aren't are well made and for rare big labels.

Once I've found what I like, Elizabeth informs me that I'm also here for a full wardrobe. Thankfully, Rebecca has a huge selection of clothes she selected based on what fits my petite body shape and flatters me the best. I'm overwhelmed by it all but also so excited by the idea of all the pretty clothes.

I'm not allowed to know the cost of everything as Rebecca informed me that Matteo has already given her his credit card and knew I would freak out over the cost.

As I'm in the dressing room trying on the beautiful dresses, all I can see is my long braid in the way. I decide it's time and tell Elizabeth I'm ready to cut my hair.

Her eyes go wide, and after I assure her twice I'm positive it's what I want, we arrive at the salon she goes to. While her normal stylist isn't available, the owner is. I'm grateful for her patience as we discuss how different lengths will look.

I exhale and tell her to take me to an inch below my shoulders. Based on the stylist's advice, it won't be a huge change. It will still look long, but losing the weight of more than four inches will allow me to do more with it.

Once she's done, I love it.

Elizabeth does, too, but warns me that Matteo might find it hard to love.

I think we're done for the day, but when she finds out that I don't have any makeup, we go to a department store makeup counter. The woman shows me how to use the dozens of products she presents me with. I was shocked by how many products Elizabeth admitted to wearing, considering how light her makeup appeared to me.

It took a few tries before I was finally comfortable with how to use everything. When I'm done, I wonder who the woman in the mirror is and if Matteo will like her.

* * *

AMY

I'm on a huge high the next day as I pack for us to leave after my therapy appointment today. I wish I could skip the appointment, but Matteo won't allow it.

Doris is almost as excited as I am to go to Chicago. She admitted she would love to go to the museum with us or be in charge of Layla and take her to a few places to explore on our own. She visited Chicago once, more than a decade ago, and had wanted to return ever since.

I was glad she was willing to give us private time. We are going to be in two different suites next to each other. Matteo was insistent we needed our own rooms. When I said a suite was us in different rooms, he shook his head as he said he didn't want to worry Doris would hear me begging him to fuck me. I didn't argue after that.

Elizabeth wasn't wrong—Matteo spanked me for the haircut last night. Then he sighed and apologized, saying it was my hair and my choice of what I did with it. It was just such a huge change, and he loved my long hair so much.

I apologized because I did know he loved my hair. He's often brushed it out and braided it for me. It was another way of him taking care of me that we both loved. I regret it for a hard five minutes, but it's still long enough to be braided, and I promised I won't cut it any shorter.

If what happened afterward was make-up sex, then I'm going to figure out how we can fight again because it was so fucking hot.

Matteo's phone goes off with an alert. He checks it. His thumbs move across the screen rapidly as he replies. "Okay, the real estate agent Mom is recommended is here. Doris, could you please take Layla either into the sitting room or her room?"

"Wait, the agent is coming here? How come you didn't tell me? Should I change?" I look down at the leggings and plain long-sleeve black shirt I'm wearing stained with paint. These are just comfy clothes for around the condo.

He's trying to hand off Layla, who is upset and clinging to him. Sighing, he cuddles her close again. "Never mind, Doris. I'll keep her. If you wouldn't mind standing by, though, I'd appreciate it."

Catching me behind my neck, he brings his mouth down on mine. "You're always gorgeous. You don't need to change. This is just a quick meeting she asked for us to have so we could meet to discuss what we're looking for. I thought the email was more than enough." His shoulders lift. "But she didn't. Since mom is insistent she's an excellent agent and can find us what we want, I agreed."

We spent an hour last night putting an email together for every-thing we wanted in preparation for tomorrow. I couldn't believe half the requirements and budget or lack of a budget Matteo insisted on. Rich, rich.

The doorbell goes off, and Doris opens it. A slim, tall man with light blond hair introduces himself as Tim. He's good-looking, and he knows it. I wouldn't be surprised if he uses it to his advantage. His teeth are freakishly white and oddly perfect as he smiles down at me, one step too close for my comfort. I have to pull my hand out of his when he doesn't end the handshake on his own.

Something shifts in the air, pulling my eyes to Matteo.

"Where is Janet? She's the one who asked for this meeting." Matteo is frowning down at Tim. The guy is tall but at least four inches shorter than Matteo. Matteo is also wider and probably outweighs him by twenty pounds of muscle. I've never thought of Matteo as intimidating—I am now.

Tim's smile falls ever so slightly. "Janet sends her apologies. The client she's been working with decided to put in an offer. They're working the deal out right now."

I don't understand why Matteo's jaw is working. Ignoring the hand Tim offers, he nods. "Fine. Make this quick. Sit. Doris, take Layla, please."

This time, Layla doesn't fight. "I'll be in the nursery, sir."

"Yes, of course." Tim spits out the words as he sits down at the dining table, opens his briefcase, and takes out a large legal notepad and pen. "Janet had a few questions."

Tension is pounding like a drum at my temples over the next fifteen minutes. It isn't until the fourth time it happens that I finally understand. Every time Tim smiles at me and attempts to speak to me, Matteo cuts him off or answers the question himself. Finally, Tim gets it and basically ignores me to speak directly to Matteo. It doesn't help—Matteo still verges on rude to the man.

The moment the door closes behind Tim, Matteo curtly tells me he'll be in his office. Before I can say a word, he's gone. Is he mad at me? What did I do wrong? Fear sends me after him.

He's stalking his office, his hand running through his hair. Shaking his head, "Leave, Amy."

It's a punch to the chest, leaving me gasping for air. "I'm sorry."

Gold goes wide down at me. "You have *nothing* to be sorry for. It's me. This is all me. And I don't—" A hand runs over his beautiful face. "I apologize, but you need to leave. Until I get myself under control…"

I'm more confused than I was before. "I don't understand."

"The fucker was touching you, smiling at you, fucking flirting with you. You were smiling back at him. You let him touch you. I wanted to rearrange his face and mess up that expensive smile—"

What? "I was only being polite. Matteo, I wasn't encouraging him —I swear it."

Turning away from me, he nods. "I know that. It's why I don't trust myself around you. Nothing I'm feeling makes sense to me. I don't recognize any of this. It doesn't feel safe to be around you when I feel so fucking violent. If I hurt you or say something wrong, I wouldn't be able to forgive myself."

Matteo is jealous over *me*? I'm in paint-splattered clothing I wouldn't go to the store in. Yet a man who clearly didn't want me smiled at me and shook my hand two seconds longer than what was polite has Matteo about to explode with jealousy? Something is definitely wrong with me for the thrill shooting through me.

I'll talk to Hillary about it in therapy later, right now, all I know is Matteo is too far away from me. I can't stand how miserable he is. Everything in me screams to touch him, to soothe him. One step forward sends him one step back. Shaking his head, he's as far away from me as he can get.

"I'm begging you, *mi amor*. Please let me get myself under control."

Is it him calling me his love? Is it how much he wants to protect me from everything in this world he thinks could hurt me? Any other man and all the beatings that Daniel put me through would have me running, screaming from the room. I'm not running. I refuse to run and *never* away from him.

The hand I raise to touch him never makes it. In the blink of an eye, he has my wrist in a rough grip. The roughness doesn't scare me—it thrills me. "I'm sorry—"

"I told you not to apologize to me." Is snarled down at me.

Something is very wrong with me for how wet I am. "I'm sorry that I cannot leave you. You need me. Talk to me, please. Why exactly are you upset? Was it him smiling at me or me smiling back? How can I make it so you never feel this way again?"

Squeezing his eyes closed, "You're mine. You belong to me. No one is taking you from me." He grits out. "I could never lose you. Promise me."

"I promise. No other man will touch me. I will never smile at another man the way I smile at you. I belong to only you. The same way you belong to me." Gold glitters down at me as air leaves him in a rush. "No other man will ever touch me again. No other man will have my heart the way you do."

His throat works. "It isn't helping. I still feel violent, like I want to break something."

The next session is going to be a long one for the way my skin becomes hot and too damn tight. "Give it to me."

"Give it to you?"

"Your violence. I love it when you lose control." I admit. "The idea that I could bring you to the brink and loss of control—I'm sorry if it's not right, but I love it. He made me feel ugly and unwanted. You're making me feel like I'm a sexy goddess or something."

"You are a goddess. I pray to you every fucking night that I never lose you, your love, your touch. If I lost you, I would lose the air I breathe."

This man, how could he think I could walk away from him? "Give it to me. Show me."

I'm thrust away from him before he bends me over his desk. He tears down my pants with my panties.

"Fucking hell, you're soaking wet," is filled with wonder.

I don't have time to be ashamed. His hand coming down on one ass cheek is harder than he has ever spanked me before. And it goes straight to my clit. "You will never let another man touch you."

"Never." I almost shout.

Another smack to my other cheek. "Promise me."

"I promise." I fight not to stiffen, preparing for him to go back to smacking my other cheek, but he doesn't. His heavy hand falls on my swollen, soaking-wet pussy lips. Oh my fucking god—it's electricity striking my clit. I wonder if I managed to come.

"You will never smile at a man like you did today."

"I promise I will never smile at another man." Sparks fly under my eyelids when he goes back to my heated ass. Holy shit. Another round of smacks to my other cheek and pussy has my legs going out from under me and begging him to fuck me.

He enters me like a man possessed hard, fast, rough. "This is my pussy. Every damn inch of you is mine."

"Only you." I nearly sob. Between the way my ass and pussy are on fire and his hot body almost entirely on me, I'm wondering if I'm going to climax without him moving.

"No other man will be inside your tight pussy. **Mine**." He growls.

"Yours," I promise him.

The leash he always keeps on himself is gone. He gives me the violence within him, and I glory in it. Hard, fast, rough, and oh my fucking god. His hands are punishing on my hips. That I inspire it in him thrills me in a way it shouldn't.

"That's it, such a good girl you are. greedy for my cock. Fuck. The way your tight pussy grips me is like a vise. Your pussy milking my every drop of come for me to breed you. I can't wait until you are pregnant, your breasts swelling—and your belly big with our love. Everyone will see you and know you are mine. That this pussy is mine alone."

"Yours. All of me belongs to you." From the first day.

"Every damn inch of you." Is blasted like a tattoo into the skin of my neck seconds before his teeth mark me. "From your cute fucking toes to the top of your hair that looks so pretty wrapped around my hand. Will they know from the mark what a dirty girl you can be for me? Will they be able to tell you begged me to fuck you, use you for my pleasure? Do you want them to know? Hm? Do you want them to know you love your ass spanked? That your pussy gushed like a water hose when I slapped your mons. They see a good girl in public, but *I* know you're so very naughty that you beg for my come and my cock."

His words are driving me crazy. I'm frantic, close, so fucking close —only I can't reach it. "Harder. Please, Matteo. Fuck me harder."

"There she is, my greedy girl. I love it when you beg for what you need. I'll give it to you." Those hands at my hips lift me up, and oh my fucking god, *right fucking there*.

Harder, so fucking hard the pain adds to the pleasure. There are no more words only the pounding of our bodies loud around us. It's rough, dirty, and so mind-blowing. And I fight not to surrender to the black all around me as he fills me with his wet heat. My body is still trembling from the aftershocks of my orgasm when he pulls out of me.

No, I want to shout. The part I love the most after my orgasm is when he stays inside me—so I can feel his heart beating inside me —in time with my own.

Without him holding me up, I sink to my knees at his feet. His eyes are closed, his head back as he fights for air. God, even limp, I can't believe how thick and long his cock is. The sight of his cock gleaming with our shared come fills me with longing and sends my tongue out to taste him, us.

A hand is in my hair, gold glittering wide in surprise. I hold the gold as I lick the head of his cock. Hmm...it's salty and oddly sweet to me. This is us. I want more. I don't attempt to take his cock in my mouth. I clean every inch of him—the taste of us is sweet to me. This man is mine. Dirty, rough, and tender, I wouldn't have it any other way.

334

CHAPTER 28

*A*my

While I couldn't do as good a job as the woman at the counter did, I'm proud of how good my makeup looks the night of the event.

Matteo frowns. "I don't remember your tits looking so damn good in that dress."

I'm trying not to laugh. "They're as covered up as they can be."

The frown deepens. "I don't think I like the idea of us going after all. Both Javier and Rafe are going. Let's stay home."

"Matteo, I spent all this time getting ready. Please, can we go?" I plead.

Gold darkens. "Fine. As long as you remember your promises to me."

I never did talk to Hillary about how wet his jealousy made me— especially when I liked it so much. My clit is tingling at the mere

335

memory, or maybe it's from the hope of another session like the first. "I promise."

We give Layla kisses before leaving, promising Doris we'll be home before ten.

Matteo opens the back door of the limo for me. We're being driven tonight so he can have a glass or two of champagne. When the car stops, I can't believe it. It's an actual red carpet. Rich, rich.

"This is city hall? Why is it so ugly?" It looks like a reverse pyramid, wider at the top than the bottom.

Chuckling, "That was pretty standard for architecture in the late seventies when this was originally built. We didn't do the initial build, just the update."

Inside, there is an enormous wide-open foyer. "My painting."

Rafe is holding court in front of the painting he bought from me. "You're going to need an agent. There are a few here who would love to talk to you. I gifted it to the city of Dallas. Looks good here, don't you think?"

The arm Matteo has around me tightens. A white card beside it has the name Amy Castillo and the title of the painting I gave the man who came to get it. "Amy Castillo? Rafe, what if she wanted to go by her maiden name?"

It's another shock, a wonderful one. It wasn't Matteo who made the assumption I would go by Amy Castillo as an artist. I wrap my arms around him. "Thank you for caring. I do want to go by Castillo."

Rafe's chuckle is loud. "I never doubted it for a moment. The same way I knew Kevin Broussard is looking to add a new artist to his portfolio."

"You're just…giving me a career." I don't know how I feel.

"Not in the least. Art is subjective except for one thing—it makes you feel something. If it doesn't, there's nothing I can say or do to get someone to buy it. Besides, what's the use in having a billionaire for a brother if he doesn't use his position to help you out a little?" His shrug is casual.

Before we leave two hours later, I meet with Kevin Broussard. He wants to represent me. From Rafe, I found that the man is one of the top agents in Texas. Rafe also assured Matteo that Kevin had a long-time male partner.

I think of Hope's words as she hugged me goodbye all the way home: "I love seeing Matteo in complete and total adoration of you. I never thought I would see it from Matteo. He was just always so…like smiling wasn't allowed. I like this Matteo better than who he was before he met you."

I understand what she means since I was what she described him as before I met him—cold and empty. I'm grateful we found each other.

* * *

AMY

Matteo took the day off so we can go house hunting together. After a week of looking with Elizabeth, I've yet to find anything I like. And I want his input on the house we're going to make our home.

When the realtor pulls up to the first house of the day, I'm wondering why we're here. I know it's not for sale. When I first saw it as we drove by, Elizabeth saw me looking at it. She told me she knew the family, and they spent the majority of their time in Aspen.

It's a gorgeous home that looks like it belongs in the French countryside. I swear it's got to be based on a castle—there are turrets at the front corners of it.

Before I can say anything, Matteo is out of the back of the SUV. Janet is on her phone. I follow Matteo only to find he's already inside. The enormous wooden door is open.

Barking catches my attention. "Where is that coming from?"

Oh my goodness, the cutest ball of fur is barking. I turn and find it running to me. Where did it come from? The dog is a twin to the one I grew up with. I'm down on my knees for the dog. I look up to find Matteo frowning down at the dog. His frown surprises me, making me doubt everything.

"Be careful. What if the dog bites?"

"You didn't do this?"

"Do what?" Another frown as he scans the enormous lawn.

"I hoped the dog was your doing." I sigh.

An eyebrow goes up. "A dog? I don't know. A dog is a huge commitment. It's a forever kind of thing."

I'm confused. "Just like having a baby together is."

"Ah, I'm glad you do seem to understand the difference." He picks up the dog and walks with it into the house.

Wait, where is he going?

There is a large two-story entrance hall. In the middle of it is a wall of green with red and white roses arranged to spell out: "Will you marry me?"

Mouth open in shock I look to Matteo and find him on one knee. The dog is still in his arms. I see it sparkling as he takes it from around the dog's neck. It's an enormous, intense blue sapphire.

"You *did* do this."

"I even went to a rescue the way you got Henry. It took them a few weeks before they got the dog they thought would fit us best. He's ten months old. The previous owner did do the buy from a breeder, so he has papers. But the owner died a few weeks ago. No one in the family was able to take him in. His name is Walter. When they told me that, I thought it fit your love of people names for animals."

I love the ring, but it means more to me that Matteo understood the breeder versus rescue debate and took it into consideration when looking for a dog.

"Well? You still haven't given me your answer. Will you make my entire world complete by becoming my wife and being the best part of me?"

I'm nodding as I fight back tears. "Absolutely."

* * *

MATTEO

I exhale in relief at Amy's acceptance. Even though I was certain, a part of me needed to hear her say it. This is the woman for me, forever.

I'm back on my feet, slipping the ring on her finger. The moment it's on, her eyes are sweeping over the foyer and into rooms.

"Want to tour this place to see if it's where you want to live and build our family?"

She shocks the hell out of me when she shakes her head.

"Why not? Mom said every time you drove by it, you couldn't take your eyes off it."

Her sigh is heavy. "It's too expensive already. Then you're going to pay for it to get the family who owns it out...no. Let's keep looking."

This woman. I keep her hand in mine as I walk into the first room to our right, a formal living room with the furniture covered in cloth to prevent dust from collecting on it. "I'm a billionaire, Amy. And now you are, too. My money is your money. Which means we could buy this place forty times over before we would feel it."

She squeezes my hand. "Forty times? Holy freaking crap."

I chuckle as I bring her up against me. I'm trying to remember the real estate agent will come in soon. There's also the dog in between us. "Exactly. The owners of this place are more than receptive to an offer."

Another sigh. "Okay, we can look at it."

Janet is waiting in the foyer, her smile wide at the flower arrangement. "I love this for you both. You ready for the tour?"

Amy nods.

It's a home modeled after a chateau in France—complete with six-inch-thick walls—I watch my woman grow softer and softer with happiness with every step we take through it. I don't love the place as much as she does. The roof in one corner needs to be redone, the owner disclosed. I can clearly see water has affected the plaster beneath it. That promises to be a pain in the ass. If one corner needs to be redone, I would rather do the whole damn thing at once.

All the large open space Amy loves so much promises to be a problem if the temperature dips below fifty degrees. At least the place was built with forced air heating and cooling, updated less than five years ago.

Once the tour is complete, I think the real reason the owner was willing to sell was the cost of maintaining it. It's more likely they spent so much time in Aspen because it was less expensive.

None of that matters, though, because Amy loves it. Which means I'm going to love it—eventually. We end the tour back in the foyer, where Janet gives us time to discuss it.

The dog is relieved all the walking is done, even though Amy carried him most of the time. He settles down at Amy's feet and stares up at her in adoration. I think I'll grow to love the dog much sooner than the house.

Her sigh is sad. "This place is going to cost us a fortune, isn't it? I saw the water stain. And—"

"And nothing. I saw how much you love this place. Let me give you the home you love." I don't want her to accept what she feels she has to. I want to give her exactly what she wants in every way.

"Okay, yes, please. Can we buy this home and build our family here?"

Janet is waiting with the paperwork. I give her the number I'm willing to start with. I sign off on it, and she can submit it from the driveway. Before we're back at the realty office, the offer has been accepted.

I was worried about the dog, but he's a chill little thing who sits in Amy's arms the whole drive.

Once we're home, Doris is surprised by the question I ask, as is Amy. "Sorry," I give Amy a peck on the cheek. "If you're happy with the way everything has gone so far? I know I am, and Layla loves you. I would love it if you lived in once the house is ready. It will probably take six weeks or so for the roof and the plaster work to be redone. We'll hire a devoted housekeeper, for when we move in. Your only worry will be Layla and our new baby we hope to have soon."

Amy rolls her eyes at me. "I'd love it if you said yes."

Doris is smiling wide. "I'd love to. Layla is a doll."

"I'm also going to need you to get your passport if you don't have it already. Over the next few years, I'll be taking Amy to sightsee art in the best museums. We will want you to go with us."

"Yes, sir. I have a passport that's only a few years old."

Layla begins crying. Amy kisses my cheek. "I'm going to go get her."

I'm saying goodbye to Doris when Amy comes back into the living room with a pouting Layla. The moment Layla sees me, she holds out her arms for me. I take her and give her kisses on her neck.

My phone rings. It's my mother. "I swear she knows we bought the house."

Amy laughs and takes my phone from me. "Hey, Mom."

I let their conversation about the house wash over me as I introduce a laughing Layla to Walter. Walter loves Layla almost as much as Layla loves him—it takes a few times to encourage her to be gentle before she figures out what I mean.

Walter hops down from the couch and runs over to the French doors. The rescue promised he was potty-trained, but that's no guarantee. I'm glad they didn't lie to get him out.

Since it's become overcast and sprinkling, I decide to let him wreck Javier's putting green. I'll buy him another one. Layla thinks everything the dog does is hilarious.

I catch the trail end of what Amy says. "—a birthday party for Layla."

I'm paying more attention when Amy's eyes meet mine and she shrugs. Since I'm lost, I shrug. I also feel bad. I forgot Layla's birthday is in a week—two days before our wedding day.

"Really, Elizabeth. I promise it's okay. You and Matteo taught me that. She's not going to remember the day. It's more for me than her. Just a day with her and her new cousins she adores and some cake is perfect for her."

I shake my head. It sure as hell isn't.

Amy sighs and hands the phone to me. "Since you and Matteo are in agreement, I'm going to let you two plan the party."

Taking Layla from me, she kisses me on the cheek. "It's her first birthday party, not her last."

I send my fist into her hair and bring her mouth to mine. "She will never look at pictures of her birthdays or special events and find them lacking compared to those of her cousins and other brothers and sisters."

"You're the best damn daddy ever." She says into my mouth.

I go into my office to get some of the information Mom needs and to write down shit I won't remember later.

As we move around the kitchen preparing dinner, I tell Amy about the plans for Layla's birthday. "There is going to be a small petting zoo and a pony. Elena and Ava loved it at the last birthday party. Mom thinks cupcakes are better than cake. Although Layla will have her own personal smash cake."

"A petting zoo?" Amy's voice goes up an octave.

"I believed loving my kids the same would be all they needed. Then the twins came over and asked if their dad would love them the same as his other kids if they didn't do what they thought he wanted them to. It was a crazy question to me. With everything I've seen from Rafe and Carrie, I didn't think for a second that the twins would question how much they were loved." I shake my head, remembering how much it hurt Rafe when I talked to him about it.

"It brought home to me that no matter how much I believed I would show Layla that I love her as much as I would our other children—she might feel or think differently deep down. I don't want there to ever be a doubt in her mind."

A hand goes up to her forehead. "I thought you and your brothers believed not spoiling them was important."

"It's not about spoiling them—"

"It is, though. She doesn't need to have a petting zoo or pony to ride on."

"This is where the whole money thing feels slippery. No, we don't want them spoiled. At the same time, by not giving them things other kids have, it feels like they are being deprived. A part of me would rather spoil Layla than have her worry that I don't love her the same as her other brothers and sisters." I admit.

Her sigh is heavy. "I remember growing up hearing that all you need is love. My mother would laugh bitterly as she said it. In my childish mind, I used to think it meant she didn't love me enough to want to be the mom I wanted her to be. If she loved me, then she wouldn't need the hit of cocaine more than she needed me. It was my own fault that I wasn't worth her love."

Fuck, how can she say it so casually? I hug her tight, the pain more than I can endure thinking of her so young, wanting her mother's love.

"Now, I recognize it for the only prayer she knew how to make. If you love something or someone as much as you do, why can't it be enough? Why is love only a fraction of what you really need? And why do they lie that it is? Why is the lie told when the honesty, as painful as it is, would hurt less than the lie?" Her words are a mere whisper as if she doesn't know if she wants the answer.

Holding her tight, I press a kiss to her forehead. "Because we want it to be enough. Love is magic. There is no denying that. Feeling loved, loving someone—it's all magic. Love changes you, how you see the world, how it feels to be in it. Except there's only so much love can do, and we have to do the rest."

MATTEO

Our discussion of love being enough leads me to my grandfather's home the next day. My grandfather's eyes go wide at the sight of me. He steps back to allow me into his home. I haven't been inside in more than twenty years. I'm looking around to find it hasn't changed much.

"Matteo, _mijo_. Is everything all right?" He gestures to the couch in his living room.

I shake my head. "I need to know, what is your issue with Amy?"

His hand goes over his mouth before running over his cheek. I've seen him do that when he needed time.

"From the moment I met Amy, I knew she was the one. I don't want to think of my life without her. If it's between you or her—I pick her."

His elbows go down on his knees. His eyes are on his hands clasped together. "It isn't about her, it's you."

I'm too stunned to speak.

Meeting my gaze head-on. "Your work was your entire world. It was something that would leave marks on anyone. You left it less than six months before you met her. There was a massive void in your life. My concern is that you're attempting to fill the void with her. Had you fallen for her a year or two from the change, while I still would have reservations about you becoming involved with a married woman—there would be no concern. Will you regret this in another four or five years, and where will that leave her and her child? That is my issue."

Since his words are much like Hillary's in therapy. I tell him the same thing I told her. "I'm not going to pretend I understand love. It's a fluid and boundless thing. When I left oncology, I can see now it was because it broke me and sent me into depression. Like anything else I didn't want to accept, I ignored it. Believing fool- ishly, I simply had to work harder to get through it. While I considered a woman and family, it didn't appeal enough for me to change my plan of filling my days so I couldn't feel the depression. Amy took that plan and shattered it."

His eyes drop from mine as his jaw hardens.

"I began seeing a therapist for Amy and Layla. They were the reason I came out of my depression. Having Layla look at me like I hung the moon did more than any pill could. Needing to be the man they deserved is why I went to therapy."

It's a battle not to allow the fear of losing her to overwhelm me. Even putting the words into the universe is terrifying. "Regret is not something I will ever have for the time I have Amy in my life. There are no guarantees in life. We're going to change and grow. Who we are now is not the same person either of us will be in five or ten years. My hope is we grow together in a way that makes us stronger because I can't imagine my life without her."

"If you're sure she's what you want. I will support you both." He promises.

"She isn't what I want. Amy and Layla are the only things in this world that I need. If you cannot accept this—us—I have no problem removing you from our lives to protect her from the pain your denial causes."

His chuckle surprises me. "As you should."

"I'm glad that's settled. Now, how about you tell me if anyone else knows you're dying?"

An eyebrow goes up at the same time his eyes shutter. "I'm ninety-two years old, *mijo*. We all have to go some time."

I shake my head. "Bullshit. It's your heart, isn't it?"

Clenching his jaw, he nods. "A few years ago, I spent time in Mexico having a bypass done. It bought me time. That time is coming to an end."

"Your doctor—"

The shake of his head is firm. "No more doctors. No more needles and blood draws, and hospital rooms. I'm done. I've had a long life. I'm content my time is coming close to an end."

I sigh. "Have you told anyone?"

"No, and neither will you. Your mother was upset I didn't tell her about the bypass before I had it. She might have figured out by my insistence she divorce your father and marry me. It was my hope I would die with her as my wife. However, she has refused. I'm not going to use it as a means to change her mind."

"That's what you two have been fighting about." I exhale the words.

He nods.

"Why won't she divorce Dad?" I'm angry with her all over again.

"Because he doesn't want her to. With the divorce, it will free him to marry his long-time girlfriend. He doesn't want to marry her, but he's also not willing to end the relationship." His chuckle is bitter. "Despite not truly caring, your mother and I are in a relationship. He's guilting her not to divorce him."

I can't fucking believe him. "What if—"

"No, don't. No, what if. Your mother has made her choice. And your father..." he shakes his head. "It would probably make him dig in his heels more. You don't tell anyone. I won't have the long faces and morose feeling." It's an order.

"You would ask that of me?"

"Yes." It's hard, firm.

I want to argue with him, fight for my family to be aware, and be here for him the way he needs. But I can't. So all I do is nod, "As you wish."

"Thank you, *mijo*. Now, tell me about this home I heard you purchased."

CHAPTER 29

*M*atteo

"Are you freaking serious? The hobby box was your mother's attempt to get us together outside of the condo so I would fall for you?" We're on our way to the cooking class we got in the hobby box.

"Yep. I didn't know about the hobby box before it showed up. When I asked about hobbies, it was to figure out what presents to get you. She decided we needed a reason to get out of the whole boss, employee thing. If we were in a class or dancing, it would remove the barrier. You could see us as something outside of that, and hopefully, you would fall in love with me."

She's quiet for so long it worries me. Suddenly, her laughter fills the car. "Your entire family is Machiavellian. Too bad for you, I scheduled the first dance class for Frida so we can get some lessons in before our wedding. I've never danced anywhere but alone at home with music blaring when I cleaned or something."

It's my turn to laugh. "Bad? Not in the least. I'm looking forward to it. My only concern is keeping my cock down in public with you in my arms."

"Matteo," she giggles. "You're so dirty."

I shake my head. "We need to go inside now. Before I embarrass us in public."

The witch laughs all the way inside.

I'm surprised by how much fun it is. The lesson involves making pasta, marina sauce, and tiramisu. Focusing on the pasta, I have my back to Amy when she lets out a cry of pain.

Christ, my heart is pounding so hard I can barely hear Amy explaining to the chef she forgot to use the potholder for the covered lid. I grasp her wrist and drag her to the sink, turning on the cold water. I'm examining the bright red line across her small palm.

"It's not bad. No skin has broken. It's a typical first-degree burn. There might be a blister." I diagnose.

"Matteo, I'm fine. Please don't fuss."

I'm trying to keep a rein on the anger boiling through me at seeing her small hand red from the burn. She's going to be fine, but the idea of her in pain is seriously fucking with my head. "We're done. I don't want you in the kitchen anymore. You could make the burn worse—"

"No, please. I'm hungry. We were having fun. Matteo, please, can we stay?" Those chocolate eyes are wide and pleading.

Fuck. I can't deny her a damn thing. "You have two choices. You sit and watch, or we leave."

Her pretty little mouth opens to argue with me before she sees I'm not having it. Sighing, she gives in. "I'll sit and watch, doctor."

* * *

Amy

I'm a bad person. Matteo treating me like I'm so fragile I'm going to break any second all day isn't something I should love as much as I do. Especially when the burn really isn't that bad. It barely hurts enough for me to use the lidocaine he put on it the minute we got home.

The only thing I'm allowed to do is hold Layla. I should not enjoy this when he looks so tortured. No matter how often I tell him it doesn't hurt, he refuses to hear it.

I'm yawning, ready for bed, when his cell phone rings. Since it's almost ten thirty, we both jump. "Who is it?"

Checking the display, he frowns. "It's Santos. If he forgot the time difference from Dallas to LA again, I'm kicking his ass." He answers. "Hello?"

Since I'm in his lap while we watch television, I can hear everything when he mutes the sound.

"Hey, Matteo. I'm sorry for calling late. But I don't know what to fucking do here. You busy?" The distress is clear in the man's voice.

An eyebrow goes up at me in question. I nod and get off his lap. "Yeah, sure. Give me a minute to get into my office."

Giving me a kiss on my cheek, "I'll be right back."

"Don't rush for me," I assure him.

Almost thirty minutes later after yawning so often it's causing tears to run down my face, I'm done waiting up. Since I prefer to take my shower at night, I figure it won't hurt to start getting ready for bed.

I'm glad I do since I have time to take a shower and braid my hair before I hear the bedroom door open. I left the door to the bathroom open in case he wanted to join me, as he often has.

"Amy?" Uh oh, he's not happy.

Walking out of the bathroom, I find I'm right. His frown is deep, and his eyes are almost a dark brown.

"Is Santos okay?"

"Santos is fine. What the hell? I told you I would help you tonight. Why didn't you wait for me?" I blink, and he's in front of me. My wrist is gently held fast in his hand as he studies my burn.

"Matteo, I told you. I'm fine. I did have to put the lidocaine on after I got in the shower. The water was a little too hot. But it's fine. You were busy with Santos. I was really tired and wanted to go to bed." The yawn is completely unplanned, forcing my jaw open so wide it aches.

Sighing, he cups my chin, running his thumb over my lips. "I'm sorry, *mi amor*. Let's get you into bed."

He catches the end of the belt around my waist from the robe and pulls it away. Gold flashes when he finds me naked. I can't be this close to him without getting turned on. A moan escapes me as I sway.

His breath catches, but he steps away from me. "Sleep, you need sleep."

I lift my hand, intent on touching him, only for him to take another step back. "Matteo?"

"You're tired. I'm going to get ready for bed myself." Before I can argue with him, he disappears into the walk-in closet.

For two seconds I'm annoyed he rebuffed me. Matteo has never told me no—for anything. Until I bend down to pick up my robe from the floor and I guess the lidocaine has worn off because my burn stings as the soft cotton finds it. Ouch, that's why he's turning me down.

This is stupid. It hurts a little, but not enough for him not to make love to me. All the arguments I could make bubble up only to die since they aren't anything I haven't already said. Mind jumbled, I reach for my lotion to put on, and the cool plastic feels good against my burn. It hits me.

When he walks out of the closet wearing only his robe for him to go take his own shower, I hold out my lotion to him. "Please, can you help me?"

"Of course." His eyes are running over me with concern.

I shrug. "The lidocaine wore off, I guess."

"I'll grab it, be right back." Once he's applied more lidocaine, he runs his eyes over me. "And some pajamas."

"I don't want to wear any." Shaking my head, I turn my back to him. "Please, can you put the lotion on? My skin is a little itchy."

"Um, yes. Sorry."

I'm biting my lip not to laugh. I've never heard him so flustered. This is totally going to work.

It's so quiet in the room I hear every move he makes, from squeezing out the lotion to applying it to his hands. His large hands come down on my shoulders.

The scent of the lotion, a mix of roses and jasmine, floats up to me as he slowly massages my shoulders. Those hands are gentle and tender as they slide over my skin. The doctor is back. There is nothing sexual in his touch. Focused and intent, they don't miss a single inch. I'm holding my breath when his fingertips graze over the top of my ass, only for him to stop.

I swallow an outraged cry when I hear him pick up the bottle of lotion again. Right. Lotion. He's supposed to be applying lotion. In an attempt to get it together, I focus on the carpet beneath my feet.

From the top of one shoulder, those large hands roam down my arm to my hand. He's gentle as he works the lotion in between my fingers. His thumb runs over my engagement ring with a small smile.

Done, he has the lotion again and begins on my other arm. It's the right one. He's even more gentle once he gets to my hand before pressing a tender kiss to my burn. If I hadn't loved him before tonight, this is the moment when it would have happened.

In a move far more graceful than anything I could hope to accomplish, he's down on his knees. I open my mouth to ask him what he's doing. Only there's no need to ask because a lotion-covered hand is running along my hip down to the top of my thighs—once again grazing the skin of my ass without touching it the way I'm dying for him too.

Down one leg, he's going too fast, or is it not fast enough? All I know is he's picking up my foot to sweep his hand along the sole. His large hand encompasses my entire foot as he works the lotion in between my toes. My hand goes down on his shoulder to steady myself.

His head comes up. "Are you all right?"

I nod, my throat too tight to say a word.

Now to the other side. Am I wrong, or does he slow as his fingers come within an inch of my clearly wet core? Before my brain can process it, though, he's already picking up my foot to apply lotion to it.

How the hell does he move so fluidly for a man as big as he is? He has the bottle of lotion again as he stands. I want to shout in delight at the way gold flashes as he stares down at my tight nipples.

One step forward brings him so close that the hair on his chest brushes against my aching nipples. I can't breathe until those large hands come down in the middle of each ass cheek and squeeze gently.

"You're a witch." He mutters as his mouth takes mine. His kiss is rough and greedy, making the world spin around us.

"I put a spell on you?" I tease him.

"An unbreakable spell to bring me to my knees for your every wish."

"My only wish is for you to never stop loving me the way I love you."

His forehead falls to mine. "You have it, my love. You are the air I breathe."

"Show me." I plead.

Sighing, his hands become rougher as they squeeze my ass—shaping the flesh before a middle finger slides down and presses into me. I shiver at the intent behind it. One eyebrow goes up in question.

Over the past few weeks, he's gone from using his middle finger to three fingers. Last night he fucked me with them while he made me sit on his face. I came so hard that the world almost went black. If I had been able to speak I would have begged him to use his cock on me then.

"I'm not going to last long enough to give you the pleasure you deserve."

I'm on my knees for him before he finishes the sentence. I lick at the slit already dripping with precome. Delicious. He hasn't allowed me to do more than clean his cock because he wanted to save his come for trying to knock me up—every time he said it, it turned me on so much I couldn't argue with him.

"Fuck, you're so beautiful on your knees with my cock in your mouth. I love how greedy you are for it." He grits out, his jaw tight.

"I love the taste of you. Every inch of you is yummy." I moan as I suck deep on the lone three inches of his cock I can take easily.

I'm using my left hand, annoyed my hand won't go all the way around. I attempt to use my right hand. Before it gets within two inches of him, his hand has my wrist in a tight grip.

"No, baby." Gently, his thumb runs over my burn. "Never mind, we'll just go really slow."

Shaking my head, I lick at the soft sac of him. "I want all of you. I've fantasized about being on my knees for you since the day in your office. Please fuck my mouth the way I wanted you to do that day."

He inhales deep and sends both hands into my hair. "I'm not sure what the hell I did to deserve you. I envisioned the same thing. But I was already worried about how roughly I fucked you and was too afraid I would scare you away completely."

Carefully, I suck the small sac into my mouth and tease him with my tongue. "I loved it so much I think of it almost every day. I'm grateful for all the ways you make love to me. It thrills the hell out of me when you lose control. How it's me that turns you from a calm, sweet man to a greedy, hungry savage."

"It's only you. No woman has ever had this effect on me. I don't recognize the man you turned me into at times." His admission sends those bees into my fingertips and all the way to my toes.

"I recognize the savage as the man who frees me from all the fears I'm not sexy or beautiful enough for someone to want me for me."

Holding me still, his cock is in my mouth. I'm wet at the growl that comes from low in his chest. At first, he's slow, almost gentle. I open my mouth wide and love the way he picks up speed. He tips my head back and sends his cock deeper until it hits the back of my throat.

Oh my god, a wet rush of heat floods my core at what it does to me. "Your mouth is so pretty wrapped around my cock. I smell how wet you are. I love it. My sweet, dirty girl drenched over me fucking your mouth—your pussy dripping down your inner thigh. All that sweet juice is going to waste. Damn."

I cling to his strong thighs, loving the feel of his muscles straining beneath my hands. Deeper, he surges, and I fight for air.

"That's it. Breathe through your nose. You can take more. I know you can."

He's fucking my mouth roughly. He pulls out until only the head of his cock remains. I suck him deep, not wanting to let him go. Oh god, he thrusts back in, and he's in my throat. Something is seriously wrong with me to love this so much.

I can't take it anymore and slip my fingers inside my soaking wet pussy. The growl that comes out of him rumbles through him to his cock as he slams it back into me. His hands are no longer gentle as he holds me in place.

"I'm never letting you go. You're every wet dream brought to life. **Fuck**."

Deeper he goes and I can't believe how deep he is. I swallow. Matteo swears as he fucks my throat in short rapid thrusts.

"Swallow again." He orders me.

I do, and his body shakes as he comes. I feel it, but he's so deep down my throat I taste nothing. Swiping my clit once, twice, I come with a small shudder.

"Fucking hell." Is an exhalation of air. Slowly, so slowly, he pulls out. I suck the head of his cock and let him go with a loud pop.

Shaking his head, his hands cradle my head. "I'm so lucky to have you."

I blink, and he's lifting me up in his arms. Gently, he puts me on the bed. I'm shivering with anticipation as he takes the bottle of lube out of the bedside table and sets it on the bed. Except he's not done. There is a small box in his hand.

I'm curious. He shows me the box. It says it's a backdoor training kit. There are three different sizes of plugs in the shape of a cock with a ridged head like his.

I tap the largest one. Removing it from the box, he offers it to me. I take it into my mouth and suck. His smile is wicked as gold glitters down at me.

"Such a good girl you are." He purrs. "On your knees."

Rolling over, I offer him my ass. A large hand runs over one cheek. Shaping it once, twice, then he smacks it hard. The sting goes straight to my core. He presses a kiss to the heated flesh. His hand goes to my other cheek, and he gives it the same treatment.

Both hands are on me, pulling my cheeks apart. The hot air washes over me seconds before his tongue is there. Oh god, he's never done this before.

Wet, hot, his tongue is teasing me. I can't keep my head up and allow it to fall to the bed. I'm gasping for air—holy shit. It feels amazing. His velvet tongue is stiff, determined, and fucking me as thoroughly as his fingers.

I want to beg him to stop or give me more. Except words are too hard to form. My knees give out. Matteo never misses a beat, following me down to the bed, keeping me spread wide for his mouth. I can't stop my body from pushing back to his tongue for more.

I'm fighting not to scream in outrage when his mouth is gone. A rough smack yanks air from my lungs. Once, twice, three, four— oh god.

Burying my face in the comforter. I'm wondering if I managed to come already when I feel it. Oh, the cool, soft jelly feeling of the small dildo pressing into my ass.

"Don't tense up, baby. You're doing so good." He croons low in his chest.

I exhale slowly. Oh, ouch, it stings. I fight against the tension at the pain. I'm a good girl. I asked for this. I want this. Once I have this, I can have all of him in every inch of my body.

"And it's in. Good girl." A hand trails up my spine from my ass to my neck. His big hand closes around my neck and brings my head up. "Talk to me, baby."

"It's good. But I want your cock, not plastic." I whimper.

"You'll get it." He promises. Gently, he rolls me onto my back. Then he comes down over me. I'm boneless and weak as his mouth covers my breast.

He suckles deep. "I can't wait until our baby is at your breast."

"You'll share my breasts with him?"

A hand traces over my stomach. "It won't be easy, but yes."

"You're such a good daddy." I tease him. Oh, he bares his teeth and tugs on my nipple.

Sucking deep to soothe, I'm lost in what his mouth is doing to me. A hand comes up and is shaping and rolling my other breast. And all words disappear.

I love the way he loves my breast. Sucking deep, teasing with his teeth. In minutes, he's pulling all the air from my lungs at what he's doing to me. At times, it's like he adores my breasts. His tongue gentle and mouth sweet. Only for me to wonder if he's angry. Torturing me with his teeth—sucking until I wonder if he'll take my skin off.

Two fingers find my weeping center and sweeps over my clitoris at the same time he sucks hard. I shatter into my climax, breaking apart into jagged little pieces.

I'm still shuddering when I feel his mouth at my swollen clit. *No, it's too much.*

Matteo is hungry, his tongue everywhere, sweeping inside and owning me. His moans of pleasure vibrate up my spine and to where the plug is buried inside me.

Oh god, he's tugging at the plug. I clench tight to keep it inside. Only for me to realize he's not trying to take it out—he's just trying to drive me out of my mind.

I can't breathe. This man is trying to kill me. Between the plug he's constantly moving inside me and his tongue—I can't fucking breathe.

Finally, his mouth moves over my clit, and sucks at the same time he pushes the plug as deep as he can.

Hitting the waves with a bone-shattering crash, I fight to stay above the water. From far away, I feel him taking out the plug. Opening my eyes, I watch him coat his cock with the lube.

Gold runs over me. "I wish like fuck I could take a picture of you just like this. So beautiful, your body soft and glowing from your orgasm. But if anyone were to see you like this, I might have to rip their eyes from their sockets."

The sweet words, followed by the too-soft promise of violence, sends a shiver through me. I don't doubt him for a moment. I'm truly messed up for loving it.

He's at my back. One hand pulling my cheeks apart. There is no tension in my entire body to fight the hot, silky length of steel entering me. Hot, so hot. I close my eyes in a bid to savor the moment.

"Eyes open and on me, baby. I need to see your eyes." Matteo growls.

My eyes fly open to meet his. This beautiful man owns my body and soul—and I own him.

I watch as sweat forms along his brow. Slowly, he presses deeper, deeper. I gasp at the pain. Looking down, I'm shocked there are still several inches to go.

"You should see it. I'm so proud of you. You're taking almost the whole thing. Such a good girl you are. That's it."

The glow from his praise hits me in the chest and spreads throughout my tingling body. He lowers his mouth to my breast, sucking at the swollen nipple. Oh god, I feel him press deeper. *No, it hurts. Ouch.*

His mouth is on mine as he begins moving, only fucking me with the inches he's been able to get inside me. Oh, oh that feels good.

"See, you love my cock. Don't you, baby?"

I nod. "It feels good. I can take more."

He gives it to me, surging deeper.

"Yes, yes." I send my hand into my pussy.

"You're so fucking gorgeous in your greed for your orgasm." He chuckles.

"More, I need more," I beg him.

Oh god, he thrusts deep. My whole body screams at the feel of him buried inside me. His hand is around my throat as he kisses me until the world is spinning.

Slow, he begins moving in and then out. So slow. Only a few inches out before he surges back inside. Too slow. He's moving too slowly.

Except I can't say it. I can't beg for more. His mouth is still on mine —his tongue fucking me the same way his cock is.

Tearing my mouth from his is agony. The air racing into my desperate lungs the only reason I dared.

With a growl, Matteo grips my hips. The leash he kept on his control is gone. He's fucking me like a man possessed. Harder, faster, I plead, and he gives me it all.

There is no slow build to my orgasm. I'm reaching for it, it's so far out of my reach I'm sobbing for it. Then I inhale, and it hits me with the force of a runaway freight train straight to my chest. The world goes black, and I tumble into the dark.

Only for a growl against my neck to pull me back seconds before he comes inside me. The boiling, wet heat sizzles up my spine, shooting sparks so brightly for a moment that it turns the world into the surface of the sun.

With Matteo buried inside me the way he knows I love and his arms holding me tightly, we drift. I'm not afraid of getting swept out into an endless ocean. His arms are my home wherever we drift.

CHAPTER 30

*M*atteo

Layla is so happy on the back of the pony that I wonder if she's going to explode from it.

"Dada, no up." She clings to the saddle.

I sigh. She's not able to hold herself up. And my back is aching.

"I've got her, Dada." Amy's hand is at my back.

"You sure?"

"Go on." She urges me.

Dropping a kiss on her cheek, I straighten and head for the deck.

Rafe has Stella in his lap. I sink into the chair beside him.

"You're getting old." He chuckles.

"Shut up. She's had me bent over that pony for almost an hour." I defend myself.

Javi appears with Joaquin, who still looks mad he's awake. "He's been sleeping all day. I had to wake him up. I'm not trying to have Hope up all night. He's got his days and nights confused."

I shake my head. "Sleep training not going well?"

"Nope, this kid can sleep whenever the hell he wants. He just only wants to from noon to eight." He sighs. "Where did Abuelo go?"

I'm tense at the question. "I don't know. He was here a minute ago."

"Him and Mom were arguing. When she got loud, he went inside, and she followed him. What the hell are they arguing about now?" Rafe sends a hand into his hair.

Biting my tongue isn't easy. All I want to do is tell them what I know. I hate being the only one who knows.

Layla lets out a shriek. I look to where she and Amy were a few minutes ago. Amy is carrying Layla away from the pony. And Layla is fighting like mad.

"What's the matter?" I'm up.

"She's soaking wet. I need to change her."

"Shit. I'm sorry. I didn't even notice." What kind of dad am I to not notice?

"Dada," Layla screams for me.

Amy shakes her head. "It's fine. I've got her. You might want to clean up the saddle, that poor pony."

I'm up, but one of the two handlers who came with the animals is already doing it. "I apologize."

He chuckles. "It's fine. I've had worse things happen with little kids. At least it's just pee. She's got some lungs on her for sure."

"That she does."

Riley is playing with Elena and Walter on the lawn. Walter comes running up to me, barks a few times, and then runs back to Elena —barking his head off the whole time.

"Thanks, by the way. Now, Carrie is talking about getting a dog. Which we don't need with Stella being so small."

"I'd rather have a dog than a cat." Javi shakes his head. "I swear the cat is trying to kill me. It's always underfoot."

I shrug. "I got the dog for Amy, but he's not so bad. Seeing Amy with him, I'll fill the house with dogs if she wants." I'm looking around. "Where did Santos go?"

Hope laughs as she sits down in Javier's lap. "Poor guy was overwhelmed with all the babies and went upstairs to take a nap. I couldn't tell if he really was or if he was just hung over."

I look to Rafe. Rafe answers. "Both. And now that Matteo is getting married the day after tomorrow, Mom is already talking about he's next."

We're all laughing at that.

"He told me last night that Mom was trying to fix him up with a date to your wedding." Javi shakes his head. "I have a feeling he's going to try and hitch a ride on the jet out of Dallas with you guys."

"Where are you guys going for your honeymoon, after all?" Hope is curious as she takes Joaquin and bounces him to keep him awake.

"Florence, followed by Spain, a week in each. We'll get Florence to ourselves, and then Doris will fly out with Layla when we go to Madrid. I appreciate you checking in on Mom, Layla, and Doris while we're gone."

"No problem. I know how anxious Amy will get while she's gone. It's not easy spending the night away from your kids. But Layla did really good last night. Doris was surprised and Elizabeth was smiling ear to ear. I think it was smart to do a test night before you guys left."

I nod. "I have to admit, I was a bit hurt that she didn't seem very excited to see me and Amy when we arrived today."

Amy is back with Layla, who is still red-eyed and sniffling. The moment she spots me, she holds out her arms for me.

Rolling her eyes, Amy puts her in my arms. "Hey, baby girl." I kiss her cheek and she cuddles into me. Then surprises the hell out of me when she pushes away to get down. Curious, I let her slide down off me. Her little hand is on my thigh, holding her up. "What? What are you doing?"

One hand is up, and she's pointing at the pony across the yard. "You want the pony? No, you've been on the pony long enough. How about a cupcake?"

She lets go of my thigh and wobbles on her own two feet. "You think you're going to walk to the pony?" I can't believe her. From the corner of my eye, I see Javi whip out his phone, and he's recording her. "Layla…"

Her hand is out and she takes one step, then another. And another. "Holy shit. She's walking to the pony."

Five steps, and then she trips over the edge of the cement patio. I scoop her up before she hits the cement. "What a big girl you are."

Amy's eyes are wide as she shakes her head. "We are not getting her a pony."

"We'll see," I shrug as I hug a squirming Layla close.

* * *

MATTEO

Tomorrow is my wedding day. Yesterday was a perfect day, celebrating Layla's birthday. I'm only in my home office checking out the prices of ponies—I'm not going to get her one. Yet.

I'm checking to find out if there's enough room on our property to build a stable when my cell phone rings.

The display has me cursing. It's Sean.

"Sir, I'm sorry to inform you that he's sitting on the address from the protection order."

Fuck.

"A little warning would have been good." I bite out.

"I apologize, sir. He never said anything out loud about coming for her. There's a woman here in the city he's sleeping with. The last time he was here a week ago—he didn't so much as say her name. This was completely unexpected."

That's not the truth. There's a reason Sean and other men were assigned to Daniel Richards. As well as men protecting Layla and Amy the moment they stepped out of the condo.

I expected him to come after Amy. Once he saw she was about to marry a billionaire, he'd be back for more than thirty thousand dollars.

369

Out of my office, I find Doris with Layla as they walk around what was once the sitting room but is now taken over by Layla's toys. "Where's Amy?"

Layla reaches for me. I take her and kiss her cheek.

"She's lying down with a headache."

"I need to run to the clinic. I'll be back in a little bit."

She nods. "I'll tell her if she wakes up before you return."

With a kiss on Layla's cheek, I hand her back to Doris. "Be right back, baby."

A drive that would normally take fifteen minutes takes less than ten.

He jumps when I knock on his window. It's a few seconds before he gives in and rolls his window down. "Yeah."

"Can I help you with something?"

A hand runs over his face. "You took advantage of me."

"I took advantage of you? In what way?" I'm genuinely curious.

Swearing, he gets out of the car. He points a finger at me in anger. "You knew if I knew you were a billionaire that I'd want more money. I deserve more money. I supported her—"

I shake my head. "You'll get nothing. Stay away from me, Layla, and Amy."

"Hey, don't fucking walk away from me. I can contest the divorce. And Layla's custody. I'll say you threatened me to get me to sign."

"That might work—if I hadn't recorded our entire encounter."

His eyes go wide. "No way. You can't be recording people. That shit is illegal."

This guy is painfully stupid. "Texas is a one-party state."

He's thinking hard.

"It means, dumbass, that only one person of those recorded needs to give permission to be recorded. I was recorded, and I gave my permission. I don't need your permission. It's perfectly legal. You're too late on everything. With your convictions of abuse against your previous girlfriend and her brother, and the evidence of you beating Amy, a judge approved all of it. The divorce is already finalized, as is your loss of rights to Layla."

Shaking his head, he opens his mouth to argue.

I cut him off. I'm done with this fucker. "Go for it. You interrupted the lawyer, warning you that if you say a word, the NDA you signed automatically gives me five million dollars. And lawyer's fees for suing your ass. Cross me, and I can tie you up in a courtroom and bury your ass in lawyer's fees. You'll never recover."

He's finally getting it. Hanging his head, he doesn't say a word.

Exactly. I turn around to leave him to stew in his stupidity.

"Asshole. Don't walk away from me. You think you're better than me? Hey!"

The fist comes where I know it will, and I let it connect. I want him to leave a bruise—the better to send his ass away for a very long time. There are men recording us from two different views.

Now that he got his hit in, it's my turn. I send my right fist into his soft middle. Then I give into the burning need to leave a mark on him and send my left fist into his face, aiming for his cheek. Hopefully, my fist doesn't pay the price for hitting all bone.

He goes down, but I'm not done with this motherfucker. I send a kick to his stomach and watch blood fly from his mouth. Almost. Grabbing him by the front of his stained shirt, I pull him up.

"If you ever even say my name, Amy's, or Layla's again, I'll bury you six feet under. I can make you disappear, and no one will go looking for you." I send him back to the ground with another blow to his mouth.

The lights are flashing on top of the cruiser behind the vehicle Sean is driving. I nod at the cop talking to Sean. He tips his cap at me as I walk to my car.

In my own car, I sigh. Fuck, my hand hurts. I watch with satisfaction as the cop pulls him off the ground and cuffs him. His head is still swimming, and the cop has to practically carry him to the patrol car.

The moment I'm through the door, Amy's eyes are on me. "Something is wrong."

I shake my head. "Everything is right. Your ex thought he was going to get to you. That will never happen. He'll never get close again to you or Layla. I promise you that."

Her eyes widen as she moves to me, her arms going around my neck. "Are you okay?" She runs a finger over the bruise on my cheek. "I'm sorry."

"I'm not. The bruise turns the charges he has on him up."

She tightens her arms around my neck. "Thank you for loving me and Layla the way you do."

"I'm the lucky one," I assure her.

CHAPTER 31

Amy

It's my wedding day, and the sun is shining brightly through the windows. Matteo is watching me with love glowing in his eyes.

"Good morning. Are you ready for today?"

I nod. "I can't wait."

Leaning down he presses a kiss to my cheek. "Me either. I had no idea when I walked into the exam room my whole life was about to change. That was the best damn day of my life until you told me you loved me."

"Thank you for loving me. Every day with you is better than the one before."

His alarm goes off, pulling us apart. "If I kiss you, we'll be late to our wedding. Come on. Hope and Carrie will be arriving soon to help you into your wedding dress."

"Oh my gosh, your dress is so pretty. You look like a princess. Now I'm sad I had kind of a plain dress for mine." Hope sighs.

Blushing, I nod. It's everything I hoped it would be with a big skirt, tight bodice in a creamy white satin and lace. And it's so comfortable that I feel like I'm wearing a cloud. "I can't believe she was able to finish it on time, and it fits so perfectly."

Carrie adds another bobby pin to my hair to keep the long lace-edged veil in place. "Matteo is going to lose it when he sees you. I wonder if he'll cry."

I chose not to have a maid of honor or bridesmaids since I only had Elizabeth, Carrie, and Hope. It felt easier to keep it simple with me and Matteo only. To Matteo's disappointment, I didn't have anyone walking me down the aisle. But I preferred it. I'm the one who decided to give myself to Matteo.

Carrie isn't wrong. When Matteo sees me, he loses it for a moment and takes a step toward me before he remembers and stops. He doesn't cry, but I do when I see the love shining in his eyes.

The judge who marries us is a family friend of Elizabeth's. He's a nice man who stays for the day.

Layla is a sweetheart the whole day, even posing for pictures with a big smile on her face. She clings to me as the day goes on, only allowing Matteo to take her a few times. So I'm shocked when Santos gets close, and she flings herself at him.

He laughs and catches her. "I swear she's only trying to make me feel bad for not giving her any more ice cream."

"Santos, you gave her ice cream?" Matteo is annoyed.

One shoulder goes up. "I had some, and she wanted some. It was make her cry by not giving her any or give her some. And I only gave her a few spoonfuls."

She buries her face in his neck, and in only minutes, she's asleep. Doris takes her from him and tucks her into the car seat.

"I'm going to take her back to Elizabeth's now." Doris nods at us. "We'll see you in a week. Have fun."

I give Layla a last kiss before Doris leaves.

"She's going to be fine. It's only a week." Matteo murmurs as he holds me close.

It's after dinner now, and I'm fighting not to yawn. Matteo's arm is around me, and he holds me close.

"Ready to sneak out of here, Mrs. Castillo?"

"Yes, please, Mr. Castillo."

On the plane, he pulls me into his arms. "Was the day everything you wanted?"

"Everything and more. I loved the flowers and the dress but the best part of the day was ending it as yours."

Eyes darkening, he lowers his mouth to mine. "You've been mine since the first day. All today was about was making sure everyone else knew it, too."

* * *

THREE WEEKS later

Amy

I sigh as I look down at the test. I'm not sure if I should take it now or wait...

"Amy?" Matteo is standing in the doorway of the bathroom. His eyes widen in surprise.

Shit. "I'm sorry. I wasn't sure if it was the right time—with Luis and everything."

His eyes darken at the mention of his grandfather. "I think now is the perfect time to take it."

"Okay." I nod and read the instructions. Once I'm done, I wash my hands and go to Matteo, wrapping my arms around his middle.

"I wish you told me you were thinking you might be already." He sighs.

"It wasn't until the last day of our honeymoon that I began to wonder. Then we got home and…you know. I forgot all about it. Then I went to make coffee this morning, and it made me nauseous."

His hand runs up and down my back. "I'm sorry. I didn't mean to sound…I'm sorry."

"Don't say you're sorry. Your grandfather just died. We're all a little out of sorts."

He pulls back. "I knew he was dying. And I didn't say anything."

My hand goes up to his cheek. "Oh, Matteo. I'm sorry."

Shaking his head, "I'm the one who should be apologizing. My mom and Rafe—"

"You didn't have a choice. Your grandfather wouldn't let you. You were doing what he wanted." I assure him. "Don't apologize for that."

"How did you know?" He's stunned.

"Because it's very much your grandfather. He wouldn't have wanted anyone aware of what was going on with him."

His sigh is from the bottom of his lungs. "He was adamant. I hated not telling anyone. If it weren't for having you and the wedding to focus on, I probably would have."

The timer he set goes off. His long arm reaches out for the test. My stomach flips a dozen times at the smile on his face. I'm in his arms with him squeezing me tight.

"Thank you. I can't wait for our next daughter. I might be the one with money, but you have shown me not a single dollar made me rich. It wasn't until you and Layla that I truly felt rich, rich."

Matteo's adoption of Layla was signed off by a judge last week. We decided to change her birth certificate after we found out Danny died in jail. His parents refused to bail him out again. So he was held in Dallas for the charges against him for hitting Matteo. He was supposed to be moved back to Temple, but before it happened, the idiot went up against a man who might have been smaller but was more than willing to make up for it with his fists. I felt awful... because the relief outweighed any sadness I thought I would feel.

"I would like to tell Mom you're pregnant today. Is that okay? I think it would help her through the day."

Today is Luis's funeral. I'm not looking forward to it. We've already made the decision that I would go with him to the church service but would not go to the graveside. Layla didn't understand what was going on and was being clingy.

"Okay, if you think it would be good for her." Anything to help Elizabeth. She was clearly under strain.

I still feel bad we missed Luis's passing. We were on the plane back to Dallas when we got the call Luis collapsed. Sadly, he was dead before we landed.

The church is packed with people. I recognize the mayor, a senator, and even the governor is among the crowd.

Through it all, Elizabeth holds her head high and her spine straight. She stays far away from her ex-husband, though. I had no idea she filed for divorce the day after our wedding, and it was signed off by a judge two days ago. None of his sons are near him. And I wonder what's going on, but don't dare ask.

It isn't until Matteo comes home late that I find out.

"Rafe is selling the entire company except what's in Texas?" I'm stunned.

Sighing, he sinks onto the couch and pulls me into his lap. "Yes. It's been nothing but a heavy weight around his neck for years. The business here in Texas is more than enough to keep us in the billion-dollar sphere. It will hardly make anyone destitute if he sells it off. My father is angry and doesn't want Rafe to sell. He swears if Rafe does then he leaves. Rafe is fine with that."

"Are you okay with that?"

He shrugs. "Hell yeah. Rafe has been responsible for everything for far too long. It's long past time he enjoyed life a little more—actually went on a vacation or two. Whatever he wants, I'm good with it."

"And Javier?" I'm curious.

"Oh yeah, he's happy. The only one who isn't is Santos. It means he must decide if he's returning to Dallas for good."

"He might not want to?"

"I think he's worried Mom will focus on him now for marriage and settling down and he's not ready for it all yet."

Running my hand over Matteo's chest. "Hm, maybe we can keep Elizabeth busy and her focus off him."

For the first time since we got back, he chuckles. "Mom has a way of multi-tasking that has me doubting we could keep her busy enough for Santos."

"Or we can find him a fake girlfriend."

Throwing his head back, he laughs loudly. "I deserve that. It was her idea to tell you I needed a fake girlfriend. She might see through it."

"Maybe, and maybe his fake girlfriend will become real the same way we did."

"Maybe. Come on, Mrs. Castillo, you should be in bed resting."

EPILOGUE

wo years later

Amy

I sigh as the wind tugs at my hair. Beneath the large umbrella, Ben kicks out as though he wants the sun shining on him, too. He's sucking on his fingers, and I'm wondering if he's hungry already. I just fed him less than an hour ago.

Layla is laughing as Matteo chases her and Walter. Matteo catches her and swings her up into the air, tickling her while Walter barks at them both. Her shrieks of happiness bring a smile to my lips.

This is the dream I had long ago. Layla running, and playing, joyful and loud in green grass. That dream didn't have Matteo in it or her baby brother watching them. Sometimes dreams don't come true. And sometimes the real thing is better than a dream.

* * *

Eight years later

Amy

"Please, Matteo?" I plead with big eyes. "You said I could have anything I wanted for my anniversary present."

He sighs. "I thought you would say a week in Chicago or the Sargent that's up for auction next week."

"I know you've already put in a bid at Christie's for the Sargent. And you're not as sneaky as you think you are. Mom told me about the condo you bought for us in Chicago. Thank you. I'm glad we won't have to stay at a hotel anymore when we go."

We both have fallen in love with Chicago, not only for the art museum but also for all the things we can do and see in the city without it being as frantic as New York. The kids love the city, too. "But I don't want things. I just want you."

I run my hand down his chest. Ten years of marriage, and he's as gorgeous now as he was the day I met him. He's finally no longer one percent body fat. He doesn't have a soft middle or spare tire yet. He simply has an all-over softness over the hard muscle he hasn't lost.

Groaning, he catches my wrist. "You should be napping. Think of the baby."

Sensing his slowly crumbling resolve, I push off the robe I put on after my shower. I love the way his eyes go gold at me naked. I'm seven months pregnant and feel like a small whale most days—except when Matteo is looking at me.

A large hand goes over my stomach. Our son kicks in response. "You should definitely be sleeping."

I shake my head as I press into his touch. "I want five minutes to taste you with my tongue. Please, my gorgeous, generous husband."

He swears. "Fine. Five minutes." Throwing himself on the bed. He closes his eyes. "Your time starts now."

"Matteo, that's not fair. It shouldn't start until you're as naked as I am."

"Four minutes and fifty-two seconds remaining."

Crap, this man. I have to use the step stool to climb onto the bed. Normally, he would help me, but I know he's trying to lessen the time I have. Jerk.

I'm beside him on the bed, and to get back at him, both hands are at the bottom of the polo he's wearing, and push it up—followed by my tongue. I giggle as he mutters a curse word.

"When your time is up, I'm going to remember you laughing at my pain." Is gritted out.

"Ah, poor baby." I giggle as I find a flat male nipple and explore it with my tongue. How have we gone all these years, and I've only managed to do this once or twice? Those few times, I was sneaky, waking up before him. Except I only ever got a few licks and touches in before he was awake and taking over.

He's so dang bossy. The evil man plays my body with his tongue and his fingers, yet I'm only allowed his cock and his mouth.

I kiss my way down to his stomach, running my tongue over his appendectomy scar and hating the sight of him ever being cut open. I finally understand why he got so upset over seeing my cesarian scar. Ben's delivery wasn't any easier than Layla's. When I had Alyssa four years ago, my obstetrician planned a cesarian with the thought a delivery via cesarian was safer than a possible rupture of the scar if I attempted a regular delivery.

It's part of the reason why there's so much time between Alyssa and this pregnancy. Matteo hated the idea of another pregnancy resulting in a cesarian. I had to do a lot of begging before he gave in. Being loved by Matteo is a gift, I know, but there are times it can be maddening.

Running my face over his stomach, he swears, and I'm flipped on my back. "That wasn't five minutes," I whine.

"Let's try it again in another ten years." He breathes into my mouth.

"I'm holding you to it next time," I warn him.

* * *

TEN YEARS later

Matteo

"You lied to me." Layla's eyes are knives cutting into me.

"We didn't lie to you. Matteo is your father. Danny never wanted to be." Amy argues.

"Bullshit. You didn't want him to be. You met a rich guy and dropped my father." Layla yells at her mother. Then she turns on me. "And you, you killed him."

What the fuck? "Look, I'm sorry you found out this way. But his brother is lying to you. I had nothing to do with his death. He beat your mother often, and the last time, he was going to hit you. Your mother left to protect you. It's the same reason I got him to sign away his rights to you—it was only to protect you from a very violent man who only cared about himself. All he wanted was money to sign away his rights, and I happily gave it to him."

"No, you threatened to kill him if he didn't sign. He was trying to stay alive. Then you killed him anyway. I hate you. I hate both of you." Before I can open my mouth to argue, she slams out of the room.

I pull Amy into my arms. She's shaking so badly, I wish like hell there was something more I could do. "We should have told her sooner."

Shaking my head, I run a hand up her back. "She'll calm down. And when she does, she'll figure out he was lying."

"You still have the recording of that day. Why didn't you tell her that?"

Sighing, "I didn't want her to hear it."

"Protecting her is only hurting us." Amy wipes her tears.

"Fine. When she comes back, if she won't listen—I'll play her the recording."

The timid knock on the door pulls us apart. "Daddy?"

"Yeah, baby, you can come in."

Alyssa's eyes are wide. "Is everything okay? Why was Layla yelling?"

"Go get your brothers. I don't want to repeat it." I sigh.

"We're telling them?" Amy's eyes are wide.

"They deserve to know. The same way we should have told Layla. Better we tell them than them find out on their own." I shake my head. "This was not the anniversary I planned for you to have."

Her hand comes down on my chest. "All I care about is that we're having another one. Twenty years with you…it's flown by, and I wouldn't have our lives any other way."

"Even if we might have lost Layla?" I allow the fear to escape me.

"We won't lose her. She had a shock to her system, that's all. She's a daddy's girl, after all. Finding out she wasn't yours biologically might not have been easy, but she'll come around."

I exhale slowly. "You're sure? Two minutes ago—"

"Two minutes ago, she scared the shit out of me. But now that I can breathe, I can see it from her side. Dan's brother comes out of nowhere and spews a bunch of lies. You're right. We should have told her sooner. For the last twenty years, we didn't think of him or that she wasn't your biological daughter because, in every way, that mattered—you are her father. She can't erase twenty years, and she won't. We just have to give her time."

"I hope like hell you're right."

* * *

THREE YEARS later

Matteo

I finish reading the report and hand it to Amy so she can read it as well. Closing my eyes, I shake my head.

"Bratva? That's like a gangster isn't it?" Amy whispers.

Nodding, I sigh. "Russian mafia."

"Maybe he's not. Just because his father Milos is…maybe he's not."

"We can't let her marry him." I bite out the words.

Amy wipes the tears trailing down her cheeks. "We have to. If we try to stop her, we'll lose her again. She goes all these years without talking to us only to invite us to her wedding happening two days after she tells us. I wish like hell we never got the condo in Chicago and let her continue to live in it after she refused to come home."

"What if she doesn't know what his father is? What Victor is. She admitted she's only known him a few months." I search for a way to protect my daughter.

"I think she knows. I'm positive it's why she waited until the last minute to invite us to their wedding."

"So what, we're just supposed to smile and pretend we don't know our daughter is marrying into a family of criminals?" I fight the urge to be violent.

Shaking her head, her arms go around me. "Why does this feel like a bad dream? If we don't support her, we're going to lose her for good. If we do..."

"I won't lose her again. These three years without her were hell. All I care about is he protects her and treats her like the treasure she is. Maybe he loves her enough to do that." I hope like hell he does. "And if he doesn't, I'll make him pay."

My cell phone rings. It's the hangar. "The jet is ready. It's time to go to Chicago."

* * *

I hope you enjoyed this story. If you did please, please leave a review.
Sign up for my newsletter and receive information about my newest releases through my website: fionamurphywrites.com

Facebook: Author Page: https://www.facebook.com/
fionainamurphy/
Regular page: https://www.facebook.com/fionaaina.murphy

IF THIS IS the first book you've read the series starts with Rafael

The Castillo Family: Follow Rafael, Matteo, Javier and their nephew Santos. A billionaire family, they made their fortune in the construction business. But all their money can't help them when it comes to building relationships with women who want what money can't buy.

My twin brothers have never been little angels, but this time they might have gone too far in crossing Rafael Castillo. Rafael wants them punished to the furthest extent of the law for trespassing and destroying his company's construction site. I can't defend what they did, but I also can't let them go into juvenile detention. All I'm asking for is another chance. But the arrogant, gorgeous billionaire refuses and cuts me down without listening. So I might have started yelling, there might have been bitter accusations on both sides, and I might have lost it and cried. Then somehow I was in his arms.

The instant lust shocks us both. Yet while I'm more than willing to act on it, Rafael refuses. Until I lie and tell him all I want are the nights in my bedroom. No commitment, no strings, just sex. All too soon, it's not enough; but will we ever make it out of the bedroom, or are we doomed to fail?

ALSO BY FIONA MURPHY

Click to order Javier's book

Javier's Castillo might be a gorgeous, brilliant billionaire but he's also a massive a$$hole. The only thing redeeming about him is how much he loves his baby daughter. I'm just the nanny with a thirty-day trial hanging over my head. I know I'm too young and curvy for him to ever be interested in me.

He's trying to get me to quit, I just know it. Except I refuse to go easily or quietly, no matter how mean or rude he gets. There's no way I am going to mess up this job, if I do I'll be homeless again. I'm positive he's just worried I'll develop a crush on him and become a clingy, love-sick pain. So why do I feel his eyes on me when he thinks I'm not paying attention? What about overhearing him warning a man away from me with a feral, jealous possessive air?

It's wishful thinking—poor, plain, curvy women like me don't get the gorgeous billionaire like him anywhere but in the movies.

I'm here for his daughter, not him. Except it isn't just his daughter who has stolen my heart and I wonder if maybe I'm not imagining things after all

ALSO BY FIONA MURPHY

His Fake Fiancée

Ivan Volkov is a wickedly intelligent, ruthless, and devastatingly gorgeous billionaire with a sexy British accent. He also owns the company I work for. The plan was simple: get his attention to show him I was the one behind all my boss's awesome proposals that have been making the company hundreds of millions of dollars for the last three years. I'm the one who should be in the big office making a six-figure salary.

It worked. I definitely have Ivan's attention. He'll put me in the big office with a six-figure salary—once he's done with me. He needs a personal assistant until he can find a replacement. It won't be long, he assures me, no more than a few weeks.

Close proximity to Ivan Volkov for a few weeks? Sure, I don't need my dignity. I wasn't using it anyway. No matter how many times I tell myself to stop staring at him with lust, I can't.

Volkov turns down the offer I never even made; he saw me staring, he's used to it by now. An unrepentant user of woman, all he wants is for them to satisfy his need, then be on their way. He can get that satisfaction from any woman. The money I make him isn't worth losing when he's done with me.

Until the moment he needs more: a shield from a woman who won't take no for an answer. He will do anything to protect his little sister from having her wedding ruined, even faking an engagement with me. Brilliant tactician that he is, he comes up with the answer to both of his problems. For the next three weeks we can satisfy the lust we both feel, while at the same time making it clear he isn't available.

But before long what's between us feels all too real. Can this lead to forever, or will the billionaire choose money over love?

This is the first standalone in a series about fake relationships. This does not end in a cliffhanger.

Made in the USA
Monee, IL
28 July 2024

62755832R00236